To Ensnare a Queen

The Hidden Land Novel 3

By Peter Meredith

Fictional works by Peter Meredith:

A Perfect America

The Sacrificial Daughter

The Apocalypse Crusade War of the Undead: Day One

The Apocalypse Crusade War of the Undead: Day Two

The Horror of the Shade: Trilogy of the Void 1

An Illusion of Hell: Trilogy of the Void 2

Hell Blade: Trilogy of the Void 3

The Punished

Sprite

The Blood Lure: The Hidden Land Novel 1

The King's Trap: The Hidden Land Novel 2

To Ensnare a Queen: The Hidden Land Novel 3

The Apocalypse: The Undead World Novel 1

The Apocalypse Survivors: The Undead World Novel 2

The Apocalypse Outcasts: The Undead World Novel 3

The Apocalypse Fugitives: The Undead World Novel 4

The Apocalypse Renegades: The Undead World Novel 5

The Apocalypse Exile: The Undead World Novel 6

The Apocalypse War: The Undead World Novel 7

The Edge of Hell: Gods of the Undead A Post-Apocalyptic Epic

Pen(Novella)

A Sliver of Perfection (Novella)

The Haunting At Red Feathers(Short Story)
The Haunting On Colonel's Row(Short Story)
The Drawer(Short Story)
The Eyes in the Storm(Short Story)
The Witch: Jillybean in the Undead World
1(Novella)

For My Ella

Chapter 1

No trumpets blared, no drums beat out a cadence for the marching feet, and no orders were bellowed. Even the whips lay like silent snakes curled at the belts of the hobgoblins. They had their orders: absolute silence. Any infraction wasn't going to be punished by a whipping this time. Death was the punishment, and it would be instantaneous.

The bodies strewn along the streets of the Demorlaik bore witness to this and their presence kept the rest of the goblins in line as they marched with their bellies shrunken by continual hunger and their eyes squinting against even the slightest light.

Their numbers seemed endless.

Out of the great black maze of the Underworld, the land beneath the Demorlaik, they came in ordered lines of tens and ordered squares of a hundred, and this in itself was unusual. Goblins didn't normally form armies so much as they formed hordes that swept everything before them. This time it was different. Where before straggling and mewling complaints were the norm, now iron discipline ruled. A discipline enforced by the harshest measures.

That discipline sent the goblins marching at the quick step, and it wasn't just the goblins either. All sorts of dreadful beasts formed the Master's army: long armed, jackal-headed gnolls, stinking ogres, tremendous trolls, and wolves by the thousands.

Even the wolves were silent, for they were not what one would find slinking through a forest. These were red-eyed and black-tongued beasts bred to serve the Master and they were altogether pitiless. They roamed up and down the goblin ranks waiting on the least word, ready to tear apart any who broke the Master's law.

For three hours the tremendous army marched up out of the black hole in the middle of the Demorlaik. They came rank upon rank, square upon square and when they had finally passed through to the Hidden Lands there was a perfect silence in the Underworld. The Master had completely emptied it, for he had bent all of his will upon the destruction of the Den, and his power was such that none knew of his coming.

His army went unseen and unheard, and the Den carried on with their lives thinking they were safe.

Chapter 2

Ella

Among the greens and browns and vibrant yellows of the forest, the unicorn should've stood out. Yet despite its white flanks, golden mane, and hocks of midnight blue, it somehow blended in with its surroundings and Ella, even with her elf eyes, could not discern it.

She had come upon it quite by accident during that morning's hike out of the town. Every day she left Hildeoven to explore, or so she told herself, but every day she found it harder and harder to come back. She felt a little like a comet circling the sun, only each of her orbits sent her further away, instead of closer, and she knew that one day she would stray too far. She would find the path that led to somewhere else; somewhere with a brighter future.

The unicorn seemed to portend such a day.

It ensnared Ella with its beauty in the first second her eyes beheld it and she had foolishly thought that she could ease up to it, whispering gently as she would with a normal horse. How wrong she was. The unicorn seemed to snort in laughter and then it sprinted off, not in a thundering of hooves, but rather in a rush of wind among the trees.

Ella gave immediate chase, running lightly through the forest with surprising speed, leaping logs and low bushes like a gazelle. Using her natural agility coupled with her magic, she kept close...at first. Then the unicorn showed her what true speed was.

In midstride it seemed to gather itself and burst forth. It was a breathtaking sight. How superb the muscles of the creature! Its great legs seemed composed of velvet over steel and in seconds Ella stood alone, panting, but happy. A unicorn! It had been real!

Wearing a grin, she reached out with her tired mind in an effort to track it, only the unicorn had mastered all aspects of the art of magical camouflage. Despite its size, Ella couldn't seem to be able to lay her mind on it. She likened it to trying to grasp a hold of a soap bubble with a set of salad tongs. It was a useless exercise, yet she kept at it until her head pounded with the effort.

And just when she gave up hope of ever finding it again, she saw its sleek body cantering along a path not far down the slope of a valley that she hadn't yet explored. Without hesitating she ran to it, and never felt more human. Her legs were like lead and her breath was a loud gasping sound that secretly embarrassed her, and she could only thank goodness that she was alone in the woods without any fey nearby to raise an eyebrow.

Though she hunted for what was probably an hour, Ella could not get close to the unicorn, regardless that the creature toyed with her. It made her look stupid appearing here and then there, always just close enough to make the sprint worth it, so that she grew splotchy and red from the exertion of dashing back and forth among the trees.

Drained of nearly everything, she eventually gave up and only stood there feeling a depression grip her, while the unicorn whinnied its laughter, the sound fading as it galloped off.

The chase had been so very much like her life of the past few months. It started with such hope and joy at the promise of something new and magical and then the promise faded, leaving...nothing, except pain and disappointment.

Ella staggered off the path she'd been on and found a patch of moss in the shade of a cottonwood. There she sat. The moss beneath her fingers was soft and cool, yet the air around her was humid. Her shirt stuck to her back and sweat trickled from her dark hair. It was annoying. She was annoyed. She never used to get annoyed at such things, but now the feeling came all too often.

With the last of her fading power she sent a breeze whisping down her neck. For the moment it felt wonderful and the annoyance disappeared...until a leaf, plucked from a branch by the light airs slid down the back of her shirt. It scratched her and she squirmed to get it out, which in turn caused her soft shirt to catch on a nearby branch. The shirt tore, and Ella slumped back, close to tears.

This happened all too frequently as well. For weeks she'd been on the verge of tears at the slightest instigation. Since the death of Generai, since her imprisonment by Darhmael, since Aric had left her; always tears were near.

When the first tear breeched the dam of her lid, she got up in a fury, grabbed a clod of dirt and hurled it at the cottonwood. It broke apart on contact in a satisfying manner yet the remains rebounded to cover her in a fine spray.

"Damn it!" she cursed. Cursing too had become a phenomenon with her and she hated it just as much as she hated the pain. For a minute she stood crying, covered in dirt and sweat. The unicorn was forgotten, as was the brief light of joy that had come with it. Only her pain remained. It sat in her chest like a vampire's stake, and in her mind like a black cloud. Her pain showed in her magic. There was an edge to even the simplest spells that hadn't been there before. It was something she couldn't train away.

Despite the hours of hard work she put in every-day, that grit upon her soul never left. She grew stronger, yet she also gained an edginess that scared her. Did it come from her father? Or was it just that her life sucked? There was no way to know and with the heat of the forest bearing down on her, she knew the answer would remain elusive. She needed water: a drink, a shower, a bath. Anything.

Placing her hand on the cottonwood, she felt the earth through its great network of roots. Water was near. A pond just to the east. Ella sighed and began trekking in that direction.

It turned out to be blue and clear through to its sandy bottom. Regardless, she gave it a now practiced eye, looking for danger. The Hidden Lands were beautiful and magical and sometimes very deadly. Just then with her magic depleted and her muscles tired, the danger was greater than usual. In that state, something as simple as a stray goblin could be hazard.

Thankfully she didn't sense anything in the water and so she took off her light boots and waded into the shallows. The water was a blessing on her burning feet and she stood for a few minutes. Then she had better idea. A swim. Finding a rock nearby she began to work the buttons of her shirt.

"Ahem..."

She jerked her head up to see the shadow of a man just on the edge of her sight among the dense foliage that ran beside the pond. In a flash her hand went to her sword's hilts.

"You need not your sword," the man said. She knew the voice. It brought back the irritating pain.

"I will decide when I need my sword and when I don't," Ella said. "I would say show yourself, but please don't."

He ignored her and came anyway and she almost laughed. Had he been anyone else she would have. She almost laughed at how this man...this king strode forward to stand in a stream of light so that the sun warmed his tan and glinted from his armor; so that the shadows of the nearby trees accented his strength instead of concealing it; so that he seemed so in command of everything around him that the grasping vines hanging from a nearby tree seemed to pull away and the bushes appeared to lower themselves...had it been anyone else, all of this would've been contrived.

For Eireden, King of the Den, it was simply how he walked.

He came to stand none to close, with most of the small pond still between them and as usual he didn't look at her, but rather he looked at the world around her. And as usual this annoyed her and so she stared openly at his sharp hawk-like features and his tall muscular figure.

She had barely seen him since the death of his cousin, and little had changed. As always he was armed; in his right he held a black sword of amazing proportions and on his face was a look of concern.

"How...how did you find me?" Ella asked, not bothering to hide her anger with any veil of civility.

"It's impossible for me not to know where you are," Eireden said. "Are you alright?"

"You tracked me down just to ask how I'm doing?" Ella's manner was distinctly American...and not at all Ella-like. She knew it—she heard it in her voice, but she refuse to apologize or taper it off. "I was doing better before you showed up."

This barb caused him pain. She saw it on his face and in the way his throat worked hard to swallow nothing. "It didn't seem like you were doing better...weren't you being chased?"

"No, I was doing the chasing," Ella explained. "It was a unicorn."

"A unicorn?" He gave a quick look around as if he could have caught sight of the nimble beast. "I wonder why you weren't able to catch...never mind. I'm sorry. That was wrong of me to even mention." He said this last with red coloring his cheeks.

"What do you mean?" Ella demanded.

"I meant nothing. Please accept my apologies..."

Ella began to stomp barefoot around the pond and Eireden, despite towering over her, shrank back at her anger. She glowered up at him and said, "I won't accept your apology until I know what you are apologizing for."

Eireden stammered, "It's...it's just that only a maiden can call a unicorn to her." When her expression switched from anger to puzzlement he added, "A *maiden*. A uh...uh a woman who hasn't uh..."

At the realization of what he was suggesting her eyes went wide. "That isn't any of your business!" She tramped back to where her boots sat limp in the sand. Furiously she began to shove her feet into the soft leather and with them still wet from the pond, it proved an impossible task, which only added to her anger.

Gritting her teeth she pulled like mad against the rebellious boot as Eireden watched in what felt to be silent judgment. First he wouldn't look her way, which had her annoyed, and now he wouldn't stop, which of course only made her furious.

"If you don't mind. Staring is impolite," Ella grunted, trying to put her back into the effort of getting on the boot. What the hell was going on? Had her feet grown two sizes in the last few minutes? Finally she gave up on the boot and flung it aside. "I could've caught the unicorn," she said without looking up. "Which is more than I can say for you."

By American standards, the Den were a prudish people. They valued honor over everything, including hedonistic desires, yet Ella couldn't imagine a man like Eireden as a virgin. Women threw themselves his way, and she didn't blame them. Eireden was handsome, and tall, and broad shouldered. He was deep in the chest, with muscles of iron, yet he was gentle and caring...

Ella blinked at where her mind was going. Flustered, she grabbed the second boot only to have that one deny her as well. She flung it just as she had its mate and Eireden watched it land in a juniper bush.

"I'm sorry," he said, speaking in the direction of the offending boot. "I did not mean to insult you in any way. With all your running around I was worried that you were in danger."

"Well, you can leave," Ella frothed. "I'm not in danger...and besides, I can take care of myself." And she could, too. In the months since her release from captivity she had been forcing her mind from her pain by turning her energies to magic. Every day she would work herself into a state of numbness and everyday she grew in power.

Eireden went to retrieve the boots; they seemed like tiny things in his large hands. "Again, I must apologize. I am well aware that you are fast becoming capable. My mother tells me you are making great strides. But I didn't seek you out in an effort to protect you. I sought you out because I am in need of information...about Aric. He's missing."

Ella smiled in a grimacy sort of manner. Could Eireden bring up a worse subject? Was there anything else he could ask that could hurt more than bringing up the man who had thrown her love away so nonchalantly? Maybe he could talk about how she was the product of rape. Or how she had been responsible for the death of thousands of fey; that would do it.

"I don't know where he is and I don't care," she hissed.

This brought his attention away from the boot. "You don't care? But you loved him."

"Yeah," Ella fumed. "*Loved.* Do you people know anything about tenses? That one is past tense in case you didn't know. I loved him, but not anymore. Besides, what do you care?"

"I care because I still love him," Eireden answered. "He is my friend."

This deflated her self-righteous anger and she took the boot without looking up. "I haven't seen him, and I don't expect to. He doesn't want to see me. He thinks I tricked him into loving him and he was right. I did. Just like you...I mean just like with everyone else. I tricked them. There's something in me Eireden, something that my father put in me that makes people..."

She bit off her words. Ella was going to say that there was something inside her that made people love her but that wasn't the truth. People didn't love her. The Den were cool to her, while the fey were curious; Eireden didn't really love her or he wouldn't be marrying Alseya, and Aric left her because she was a half-breed. Even her mother didn't love her. Elleni was little more than a breathing corpse and had feelings for no one.

"I haven't seen him," she finished lamely. "How long has he been missing?"

"It's been a couple of months," Eireden answered. "It's like he just disappeared off the face of the earth. I worry for him and...I was hoping that he would stand for me at the wedding."

There it was. Eireden had found something even more painful to talk about. Ella studied the boot hoping not to cry, hoping to be strong. "Nope," she said in

a choked voice. "Haven't seen him. I should be going."
She dropped her boot and started away, thinking that
she would simply go barefoot. It was something she
used to enjoy back in her old life.

Eireden held her back. "Are you all right?
You...what is that?" With a strange look on his face he
pointed at her chest where her shirt was squirming.

"Oh that," Ella said with sudden embarrassment.
She turned away and unbuttoned the top of her shirt
and loosened her *Woman's Bindings*, what the Den
called a bra. A glow came even in the light of day. "I
was going to tell you, but you've been busy." Ella
turned back and held up her hand and there upon it
was a tiny fairy, just over three inches in length.

Eireden stared at the fairy and the fairy stared
right back. "She looks just like Whip-wip," he said. "I
mean exactly like her. Even her little dress is the same.
May I hold her?"

"She won't go to you," Ella said. "She stays close.
I think she believes I'm her mother. Isn't that funny?"

"Her mother, really?" Eireden asked with a smile.
They locked eyes for the first time in months, though
judging by the force of the connection between them it
might as well as have been seconds since the last time
they had smiled on each other. She felt it deep inside
of her. It melted away the last of her anger and she
could suddenly no longer feel her limbs.

After a few seconds Ella dropped her eyes. It was
unfair to him. He was a good, kindly man and didn't
deserve to be tricked into feeling something for her.

"Yeah, her mother," she said. "I think I've im-
printed myself on her like a mother bird. That's why
she won't go to any..."

Eireden interrupted, "Whip-wip swirrp."

Ella began, "Her name's not..." But then the fairy
actually flew over to the King's hand and stood upon
the flat of his callused palm.

He boomed out a laugh and the fairy giggled along. "This is Whip-wip!" he cried. "How is this possible?"

"She's not Whip-wip. I think it's her daughter...and how'd you do that? She doesn't go to anyone. Really she's very shy."

"They don't call me the Fairy king because of my penchant for wearing dresses," Eireden answered, grinning. He brought his palm up to his face and blew lightly, sending the fairy spinning in a gale of laughter back to Ella.

"Careful now," Ella said anxiously, catching her in both hands. "She's very delicate."

Eireden scoffed at the idea. "You do sound like a mother. Not mine of course but a normal one. I wish you had told me about her before this. There are people back in Rhyoeven who would love to know that she's still alive...you know what? You should bring her to the wedding. Consider this an invitation, Whip-wip. I only ask that you refrain from high jinks; no throwing grapes at Furen."

"Her name's not Whip-wip," Ella said. "And we're not going to the wedding." The decision came to her in that second. Being so close to him was pain. There was no other word. Her chest hurt. To go to his wedding would probably feel like an hour-long heart attack. And if Aric was there as well...she didn't think she could take such a thing.

As well it wouldn't be fair to the bride. Alseya had done nothing wrong, not really, in fact she had done everything right. She had seen what she wanted and had gone for it like a laser, an attitude that Ella envied.

Eireden seemed stunned and Ella made it worse, "And I think I'm leaving the Hidden Lands for good. I'm going back to America."

"Ella, you won't be safe there," he said taking her hands.

"I was perfectly safe in Seattle before I met you," Ella said, pulling away. "You're the one who introduced danger into my life...and pain. Before you I was happy."

Chapter 3

Ella

After announcing that she was leaving for America it should have been no surprise that Ella would receive a string of visitors begging her to stay. The first to come knocking was the prince of the city.

"Have I done something to offend you?" he asked, glaring down at her fiercely through his one remaining eye.

"Of course not, my Prince," Ella replied, curtsying. She then offered her hand, which he kissed with his disfigured lips. "When are you going to let me fix you? I can leave a couple of scars to keep you looking rugged. Maybe one along each cheek? I'm sure it would give you a rakish air."

"This isn't about vanity," Prince Lienhart answered, touching his face. He had survived the fight with Darhmael, but only just, and the scars of his burns were outrageous. They pained Ella every time she looked on them.

"It's about pride, which is almost as bad," Ella said. "Where I come from people with such scars would kill to have them fixed in the manner in which I am able."

"Why?" Lienhart asked, coming into the candle-maker's home and settling himself down on one of his threadbare couches. "So they can look like everyone else? Why would I want to look like everyone else when I can look like me? I have heard rumors of your America, and why you'd want to go back there is beyond me."

This was the common refrain. No one could understand what the draw was for Ella to live amongst such people. In truth there wasn't a particular draw for Ella; rather she was simply repulsed by her current situation.

Some of her visitors exacerbated the issue such as when Alseya showed up the following day.

"You can't leave!" the queen-to-be demanded with barely a token greeting. This was so out of character for her that Ella failed to even invite her inside. Alseya didn't notice and walked in anyway.

"Would you like some tea?" Ella said as the white-haired, opal-eyed fey plopped herself on the same couch Lienhart had sat on the day before.

"No, I don't want tea, thank you," Alseya, said. "I want you to stay here in the Hidden Lands. In fact I don't just want you to stay, I need you to stay. Eleanor, it's important that you stay and not just for me and the baby, but also for the King."

All thought of tea went out the window. The baby! "You're...you're pregnant?" For some strange reason the image of the unicorn she had seen came back to her—if Eireden hadn't been able to catch it before he definitely wouldn't be able to now. Ella sat down; her legs had gone wobbly.

Alseya looked shocked at the question. "How could I be? I am not yet married." In answer Ella could only wag her head, confounded at the direction of their conversation. "I meant my future baby," Alseya explained. "He will need you. Who, other than you knows what it's like belonging to two races at once. I am so fond of you Eleanor that I am sure you'll be just a wonderful influence on him. Promise me that you'll stay to help guide him."

Though she had just sat, Ella couldn't stay in one place for long. She hopped up and fidgeted with the candle-maker's belongings. With her back turned to Alseya, she said, "I can't make that promise. And besides I think it would be wrong to be too close to your family."

"Why, because the king loves you?" Alseya asked.

Ella choked on the glib answer the fey had given. "Yes," Ella replied. "It's not right...and it's not his fault, so please don't blame him. He's a perfect gentleman."

This had Alseya laughing. "Of course he is. Yet I don't understand you. Why should I blame him for loving you? You are sweet and kind and beautiful. How can anyone not love you?"

They couldn't. It was a simple nasty fact: Everyone loved her because she had been engineered that way. Her father had used magic in her creation, so that she emitted frequencies that made people feel for her.

"That's just it," Ella said. Her hands arranging the books on the candle-maker's shelves. "He can't help it. He has to love me."

Alseya moved with the stealth of a midnight breeze and was there behind Ella before knew it. The fey put her small hands on Ella's shoulders and turned her around. "Do not think the King is so weak as that. I know of the incidence of your birth. Aric told me before he left."

"Then you know that I emit frequencies and that I was engineered..."

"Stop it," Alseya chided. "We are all engineered in some fashion and we all emit frequencies. Yours were just more deliberately planned."

"For an evil purpose," Ella said, fighting back a need to throw one of the books at a wall.

"A purpose which failed," Alseya shot back. "Remember that. The same love that was supposed to destroy the fey, instead saved us. Every day I am thankful for that love."

"Is that how you justify marrying a man who supposedly loves another?" Ella asked, stiffly. She hadn't been mollified in the least by Alseya's words. Ella figured that If Eireden loved her it was because he had to, not because he wanted to. Just like Aric.

Despite the biting words, Alseya pulled Ella back to the couch and sat down, gripping her hands in a way that made it clear she wasn't going to let go. "I love the king. I didn't think I would or even that I could. He is Den and I am Fey. Yet that doesn't seem to matter anymore. He is a beautiful person on the inside where it counts." She touched Ella's breast. "In here, one is neither Den nor Fey nor any combination. It's that person whom I love."

"And yet you want me near?" Ella asked. "Why would you want to tempt him so?"

"How did we go so far off subject?" Alseya wondered aloud, looking up at the ceiling. "It's not temptation I fear. It's the future I fear like I've never in all my life. I want you to stay in the Hidden Lands. I have my reasons and all are selfish. I want you to stay for my child's sake and for the king's sake and for my sake. I am bound by duty, but in this you are not. I can only beg that you reconsider leaving."

Ella could make no promises not even when Furen Traganfel came the following afternoon and begged as well. And he did so weeping in the stoic way of the dwarves—he acted as if his tears weren't even there—even when Ella offered him a handkerchief.

"For what purpose?" Furen asked, despite that tears had made their way to his chest plate after navigating the dense jungle of his beard. "You make no sense. And you can't take Whip-wip away," he moaned. For some reason the shy fairy had crept out of her hiding place at the sound of Furen's deep voice; her presence only adding to the Dwarf's tears.

"Her name is not..." Ella stopped with sigh. The fairy had no name; Ella had taken to calling her Little Fairy, which was not only silly but redundant. When she had first emerged from her shell in a blossoming of light, Ella had still been too aggrieved to use the name Whip-wip, but now it seemed proper. "I guess we should make it official. From now on, Little Fairy you shall bear the name Lady Whip-wip of Hildeoven or America I should say."

"Not America!" Furen cried, again with real tears, "I can't abide it. You belong here."

"I can't," Ella said quietly. "It hurts too much to be so near."

"What happens if Aric comes around to some right thinking?" Furen asked. He tapped his hammer. "I could knock some sense into him. It would be no problem."

"I can't force him to love me..." she hesitated. What was she saying? Of course she could force him to love her. All he had to do was stand too close to her, or maybe it was her smile that would ensnare him, or perhaps a bat of her eyes.

"Who would need to be forced into loving you?" Furen said. "Aric's just a little mixed about your ancestry. He'll come around. I don't think you have anything to worry about in that department."

"I don't want him to come around," Ella said. "Aric's love wasn't real. It was conjured by magic. And so was Eireden's. It's why I'm leaving. It's too dangerous for a girl like me to be hanging around in the Hidden Lands. You know people die for me here? People risk their lives for me...for nothing. But in America, what's the worst that can happen? Someone might spend their paycheck on me. Big whoop."

"Slow down," Furen said, holding out his huge hands. "There is another option—you can come back with me to my kingdom. Yes Gargefrel might be a little jealous at first, but I'm sure she'll warm to you over time. And it'll be just for a little while until you and Aric come to your senses." When Ella started to shake her head, Furen was quick to launch into a very, very, lengthy description of his underworld kingdom that he figured would change her mind.

In the end, she declined and he went back to his kingdom a saddened dwarf.

And this left only one other visitor, or so she thought. Ilenwyth, the mother of the King came on the day before Ella was set to leave.

"My machinations have come to naught," she said after breezing in and letting the candle-maker kiss her hand. "I have plotted all that I can plot. I have intrigued and schemed and maneuvered and still you insist on leaving?"

"Yes, your highness," Ella replied. "Though why you would go to any trouble is beyond me. Alseya is a fine woman and a powerful fey. Your grandson will be a very great man...like his father."

Ilenwyth glanced down at the weathered couch and turned her nose up at it. Instead she went to the bookshelf and eyed the books that Ella couldn't seem to stop rearranging. "Alseya is a fine woman, but she is not right for my son. A marriage is not just about honor and duty, it's about love. I loved Eirolden, the king's father, with all my heart."

"I remember," Ella said. "Alseya tells me that she loves Eireden. She acted surprised that she could."

The king's mother snorted at that. "And what of Eireden? You saw him the other day. Was he a man in love?"

"No," she said, though the answer was in truth, yes. Eireden was still under her spell and Alseya didn't stand a chance as long as Ella hung about. How come Alseya didn't see that?

"And what of you?" Ilenwyth asked. "Do you love my son?"

There was a time only a few months ago that she would've said yes, without a second thought. However, time and again, fate had intervened and had nudged Ella away from Eireden and into Aric's arms. Yet no matter how happy she had been with Aric, Ella couldn't look upon Eireden without getting a hitch in her chest.

"Yes. I've always loved your son. Perhaps in the manner in which a subject loves her king."

Ilenwyth eyed her doubtfully. "And yet you would leave him behind because of some misunderstanding?"

Ella sighed at the simplicity of the word misunderstanding. "Yes."

"Though you will never find his equal in America?"

"Yes. What would you have me do? Your son is marrying another woman. I won't get between them. And Aric has left me. I think I'm still a pawn. Remember when you called me that? You said if I could make it to the other side of the board I could be anything I wished. Well, I've made it. I could be a queen of the Den if I wished or maybe even queen of the fey. But, I think I'll stay a pawn."

"You're hopeless." When Ella nodded, Ilenwyth blew out angrily and added, "You must know that you are relegating yourself to a most unhappy life."

She knew that she would not love again, that was for certain. How could she when always in her mind would be the idea that the love was just a gimmick; a trick, a mirage, an illusion. No one could love her for real.

Yet that didn't mean she couldn't be happy. She had been happy in her garden, working for Cascade's

Nursery, before all of this had started. Ella could always go back to that. That was her plan at least.

The following morning she got up before the sun. It was her worry that there would be more people lined up to stop her and she wanted to slip out of town before they could make it to her door.

Only the candle-maker was there and he had tears in his eyes. "I have lost my daughters in battle," he said. "And your presence has been a salve for my heart. I will miss you."

These simple words were greater in effectiveness than all the rest put together. They turned her feet to stone and it was with some difficulty that she made her way into his arms to hug him. "Thank you for allowing me to stay."

"I will keep a room for you if you ever wish to come back."

Chapter 4

Eireden

The view from the tower above the palace, with a great sweep of the Hidden Lands in all their splendor laid out for him was beautiful, magnificent, breathtaking, and many other superlatives that were lost on the king. For him it was enough to see that the battle plain was empty.

Every morning he came to look out upon it just to reassure himself. Darhmael had been checked, not defeated, not destroyed. He was still out there and what sort of army he possessed was a matter of question. There were some that saw the threat posed by the elf to be negligible; that he wouldn't be more than a nuisance for years or even decades to come.

There were others, Eireden among them, that saw the elf as a very real threat, despite the loss. Before the great battle, the maug surrounding Hildeoven had been beyond count. The plain surrounding the city had been literally black with their bodies. Yet after the victory, the corpses of the maug had numbered just over twenty-two thousand.

It was an unquestionable victory, yet it was not complete. Far too many maug had escaped to be dismissed out of hand, not with the power of an elf behind them.

Eireden turned from the pretty view and shook his head to clear the dour mood that had set in, and as usual Ella's face came to fill the vacuum of his thoughts. Always the vision of her gentle beauty would creep into his mind if he didn't hold himself rigid against the intrusion. Even then, with his bride-to-be staring at him with her sparkling opal eyes he could barely push Ella from his consciousness.

"Ella wouldn't stay," Alseya said. "I'm sorry; she left for the Americas this morning."

Along with the fey, Eireden's mother, Ilenwyth-Eden had joined him in the tower that morning. He frequently met in odd places like the tower, or the kitchen, or sometimes even the stables. He was uncomfortable using the throne room for anything but the most official of business. It had always been his father's and it brought back hard memories.

"There's no reason to be sorry. If Ella will find happiness in America we should not interfere. You know that I did not want you to even ask her." This wasn't exactly true. He wanted more than anything for Ella to stay, however he had a duty to perform. Alseya turned her opal eyes in Ilenwyth's direction and they shared a look. "What?" the king asked.

"She won't be happy there," Alseya said. "We all know that."

Ilenwyth agreed and added, "And she may be in some danger."

"Yes, perhaps, but I don't have anyone I can spare to guard over her indefinitely," Eireden said. He stroked the stubble of his chin. "If only Aric hadn't left her like that. What was he thinking?"

"I would say that *thinking* was his problem," Ilenwyth answered. "He should have listened to his heart. And before you ask for the tenth time, yes I've searched for him again. Just as Alseya has. He has disappeared off the face of the earth."

Eireden paced the room feeling antsy. He was new to the kingship and hadn't yet come to terms with the idea of delegating. He wanted to do something, though what, he wasn't sure. Taking a turn around the tower, he paused at the window—again the view was lost on him—his mind far away.

"Mayhap he is under the earth," Eireden said with some apprehension.

"Yes, we've thought of that and there are only two places with the strength to resist our vision," Alseya said. "And we've already ruled out the dwarven Kingdom, which only leaves the Demorlaik."

"You will not go there!" Ilenwyth commanded her son with a sudden flare of her eyes. "This has long been my fear: that you will make another attempt on the Demorlaik. So I'm ordering you now to stay away. I'm not ordering you as a former queen, but as your mother. And in this you will obey me."

Eireden chuckled at her stern look. "Yes Mother, but you have nothing to worry about. I will not enter the Haunted City again, nor will I order any to go in my place, not unless there is some prospect of actually finding and defeating Darhmael."

"Which is impossible," Ilenwyth was quick to point out. "The lower depths have never been plumbed; not even by the greatest names in our history. It's a black maze that none could hope to fathom."

"Lay your fears to rest, Mother. I will not make the attempt unless compelled by something greater than my love for Aric. He is a true friend, but his life or even mine is not worth the thousands of Den who would perish in an assault. I've learned my lesson." Ilenwyth stared hard with pursed lips trying to fathom his mind from without. She kept up the attempt until he added, "What about the Americas? Have you searched there?"

"Yes," Alseya answered, looking dejected. "It's difficult and wearying because of the great expanse of the land, but I am slowly working my way through it. But..."

"But what?" Eireden asked.

"I don't understand the reasoning behind expanding so much energy on this. It is Aric's choice to remain apart. We should not interfere. That is the way of the Fey."

"It's not *my* way," Eireden replied. "Aric is the strongest of the fey and a great ally. He will be needed...or so I fear."

"He may feel that his own needs come before others at this time," Alseya replied. "He may also feel that his time upon the earth is at an end."

"You mean he might kill himself?" Eireden demanded. "Why? It would make no sense. His main problem seems to stem from the fact that he loves a woman and she loves him back! That hardly seems reason enough to kill yourself."

Alseya dropped her eyes and said, "The lord Aric feels that his heart has been bound by the mind of another. Enslaved if you will, and that his feelings are not legitimate. He also believes that the union of man and fey is an abomination. Though in this he is short sighted. The Lady Eleanor is proof that the races may be adjoined in a positive way. In my opinion our efforts would be better served in bringing her back instead of him."

Eireden disagreed. Having Ella around would be too much for him to bear. Every time he heard her name his heart leapt. Every time he saw her face his soul burned with need. It had been truly difficult for him in those days after her rescue from the dungeons. He couldn't stand to be in the same room with her; her very presence tied his tongue and made him sweat. The guilt he felt had been fantastic. He was an engaged man and he could barely spare a thought for his future wife.

When Ella moved to Hildeoven things had been better, but not by much. The tower window that over looked the battle plain also faced south—toward Ella. Yes he came every morning to look out over the plain to assure himself that it was empty of his enemies, but he also came to peer southward, the direction his heart pointed.

He could feel her even then. She was moving slowly south and west.

"Ella should stay in the Americas," the king said and then held up his hand to forestall Alseya who had opened her mouth. "I understand the danger she faces out there alone; I warned her myself...yet I might have over-stated that danger. Rationally it would make no sense for our enemy to go after Ella when she is re-moving herself as a threat to him voluntarily. I think it best if we just left her alone."

"The same could be said for the Lord Aric," Alseya put in.

Eireden gritted his teeth. "It's not the same at all. There are reasons that he should be found. First of which is that he is my friend. He is also a great warrior of proven valor and strength. And for his sake he shouldn't be alone. We know that he blames himself for the destruction of the Feylands."

"Again you have described Eleanor and the state of her mind," Alseya remarked, pleasantly. "She blames herself just as Aric does. As well she has dis-played courage, and her potential as an ally is even greater than his. Also you view her as more than just a friend. You love her."

It felt as though all the air left Eireden's lungs and it took a moment for him to pull himself together. "In that you are wrong. I loved her...if I ever really did. Past tense," he said, echoing Ella.

Alseya raised an eyebrow and made to reply, but Ilenwyth interceded, "There is one place we haven't looked for Aric, though I am loath to name it: The Feylands, the home of the Fey. I didn't think about it until just now when you mentioned it. Its protections are proof against any scrying. Unless there is some power of the Fey's that can reduce the illusions?"

Alseya looked queasy at the very mention of the words: the Feylands. Her hand went to her breast and she took a deep breath before saying, "There isn't any way to circumvent the barrier, save by the physical presence of a fey. Scrying would be useless. Someone would have to go through the mists."

Thankful that the subject had been changed, Eireden asked, "Would you be willing?"

Her queasiness increased and she kept her eyes to the floor. She shook her head. "Not unless you ordered me to, my Lord. I would rather risk the Demorlaik than see the hell that has become of my homeland for a second time. It is too much to bear."

He would not order his future wife...the woman that would bear his children to go into a land of death, where every breath was poison. "Would Feylon go if she thought her son was there?" Eireden asked.

The answer was a firm no; Alseya shook her head emphatically. "Feylon believes as I do. We should not interfere in the life of another simply for our own sake. The same is true for all the fey. None would volunteer, however none would refuse an order from you either."

"Then I will go myself," the king said.

Ilenwyth's eyes shot open. "If you go you'll take a company with you of course! Or three companies of soldiers. You will not go alone."

"I cannot ask any to accompany me," Eireden replied. "I saw what the Forest of Mists did to even the hardiest of the Den. It was too sore a trial and I won't put any through it again."

Alseya's inherent racial calm seemed to crumble around the edges. "You endanger yourself for nothing. There is no saying that Aric is even in the Feylands. And if he is there then he went to die. You have been there. You know what it's like."

"I would not say that saving a life, especially the life of a friend is an act of nothing," Eireden replied stiffly.

"My apologies, my Lord," Alseya said, dropping into a curtsey, and remaining there with head bowed.

Eireden sighed. "There is no need for that," he said, taking her hands and pulling her up. Her skin was the velvet of a butterfly's wing and her beauty smote him as it frequently did when he wasn't prepared. *Maybe I could love her*, he thought. *If I ever gave her a chance.*

Aric was key to giving her that chance. It had been easier on Eireden when Ella and Aric had been a couple. Out of respect, he had bowed aside as the man unchosen. "I will leave this morning. The sooner I find Aric the better."

Alseya restrained the king as he headed for the door. "Perhaps before you leave we can discuss our wedding? You have put off setting a date for some time now."

A pain flared in his chest at the thought of his wedding. "When I find Aric. We'll set a date. I promise." He left them and alone went to the stables.

Chapter 5

Ella

The little fairy happily greeted the first rays of morning as she always did—with the energy of a jet engine. She squirmed from Ella's bosom, where it was warm and close to her heart, exploded like a tiny nova of light, and then shot away only to come right back to sit on Ella's shoulder, confused at her surroundings. This wasn't the candle-maker's home; this was the forest three miles west of Hildeoven.

"We're going on a trip," Ella told her. "To America." Whip-wip whistled a question and Ella answered, "It's not far. Just a couple of days walk." This elicited another question from Whip-wip, which was dutifully replied to. "Don't worry, *you* won't have to walk. I know how you hate it. I'll carry you or you can fly."

There were more follow-up questions of course. The fairy's curiosity on all subjects was boundless and only exhaustion or a momentary distraction would give Ella a break. Thankfully both came at frequent intervals.

The fairy wasn't like her old self, who had slept with the regularity of an aging tomcat. This new Whip-wip was like a recently birthed kitten. She snoozed half the day away but in short bursts and then tried to spend as much time eating during the other half.

"*Zooti*?" Whip-wip whistled hopefully. Just as she would an infant, Ella babied the tiny thing; she produced a blueberry and handed it over. In a minute the fairy was covered head to toe in blue juice and her whistles came out garbled and tiny bits of pulp flicked onto Ella's face.

"You shouldn't talk with your mouth full," Ella scolded gently. "We're going on the trip to get away. I don't like the Hidden Lands any longer. This adventure didn't turn out like I thought it would. I thought...I thought it would be fun. I thought I could find out who I am and where I came from. And who my parents were. Now I wish I didn't know."

Whip-wip threw the peel of the blueberry away and began cleaning herself—cat like, licking her fingers and hands and even her arms; somehow she even cleaned her elbows. She whistled as she did.

"And don't talk while cleaning yourself either. I can barely understand you. I wish I didn't know about my parents because they aren't..." Ella paused and stared down at the new shadow she cast which was flung out to the west in front of her. "They aren't what I had hoped for. My dad is evil and my mom is ill. You saw her. Wait, that was the old you. Do you remember Elleni?"

Whip-wip nodded, though that didn't necessarily mean she remembered. The fairy was always trying to please Ella and would lie without hesitation in the most bald-faced manner if she thought that it would make Ella happy.

"If you remember her, tell me what she looked like?" Ella asked. Whip-wip squinched her face for a moment, thinking. She then went rigid and blank-eyed. Ella nodded and said, "Yeah, that's her. It's one of the reasons why I didn't stay. I couldn't look at her without wondering what sort of pain she was going through and not being able to fix her. The truth is I wanted to put her out of her misery."

The fairy cleaned the last of herself and immediately asked for more zooti and of course asked another question.

"Misery? It's when someone is very unhappy," Ella said. She then dug out another blueberry, to which the fairy made a face. Ella tried her bag of assorted nuts and offered a cashew. This Whip-wip took and began to gnaw on it like a dog would with a bone.

It took over an hour before Whip-wip tossed what remained of the nut aside and then, exhausted from eating, she settled down for her first nap of the day. With her nestled, snug and secure, Ella walked along singing a lullaby of her own creation.

It was a peaceful morning yet that did not stop her from periodically checking the forest for danger. In this way she felt the presence of a variety of creatures including a badger, a doe and her fawn, and most interesting a small bi-pedal humanoid that she could not name by feel alone. Whatever it was it was smaller than a dwarf and walked with extremely light steps.

Unable to resist temptation, she went off after it to see what it was, however the thing effectively disappeared before she got close, and she decided against trying to find it through magic. She wanted to save her power just in case of an emergency; after the fiasco with the unicorn she wasn't going to chance draining herself uselessly.

Thinking on the unicorn she breathed out a sigh. If there was anything in the Hidden Lands that could entice her to stay it was the prospect of riding a unicorn, but none presented itself and she continued to plod along on foot. It had been a conscious decision to walk out of the magical realm and it wasn't a stretch to say that she was dragging her feet as she walked.

America didn't beckon as a beacon of hope, it was a place to lose herself in, and thus she wasn't in much of a hurry. At a stretch of hills she allowed herself to be turned south and though the hills began to run somewhat eastward she didn't bother trying to crest them. It seemed like too much effort and with every step her depression grew.

By afternoon she was tired and thirsty. Before kneeling in a little patch of valley tulips, Ella sighed for the hundredth time that day and then she reached out to touch the delicate petals and her mind arced through its fine stem and down into its branching roots, tracing a path, searching for water.

Water was near, just to the west. She could feel it in her mind, but there was something about the water that was strangely familiar. It felt like rain on a pond. Many high, leaping notes going all over the place.

"That reminds me of when I first met you, Whip..." Ella stopped in mid-sentence, her hand still on the tulip. It was the grotto that her mind had connected with. Whip-wip's grotto. Somehow Ella had allowed herself to be turned more southward than she had thought.

Now she hurried. Ignoring any possibility of danger, Ella ran light through the forest, noting the spot where Furen had tumbled down the hill and where Eireden had put her hand on his on the bole of a tree and she had felt his heart truly for the first time. And now she was up over the crest and there was the shaded pond below.

Whip-wip had been idling on Ella's shoulder, playing with her thick hair, but now she sat up and sniffed at the wind. Suddenly her sapphire eyes went wide and she began tugging at Ella, explaining unnecessarily that her family was close by.

"Yes I know," Ella said, smiling, allowing herself to be pulled along by a creature that didn't weigh over three ounces. Hooting and piping, Whip-wip called to her family and then her brothers and sisters and cousins beyond count swarmed Ella and she was laughing and they sparked and laughed as well. All the fairies were whistling at once so that nothing could be understood and it was all such a cacophony.

Fairies were crazy about seeing other fairies, all of whom they regarded as kin in one manner or another. And it was common practice among them to touch each other on the chest for luck or for greetings and thus they were all swirling about acting as if each was new to the other, when they had been playing together just the second before.

Then they coalesced into a spinning shimmering vortex and spun up over the pond lighting its surface and bringing the nymph up from the depths. Ella backed away from the water. Though nymphs ignored females as a rule Ella didn't quite trust the thing that had ensorcelled Furen and had nearly done the same to Eireden.

Ella sat up the hill on a log and watched Whip-wip playing and singing and dancing. "You should take it easy," she warned the fairy, when Whip-wip came up to her breathless and sweating. "You'll be too tired to even eat."

This struck all the fairies as the height of hilarity and they snorted laughter and some dropped from the sky to roll about on the ground clutching their little bellies. The laughter was so infectious that soon Ella was laughing so hard that tears streamed down her face and she wished that she could give up her troubles and live the carefree life of a fairy.

And then the tears of laughter turned to tears of pain. How could she take Whip-wip away to America? A fairy didn't belong there. She'd have to hide herself constantly. She'd have to limit herself. She'd be unhappy, maybe as unhappy as Ella was going to be.

"No," she said. "Whip-wip will be happy, even if I can't be."

The fairies carried on in their manic way for some time, but eventually Whip-wip, as the youngest, tired first and came to sit on Ella's knee, yawning hugely, showing her tiny fangs and pink tongue.

"Here you go. Bed time," Ella said, holding out the white linens of a lily, trying to hide her sadness. The petals were long and soft and Whip-wip sighed contentedly as she snuggled in. A second later she was snoring—a surprising sound in so delicate a creature— and Ella placed her in a tree bough.

"Don't let her follow me," she said to Easa-see, the leader of Whip-wip's family. "It's dangerous where I'm going." This had the little fellow laughing. "I'm serious. Whip-wip will be safer here and happier too. So keep her here when she wakes up."

Easa-see only laughed harder, which wasn't wholly unexpected. Fairies liked to laugh and would find any excuse in order to do so. Ella left him there chortling and looking sleepy. The family would all slumber for the better part of what remained of the day and then as sunset neared they'd wake for more play and eating.

It was a wonderful life and Ella knew she was right not to keep Whip-wip from it...even if it hurt so much. With tears streaming she marched straight away, heading west over the hills, and she didn't slow to check for danger or even to eat or drink. She walked for hours with her eyes pinned to the forest floor; a unicorn could've walked by and she would not have noticed nor even cared.

Now she was alone; more alone than she had ever been. And friendless as well; no Whip-wip, no Eireden, no Aric, no candle-maker. No Generai...the thought of brave Generai was too much and Ella staggered along in a misty haze of tears with only the setting sun in her face guiding her.

Generai had loved without hope. She never had a chance with the king yet she had been willing to lay down her life for him. That sort of helplessness was a sensation that Ella had never known nor would ever know. Whomever Ella picked would love her forever. Would die for her. Would kill for her. *He* would be the one who was helpless.

What about Aric? He left you, remember? The question came and was easily answered: Aric was as helpless as anyone else.

"I could have him," Ella spoke aloud with sad confidence. "If I really wanted him, I could have him eating out of my hand. It's why he left. He knew it was true...wait...wait. What am I saying? If I really wanted him? What does that mean?"

She stopped and gazed about with her mouth hanging open. Though her eyes were clear she didn't see the forest or the hills or empty sky, she only saw the king as he looked on the day she had seen the unicorn, striding through the forest with the sun dancing off his armor and his steel-grey eyes full of...

"Stop," she whispered. "I'm being stupid. It doesn't matter who I love or who loves me, not anymore. I had my chance with the king, but I was petulant and unforgiving, and now he's getting married. And Aric. I felt him pulling away. I knew it the second he saw my human mother. The truth is I let him go. I didn't even fight. Generai at least fought. She stayed by the king's side no matter that she had to know she was going to die...damn it! I have to stop this."

Ahead of her was a river. She ran forward and leapt it gazelle-like and then continued to run. She ran and ran and only when the moon had long been in the black sky did she bother to slow.

Thirsty, she drank from her water bottle, finishing it off. She then dug in her pack for food and the first thing she came upon was a small bag of blueberries. Ella broke down and cried in the dark, under the stars. She would be forever alone. There was no going back to the nursery or her old life in America, and there was no going back to the Den or the Fey.

Neither wanted her. She was both and so she was truly neither.

And there was no going back for Whip-wip. Ella wasn't a fairy. She wasn't a human either, nor a fey and not even an elf. She was Ella. She was no one.

Chapter 6

Eireden

The King rode through the main gate with a great deal of fanfare and perhaps an even greater deal of whispering. The city feared for its king. That he rode away alone wasn't taken as a good omen in most eyes.

Yet he wasn't alone for long. Eireden had barely left the wide battle plain behind and was riding with an easy canter along the South Stream road with his mind adrift when he heard a steady beat of hooves coming up quickly behind him.

Instinctively and perhaps eagerly he loosened the black sword of Aug-Raumon in its sheath and his hand gripped the hilts with anticipation. Being king was who he was by blood and birth, yet he was also a warrior by inclination and long training, and it was not a stretch to say that he was spoiling for a good a fight.

He had chosen a charger with the same disposition and he had to hold the beast back with a firm hand as it burned to rush against any foe. Checking the stallion he waited with his body leaning forward, his knees holding him in the saddle, ready to explode at the first hint of danger.

Yet the person following him was no enemy. Alseya sat atop a pretty little grey that seemed keen to show off her delicate gate, flirting with her stride. Again Eireden had to hold the stallion in check, this time for a different reason.

"Milady," Eireden said with a small bow from in his saddle.

She accepted his greeting with a smile and then inclined her head. "My Lord King."

There came a pause then as Eireden gazed at her lithe aspect and said, perplexed, "You seem arrayed as though for travel. Have you an errand? If so, you should not travel unescorted. It isn't safe."

"It is your safety that I fear for," she answered. "I can journey unobserved if I so wish. You, on the other hand, on your fine horse, with all your armor, are too great a figure to go unnoticed. I'm sure all the Hidden lands know of your passing."

"And you came to protect me?" Though he said this with a smile it wasn't out of the question. Next to Aric, she was the most powerful of the fey and a dangerous fighter in her own right.

"No. I came because you seemed lonely when you rode away."

"Oh," the king replied quietly. Could he deny it? Not even to himself. "I'm used to it," he said, which was true. Five years as a *Gada*, as a nameless one, had been lonely in the extreme and had inured him to the sensation. The truth was now crowds made him edgy.

"The world is more joyous when it is shared," she said, moving her grey along side of his and nudging it south. "We were not made to live our lives as hermits."

"Does this mean that you are coming with me?"

She bowed her head again, letting her milky white hair shimmer before her face for a moment. "With your permission."

"My permission?" Eireden smiled. "You are to be queen. You do not need my permission." Just then the idea of her being queen seemed strange to him. She was so tiny—barely five feet tall—and on the little grey she was almost child-like, except when he looked into her opal eyes. There were many years, many hundreds of years in those eyes. They held wisdom, and knowledge, and power...and strangely, a faint touch of frailty that he had never seen before.

"It is not the way of the fey to assume," Alseya remarked.

"A queen of the Den may assume much. However manners are always appreciated," Eireden said and then went silent for a long stretch of the dirt road.

Alseya was also quiet before she worked up the courage to ask, "And do you still plan on traveling to the Feylands?"

"I am, and right away." His heart told him this was where he would find Aric.

Her smile became strained. She then pointed south, saying, "Yet you follow the road to Hildeoven?"

"So I am!" he said with an odd guilty laugh. Was it inadvertent that he was following Ella instead of heading straight west for the Feylands? Hardly. She was like a magnet pulling at him. "I guess I wasn't really paying much attention. Yet since I am on this road I should pay my respects to Prince Lienhart now that he is well enough to receive visitors."

"Where you go, I shall follow," she said in answer, nudging the grey closer. "Though to be sure, I would that you were on this road in order to find our Eleanor."

Could she read minds? Or was it the heart that she could read? Either way the remark hit too close to home for the King. "I know your wishes, though I do not understand them."

"You will, one day. But since that day is not this one I say we ride! This little filly has a head on her. See how she flirts." The fey gave a sharp whistle and her steed shot away, kicking up dirt.

Eireden couldn't help but be impressed by Alseya. Like a feather on the filly's back, she rode south with her white hair streaming behind and her laughter on the wind. Effortlessly she sat astride the animal, undulating from the waist down, speeding faster than Eireden thought possible.

"She is beautiful," the king said, as if just noticing. "And kind. Why do I delay the inevitable? Why am I being unfair?" *Because you don't love her.* "That shouldn't matter. I have a duty to my people to marry...and I made a promise that I intend to keep. And there's no use putting it off. I will marry her."

His mind made up, the king unloosed the stallion and gave chase. The stallion was a marvel and blazed after, though with a knight in armor atop it, especially a knight of Eireden's size it struggled mightily to make even a dent in the lead the grey had.

When it was clear that the stallion wouldn't be able to catch the fleet grey Alseya slowed, laughing like warm wind on sunshine. "Your poor horse will never be able to catch up, not with its burden. It's all that silly metal you wear about, my Lord. You seem more a beetle than a man! Though a shiny beetle you appear and a handsome one as well."

"We should talk about our wedding."

"I've been saying the same thing for some time. It's good you caught up with me on that at least."

"Are you looking for a big wedding?" he asked. "We could fit half the kingdom in the Great Hall of Rhyoeven, if you wish."

She had been smiling, but now it failed. "If I wish? I don't get to...I mean...I think maybe it would be better if we do something small."

The king looked at her sharply. "This is your wedding. You can have it any way you want."

"Then I want it small."

"Ok. But you have to know that small is a relative term. I have to receive the five princes and their families. Then there's Ilenwyth. I can tell her small, but she is...how do I put this?"

"She's your mother."

Eireden laughed. "Yes and soon to be yours as well. You may be three-thousand years her elder, however you should prepare yourself for all the advice you can stomach."

Alseya's smile came back, though it sat a weak little thing on her red lips. "I would be honored for your mother to impart her wisdom."

There was something wrong. "Are you alright?" he asked. She nodded and attempted more at her smile, though the effort wasn't lost on the king. "I thought you'd be happy."

"Oh I am happy," she said as their horses crested a small rise.

They looked down at a long valley through which the road turned eastward gently. Eireden knew this stretch of forest. This was where Lienhart's company had been attacked—the spot where Olawe, sister of Generai had died; her body riven with spears. It was the spot where he had saved Ella. The spot where he discovered the connection between them—the one she despised and the one that doomed him to a life of heartache.

He blinked away the image; not of the valley, but of Ella's face.

"Happy people usually smile," he said, though his tepid smile was a match for hers.

She brightened the day by unfurling a large one. "How's that?"

"Little can compare," the king said and meant it. "Even when it's so false. You know this marriage isn't necessary. You're the only one that seems to be pushing for it."

"It is necessary," she insisted. "And you are right that no one seems to be pushing. The fey do not push. Yet this doesn't mean they are against our marriage. The opposite is true. There is an unspoken agreement that out union is the correct course of action."

"Union," Eireden said, quietly, uncertainly.

"Yes union. The only question is when? I think soon would be best."

Shifting in his saddle the king asked, "Soon? Is six months soon enough?"

"Sooner. I feel an urgency like I've never felt in my life. It's as though the air demands that we act now! I think one month is too long."

Eireden felt that need as well. It came to him every morning as he looked off to the south. But one month was just too fast. "I think a month's notice is unfair to our guests. Can you settle for three?" Her look told him that it wasn't. "Ok a month it is, but you're going to hear from my mother."

"Thank you," she said, nudging the grey closer and looking up at him. Her eyes were on his and he hesitated, which brought a chuckle from her. She held out a tiny hand and he took it in his huge paw. His instincts screamed for him to kiss her, but his heart rebelled. Yet he still had a duty to her and that included a physical duty that shouldn't have been this hard.

Alseya tilted her head upwards, waiting. It was clear that not only *could* she wait forever for him to kiss her, but that she *would* wait forever.

Well, if I'm going to do this, he thought, *I better do it right*. Since the king, high up on his stallion, would have an awkward time of it bending so low he decided to bring Alseya to him. Gripping his horse with his thighs he pivoted and gently lifted the fey up and sat her before him.

"My goodness," she said in a low voice. Then the king kissed her for the second time. It was deep and long. His hands went to the silk of her hair and then along her neck. His body pressed to hers. His heart beating so strongly as to send a thrum through her skin. His mind far away on another woman.

Chapter 7

Ella

Covered in morning dew, Ella woke chilled to the bone. She blinked around at the forest trying to wake up enough to tell where she was exactly, while at the same time her mind lingered on a dream she'd been in the middle of. In the dream she had been a bird high up in a tree, watching as a pair of riders came to a stop below her and...

Suddenly a sharp light struck her, interrupting her memory, and a tiny voice cried, "Zooti?"

"Gah!" Ella cried, blinking harder, confused at the presence of... "Whip-wip? What are you doing here?"

"Zooti," the fairy explained before tugging at the straps of Ella's pack. "Teefa es zooti?"

"What do you mean, where's your zooti?" The girl sat up, pulling back the layers of fronds she'd used for warmth and cover. "Whip-wip, your zooti is back at the grotto, that's where. You have to go back."

"Way?"

Ella's brow came down. The fairy hadn't whistled this, she had spoken in English. "Way? What do you mean? Do you mean why?"

"Sis, why?"

"Why?" Ella asked, bemused and exasperated. "Because, that's why. You belong with your family."

The fairy finally got the strap undone and after a second of digging came away with a blueberry, which she immediately tore in half with her sharp fangs. "Why?" she asked again around a mouthful.

"Because you belong with *them*! Your family. And don't ask why anymore."

Whip-wip considered this as she finished off the berry and then she said through purpled lips, "Es famry...famery. You famry."

Ella's shoulders slumped. "It's Fam-il-ly. And I'm not it. I'm not a fairy, and I'm not your real mother. Go back to where you belong, with Easa-see and the rest of your brothers and sisters. Please go away." Ella hung her head to hide her tears. Whip-wip would not understand them.

Irrepressibly curious, Whip-wip asked again, "Why? Why go away?"

Ella wanted to say: *Because I love you.* However that would never do. Fairies only understood the absolutes of emotions, never the nuance. Ella had to settle for the time-honored response of all mothers. Wiping her eyes with her sleeve she answered, "Because I said so. You go back to the grotto and to your family right now."

"No," Whip-wip said and then began a bath to remove the berry juices she had covered herself in.

"What? What do you mean, no?" Ella spluttered. "You're not allowed to tell me no."

"Why?"

"Because! Stop asking why about everything."

"Why no ask?"

A little noise of frustration escaped from Ella's throat. "Because...please go back. You won't like it where we're going. It won't be like before. You'll have to hide all the time, especially in the day, and you won't be able to fly around or anything."

"Why?"

"Whip-wip!" Ella stormed. Her anger grew so much that she blew a great gust of air at the fairy and sent her flying away, laughing. Ella sagged again, defeated. "What am I going to do with you Whip-wip?"

"Lerve," she answered easily.

"Do you mean, love?" When Whip-wip nodded Ella asked, "Since when did you learn English?"

The fairy shrugged her tiny shoulders and answered, "Thes-si." This meant now or present in the sythie language. For fairies, most everything occurs and has occurred in a coalesced term they describe as *thes-si*.

"Speak always and good," the fairy added, taking strands of Ella's hair and braiding absently.

"Oh really?" Ella said. "If that was true then you would have said: I've always spoken English."

"Sis," Whip-wip agreed, pulling together a couple of the braids and tying them at the ends. She then sat where the two joined and began to swing, kicking her feet.

"It doesn't matter if you speak English or not. You can't come." Ella bent so that the fairy could swing easier. It was only then that Ella realized how long her hair had grown. She'd not had a proper cut since coming to the Hidden Lands months before, and now it hung all the way down her back.

Whip-wip went back and forth merrily and said very plainly, "I go wit you. I do."

Ella realized that stopping this little wild creature would be impossible. The fairy would stalk her relentlessly. "If you come with me you'll have to do what I say. No questions asked. If I say hide, you'd better do it or I'll make you go back to the grotto."

Just like that, Whip-wip seemed to fade among the deep cherry-brown of Ella's hair. "Whip-wip hide," she said.

"Yes you did and really well...hey stop that!" Ella cried giggling and squirming. Whip-wip had begun tickling her neck.

Of course Whip-wip didn't stop. Laughing and joking was her natural state. To get her to stop Ella had to comb her out with hooked fingers at which point the fairy buzzed away, cackling and dodging back and forth among the trees showing off her speed.

"Come back, you silly," Ella called. "You're going the wrong way." Whip-wip had shot northward, while Ella was going south and west toward..."Where am I going?"

Her original plan had been to re-join her old life, but that would mean putting her friends in danger. She couldn't do that. So that left...what? A life as a wandering vagabond?

"Maybe not. I can help people. I can heal people. That's something." Just then it didn't seem like much of something. It seemed like a life of loneliness. She made to sigh, however Whip-wip came back, flying erratically, chasing after a jigging and jiving butterfly. Ella had to laugh. The natural chaotic movements of the butterfly were utterly baffling to the fairy who tried to emulate the herky-jerky motion but who could never catch up.

Finally an exasperated Whip-wip shot a beam of light at the insect and it dropped to the forest floor.

"Look," Whip-wip said, hauling the butterfly up to Ella by one of its legs.

"Yes," Ella said, putting out her hand. The butterfly was half Whip-wip's size and the strain of carrying it was evident. "It's an emperor."

"Em-per-per?" Whip-wip asked, taking a seat on Ella's thumb.

"Em-per-or," Ella explained. "Isn't it pretty? I just love her purple wings."

The fairy's eyes went wide and consciously she sat up straighter, letting her four wings flare. "*Ma ta sss*," she said disdainfully, meaning: *Her* wings are ok.

A laugh escaped Ella. "Yours are still the prettiest. Gold and silver, what's prettier than that? You should know that..." A raindrop splashed down upon Ella's wrist and she blinked up at the sky as more came falling. "We should let her go. She has to get under cover."

With a gentle breath, Ella blew on the butterfly and the stunned creature seemed to come awake. It beat it's two large wings and then flew off dodging the rain drops. Whip-wip too hid. She tucked her wings in and burrowed down into Ella's shirt to stay dry.

Ella didn't have the luxury of escaping the downpour and she had nothing more to protect herself with than a hooded coat. Despite this she remained warm. Her magic was like a volcano within her and it was nothing to let it heat her as she went.

All that day she walked in the grey showers and the journey could not have been more depressing. Whip-wip stayed hidden, tucked away in Ella's bosom. The hours slipped by slowly.

By evening she crossed a wide river and climbed the hills south of Tayoeven. The city was brightly lit, strangely so, and its warmth beckoned, however Ella turned away. She slipped and slid, following the mudding streams that ran down the hills until the lights were lost to her and the coming night hid any mention of her passing.

Just as the night before she went on long beneath the stars before weariness had her stumbling. Only then did she search for a place to stay, and she did so with a sense of foreboding. Nervous, she touched a pine and through its roots felt the world about her.

That nervousness extended for miles. It was felt by the flowers and grass and as the night went on, the very air carried it to her.

"Do you feel that," she asked Whip-wip. "There's something wrong."

"Sis."

Again Ella tried to touch the world, to follow the anxiety to its source, but it proved fruitless. Whatever was the issue was too far away for her to sense. The anxiety built up upon her and grew into cold a fear, which made the air difficult to breathe. She grew wide-eyed in the dark while Whip-wip shivered...and then it ended.

There was a burst that nearly stopped her heart and then slowly the fear left the air and left the roots, leaving her drained. Exhausted, she covered herself in pine needles and fell asleep beneath a rock over hang.

Only a few hours later she woke to a grey dawn and a hungry fairy. "Zooti?"

Ella tried to hand over a blueberry, however they were three days old and mushy. Whip-wip made a face before saying, "New zooti?"

"We'll find some," Ella said. She went to put her hand out to another tree to search, but paused with it inches away. The fear from the night before holding her back. What had that been?

Had Darhmael been up to something? Should she go back and warn Eireden?

"No," she said. He would know already, or at least Alseya would know. She was very powerful and fully in tuned to the world. What happened last night would not have been lost on her.

Resolutely Ella touched the tree and within a minute felt the fury roots of an early season peach tree not more than a mile off. "Here go," Ella said ten minutes later, taking her knife and slicing off a little of a peach. Whip-wip was soon slurping the juices and gorging herself on the meat of it. Ella grabbed two for her breakfast and another couple to nibble on as she walked.

She'd be leaving the Hidden Lands that day. The border wasn't more than eleven miles away and despite the rain it was well before noon that she stood gazing at the thin veil of illusion that helped to detour the Americans away.

It made her smirk. Where once she had been in awe of the magic, now she saw gaping holes—holes that no one would ever notice. "I should tell Eireden. He'd want to..."

She stopped in mid-sentence as her far seeing eyes swept north where the handsome king ruled in his city of white marble. Her breast heaved a great sigh as she pictured his face.

"No. That's done with. It's all done with." Clamping her mouth she passed through the veil and tramped along the edge of the hills and the rain went on and on.

By sunset she was soaked through and even Whip-wip was wet and shivering. The fairy had her wings wrapped about her while her fangs jimmied up and down.

Suddenly Whip-wip pointed and cried, "Ssi meach!"

Among fields of turned soil sat a lonely farm-house. It was the first sign of civilization they'd seen since they had spotted the lights of Tayoeven the day before. Whip-wip wanted to go to it straight away, but Ella knelt and felt the world around her.

There was a town further on. That's where they'd go, she decided, hoping to find a motel. It was an hour walk and all during that time she coached Whip-wip on how to behave: when she could come out of hiding, and when she could fly, and when she could display her light.

"I warned you this would be how it is," Ella said as Whip-wip looked more and more miserable.

The town was worrisomely small; not even rating a single traffic light. And there wasn't a motel, however there was a bed and breakfast, which was doing a surprisingly brisk business.

"You've got the last room," beamed a cheery white-haired, matronly sort of lady. She was stout from the ankles on up. Despite the cheeriness she gave

Ella's bedraggled appearance a queer look...and then her eyes went wide.

After all of her warnings to Whip-wip about staying out of sight and being careful, Ella had forgotten to hide her own short sword. It had hung from her hip for so long that it was strange not to have it on her side.

"It's for protection," she explained. "I...I don't believe in guns."

"Oh." The cheery smile went crooked. "Well, uh, I hope a full sized bed will be big enough. Like I said, we're booked."

"A full is fine," Ella said, distractedly. Whip-wip was squirming about in her hiding spot, trying to peek out.

"It can be quite snuggly, but I suppose that's one of its benefits."

"Benefits? I don't understand what you mean by..." A quick glance around answered her question. The main sitting room was populated by twelve people—six couples. "It'll be just me," Ella said quietly as if admitting to something wrong.

The woman's smile nearly failed altogether. The remnants sat on her face as though held there with string. "For the weekend?" she asked. "Just you?"

"No, just for the night."

Now the smile was done. "We only rent rooms by the weekend. There's a motel out by the highway. What you want to do is go back the way you came and take a right on county road eight. From there it's only seven or eight miles."

Ella looked out at the night and the rain. Suddenly she felt a little of the fear she had from the night before. It wormed in her gut. "I, uh...walked."

The idea of someone walking seemed strange to the lady. "You walked," she asked open mouthed. "You didn't drive?" When Ella shook her head the lady nodded and then took Ella's hand saying, "Ok. We'll take care of you. You do have money?"

Ella understood the woman's worry. She looked a mess, wearing rain soaked clothes that were a mish-mash of styles: the outfit she'd worn into the Hidden Lands long before: jeans and a white blouse, with a magenta cloak—given to her by Ilenwyth, and a pair of tall leather boots that had once been Generai's.

"I have money, or a credit card."

The lady swiped the card and then ushered Ella to a back room on the second floor. It was cramped with a sloping ceiling, but it was also warm and cozy. Whip-wip loved it. When the lady had left she wiggled her way out of Ella's bosom and then streaked around the room investigating everything, demanding that each drawer be opened for her to scrutinize.

While the fairy was busy, Ella undressed and hung her clothes up to dry. She then made a cage out of her slim fingers, caught Whip-wip and stuck her in the pocket of her robe and went to take the longest, hottest bath she had taken in a very long time. While she did Whip-wip dangle her feet in the water, and sang a song about her grotto back home, somehow insinuating that Ella was a nymph with her lyrics.

It was a relaxing time, that is until Ella went to wash up. The fairy had been eyeing the soap with sus-picion until Ella ran it under the water at which point bubbles formed and Whip-wip went nuts.

She squealed with delight as she flew about at-tempting to shoot through them or attempting to wrap her arms around them, or standing on them while her wings beat like mad. This went on until Ella was pruney and waterlogged.

"Mow?" Whip-wip begged.

"No. I'm done. Look at my fingers. They're like white raisins." Of course this had to lead to a descrip-tion of what raisins were. Ella explained as she went back to her room and brushed out her hair.

"Why?" Whip-wip asked. "Grape is gud."

"A dried grape is also good." Ella said, into the mirror. "When we get to a real town, one with a grocery store, I'll get you some. That way..."

A sound interrupted her. It was the sound of a horse trotting. Fear smote her and quick as a wink she flicked off the light with her mind and ran crouching to the window.

"Oh my God! It's him. What's he doing here?"

The King on his black charger rode up the muddy track. Even in the dark his armor shone, but as she watched he swung a black cloak over himself and now all she could properly make out was the steel of his eyes.

Chapter 8

Eireden

The kiss lingered on Eireden's mind, and upon his lips. Even hours later he could feel the warmth of it. Unfortunately he could also feel the guilt of it squirming like something rotten in his stomach. It made what should have been an enjoyable dinner with Prince Lienhart, less so.

Lienhart was overjoyed at the news of the upcoming marriage, yet also surprised at how rapidly it would be upon them. "That is quick. I mean it's quick for us...for the Den. How about for you?" he asked Alseya. "For your people?"

"*Our* people," she asserted, touching his scarred hand. "That is what this marriage is all about." Though her eyes were warm, the words were bereft of any sort of romance or love and the king couldn't look at her. She glanced his way and then back to the prince. "Our peoples have always been entwined by destiny, yet destiny can be fickle and harsh. This marriage will ensure that we are tied together with a bond stronger than destiny. The bond of love." Eireden's lips became a thin line and this she caught. She smiled at it. "You will see, your Highness. When your son is placed in your arms you'll feel love—so much love that you'll think your heart will burst."

"Yes, I'm sure you're right, Milady," Eireden assured, honestly. "I couldn't imagine it otherwise."

"And neither can I," Lienhart cried jovially. Throughout dinner he'd been easy with the wine and now his cheeks were red and his one eye half closed. He stood with his glass raised. "A toast! To King Eireden and Queen Alseya!"

Eireden raised his own glass but before he could say anything Alseya said in a small voice, "I'm not queen yet." The words struck the king and the guilty sick feeling came stronger than before while the air turned thick between them. Generai had said that very thing—*You're not queen yet*—not long before she had sacrificed her life for Eireden. "I'm sorry. I don't know why I said that," Alseya said quickly.

For the first time since they sat, Eireden looked her way and saw the sudden sadness in her eyes. He also saw in her a sharp edge of guilt, as well as a hint of desperation—yet he did not see love. That was something he had never missed when looking into Generai's eyes. She had loved him to death.

"To Generai," the king said and finished his wine at a gulp. Lienhart, looking confused followed suit while Alseya nodded.

"To Generai. To sacrifice," she said, and though her glass was nearly full she drank it all. "Excuse me. I am tired from our ride and I fear the wine has gone to my head." As she stood the two men did as well, the prince bowing. She offered her hand, which he took to his lips. "Thank you for dinner, Prince Lienhart. As always your hospitality is unmatched. I do hope we can make a week out of it. I have family still in Hildeoven and would love the opportunity to meet with them to plan for the wedding." She gave Eireden a significant look.

He shook his head, which Lienhart missed. "Of course!" the prince cried. "I would be overjoyed."

"You may stay if you wish, Milady," the king said. "You know I cannot. Lienhart, I must be away by sunrise. See that my horse is..."

"Our horses," Alseya interrupted. "You cannot cross through the Forest of Mists without me. And I will not be parted from you again."

Despite his wits dulled by the wine Prince Lienhart's face showed his shock at the mention of the Forest of Mists, a place where his courage had failed him. "Do you require a guard? Should I accompany you with a squadron of cavalry?"

"No my friend," the king replied. "The Forests are too sore a trial for man and beast alike. I shall be safe enough with the Lady Alseya by my side and she'll be safe with me by hers."

The king could not fail to catch the look of relief that swept the prince's face, but he was tactful enough to pretend not to have. Alseya demonstrated equal discretion and took her leave with a gentle smile. Despite her admission of exhaustion she did not sleep that night and instead went to find her relatives. The king, on the other hand, felt a great need for sleep though he knew not why.

The following morning the pair took their leave of Hildeoven and rode in steady silence toward what the Den called the Feylands and what the Fey called Istranane. It was an absolutely beautiful morning and yet despite that the land was steeped in magic and consisted of impossible plants and gorgeous views neither the Den nor the Fey seemed at all pleased on this easy journey.

The Feylands had become a land of death and it's very thought was enough to ruin even such a pleasant ride. Though it didn't stay so pleasant all day. As afternoon came on clouds built up and now a steady rain sent little rivers running from their cloaks and down the backs of the horses.

"Last chance," Alseya said as they stood on the verge of the forest. She held a delicate hand to her face. There was a smell of rotting flesh drifting along with the mists and the horses had to be held in place by stern hands.

"Lead on," he said simply. She complied and the two followed along an easy dirt path and as the minutes ticked by the smell grew worse. It became a stifling, stomach-churning nightmare and the King had to dismount in order pull the horses along.

"Don't look, Milady," Eireden said as they came up over a rise. Before him was horrendous mound of decaying goblin corpses. All of them bore obvious wounds attributed to death in battle, however a number had been partially eaten by something of great size. Eireden's hand went to the hilt of his black sword.

"There is no need for your sword, Den," a voice hissed out from behind the mound of bodies. It took the King a moment to see the strange face with its long teeth and plated skin—it was the mist dragon. Without the foggy illusions it normally hid itself in, it wasn't nearly as formidable appearing as it had on the one other time they had faced each other. In fact it looked distinctly undernourished.

"Is this the fare of a dragon?" Eireden asked. "I would have thought a beast of your magnificence would dine upon something...tastier."

The dragon sighed, shooting out a long plume of steam that obscured it momentarily. "Aye, aye, aye. You would not be wrong on the average evening. Only there has not been an average evening for many days. Not since the elves came. Curse them. Curse Darhmael!"

Alseya, looking whiter than usual, spurred her horse forward. "Please tell me Thayonra, have you seen the elf? Is he within your borders?"

The dragon dropped his head and answered, "No Milady. Only the lord Aric comes to the Forest of Mists and he for not much longer. He is ill. He drinks the poison waters and sips the poison air. It will be that I feed upon him before many more days pass."

Eireden, who had been feeling a strange pity for the monster, felt his anger grow quick; he drew his sword and came on with death in his heart, but Alseya held his arm.

"It is the way of dragons," she told him, simply. Her touched held magic, which he did not resist. It calmed him and he slid the sword back home.

The dragon did not seem much concerned with Eireden, in fact he heaved out another grey billowing sigh and rested his head upon the stinking hill. "But for how much longer will it be the way of Dragons?" it asked plaintively. "The elf poison is emptying the forest. Everything that I love so much to eat is no more. The gnomes have fled the vapors. I haven't had gnome in weeks. Nor adar, or 'corn, or dryad, or dwyr, or anything crunchy. Look at what I'm reduced to. I subsist on carrion! I'm no better than rat or roach."

"There are other forests," Alseya said. She turned to Eireden. "Maybe you could partition off the forest south of Tayoeven? From what I understand it is relatively unused."

Eireden stared at her in disbelief. "Partition? What do you mean? Would you that I allow this beast to range upon my lands?"

"Yes, exactly."

"That's...that's absurd. First off, there are woodsman and huntsman working those forests and secondly, he's dragon!" Eireden pulled her close and whispered, "We kill dragons. The Den that is."

"It's true," the dragon said. "They do. It's the way of the Den."

"Perhaps you can make an exception. The mist dragon is a singular being. He should be protected."

Eireden rubbed his forehead. "We'll see. Maybe I could cordon some land for him, but there would have to be strict rules in place against poaching by the beast. Really, the thought of him eating a unicorn or even a gnome is repulsive."

"I agree, my Lord. Perhaps if we were to supply him with an occasional goat or sheep?"

The dragon perked up at this. "Yes. Or horse. One of these would do nicely for a start. If you must know, rotting maug is hard on my innards. I am sure you understand."

"I understand perfectly," the king replied, fingering the black hilt of his sword again. The dragon had started forward with a green glint to his hungry eyes, but at the king's gesture it flinched back. "It'll be maug for you for a little longer, Sir Dragon. I am still in need of my mount. And yet I am not unmoved by your plight." Eireden glanced away from the pile of dead and smiled at Alseya. "As a gesture of affection to my bride to be I will acquiesce to her desires and provide for your upkeep for as long as she lives."

The dragon showed his pleasure in his deadly manner: exposing his foot long fangs in an imitation of a smile. Alseya on the other hand seemed less pleased. As the king puzzled on this she waved her hand.

"Mayhap it would be wisdom for you to set an actual time limit," she said. "Destiny's hand is fickle after all. Would you agree to a thousand years?"

"Of course," Eireden replied, suddenly concerned. "Is there something wrong?"

"Maybe it's just the smell," she answered evasively, holding her hand to her face. "Oh Thayonra, I cannot abide the stench any longer. Please don't be offended, but I must take my leave."

The dragon, a huge beast of many tons of muscle, bone, and shearing claws actually bowed its head to the tiny fey women. He did not do the same to Eireden. Instead, the two natural enemies eyed each other as the king escorted Alseya away.

"That's better, don't you think?" he asked after they had ridden a few miles.

She shook her head. "Can't you smell that? The chemicals? We're getting close."

Alseya wasn't wrong. Within minutes the horses began to yank back on the reins. They snorted, stamped, and generally made such a fuss that the king had to dismount once more and pull them along through a quickening rain. The evil smell mounted until Eireden tore his cloak and wrapped the muzzles of the horses. The remainder of the crimson cloth he gave to Alseya who looked a light green.

"What about you?" she asked, coughing weakly.

Though the king found the smell noisome and repellent he wasn't nearly as affected as Alseya was. It was as if Darhmael had concocted some poison that was particular to the fey. "I'll be ok at least as long as it takes to find Aric."

It was easier to find the lone fey than he had expected. Time had not healed the Feylands, if anything it appeared worse. The air shimmied with reeking fumes that choked the lungs and stung the eyes. With the rains, the land itself had turned into a black bog that made every step treacherous. Yet that same rain gave clues.

Toward the lower part of the valley they found footprints and strange criss-crossing ruts in the slime. These the king followed until he spied a stooping figure pushing feebly at a wheelbarrow, trying to man-handle it up the side of hill. The wretched creature was covered head to toe in the muck and seemed thin to the point of starvation, still the king recognized his old friend.

"I see Aric," Eireden said. Alseya had been walking essentially blindfolded and now she tried to pull back the material covering her eyes, but the king stayed her hand. "No. There is no need for you to go further. Take the horse back up into the forest. Just keep your head down and follow our tracks back out."

"Nay. I would…" she paused to cough and then finished, "I would not be separated from you, Milord."

His first impulse was to command her to leave as though she were one of his subjects, which technically she was. She was also his fiancé. "Please?" he begged. "There is no need for you to feel further pain."

She nodded which he mistook for agreement but she was only trying her best not to break down coughing. In a choked voice she said, "The wind...is wrong. The air in the forest spoke of fear. I will not be easy in my mind without you by my side. There is danger."

He had not felt any fear, but held his tongue, trusting her greater abilities. Taking her bodily he propelled her with one hand while hauling on the rebellious horses. They were in no way quiet, yet Aric ignored them as he struggled with the burrow, which he had piled high with black muck.

"Aric? Aric?" Eireden called, yet it wasn't until he had closed the distance and actually touched the fey on the shoulder that Aric turned in dreadful daze.

"Auh?" Aric said.

Eireden recoiled at the sight of the fey. Aric's face had mostly rotted away so that the few teeth he had left could be seen sitting like little grey boulders in a ragged wet landscape. His nose was gone and now only two black holes bored into the center of his face. And his eyes had been eaten away by the poison in the air, leaving runny pits.

"Oh no," Alseya whispered. Aric tried to speak, but without tongue or lips he only made sloppy grunts. She touched him, quieting him, and then a blue light streaked out of her fingertips and blanketed the fey. He tried to struggle but Eireden, with his great strength, held him in place until he had been fully healed. Alseya swooned and the king left Aric and caught her.

"She should not have done that," Aric said without emotion or even a hint of gratitude. He then picked up the handles of the burrow and began to trudge away.

"What are you doing?" the king demanded. "How can you walk away from her like this? She just saved your life."

"I didn't ask to be saved," Aric replied, without turning.

"Stop!" Eireden demanded.

Aric dropped the burrow and turned insolently. "What?"

Eireden felt a fury at Aric's actions like he hadn't felt in a long while. "You are being rude. It's unbecoming." Aric gave a shrug and Eireden seethed, "You're not thinking straight, I'll make an allowance for that. It's the poison in the air. You should come back with me to Rhyoeven."

"My mind is *straight*, as you put it," Aric replied. "And I will come back to Rhyoeven—when I'm done here."

He turned and began again to work his burden. Eireden hefted Alseya to his chest, covered her face against the acid rain and hurried after Aric. "When you're done here? What does that mean? When you're done dying?"

"Hardly," Aric snorted. "I'll leave when I'm done fixing the wrongs I have wrought."

"Not your...fault," Alseya whispered.

Aric laughed at her in harsh anger. "Then whose fault is it, Alseya? Gada's? Hardly. He saw the truth when I only had the eyes of a child in love. Ella's? No. She had no idea what she was…" he left off with a snarl.

Alseya pulled back the strip of cloak Eireden had covered her face with. She was white like he had never seen a living creature before. It looked as though her skin had been bleached to the point of death. Still she rallied what little strength to admonish Aric. "His name is Eireden, and he is your king. You would do well to acknowledge this."

For some reason this got through to Aric, who dropped the handles of the burrow and made to kneel. Eireden grabbed him and said, "No. Not here, not like this. You're my friend, Aric. I've come to find my friend not another subject."

The fey fought him off and then knelt. He did so with a drooping shrug. "You are king. You are my king no matter if I can cure these lands or not. In every way I have proven myself the least fit of your subjects."

"Stop," Eireden said hoisting the fey back to his feet. "Your strength has always overwhelmed me. If any should be king of the fey it should be you my friend."

Both Aric and Alseya shook their heads.

"Look about you," Aric said ruefully. "The Fey-lands are a testament to my weakness. A monument, dedicated for all eternity, to my short-sightedness."

"Aric, damn it!" Eireden thundered. "You make no allowance for mistakes. Know that perfection isn't the journey but the goal...the unattainable goal. Yet if any could attain it, I would guess that it would be you. I know your heart and your mind. If any would be a great king of the fey it would be you."

Alseya shook her head weakly, but Aric stood straighter and said, "Yes you're right! I would be a great king—far greater than you, my friend. I'd rebuild all this land. I'd turn it back into the pristine land it once had been and then I'd gather all the fey to me. Picture it!"

Aric waved his hand, indicating the valley, with an insane gleam in his eye and a deadly smile on his lips. Alseya began to moan. He ignored her and went on, "And when our strength was full upon on us once again I'd do the world a favor and rid it for all time of the menace in the Demorlaik. I would slay them all. Every ogre, goblin, troll. Every gnoll, every demon, every dragon, everything that got in my way would have to die, because that's the only way to true peace."

"No," Alseya whispered.

"Oh yes! The fey would flourish and be great as they were meant to be. And the world would be perfect....and you'd see peace spread across it...or you would if it weren't for those pesky humans. Right Eireden? Weren't you the one who warned me of the danger they pose?"

Eireden felt the poison in his mouth, but thought it would be dangerous to spit it out just then. Aric was practically manic and there was no knowing what he would do. The king swallowed the poison with a grimace and then said, "The humans can be contained."

"But for how long? The Den are long lived, but the fey are immortal. A threat to you that is centuries away is for us just a blink of an eye."

"And what would you do?" Eireden didn't like the look in Aric's green eyes. There was a fever burning in them.

Aric shrugged uncaringly. "They are only humans. I could have them at each other's throats without much effort. I'd let them kill themselves off and those that managed to live…" he finished with a knowing look.

"Murder?" Eireden asked. "And what of the Den?"

"What can I say? We'd still need servants."

Eireden's teeth ground together and his hand was on his sword, but he managed to hold back. He did not fear Aric, certainly not in that poisoned land. Aric was growing weaker with every passing second and Alseya had already slipped into what looked like a coma.

"You speak like an elf," Eireden said.

Now Aric laughed with his head back and he seemed to have gathered his strength. "Yes!" he cried. "And why should I not sound like an elf? What is the difference between elf and fey but the temerity to rule?

To claim authority over another. To claim a moral and genetic superiority over all others? Were I to claim kingship then I'd be claiming supremacy over all the world."

"Is that how you see me?" Eireden asked. "I am king after all."

"No," Aric replied easily. "You rule out of a sense of duty only. The Den are different and thankfully so."

"Come, we are not so different, Aric. All this you just said is not you. You are kind and gentle. You would not rule in this manner. I know you."

Aric sighed, drooping. "I wish you were right. However it is a fact that any fey who would seek power over another cannot be trusted."

"Yet you trust the Den?"

"I trust you," Aric answered.

"You claim me as your king. What would be your answer if I commanded you to come back with me? I need you. Darhmael is not yet defeated. His army is still very great...and what's more, I'm to be married."

"Darhmael would be a fool to try to take you on again. As for marriage..." A sad laugh escaped Aric. "I suppose a congratulation to you both is in order."

"It is. Think about it for me. You could take a break in a couple of weeks. Come out for the wedding. We'd heal you up; get some food in your belly; you'd have a great time."

"And Ella?"

Eireden sighted his heart on Ella, she was south west near Tayoeven. "She's going to the Americas and doesn't plan on returning. Now promise that you'll come."

"I cannot make promises I have no intention of keeping. I won't leave until I'm done here, now please take your bride to be and leave this land. She is weak and will die soon if you do not. It takes a certain hard-headedness that very few possess to last for long here."

Eireden actually laughed before saying, "I'm not done with you. I'll leave for now but I will not allow you to waste away out here."

Aric pointed to the misty forest. "Take her and love her. Do yourself a favor and forget about me and Ella. Love this girl while you can. Alseya deserves it."

Chapter 9

Ella

The sight of the king in his glittering armor, astride the black charger galvanized Ella. Her eyes went wide and she stood frozen for a full three seconds as he drew nearer with the horse's hooves kicking up mud. And then she flew about the room, snatching her drying clothes and throwing them on with little regard to anything but speed. She then dashed around in a mindless furor tiding up as fast as she could.

"Why are you do?" Whip-wip asked in a sleepy a voice. The fairy hadn't budged from the bed of wash-cloths she had fashioned for herself as a nest and it was clear she wouldn't.

"The King! Eireden's coming," Ella cried, kicking her pack beneath the bed. When it got jammed, still partly showing she went down and pushed it further out of sight. She then grabbed up the damp towels and shoved them unceremoniously into any available drawer.

"Why he want?" Whip-wip asked. She only had one eye open and even that was a slit.

"What does he want? I don't know. Probably to..."

Ella's quick ears caught the soft tread of the king on the stair. Despite that he was so big he could he could move like a cat when he wished, yet little got past her when she was alert.

And then he was just outside the door and there came a soft knock.

"Come in," she breathed, before turning to mirror one last time. Her eyes went wide at what she looked like.

Yet when the king came in, bigger than life, he took away the panic she had felt at her appearance. Though it had only been a few days since she last saw him, his smile still dazzled her, while his eyes smoldered right to the hidden part of her that ran her breathing mechanism and it shut down momentarily.

She forgot her manners completely and only stood there with her lips parted and her eyes growing wide. He was last person she had expected to see and the shock left her nearly speechless.

"Ella," he said her name easily as if this was only a social call. When she did nothing, but open her eyes wider he asked, "May I come in?"

She swallowed. "Of course, your Highness. Come in. Have a seat on..." There was nowhere for him to sit save the bed and the idea that this man would be on her bed stopped her words.

He noted her floundering and said kindly, "I'll stand, thank you." Stand he did—very close—looming would be a good way to describe it. Ella backed up to the dresser. It was one thing to confront Eireden in a sprawling palace or a vast forest, but in the cramped little room he seemed larger than life.

"How may I help you?" she asked, nervous at his proximity, yet curious as well.

He knifed her in the chest with his answer. "I'm here concerning the Lord Aric. Has he tried to contact you?"

She blew out noisily, her curiosity gone, replaced with the familiar self-pitying anger she'd been carting about within her. "In the last three days? I haven't seen him and I don't want to. Wherever he is, isn't far enough away for me."

The king saw her pain and gave her the sad smile that he'd worn so frequently as a *gada*. "I had to ask. Sorry."

A silence, broken only by the light snoring of Whip-wip came between them. Ella grew more and more uncomfortable until she finally gave the king a half shrug and said, "If there's nothing else..."

"There is something," he said, suddenly uncomfortable. "There was something between us once and now there isn't. That is a correct statement?"

She blinked widely and then answered guardedly, "Yes, I suppose."

"I need you to explain that to me," he said, clearly honest in his request. There wasn't a touch of bitterness or anger in it, only simple curiosity.

"What...you want me too..." Ella said, spluttering her words, feeling her facial muscles pull about in confusion. Eventually she turned her back on him, but unfortunately she had faced the mirror and there was the king staring at her in puzzlement.

He raised his hands in an odd shrug and said, "Honestly, this concept of love is beyond my ability to comprehend. One day you people give your lives for love...for each other, and the next day the feeling is just gone. How does that happen?"

Ella couldn't believe she was hearing this. "Hold on, *you people*? What about you? Why don't you count yourself in this?"

"I am king. I am different, but you are a girl. Love comes to you naturally. So I ask again: How can you give up love? Is it just a transitory feeling? Is it simply a tangential outspur of lust? Can it be controlled?"

"Amazing! How can you of all people ask this?" Ella barked furiously, her blue eyes flashing with ice. "In case you forgot, you're the one who turned his back on me!"

"Yes, and I explained why," he said as if her anger was nothing but a child's tantrum.

"You explained? Do you think your explanation was near good enough?" Ella spat out the words with the intent of hurting him. "Well it wasn't. Not even close. You want to know if love can be controlled? Yes, but only by a robot like yourself."

"Robot? I don't know this word."

Was he putting her on? She thought he'd been to America enough times to know what a robot was. "It's a machine in human form, duh."

The king got a faraway look in his eyes and then smiled suddenly. "Humans can be as clever as gnomes at times. So, you think your king is a robot? What about you, Milady? Are you a robot as well since you no longer love me?"

"Hardly...I still have *some* feelings for you," she said as her anger began to slip. "But it's not meant to be. Our love is, I don't know, wrong maybe. Don't you feel it too? It's like fate doesn't want us together...and besides you're getting married, so why do you care?"

Eireden ignored this last. "And the Lord Aric. He left you because of your half-breed status. Do you still have the same feelings for him? The same love?"

"Half-breed?" Ella's lips disappeared and her teeth flashed as she snarled, "Get out! You may be king in the Hidden Lands but here in America you're nothing but a jerk and we have plenty of them already. Now get out."

He did not leave, nor did he budge in his stance and Ella felt somewhat powerless when he didn't. It turned her anger into fear and it was she who edged away from him until her back ran up against the dresser.

"I'm just trying to understand the nature of love," he said innocently, ignoring her discomfort and the fact that she had retreated from him. "Love is at once equally mysterious and powerful. It springs from a source unknown yet contains the energy to move mountains. And it's my conjecture that if one were able to unravel the puzzle that it is, then that person would have control over powers unseen since Aug-Raumon."

"Control love?" she asked. "Are you talking about a love spell? To use on who? Alseya?"

He shrugged. "Maybe upon myself. I don't know exactly how it will work in the end, and I'm not talking about a simple love spell either way. My goal is capturing the power of this most powerful of emotions. Though to be sure I'm not exactly positive it even exists outside the imagination of the individual."

"It exists," Ella asserted, her fear growing. The king was being exceptionally odd. His mannerisms were clinical to the point of being inhumanly cold and the steel-grey of his eyes were now mostly steel. "Love exists, but it's not something that can be measured. It's there or it's not."

"So you still love me exactly as you did before?" When she paused in her answer he reminded her, "You just mentioned that you still had feelings for me. Can you describe them?"

For Ella the conversation had been like a five-minute car crash and now she was being asked to confront what she had been fleeing the Hidden Lands for in the first place. "I loved you. I know that for a fact. And when I saw you coming up the road on Lienhart's charger I thought for a moment that I still did." She recalled how her heart had swelled within her at the sight of the heroic king. How a great part of her wished that he'd come to take her back with him, that he was there to proclaim his love.

"What about now," Eireden asked, looking into her face closely.

The honest, but hurtful answer was that the warm feeling within her had faded with every word he had uttered. He seemed to read this from her expression. "The feeling has dimmed?" he asked.

"Yes."

He gave her a nod of understanding, not of disappointment, which in itself was a disappointment for Ella. "So, my visage is pleasing to you," he said in his clinical way, "yet my mannerisms are not."

"Yes."

Another nod and then he took a sudden step forward so that he loomed over her. "Would a kiss bring forth any feelings?"

Ella, with her heart jumping quick in her chest at how close he was thought it likely. "Maybe, but it would be wrong. You're to be married and I..." Her words faltered as she pictured Aric's perfect face and she knew another stab of disappointment in her breast.

"This is about understanding love," the king explained. "It's not the time for worrying over right or wrong." He bent down to kiss her, but she dodged away, slipping along the side of the dresser, ending with her back to the door.

"Look, I don't know what I'm feeling, really," she said, growing ever more anxious. With her left hand she searched for the doorknob at her side.

Eireden smirked and covered her hand with his and when he did she caught his scent. It was different...or rather it was strange: he had no scent whatsoever. This was terribly puzzling and Ella gave another sniff. Nothing. How could this be? Everyone had a scent, even people using deodorants or perfumes; their personal scent was always there layered beneath. Yet Eireden was altogether devoid of any smell and the only way that was possible was if he was magically concealing it.

Now Ella breathed in with purpose, letting the air fill her, searching beyond the unnatural barrier he had erected, hoping with a gaining anxiety that it was only body odor the man was hiding.

The acrid smell of burnt flesh struck her nostrils and she gasped.

This wasn't the king of the Den at all. This was one of Ella's half brothers—an elf! Panic leant her strength and a wave of pure energy rushed down her arm and into her hand. Almost gently she put her hand out and touched her palm to his chest.

There was a flash of light and a deafening explosion, and then the elf was flying backward through her bedroom window in a shower of glass and wood.

"Whip-wip!" Ella screamed as she turned and threw open the door. Just as she did the door across from her opened inward and there was one of the guests, a middle-aged man with a receding hairline and a gaining paunch. His mouth came open to ask Ella about the noise but then the fairy came bursting from the room, her wings glowing in her excitement and fear.

"Why is noise?" Whip-wip asked, her blue eyes big with fright.

"Elf," Ella answered. There was no need to explain further.

The man stared at Whip-wip as if she were some sort of giant glowing bee. Then Ella stuck out her hand and her short sword flew through the air and smacked into her palm. The man's eyes went wider still and he made to shut the door but Ella stopped him.

Her mind raced ahead of her thoughts. It had already mapped out the Bed and Breakfast; she knew where every guest and staff- person now stood, most looking upward with mouths hanging open, and she knew that to take the stairs would only slow her down, and she needed every second.

From her hand shot a burst of pure energy; it knocked the door back into the frightened guest sending him reeling to the floor. Ella raced in after him with Whip-wip above her. A woman on the bed screamed, however Ella didn't slow to cast even a single glance her way.

The elf was coming.

It had deflected much of the energy she had sent into it and absorbed the rest. She could feel it on the other side of the building where it had landed in the wet grass of the front yard; it was getting to its feet and even from where she stood she could feel its excitement at the thought of a fight.

Ella knew she couldn't stand for long against such an opponent. Yes, she had grown in power, yet hers was a raw energy and quickly depleted, while his was expertly wielded. Her only chance was escape.

She gave a shove with her mind and the window in front of her blew outward. A half-second later Ella flew through the cascading remains, her magic guiding her, slowing her fall. Parked below her was a Cadillac. She landed on it feet first, barely denting the hood.

To her left was a row of parked cars: Volvos and Toyotas, none of which suited her needs. Across from her was a pick-up truck afflicted with a bad case of rust. That was the one.

Ella ran to it, sending up mud with every footfall. The locks on the driver door popped up when she was fifteen feet away and just as she neared it, the door itself sprang open revealing an empty cab. First Whip-wip then Ella shot in.

"Make it go!" the fairy demanded, urgently, pointing at the steering wheel.

"I'm trying," Ella said with her eyes closed. She needed to concentrate. Her mind could feel the odd grooves of the ignition where the key should go, but when she used her magic to turn it, nothing happened. After a third try she swore and opened her eyes to see if there was something blocking the keyhole.

There wasn't, but she did see a switch taped to the lower part of the dash. There were green and red wires running from it that snaked into the engine compartment. "Oh jeez," Ella whispered as she flicked the jury-rigged switch upwards.

The truck rumbled into life, coughing out a blue smoke from its tail pipe. More of the smoke exploded outward as she yanked the transmission into drive and stomped the gas. Whip-wip screamed, grabbing the headrest to keep from flying backwards and then the truck was fishtailing through the parking lot. With the rain and the mud its rear swung way out to the left before its tires caught some traction and Ella was able to fight it back to center.

The most direct way to the soggy main road was across the front yard of the Bed and Breakfast, Ella didn't hesitate. "Sorry!" she called out as she sent the truck through a flowerbed and across the lawn. Behind her people were yelling and then there was only the sound of the wipers slapping back and forth, and the rain beating on the roof.

A minute later Whip-wip pulled on Ella's hair and whistled in a panic, "*Zee! Zee!*" Ella turned and saw the danger that the fairy was warning of. The elf was on its black horse and was riding hard after them.

"It'll be ok," Ella said. Despite that the road was more than half bog, the truck was gaining speed. "We're going to make it. Just watch."

"Ok," Whip-wip said. She didn't sound convinced. Nor did she look it as she sat on the passenger side headrest facing back.

Ella's lead continued to lengthen until she neared the two lane main road that ran through the little town. She slowed only enough to keep the truck from going over on its side but still she lost half of the lead she had built as the elf took his horse across a field to cut her off.

"It'll be ok," she said again to reassure Whip-wip, who was hooting and pointing as the horse and rider drew closer. "The truck's old but it'll make sixty easy."

The truck began to rattle along faster and faster, and Whip-wip smiled. But then the air suddenly shifted in the cab and the wheel gave a jerk beneath Ella's hand.

Just as she had attempted to use her magic to start the truck, the elf was using its own to stop it. The windshield wipers flicked on and off, the radio blasted country music and then ran down the dial in a hissing fuzz. The heater turned on and the lights flicked from low to high beam.

Still they pulled away, until the elf discovered the brake and then the truck's tires locked sending out a scream as rubber dug into the road. Whip-wip shot forward to smack into the windshield and Ella's face hit the steering wheel and she only just managed to keep the truck on the road.

With her right foot she kept the gas going for all she was worth so that for a time the truck was fighting itself—gas against brake. And then Ella managed to snake her left foot beneath the brake; she pulled her toes up.

The physical proximity overrode the elf's magic and the truck lurched forward. Then the elf was beside her galloping like mad. She could feel his mind searching for any weakness in the truck, any way to slow it down, because it was clear that his horse was nearly spent.

Ella wasn't going to wait for him to find one. She swerved the truck to her left hoping, for the first time in her life, to hurt an animal. The elf was too good a rider for that and ran the horse up the embankment out of danger.

But Ella wasn't through. She had her own magic. In the bed of the truck was a rake and a couple of blocks of wood. These she picked up with her mind and flung at the horse. Though the elf swatted them aside with ease, it was clear the horse had run its race and was even then slowing.

"Ella!" Whip-wip said from the dash. The little creature was pointing ahead. "Sythie."

"Fairies?" Ella asked, squinting through the rain soaked windshield. There were lights ahead of them and for a moment she felt a touch of elation. However when she found the windshield wipers and flicked them on her stomach went sour. It wasn't fairies ahead, but the winking lights of a police cruiser.

It slowed a half mile from her and turned broadside, effectively blocking the road. "This is why I chose the truck," Ella commented mostly to herself. She braked hard and then swerved off the road and into a field. This she had hoped would be a complete quagmire, instead the field was relatively solid and though she was able to bounce along faster than the horse it meant the police cruiser would also be able to drive upon it.

The policeman swung out after her and the cruiser turned out to be amazingly fast. Within a minute it was ranged up next to her, its lights spearing the night. Ella had one option, to stop the cruiser in the same manner that the elf had tried to stop the truck. Unfortunately she couldn't stop the cruiser and at the same time protect her own vehicle.

Just as the police cruiser went dead, her truck's engine hitched and sputtered. She stomped the gas, which did nothing but send up a cloud of blue smoke. In seconds the truck had stopped and began settling into the mud.

"Whip-wip go! Get of here," Ella screamed. The fairy was sitting groggily on the dash watching as the elf swung out of the saddle of his blown horse. She started to shake her head, no, but Ella wouldn't have it. "Go home my love. Go back to your family." She gave a gentle push with her mind as she said this and Whip-wip's face went slack.

"Home?"

"Yes. Go play," Ella said fighting to keep the panic out of her voice. "Go on home, it's almost time for bed."

The police officer was issuing orders through a loudspeaker but the words were lost on Ella. She hand cranked the window down and nudged the fairy out.

"I love you, Whip-wip," Ella said and for some reason added more of her magic to these words.

"Love you too," Whip-wip answered back as she slowly drifted away into the night like a lost balloon.

Ella gave her a final wave and then unmindful of the policeman and his drawn gun, she stepped out of the cab of the truck with sword drawn. If she was going to die, she was going to die fighting.

Chapter 10

Eireden

Alseya's breathing stayed ragged and phlegmy until long after Eireden had left the Feylands and the mists miles behind. It was even longer before she even had the strength to open her eyes. In all that time Eireden could barely keep his eyes off her as he pondered Aric's words.

"Love this girl while you can."

They were strange words. Perhaps wise words as well. In this day of battle and blood it was smart not to dismiss love so easily. He had dismissed Ella's love and now she fled the very sight of him. He had dismissed Generai's love and she had chosen death over living with her feelings unrequited.

Still it was a wisdom that he figured would be nearly impossible to follow.

No matter that he looked upon Alseya as beautiful and precious, kind and sweet, and also resolute like no woman he had ever met, save perhaps his own mother, there was always Ella to compare her to.

Always Ella.

The fey woman stirred. She rode cradled in the king's arms and now she blinked up at him. "What is that?" she asked in a whisper.

Feeling a sudden relief that she'd regained consciousness, Eireden smiled down at her. "You're going to be alright. It's the residual effects of the poison that you're feeling. It would be good that you rest."

"But what is that?" she insisted.

"What exactly do you mean? Do you hear something?" Eireden craned his head around trying to pierce the long shadows thrown out by the setting sun.

"No it's..." Alseya tried to sit up but was so weak that her eyes rolled back in her head and she slept again. The moon was over the trees and the lights of Avargard were in sight before her eyes fluttered open once more. The king read panic in them.

"What is it?" he asked.

"I...I don't know. It's in the air. Do you feel it? There's fear. And death. There's blood on the air. Can't you feel it?"

Eireden gazed about him at the dark. Nothing seemed amiss. "No, I don't. Is it Darhmael?"

"I don't know," she answered in a hollow voice. A fear seemed to grip her and she clutched at him.

He disentangled Alseya's arms and set her on the grey she had ridden. "Can you ride? Look! Those lights are Avargard. The city is very close. You can do it."

She nodded. "I can ride for a little while at least."

Before the king leapt into his own saddle he knelt and felt the ground searching with his mind for anything that would cause the intense fear that enveloped her. Unfortunately, whatever it was lay further than he could sense.

The two rode, slowly in Eireden's opinion, and all the while Alseya's strength grew at the same rate as her fear so that she was positively beside herself by the time the gates came into view.

It was a strange view for the king. Avargard was the most southern of the five cities. It lay nestled among the sharp peaks of the eastern Cascades and was famous for its high walls, scenic views, and goat's milk.

Maybe because of its walls or its seclusion it was generally a quiet city and was not considered militarily significant. Which was why the fact that the battlements were lit with every available torch and the walls teemed with men had Eireden anxious.

"Who goes there?" a voice called from the gate tower. "Declare yourself!"

"Eireden, King of the Den."

This caused a stir and voices cried out: "The King! The King!"

A soldier at the gate ordered, "Raise the portcullis. The king has come."

"Belay that order!" commanded Eireden. "Do not be so quick. Do not trust even this pretty face," he said to the soldiers who crowded the bars. After Darhmael had so easily infiltrated Rhyoeven, standard operating procedure was for everyone entering the city to be screened for illusions.

Their relief at having the king near was evident; they laughed and jostled each other until one among them pushed the others out of the way and stared at Eireden and Alseya.

"I say the Lady can come through, there is no illusion that is so becoming as she. But the man? Eh, he looks a might dodgy." The soldiers laughed and slapped the man on his back.

The king smiled. "Prince Jarlen, I don't think you can handle this lady."

The prince of the city made to reply, but Alseya held up her hand. "What is happening?" she asked, desperately. "Is it some great misdeed?"

Jarlen looked to Eireden before answering, "We know not. Come sundown the fey of the city became worked up though none would say as to why."

"Have they not a seer among them?" Eireden asked.

Prince Jarlen shrugged and it was Alseya who answered, "No. The line of Me-ayfa came to Avargard at the king's bidding. They are masters of song and their healing is well known, but of far-sight they have not the taste."

"What good are they?" A soldier commented. He shrank back into the crowd as Jarlen glared hard at him.

"My apologies," Jarlen said. An uncomfortable silence settled at the gate which was only broken when one of the fey finally came to verify the King was indeed the king.

"Has any made an attempt?" Alseya asked the fey, a soft-skinned male who barely looked eighteen in Eireden's eyes, though who was likely over a thousand years old.

"None has the temerity," the male whose name was Pansfor, replied.

"I understand."

"Will you cast your gaze?" he asked.

Alseya gave Eireden a look of uncertainty, which had him wondering. "What is at issue?" he asked. "Why is there trepidation at using your magic?"

"When one cast their gaze, the subject can look back if he has the skill."

Prince Jarlen had been following the conversation. "And Darhmael has the skill?" he asked.

The two fey nodded in unison and Alseya added, "He does and if he were to look back there'll be a connection, one that only the most powerful may break."

Pansfor looked into Alseya's face. "You are greatly skilled. Greater than any. You could do this."

"No," the king said, stepping between the two fey. "She may be skilled but she is worn and only just recovered from poison. We'll send scouts instead. Lord Jarlen have them sweep the entire valley north and west. I have just come from The Feylands and saw no sign of an enemy along our route."

"Already done. Three squads went out an hour ago. I don't expect them back for another two hours. In the meantime we're buttoning things up here."

"Good," Eireden said. "I joked about not letting us through yet your walls are devoid of your fey compliment. Did they not answer your summons?"

He shook his head. "In this I am at fault. I had decided not to tax them as yet; they seem to be weak in their constitution."

"By all means, Lord, tax them," the king said putting a heavy hand on his prince's shoulder. He gave it a squeeze and added, "The fey are stronger than they appear."

"We are," Alseya agreed. "Which is why I will see what is amiss myself. I only ask for a few minutes to rest."

"That can be arranged easily," the prince said eagerly, hoping to repair any damage he had caused in Fey-Den relations. "My palace has room for such a lovely creature as yourself." He pointed up a steep hill at a grand building that dominated the city.

She eyed the climb and blanched at it. "Is there anything closer?"

"I'll clear a barracks room for you," the prince said before hurrying off, giving belated orders concerning the fey.

Alseya rested and took a light meal. While she did Eireden went to the walls and inspected the fortifications and as always he saw the lay of the land as an invader and not a defender.

Unlike at Hildeoven any invader would have a tough go of it at Avargard. The land sloped steep up to the high walls and these were not a simple wooden palisade. The walls were constructed of sturdy masonry.

Still the city had two glaring weaknesses: First: the gates had been magnificent when first built three hundred years previous. Now there was rust at the joints and the metal had likely weakened over time. The second, and greater issue, was the dearth of trained soldiers. Avargard was a mountain city with limited living space and thus could not support a large population.

The king had far fewer soldiers to work with than he had even at Hildeoven. And the numbers of fey were insignificant. After becoming King, Eireden had asked the fey people to migrate to the other cities of the realm not only to relieve the burden on Hildeoven but also to help guard against the illusions of the enemy. Only very few of the fey could look upon the confines of the mountain city with anything but unease.

He was mulling this over when a runner came to him to say that the Lady Alseya was going to work her fey magic.

"Good. Thanks," Eireden said to the man, absently. His mind was on the problems involved in keeping a city alive throughout a siege and whether it was better for him to be within the walls or outside of them if it came down to it.

He was so preoccupied that he was surprised when a scream burst from the barracks just as he came walking up. He dashed inside to see Alseya's white eyes bright and fevered, staring right at him.

"This is for you," she snarled. "See what I have done so easily. See what I've wrought without effort. And know that I will crush your every city, your every village, your every dirty little house. I'll crush them all! I'll lay waste to your every…"

The room was full of fey, yet they only sat and stared. Eireden dashed forward and shook the fey woman. "Alseya! Alseya! Throw him off. Come back to me. Come back to me."

He looked her in the eyes but it was not Alseya who looked back. "You want your fey whore? Is it because you tired of the half-breed so quickly?"

"Leave her," Eireden commanded. "Face me. Leave her and face me!"

"What a joke," it said through Alseya. "You'll not face me, not alone, not in single combat. I know your line. I know your cowardice. I know your excuses. I've heard them all before. Here, take your whore back and tremble. Tremble with…" Alseya stopped her talking. She gritted her teeth as if she had swallowed something unwholesome and then she gasped.

"Alseya?" Eireden asked staring into her face.

She began to nod but then she shook her head and closed her eyes. "He's destroyed Tayoeven. The entirety of it. Even now his army is raping and killing…and worse."

"How?" Eireden asked. "Tayoeven is a strong city. Their walls are…" he left off envisioning the beautiful city, the white marble, the ivy, the fair little streams that criss-crossed in every direction.

"Darhmael's army is immense," Alseya said with a hollow voice. "He showed me everything. His forces are…they're countless. He says over a hundred thousand, but it may be more. And the ogres. So many ogres. And the trolls. He has trolls. They tore down the gates. They bent the bars with their bare hands!"

Eireden straightened, standing over Alseya with a sweat on his forehead. He spoke to Prince Jarlen, "Send scouts to Tayoeven. We need a count on that army and we need to know which way it's headed next."

"They're coming here," Alseya said. "It knows where we are. It wants to trap you, Milord. That's its plan. It wants to trap you. And then destroy you."

"Well that helps," Eireden said calmly. "I need runners sent to every city. If there are fairies use them. I want a full mobilization. Every man will report for duty regardless of age."

The prince hesitated. "What about us? Our walls are strong but we cannot stand against a hundred thousand maug, not to mention the trolls."

Eireden's head spun with the numbers and the ramifications. "I...I don't know. For now we wait for more news. Could you be wrong?" he asked Alseya. "Could Darhmael have fooled you? Could he have shown you things that weren't true?"

"No. You will see. He will come and kill us all. You will see..." she stopped and began to cry.

"We will find out soon enough when the scouts return," the king said. "In the meantime I want all preparations made to abandon the city. The populace will only take with them what they can carry and what is of value militarily. Everything else will be left behind, or, if it will be of any use to our enemy, burned or destroyed. No exceptions."

The next morning, after riding their horses near to death, the scouts returned with the dismaying news that Alseya had not been wrong. The maug were swarming the remains of Tayoeven, wallowing in pools of blood and gore. For Den, the scouts were practically in a panic and they constantly spoke over each other when giving their report, embarrassing Prince Jarlen.

The king pretended not to notice. He didn't blame the men, there was much to panic about. As a remedy he remained stoically calm and over the next two days, while the maug marched the forty miles between the two cities, the king's orders were delivered with cool precision that hid his own panic.

In all the long history of the Den it was that cities had been lost, burned, captured. Times of plague and famine and war had ravaged them, yet these were setbacks only and in the end the Den had always prevailed and had always rebuilt.

This time it was different. Far worse. Only Rhyoeven, high on its plateau with its great walls, could hope to hold out against a hundred thousand goblins. Every other city would fall one after another and its people butchered or enslaved. All the Den lands would be overrun and subject to Darhmael's revenge.

His choices were limited to just two: hide in Rhyoeven while his lands were destroyed or gather every available man and offer battle. With the companies of Tayoeven destroyed the king could hope for maybe thirteen thousand soldiers and that just wasn't enough men. Not with Darhmael leading them, and there were the half-elves to account for as well, and who knew how many trolls and ogres?

"You have the fey to help," Alseya said, reading his mind. "And the dwarves. Furen would never let you down."

Eireden knew all of this. "I am loathe to even ask Furen. To make any difference he would have to send his entire army. He would be staking the future of his race on what may come down to a coin toss."

"A coin toss?" Alseya looked taken back. "Is it that you have so little confidence in your men or your ability to lead them?"

"Neither," Eireden replied. "It's Darhmael that worries me. I won't get lucky again as I did at Hildeoven. He'll be prepared against the sythie this time, and I'm sure he will have new tricks up his sleeve."

"Still he leads a goblin army, while you lead warriors of proven nobility and courage."

The king walked away—stalked away more like —he was in the highest tower in the palace at Avargard, a place where he could see for miles, a place he had gone for the last two days to brood. In those two days the king had barely rested. His mind was a fever of thoughts and ideas and possibilities, every one of which pointed to the fact that not only would Avargard have to be abandoned, every den city would have to be left open to the hatred of the enemy.

He looked west toward the dead city of Tayoeven. For now the hills in the west were empty. "Do you so soon forget the magical blackness at Hildeoven?" he asked his fey lady. "Or the attack on the Feylands itself? Or the treachery within my own family? Darhmael has been one-step ahead of us...no, ahead of me for months, and all it'll take is a single slip. A single error in judgment. Hell, even a single moment of bad luck and he'll win. All this will be destroyed and the earth laid bare to his wicked heart."

Alseya brooded on this truth for a while

"So yes, we may be looking at a coin toss," Eireden finished.

"And your plan is to retreat to the capital," Alseya said. She too stared out, but her eyes saw nothing save what Darhmael had shown her. "It's what he wants. You are falling into his trap by not fighting him. I know it as fact."

"Thinking that we won't fight is where you're wrong, my Dear. We will fight. I ride out at sunset to contest Darhmael at the river Ixreal. And then we'll pull back and fight him along the Holly-back ridge just north of here. Then we'll fight through the forest just south of the Feylands and maybe every step of the way back to the capital. We have to slow him down if we're to get everyone to safety. So you see we'll fight plenty."

"But you won't stake your entire army on a single battle?"

He turned full from the sad view and came to hold her in his arms—the first tender moment he had spared for her since they had ridden into the mountain city.

"No, not if I can help it. Darhmael is no fool. He has learned the hard lessons I've taught. In the Feylands he learned to lead in person and not to trust in subordinates who are more interested in bickering among themselves than fighting. And at Hildeoven he learned not to trust in the sheer weight of numbers. He's learned to exercise control and nothing can be more dangerous for us."

"Though it be dangerous you must risk it!" she cried and her eyes were wild. "We can't be trapped. It will be our death."

Eireden pulled back to arms length so he could see her clearer. The fear emanating from her was unmistakable. "Your worry is unfounded. Rhyoeven is too strong to be taken by assault and by the time we pull back it will be provisioned with enough stores to withstand a siege of many years."

"I suppose," she replied uncertainly.

"It's more than supposition. I know your power is great, but Darhmael is greater still. He may not have shown you falsehood for you would have seen through that, but maybe he edited what came through the connection. What he fears most is us holing up behind our walls where he can't get at us…"

"But…"

"Hold your tongue for a spell," Eireden admonished gently. "The reason our enemy fears this is that he knows he will dash his army to pieces if he attacks. And if he tries to wait us out, his army will disintegrate around him. You know what sorts of creatures he considers soldiers. They're bloodthirsty even among themselves."

"They are," she agreed. "But about the rest… about the trap I was so sure."

"Something we've all learned is that nothing is certain with Darhmael," the king replied and then paused, second-guessing his decision to retreat to the capital. By his very own reasoning: the certainty that Darhmael feared him holing up most meant it was what he feared least…but that just couldn't be!

Eireden blinked and shook his head. "All this talk has made me forget why I called you here."

Alseya gave him a close look. "You aren't think-ing of trying to postpone our wedding again?"

"No," the king answered truthfully. "A long siege is the best time for a royal wedding. Our people will need something to help cope with the stress, and the pageantry of a wedding is just the thing. Of course this means the actual ceremony will be much, much larger than we ever could have conceived."

"The entire kingdom?" she asked with a laugh that lit up the tower.

He shrugged. "Who could I not invite? I'm related to every one of them in one form or another…but the wedding is not what I asked you here to discuss. I meant what I said about fighting. I'm going to lead every available man out to the river, which means there'll be no one to lead the women and children…"

Alseya's smile disappeared and she interrupted, "I can fight. I know the sword. I am an artist with it." As usual for her, she wore loose linens of snow white. These she swung back to reveal her sword girt to her hip, the pommel of which she rested her small hand upon.

He knew her strength, though her diminutive size was such that he couldn't help but smile at her grim yet delicate appearance. "I have heard of your skill and doubt it not."

"But?"

"But, I am to command. My mind cannot be so split as would be if you were among those battling our foes." Even as he said this he pictured Ella's face and her large sapphire eyes. The truth was his mind was split enough already and Alseya would be just another distraction that he couldn't afford, not with lives at stake. "I would worry over much for you and I fear that it may cause a lapse in judgment."

"I see," she replied studying his features. With her abilities so great it was an uncomfortable moment for him. How much did she suspect of his true feeling?

"And there is no other to lead the women and children?" she asked.

"No one near as capable as you."

"I have no taste for battle, even one forced upon me. I will lead your people."

Now it was the king's turn to smile. "Our people you mean?"

She touched his hand. "Yes, our people." Their eyes locked and again he heard that voice: *Maybe I can find love with this girl*. His smile grew.

It was the last smile that would turn his lips for some time. That evening, at twilight he waited on the walls as the last of the inhabitants marched out of the gates of Avargard.

He had given up the city without a fight. With his stomach knotted he mounted his horse, kicked it into a gallop that sent echoes rolling along the empty streets, and hurried to catch up with the paltry six hundred men he had to contest Darhmael's grand army.

Chapter 11

Ella

Ella pushed the door shut behind her and now that the engines had ceased their roaring and there was only the steady lip-lip-lip of the rain coating everything, the creak of the rusting metal made an ominous noise.

"Put the swords on the ground," the police officer cried. He had his gun drawn on Ella, but his eyes flicked constantly to the left where the elf stood next to his gasping horse. He still wore the illusion of the king of the Den and was quite a sight.

"You'll let the human go," Ella demanded of the elf.

He swaggered forward, filled with confidence and shrugged as if Ella's demand was nothing to him. "Kneel before me and beg. Only then will I even consider..."

The officer swung his piece toward the elf and menaced him with it. "I said drop the sword!"

Neither did. The elf wore a nasty smile and Ella had the desperate wish that the officer would just shoot. Instead the elf lifted his hand and in the next second the gun flew toward him. Ella tried to leap after it, knowing it was the only thing that could stop the elf. She was too slow and the elf caught it. He gave the steel of it a sniff and then nonchalantly tossed it into a puddle.

Ella's mind went to it, but the elf had expected just that. The two locked their powers together and it was an odd and frightful feeling. Around them, the air spun sideways and the rain stopped falling, instead it went this way and that, and it made a noise out of proportion to its size, as though a thousand drums beat at once. The power of the elf was amazing and Ella was soon gasping on her knees, her opponent was simply too strong for her. It had crushed her pathetic defense in seconds and could break her mind with only a thought.

"Ok I'm kneeling and...and I'm begging," she said, breaking the connection and dropping into the mud. "Please let him go. He's not a part of this."

The officer only stood there with his mouth open and a fearful, confused look to his eyes. A shotgun poked up between the seats of his cruiser, which he seemed to have forgotten about.

"The human must kneel as well," the elf said. The creature then let his illusion drop and his charred skin had the officer blanching back. "Come kiss my hand and beg for my mercy. I can be generous."

The man began to shake his head so that his slack jaw swung gently. To save him Ella spoke and there was power in her words, "Go to him and kneel."

Dazedly the officer started forward but the elf thundered, "Stop! He has to come of his own volition. Come human, kneel before me."

"No," the man whispered. He'd been walking forward in a stiff-legged imitation of a robot, but now he stopped. "I...I'm an American. We don't kneel for anyone."

The elf smiled at this bit of foolishness and the burnt skin of his lips cracked. Clear pus ran down the cracks, making Ella shiver at the sight. "That's commendable," he said. "But your choices are kneel or die."

The man hesitated and there was really no knowing what he would've done because the elf took the pause as a decision not to kneel. He raised his right hand and a gout of flames shot out toward the officer. Instinctively Ella leapt up and threw herself in front of the fire, using her mind to shield her and the human.

Now the intuitive move startled the elf and for a moment Ella was able to push the flames back at him. He quickly rallied, however. With a laugh in his high, childlike voice, the elf exerted his full power and the flames rushed to cover Ella. The air roiled around her, the heat turning the rain to steam and baking the mud hard beneath her feet. Her sword glowed and with a shriek she had to let it go and then her cloak went up. It had been soaked through, but the heat had dried it and now it was in flames.

Still fighting with every ounce of energy, Ella shrugged her way out of the cloak and then holding it up she turned to the officer and cried, "Run!" It was his only chance, Ella was down to her last reserves.

The officer had been standing dazedly, watching the uneven battle in amazement while his courage drained away. At Ella's cry it failed him altogether and he ran—not a moment too soon. The flames had consumed the cloak and now she could feel her hair curling and there was smoke rising out of it. She was seconds from dying...only, suddenly, blessedly the flames miraculously disappeared. Powerless to stop herself, Ella fell forward to her knees and knelt blinking at the phantom glare where the flames had just been. The elf hadn't killed her. It had known exactly when to stop. It was an expert at death and a master of torture.

Still she couldn't help feeling the least bit of gratitude; the pain had been that great. She gulped the cool night air for a few seconds until a scream brought her around. High and soul piercing, the scream had Ella pulling herself up once again.

The officer was on the ground awash in flames. "No," Ella cried as she staggered to the man. His clothes were burning bright and his skin was already charred. Unthinking, Ella used the last of her power and extinguished the flames.

This did little to help him, however.

"He looks like me now," the elf cackled as he leaned against the cruiser, smiling his deadly cracked smile. "And you will too soon enough. Father can't abide the humans. He hates their thin skin; their dull eyes. He just hates ugliness in all forms. And who can blame him?"

"Then why does he keep you around?" Ella sneered.

"Yes! Good," the elf clapped. "Keep hating. Father appreciates hate. It's a driving force. It gives us power. Now show me some more of that hate you have burning in you."

Burning. The smell of burnt hair and flesh made Ella's stomach spin. She turned back to the police officer. He was horrid to look upon and surely dead. "I'm sorry," she said to the man, wishing she had been able to save him. Then louder she apologized to the elf as well. "I was wrong, I should not have said that to you, Elf."

"Oh what a saint," he retorted sarcastically. "I wonder if you'll be so forgiving after I torch you like I did him. Will you? Would you like to wager on it? Because I'm pretty certain you won't be in much of a forgiving mood. You'll curse me. I know, oh yes I know."

Ella ignored the elf. She stared at the officer instead, feeling the greatest pity for him...and then the greatest shock. He opened an eye. Just one gleaming eye stared out of the black ruin of his face. Tears streaked down Ella's hot cheeks and she was desperate to heal the man, but she was bereft of any strength.

"Can you hold on?" she asked.

"No, I don't think so," the elf replied, thinking the question had been for him. "I think it's time for you to begin learning a valuable lesson about what you really are, and there is only one sure way for you to discover what that is. We have to rid you of this pretty facade of yours. We have to burn it off."

"What?" Ella said. She hadn't been listening close, but the word burn had gotten through and now she looked to the elf in time to see him send a blast of fire straight at her. She was without power, but not without her natural agility. Yet she did not dive out of the way of the flames. Instead, instinct took over a second time—the instinct to save and to protect. She threw herself over the police officer trying to shield him with her body.

No pain was ever so intense. The flames set her shirt alight and her beautiful dark hair went up. The night air crackled and stank. Ella screamed, tearing her vocal cords as her skin seemed to melt, and the elf laughed gleefully...

...And then there came a sudden explosion, which jarred her from her misery and ended the screams and laughter and fire crackling. All that was left was a hissing as the heavy rain put out the fire on Ella's back.

She blinked the water from her eyes in confusion at what had just happened. In the officer's hand was a small pistol, which he had pulled from an ankle holster with fingers burnt down to nubs.

"Uh-uh," the man mumbled pointing the gun past Ella. It was pointed at the elf who lay on his back with rainwater filling his open mouth. A small hole had been dug just above his right eye and that didn't fill; instead it drained blood that seemed abnormally bright.

"Uh-uh," the man grunted.

Ella turned back to the police office and cried out in pain—her shoulders and neck were a misery and every movement sent waves up and down her that nearly had her blacking out.

"Il-ee," the police officer said. The night swam in Ella's vision and she tilted over and her hands went into the mud. She began gasping to keep from throwing up. "Il-ee," the police officer said again.

"No. Don't talk," she said in a raspy voice. "I'll—I'll do something. It'll be ok. I can...do something." She searched her soul for the least strength to heal the man, however her soul's energy was only a whisper within her.

"Il-ee," the police officer pleaded, and then held up the gun slightly. He seemed to lack the power to do anything more.

"Kill you?" Ella gasped, catching on suddenly. "No, I can't do that. I can heal you. If you can just hold on for..." How long? Ella had never depleted herself so completely. And then there were own injuries to worry about. She was on the verge of passing out with every breath.

"Eese," the man begged. He tried to raise the gun again but it slipped from his hand; upon the grip hung a crispy, foul smelling slag of dead skin.

Ella's head hung down and now tears joined the rain. She would have to kill the man. If his pain was anything like hers it would be a mercy. "Make your peace," she said. "Blink twice when you're ready."

The officer closed his eye for a spell and then opened it long enough to blink once and then again. "Find happiness," Ella whispered. The man nodded in the slightest and then closed his one eye for good. She shot him once in the head and then cried harder than she had ever in her life.

Chapter 12

Eireden

"They're stretched out for two miles or more along the ridge," Prince Jarlen said as if the fact wasn't the least troubling.

"Yes," Eireden agreed. He picked at a stray run of golden wheat that had survived the winter. Next to him the horse he had ridden out of Rhyoeven searched the hillock for tasty leftovers as well.

"That's a rather large number per mile. Quite a few. The ratio isn't really in your favor for a fight on the open plain. I'm just saying that the numbers don't suggest your plan, not with your wings hanging on nothing but hills and grass."

"Yes," the king agreed a second time.

When he didn't expound a runner who wasn't supposed to be as near as he was asked in a shy voice, "What does the king worry about ratios for when he has a plan?"

The runner was nothing more than a boy and one that the king recognized as the prince's youngest son. While the king smiled and coughed out a laugh, the prince gave a glare and growled, "Don't you mind what the king does and how he does it. Just be glad you still have a king at all."

Eireden held up a hand. "And were I to fall should not the next generation of Den be privy to my wisdom? I will answer young Roydol. Numbers are very important in battle. With everything else equal: open land, simple leadership, a straightforward hand-to-hand fight, a den company of one-hundred men can expect to win a battle against four-hundred maug. So the *numbers* suggest that a Den captain shouldn't attempt to fight five hundred maug straight up. Do you see?"

"Yes, Milord," Roydol answered. "They should use ruses or stratagems."

"Very true. Stratagems have their place, but so does the land. The *numbers* change when the captain uses the terrain to his advantage. If the maug have to cross a river then the odds go way up. The same hundred men could fight off a thousand maug. And if the maug have to battle uphill like they did along the Holly-back ridge this morning a hundred Den could expect to win out over six-hundred or so."

"Yes sir," the lad said enthusiastically. "We really womped them good didn't we?"

Eireden nodded along though his view of the fight hadn't been as rosy as Roydol's. The Maug army hadn't charged up in the simple-minded way that had been expected. Nor had they crossed the river Ixreal in endless dull waves that would've meant the slaying of thousands. No, Darhmael had his forces disciplined and well in hand.

Like a thousand streams, the maug had flowed around any point of resistance and it was Eireden who was constantly in danger of having his tiny army overwhelmed by flank and rear attacks.

"We did well enough," Eireden answered the boy. This was true. His own six hundred men had suffered very few casualties, however he was doing absolutely nothing in slowing down Darhmael. The maug army was rolling on unchecked. The king had to go against the "numbers" simply to give his people time to escape to the capital.

"Your father understands all of this," the king went on. "And he sees, correctly, that a fight on this open plain is just not as good as falling back to the capital where, if we gathered all of our people, we could hold out against all the maug! They'd never be able to take us there."

The boy looked with new wonder at his father. "Then why do you fight here?"

They were on the plains five miles south of the Feylands and the Forest of Mists, a day's ride to either the capital in the northeast or Hildeoven to the south-east.

"We fight for two very important reasons. The more time we give the other cities to evacuate the less we will leave in the hands of the maug. You see, all those maug have to eat. They're like locusts. They'll eat all this land bare and then they'll starve. So every-one in the cities, all the soldiers and men and women and children are rushing about picking whatever fruit they can, pulling up potatoes and carrots, basically leaving nothing in all the Hidden Lands for the maug."

"Good, they should starve, the vile beasts," Roy-dol said savagely. "They deserve nothing more."

"And the second reason," Prince Jarlen asked, cocking a keen eye.

"I need to test Darhmael," the king replied. "He is unpredictable. It is a certainty that he has his own rus-es and stratagems, and I can't wait around to see what he plans to spring on us at the times of his choosing. I need to force his hand."

"With six-hundred men?" Jarlen asked.

"I don't even want to risk that many, but it is what it is."

"We may not have to," Jarlen said. "The main army has turned south toward Hildeoven. Lienhart will most certainly follow your orders and torch the fields just ahead of them. It's likely that we'll be able to slip back to the capital and whatever he plans there will only end in his ruin."

"Aye," Eireden replied, tepidly, feeling how his situation had been reversed. It was only two days previous that he had been extolling the virtues of "holing up" at the capital. Now he was uncertain. Darhmael's actions so far had been methodical and perfect; it wasn't likely that he would burn every Den city only to throw himself on the spears of Rhyoeven.

So what did the elf have...other than a hundred thousand goblins that is. What trick up his sleeve did he have to deal with the fortress that was Rhyoeven? The best way to find out was to get close, within striking distance.

"Your Highness!" Roydol cried, pointing. All along the thin line, fire arrows streaked upwards as the advance scouts shot their arrows and rode back to friendly lines with all the speed they could muster. The arrows meant that the twenty-thousand maug of Darhmael's screening army had broken camp for the day and were advancing. Eireden glanced nervously at the threatening heavy black clouds above and whispered a prayer.

"We will be tested tonight," he said to the prince. "And we will not fail. Prepare your archers."

"Yes sir," the prince answered with a steady voice. Fear had never stained Jarlen's soul. He rode off issuing orders.

Six hundred men hunkered down along a stretch of a mile. A bare hundred of them were actual knights, another hundred were scouts, and the rest were men-at-arms eager to ride with the king, eager to prove themselves, eager to do their duty. Yet they weren't trained to fight on horseback.

Many were nervous over this, and with good reason. It was one thing to fight from the battlements of a castle or stand in formation trusting to your captain and your fellow soldiers. It was another thing to ride at full speed swinging a sword or charging with lance knowing that you'd be accepting the brunt of a collision on a thin pole of wood with a point shod in steel.

Still they were Den and they did not shy at the chance to set blade to their enemies. Though that would not come first. First would come the signal from their fairy allies and then would come a storm of arrows the like of which these goblins had probably never tasted. All Den soldiers were well trained in the long bow.

The men waited tense. Minutes slipped by and sweat began to trickle down from steel helmets. The enemy never hurried. They came on slowly like a steamroller crushing anything that stood in their way.

And then the fairies began blinking. Thirty had answered the king's call and their job was simply to give the Den a target to aim at. They hovered above the advancing maug army and when it was within extreme arrow distance they swooped down, blinked three times and then shot back up. It was the only way in the pitch black for the soldiers to use their arrows at the greatest possible distance.

The six-hundred men fired twice in quick succession and then paused as the fairies swooped in again. A second time the blinking started, only this time there also came high-pitched whistles and cries, and now the fairies were flashing their lights everywhere. Something was happening to them.

"Keep shooting!" the Prince roared so loudly that the individual captains didn't need to add a thing. Arrows went out into the darkness but if they were hitting anything, none could tell. The fairies were no longer holding position above the advancing army. They were zigzagging all over the sky, screaming in terror.

"Come back!" the king yelled to them, his heart breaking for the innocent little creatures. "Come back!" And they did, rushing at him as if he were the only one who could save them. Right behind the fairies, things like flying shadows raced, dipping and wheeling whenever a fairy dared to show the least light.

"To me," the king called and soon he felt them clinging, invisible to his armor, while he swung his sword uselessly at wheeling bat-like creatures that hissed and spat, keeping just out of reach. Finally he swung his cloak off and waved it in the night sky until the things flew off. They didn't go far, they flew lazy circles above his lines effectively turning the tables on the king. Now the Den were blind to what their enemies were up to, while their own movements were plain as day to the flying night creatures.

"Our fairies have met their match," Roydol said as he swung the king's banner at the odd things to keep them away.

They had. Eireden counted and found only thirteen of them clinging to him; they shivered in fright. "I'm sorry," he whispered to the survivors. Then louder he ordered, "Loose three more flights then order the first repositioning."

Signal whistles blew and riders were dispatched and within a minute the Den soldiers, having fired their third flight were mounted and riding hard eastward. They paused a mile from the maug until the six hundred had formed, then they split again, though this time the king kept them closer together. Without his fairies to act as guides he would have to let the goblins get dangerously close or risk wasting his arrows shooting at target too far away.

"Have the scouts give us a range with a flight of fire arrows," he ordered. The arrows went out and the Den were shocked to a man: the plains were teeming with goblins. They had come racing after the Den in a silence that couldn't have been anything but magical.

"Rake 'em three!" the king yelled. The soldiers loosed their arrows at near point blank range and the leading goblins were laid flat while those behind quailed. The third line, however pushed on—to their death under the hail of the next flight of arrows.

"North flank at four," a voice called out.

And another voice, this one with an edge of panic yelled: "South flank at seven!" Even as the Den were dealing with the horde in front, Goblins by the thousands were racing on either side to trap them. They'd be completely encircled when both goblin wings met at the six o'clock position directly behind them.

Thankful that the dark hid his shock, Eireden cried out, "Position two! Position two!" The order to retreat to the next pre-arranged site came almost too late. Most of the men turned and leapt into saddles and charged off with the goblins nearly within reach. Some of the Den soldiers disobeyed the command, maybe forty or so in all. These hearty souls drew their bows one last time and fired into the face of the advancing goblins and then with bloodthirsty howls they pulled out their swords and died hacking and swinging to make sure their brothers could get away.

The king rode watching back, cursing and gnashing his teeth. "Stop it!" Prince Jarlen growled at him as the two rode past the fast closing goblins who had swung in to trap them. "I can tell what you're thinking. You blame yourself for their deaths. Don't."

"I should've called the retreat right away," Eireden said.

"Don't do this," the prince cautioned. "Don't second guess yourself on every little thing. It's what our enemy is hoping you'll do."

"It's a little late for that. I'm second-guessing everything. Darhmael has a counter for each move I've made and I can't help feel like I'm being cornered."

"Look at it from his point of view. He's tried everything to destroy us and has failed at every turn. Sure we haven't hurt as much as we wanted but he's getting nicked up but good. I'd wager you're getting under his skin. I'd even wager he's showing you more of his tricks than he intends."

"Perhaps," the king allowed.

"Perhaps nothing. You'll see, Milord. The stinking elf will try something new and wish he hadn't."

Eireden grunted noncommittally and stared back at his men. They were hard men, yet they rode the four miles to the next position in an uncomfortable silence, each uneasy in their hearts about how their enemy was being handled so expertly. None was more uneasy than the king.

"Give me lines two deep and pickets at three hundred yards," he ordered when they arrived at the string of low hills he had chosen that afternoon as their next position. "I want a tight formation. Shoulder to shoulder. All bows at the ready."

The orders were carried out with quick precision, yet the men had barely took up their weapons before the pickets in front came pelting back with news of the advancing goblins.

"My goodness!" Jarlen exclaimed. "The elf must be plying the whip with a will. You see, Milord? He's too eager; he'll wear those lazy ol' maug out."

Again the king only offered a simple, "Maybe." He didn't think it bode well that the maug had come on so quick a second time. He felt the new trap closing in. "I want fire arrows staggered by platoon. Let's get a range on them." The first Den archers lit their arrows, however before they could fire, the storm that had been threatening broke loose.

Jarlen blinked up at the downpour and yelled over the din of the heavy rain, "This is a little too coincidental."

If it was purposeful, then that meant the maug were well within range and every second brought them closer and they wouldn't know until it was too late.

"Mount up! Mount up!" the king roared, swinging up into the saddle. "To me knights and men of the

Den! Forget your arrows, all of you. Let us set steel to them and don't be slow!"

Eireden charged down the hill at top speed, attacking when his opponent supposed he was just sitting there getting wet. He blazed forward to gather all the momentum he could and then veered to the right hoping to hack into the wing that was undoubtedly folding inwards, thinking to catch the Den in a vise.

And there it was. Maug in long lines, running tiredly with their heads down and their mouths open and panting. Too late they realized that what they mistook for rolling thunder was the cavalry charge of the entire Den force.

Unprepared and tired, Eireden ripped into them and set them screaming all over the plain. Two thousand died under the deadly hooves and flashing swords before Darhmael countered. He had a counter for the King's sythie allies. With the magical rain he had a counter for the fire arrows. He had his magical silence and somehow he had instilled an unbelievable endurance into his goblins. And now Darhmael had the perfect counter for a charge of heavy cavalry.

The howl of wolves suddenly went up all around the battlefield and every Den took notice and not a few shivered at the sound. "To me!" the King ordered in a voice that shook the rain. "Light me up," he said to the fairies that still clung to him. "Do not be afraid."

One by one the fairies began to glow and now the Den could see their king on his stallion. They raced to him and gathered behind in a V formation. Out in the dark the howls continued and grew in number and force and soon the shining eyes of the wolves could be seen—there were thousands, ringing the Den. The trap had closed.

Now Eireden grew greatly concerned. Unburdened, a horse was only slightly faster than a wolf, but with an armored man atop the horse, the wolf had the edge. As well the wolf was quick and its jaws strong;

one could slash out the tendons of a horse's leg, or dis-embowel its underbelly in seconds.

The king tried a charge at the wolves, rushing down on them in a fury, but the agile wolves simply melted away in front while they converged on his flanks. Horses whinnied in terror as they were pulled down and eaten alive. The men leapt off but were overwhelmed by white fangs and grey bodies.

Everyone knew there was no going back for the soldiers. To do so would be to risk the rest. Yet it hard-ly mattered. The king put spur to his horse and raced on, however the wolves kept pace easily and more men went down.

When it was obvious there was no outrunning the beasts the king pulled up suddenly. "Form a perimeter!" he ordered. "Face out. Bows at the ready."

The Den made a hasty perimeter that was shaped somewhat like a comma. Each had their bows trained into the rain and many had fingers that shook. The wolves were there just out of range, howling and howling calling to the main maug army.

In the black, the king toured the lines with his fairies shining bright and he seemed otherworldly and the men rallied. "We'll give them hell when they come," a man called at the sight of his leader, while others cheered.

"I'll take ten with me," another boasted.

"You bet you will," Eireden said giving the man a nod.

Prince Jarlen sidled up close and whispered, "We can't stay here. When the maug arrive the fight won't last but a few minutes."

"And your council is?" the king asked easily. He had looked his death in the face enough times not to get overly worked up over its proximity.

The prince shrugged. "I don't know. You're the king."

"Aye, I am that," he said wiping away rain that had run in his eye. Eireden continued on down the curving line with the prince and his son riding along anxiously. He was just about to order the line be pulled in when Roydol spoke.

"They're following us. Look at them."

His pointing finger shook as he indicated the wolves. The wild beasts had formed a huge pack and were milling about eyeing the king hungrily.

"Interesting," the king commented. "Wait here." Alone, he rode back to the fat part of his lines and sure enough the grey mob moved with him. Dismounting the king called for the prince and then began tugging off his armor.

"Am I to guess you have a plan," Jarlen wondered. "Or have you gone mad? Do we all have to get naked?"

After stripping down to his tunic, Eireden went to work pulling the saddle from the stallion. "No. Just me. I'm going north into the Feylands...alone."

"No, you can't leave the line!" Jarlen cried.

"I can and I will. Those wolves aren't thinking for themselves. They're spell-struck and I am their target—all else is incidental. It's my guess that if I ride out, I'll have the entire pack after me, which will give you a chance to save the men."

"And what of you? Do you expect me to leave my king?"

Eireden came up close and looked into the dark eyes of his prince. "I expect you to follow orders. Save your men. They're too valuable to waste fighting on this plain. Get to Hildeoven. Do what you can there to help evacuate."

Jarlen stared and said nothing. Unencumbered the king leapt onto his horse. He strapped the sword of Aug-Raumon to his back and then called to the fairies who had flitted away when he had removed his armor. "Light me up. Jarlen, make sure the wolves are clean after me before you move and then move fast. The maug will be here any minute."

"What if they don't follow you?" Roydol asked and was elbowed by his father for his temerity.

"I won't leave you, if that's what you're asking. I will share your fate. Now, hand me that standard. Good. Fare thee well young Roydol." The king made a great show of himself so that he was in full view of both his men and the wolves. "Till we meet again in Rhyoeven!"

He then turned and spurred his horse, racing through the perimeter with the wolves tracking him in a great rush of shaggy grey fur. There was no doubt that they would follow. The only doubt was if he could get even a mile away before they were on him.

In this the stallion was tested. It's long legs stretched and its heart hammered so that Eireden felt it coming up through the great muscular back beneath him. He made for the Feylands, a race of five miles in the dark and rain with wolves snapping at his heels.

Very quickly Eireden jettisoned the standard as useless weight, casting it behind him to disrupt the onrushing wolves. Then he leaned in close and urged the horse on and still the wolves closed. They seemed to have an unreal endurance that allowed them to keep pace when any other wolf would've dropped back from exhaustion.

On and on they came. Out swept the black sword and this Eireden swung all about, striking the meaty bodies of the wolves, desperately trying to keep the beasts away from the horse's unprotected hindquarters. Again, unnaturally, they did not fear the great sword. They accepted the wounds and kept coming.

Now wolves raced on either side, pulling ahead. Soon they would close in and attack from the front. "Time to go home, my friends," Eireden said to the fairies that clung to him against the head wind generated by the speeding horse. "Go on."

They seemed uncertain what to do until the leader of this little family let go. He flew next to the horse and rider for a moment and then turned and shot like a tiny rocket right at the lead wolf. Surprised, the beast yelped, lost its footing and fell, bringing down a large part of the pack like a series of dominoes.

More came on, but the other fairies left the king and began to zip around, blinding the wolves, though they did so with frequent looks up to the sky. It was a good thing they did, too. One of the bat things came streaking in to gobble up a fairy, however it was so intent on its meal that it didn't see the black sword until it was too late.

Eireden speared the thing—a bizarre cross between a bat and giant spider. With a look of revulsion he whipped the sword, and sent the dead creature out into the night. As he did he saw a strange sight ahead. The black night was broken here and there by what looked like low white clouds or fog or...mists!

How long had he been riding this great horse that he was so close? Ten minutes? Eleven at the most. And it was beginning to show. The stallion's breathing came ragged and frequently he began to make a *Hu-uragh* noise. The horse was dying.

"Keep going!" Eireden urged, slapping its rear with the flat of his sword getting a tiny extra burst as the mist came up. It felt cruel of him, but the alternative was for the steed to lose this fantastic race so close to safety and die under the gnashing teeth of the wolves. Yet would the mists actually mean safety? It didn't seem so. The stallion stumbled just as they came upon the mists and the first of the trees. It kept itself upright for a few more paces and then its heart gave out. The poor thing gave a twitch and then its legs went loose. It's head lolled and it fell forward in mid-stride, pitching the king into the wild woods and vile illusions of the Forest of Mists.

The King of the Den took the fall easily, rolling with the momentum kicking up billows of fog, and then he was springing up with sword at the ready. All around him were hundreds of ferocious wolves, they glared and showed their dreadful teeth, still they weren't the most terrifying thing in that forest. Screams echoed all around, while fiendish specters sprung up out of nowhere and came at him with grasping claws and hungry mouths.

Eireden turned to run, thinking to escape deeper into the forest, only he discovered he was already lost. And this time there was no Ella to draw him on.

Chapter 13

Ella

With the elf's sword sliding about the floorboards and the policeman's pistol sticking out of a cup holder, Ella drove the stolen truck in a haze of pain and despair. She drove throughout the night, sitting far forward, leaning on the steering wheel and gasping or cringing, and sometimes crying out, until exhaustion swept her and she could go no further.

Needless to say her sleep was fitful, she slumped in the cab, careful not to move or allow anything to nudge her shoulders or back and she woke with the sun turning the truck into an Easy-Bake Oven. "Oh, jeez," she groaned in misery. Her head thumped and her back was a horror of blisters and charred flesh.

"Water," she said through cracked lips.

Whip-wip, with tears on her small face pointed out the window. The night before she hadn't gone far in her daze and when the gun had gone off for the last time she had crept back to Ella to see what had happened.

"Yeah?" Ella asked. The image of the fairy blurred, became two and then disappeared in a haze of grey. Ella had fainted. She woke sometime later with a breeze going through the cab of the truck and the distinct and wonderful feeling of water on her back.

Just then Whip-wip floated in through an open window, hauling a small basket that she had constructed of grasses. It seemed heavy for the tiny fairy, and for good reason. It was filled with water, maybe an ounce worth and this she dumped on Ella's shoulder.

"Whip-wip?" Ella asked, uncertainly. "Are you real?"

"Sis! Real. Get drink." Ella blinked once and the fairy was gone. It felt like she only blinked once more and Whip-wip was back with her little basket of water. Gratefully Ella opened her mouth. It took the exhausted fairy ten more trips before Ella had the strength to back awkwardly out of the cab, sliding on her stomach.

She cried as she did and only partially from the pain. Her heart still hurt for the poor police officer whom she had shot. And her heart ached for herself. Her life was ruined.

The attack by the elf had solidified that like nothing else could. She had no chance to go back to her former days with Cascade Nursery. She couldn't go back to the Den and watch the one man who had loved her no matter what, marry another woman. And she couldn't go to the fey and have them look down their noses at her as some sort mongrel—half evil elf, half monkey.

And she didn't really want to be around normal people either. Ella Belmont was bad luck.

A small, and very cold stream, ran next to the road she had been travelling upon. Ella went to it on hands and knees. It was a wonder on her burns, though the rest of her shivered. She drank the water uncaring if it was clean or not and soon her strength returned enough for her to heal herself in the smallest way.

"That's a little better," she told the fairy.

"Sis," Whip-wip agreed. "Go home now?"

Ella shook her head. "No. Not yet."

Now Ella looked around at the environment she found herself in and discovered that she had no idea whatsoever where she was. The only thing she knew was that the truck had come to a stop on a dirt road and it was currently pointing into the new sunrise.

"Zooti?" the fairy asked.

The girl patted her pockets and came away empty. Everything she owned was back at the bed and breakfast. "We'll get you something." Ella went back to the truck, but in her weakened state she couldn't start it, and in fact fainted trying.

A few hours later she woke, again with a fantastic thirst. Again Whip-wip carted water to her from the stream in her little basket until Ella could make it on her own. This time her strength returned to a greater degree and when she healed herself as best she could she felt much better.

The truck was out of gas, which meant she would have to hoof it and that was really ok with her. She had nowhere to go and thus wasn't in much of a hurry. "After a nap," she said to Whip-wip. "We'll go then."

The fairy answered with an agreeable yawn.

It was late afternoon before Ella woke. Her first act was to heal herself as best she could with her depleted energies; there was still pain, but now it was at least manageable and it allowed her to thrown on an old sweater she found in the truck. The second thing she did was to drink until her belly felt like it was about to burst. Her third was to swallow the three little berries Whip-wip had brought for her to eat.

"Thanks," she said. "But I'm going to need something more."

Fish sounded good to her and so Ella plodded wearily down the road until her stream joined a second. The two together made for a sizable creek and it wasn't long before her mind felt the vibrations of a fish that had enough meat on it to eat. Even tired it was an easy thing to pop the fish out of the water using magic.

"Well what are you?" Ella asked it as it lay upon the grass, working its gills uselessly. Over a foot long and at least three pounds, the fish had two tall fins upon its back and an ugly mouth. "Don't get too close," she warned Whip-wip who was trying to peer down into the hard-ridged mouth.

The fairy wisely backed away. "You know what this fish needs?" Ella asked.

"Water?"

"No, silly. It needs some herbs. Some parsley or dill. Heck, even some salt and pepper would be nice. Do you know what dill is?"

Whip-wip considered the question for a moment and then answered, "Zooti?"

"No, dill's not a fruit. It's an herb. Like a smelly plant. Could you go scrounge around for some smelly plants while I make a fire?"

"No zooti?"

"Actually if you happen to come across a lemon tree, definitely grab a lemon. And if you find a butter tree, get me some butter." When the fairy looked un-sure, Ella said, "I'm just playing. Except for the smelly plants, I need those."

Just as Ella got a fire going, Whip-wip returned. In one hand she had a sprig from a juniper bush and in the other she had a bottle cap. "Thanks," Ella said, placing the two items next to the fish as if they were going to be of some use. The fairy watched Ella pre-pare the fish using her sword and when that proved clumsy and inadequate, she resorted to a bit of magic —the magic reminded her, she had other powers that could help in making her dinner complete.

Placing her hand in the grass beside her, she closed her eyes and felt the world around her. The feel-ing emanated out from her in ripples, each one a dis-tinct need to know and categorize the world. The feel-ing ran up the hills and along the forest floor spreading further…until she found what she was looking for.

After a quick walk and she came upon an old onion that had been good the fall before. It was soft and spotted, however when she cleared away a fibrous network and pulled back the layers there was still a core that would do.

"What else is there?" she murmured, again reaching out with her mind. Nothing near, and so she stretched further. At two hundred yards she discovered mint and something else—the soft step of a person…a little person. Concentrating harder she discovered the person wasn't quite a person at all. It was a gnome. She could picture it square in her mind: three feet, two inches tall, with a long nose and tall ears. It had spindly legs and arms, and a torso that was longer than both.

Her mind swept up the gnome, exploring him and too late did she realize what an invasion of privacy her actions were. Suddenly her mind went numb as a blast of radio static went through her brain, ear to ear.

"Oh…oh my." She clutched her head until the noise fuzzed into nothing. "What was that?"

"Hmm?" Whip-wip asked.

"That noise. What was it? And what are you wearing?" Using her near invisible filaments the fairy had the bottle cap tied onto the top of her head.

"Hat," she said pointing with a tiny finger. "Me American."

"You're strange is what you are," Ella countered. She began walking carefully in the direction she had felt the gnome in. "Tell me. Do you know what a gnome is?"

"Sis," the fairy replied and then hunched her shoulders in tight and made a face that looked as if she had eaten something sour.

"Are they evil?" When Whip-wip only gave a shrug, Ella asked another question, "Do you know why one would be so far from the Hidden Lands?"

"No. Gnome is strange. More than Sythie. Sythies is no strange. Sythie is pretty. See?" Now Whip-wip pointed at her own face.

"Yes very," Ella said after a single glance. She came into a little clearing in the forest and paused gazing about. "This is where the gnome was. Something is strange here. I can't even smell him. And there are no prints anywhere." She wanted to ask Whip-wip if gnomes could fly, but the fairy was yawning and looking about with slow eyes.

"Mr. Gnome?" Ella called. "I won't hurt you. I just want to ask you a question." No answer came and after waiting for a minute Ella went to find the mint. She wasn't healed fully, as well she was hungry, tired and in pain. It wasn't a good time for a gnome hunt.

Still the gnome occupied her mind for the rest of the evening as she cooked the fish, which was surprisingly tasty. What could possibly bring the little fellow all the way out here? Was it on an adventure? Had it been banished? Was it just curious? Ella certainly was.

Though hers was a necessary curiosity. When she wasn't dwelling on the gnome her mind went to Eireden and Aric and Darhmael. She thought of her mom in her dreadful state and while she sat watching the flames she thought of the poor police officer.

"I think it's bed time," she said to Whip-wip who was already snoring.

"Sis."

In the morning Ella finished healing herself. Her strength had come back to such a degree that she also went so far as to re-grow the hair that had been burnt from the back of her head.

After this bow to vanity she had a few bites of cold fish and began walking. Purposely this was in the direction the gnome had been in. When she got to the clearing she studied it closely and again she could discern nothing. However, when she widened her search she came upon two tracks that didn't belong in that empty forest.

They were wheel tracks. Thin ones like a bicycle would make. They ran parallel through a little mud puddle and then they up and disappeared. At once Ella set off in the direction they pointed. She had nothing better to do and no better direction to travel.

Curiosity pulled her along.

"Curiosity might have killed the cat, but I should be ok," she said to Whip-wip.

Immediately Whip-wip clutched at Ella. "Cat? Where? Is dead?"

"It's only a saying. There's no cat. Or actually in this case I'm the cat and the gnome is…never mind. Just trust me there's no cat."

Whip-wip assured Ella that she did indeed trust her, yet for the remainder of the morning she kept near and had a sharp eye out. Unfortunately for her there wasn't much to see. At some point in history the land had folded in on itself so Ella found herself trudging up and down hills and the air grew hot and dry. Ella guessed she was somewhere in the middle of Washington, but hadn't passed anything that resembled civilization for so long it was hard to tell.

With her nose pointing at the earth and her head swaying left and right searching for clues, Ella walked and walked. All afternoon she kept going, spying a drop of oil here, or a tire print there.

Eventually the day wore away and near sun down Ella finally found a road. It was a dirty little thing, still it had a sign posted: BIA-118

"What does that mean?"

Whip-wip looked at it close and then looked down at the trail. "It a road. Sis."

"Yes it is," Ella remarked. "Thanks for that. Let's look to see if the gnome came through here. Holy cow! Look, right there." Ella pointed at two tracks that cut across the dirt road. "That has to be him."

Doggedly the gnome was travelling straight across the state without deviating for hill, river or mountain. Buoyed by her discovery Ella went on until the sun sank and stars came out. She camped on a bald hill and after a dinner of roasted acorns and chestnuts she fell asleep watching shooting stars slash the night sky.

In the morning, after she waved goodbye to Whip-wip, who was off on a zooti-hunt, Ella went to a stream to drink and bath her face, and as she did her mind reached out almost on its own. It ran down the water like an electric current and there, not more than a mile away was the gnome doing just the same as Ella.

Quickly Ella hopped back, breaking the connection. Here was her chance. Using all of her elvish stealth, which was considerable, Ella stole along the banks moving with all the noise of summer breeze and found the odd creature in a clearing with an even odder contraption in his hands.

It reminded Ella of an upright vacuum cleaner, except there were billows attached which the gnome worked with gusto. When one billow blew the other sucked and the contraption made a sound like a wheezy donkey.

"Excuse me…" Ella said from the edge of the trees.

The gnome jumped and cried out, "Eeee!"

"Sorry," Ella said, holding her hands out. "I didn't mean to scare you. I was just wondering what that device does."

The gnome looked from the contraption and then to Ella. He then screamed "Eeee!" a second time and then bound away. Despite his spindly little legs he was quick and was in the brush before Ella could gather her wits.

It was like chasing a ground squirrel. They ran round and round, from tree to bush and back again, and all over the forest. Finally Ella caught it and threw it down, incongruously saying, "I won't hurt you," as she did.

"Let me go," squeaked the gnome all in a fright. "I do the master's bidding just as you."

Ella had been feeling a powerful sense of shame at having manhandled the gnome as she had, but now her eyes narrowed. "What master?" she asked in a quiet voice.

"*The* master," the gnome replied, clearly thinking it was speaking to someone of limited intelligence. "So that is that. If you'll regain some manners I'll be leaving. I do have an errand."

Ella was just letting him up and now she paused. "What is this errand?"

"My own, Lady Elf. If the master does not deign to explain what is what to you then I most assuredly will not either. It is what it is after all."

"It is what it is?" Ella asked in a gathering heat. Her hand stole to her sword. "Before I let you up… who is this master you speak of?" She knew already and the perfect features of the pureblooded elf, Darhmael came into her mind.

The gnome refused to answer outright. His tall ears swiveled and his eyebrows went halfway up his head as he said in a whisper, "*The Master*."

"Darhmael," Ella said without question. The gnome agreed by dropping his eyes. Ella's lip curled at the creature and before she knew what she was doing her sword jumped from its sheath and sat in her hand, glittering in the sun. "You will tell me of this errand, now!"

"Eeeee!" it screamed, shaking in unfeigned fright. "It is what it is and what it is, is a trinket. Please. I'm just to fetch the Master a trinket. Please. I am to do what I'm to do or my family will die."

Ella blinked at this trying to make sense of the things squeaky little voice. "Your family? Darhmael has your family?" The gnome, so stiff through its odd body could barely nod. Ella came to a decision at once, sheaved her sword and then proclaimed, "Then you have nothing to fear from me. Darhmael is my enemy and I won't have anyone hurt on my account. So what sort of trinket is he after?" In her mind she pictured fanciful pendants of diamond and ruby.

The gnome, who had just been afraid to the point of crying, now gave Ella a sharp look with his baggy eyes. "You'd help me? But you are not within my instructions. The Master did not mention much that was not and this includes you, lady Elf."

"Don't be stubborn Mr. Gnome," Ella countered. "I'm offering my help and whether it was or wasn't *not* mentioned hardly matters. I can be stubborn as well. What's to stop me from just following you and helping you as I see fit?"

"This will," the gnome said holding up something that looked remarkably like a mouse made of string and buttons. He held it up for Ella to see.

"How would that…?"

As she spoke he squeezed the hind end of the mouse and out of its little nose a fine powder blew straight into Ella's face. She opened her mouth to cough and then froze with her mouth open and her face contorted. Ella was completely paralyzed.

Chapter 14

Eireden

Never had the Forest of Mists been as chaotic and dreadful than on that storming night. Eireden battled with wolves all around him. They leapt and bit and frothed in a mad fury. Sometimes they attacked Eireden with gleaming fangs; other times they turned on each other and tore one of their fellows into red shreds of gore.

But mostly they attacked the forest, and this was because the forest was defending itself in its own ghastly manner. Though Eireden was encircled by tremendous timber wolves, the wolves were themselves ringed by creatures that were far worse.

Ghouls with white eyes, and undead trolls with hammers of bone walked among them killing as they would. The forest floor was alive and undulated with snakes and yellow-toothed centipedes that were longer than a man's leg, while a toad the size of a bus leapt about snatching up wolves with a slapping pale white tongue. Above, the skies buzzed with black flies each the size of a pony.

Alone in this madness Eireden battled, hacking away at the wolves. Of the fiends wrought by the mists he ignored completely though they pressed on him and he could smell their filth and feel the decay of their rotting bodies.

To do anything but ignore them would be to give manifestation to the fact of their illusion. And then they'd be real in his mind. Illusions couldn't kill unless he believed that they could. Only then were they dangerous.

Still they were a horror to behold and he felt his mind like a teeter-totter going back and forth between the real and the unreal. And worse, he began to tire.

Time in the mists could not be counted. How long did he battle? How many wolves had he slain? How many were illusions and how many real? That was his great fear. How could he tell a real wolf from a fake? He couldn't risk second-guessing himself and so he fought and fought. His blood came easily from a score of wounds and still the undead and the snakes and the wolves bit and clawed and screamed.

And then he couldn't take it any longer. His sword arm felt to be weighted by iron and he could barely lift it. Just then one of the fairies that had clung to him throughout the fight screamed and fled into the hellish night.

"No! Come back!" he screamed. It didn't and after a second it was swallowed by the maelstrom that surrounded him. Eireden had to get out of there, but which way could he run when the world had become hell all around him.

His heart knew. He felt Ella far away to the south. He could get out of the Mists simply by following her beacon! Eireden hacked at a wolf, shearing through fur and bone, feeling the meat of the thing and not at all knowing if it was real. He took a step south and then stopped remembering suddenly what lay beyond the mists, between him and the girl—one hundred thousand goblins, and who knew what else.

To go that direction would be certain death and perhaps not even a sane death. What tortures did Darhmael have in mind for him if…when he was caught?

"But this isn't any better," he commented as fangs sunk into his sword arm. Grimacing he switched the sword to his left and ran the wolf through.

Just then one of the fairies began screaming and pointing behind him. Eireden spun to see one of the black and charred elves bearing down on him with a glittering sword. "Nice try," he said and then, purposely not thinking, ran straight for it and ignored it as it took a great swipe at him.

And then he was alone in the mists. The elf had been a fake. Behind him the wolves continued to fight. They could not tell friend from illusion and they would all die. This was a certainty. Eireden watched the bizarre battle as he backed away and then wonderfully the trees interceded.

"Thank goodness," he breathed, and then he paused as the mists began to send more illusions his way. "Just don't look at them," he told the fairies—and himself. Keeping his head down he began to march through the forest always keeping Ella's beacon behind him. In this he had one sense of reality: he knew a single direction. This one thing was his only reality. The mists would not stop. More creatures came his way. Bizarre things that made him sick to his stomach. The fairies quivered in fright at them but the king went on, walking through pools of blood or over bodies that writhed beneath his feet or up hills of piled skulls.

After an hour he was tested unexpectedly. A wolf, red eyed and snarling came barreling at him from out of the mists. The king waved it away blithely, only to be knocked sprawling, his black sword spinning from his grip. In a flash of hot grey the wolf was at his throat digging his fangs into the king's flesh. Eireden got one hand up in time and felt the bones in it snap and crunch beneath the power of the wolf. He grunted his pain and struggled to push the beast off of him, however the wolf was too strong and clung tenaciously.

The fairies gave him a reprieve. Startled off of him by the attack, they closed quick and shot light into the eyes of the wolf but that only set the creature's insanity on edge and it gave a great shake of his head taking half of Eireden's hand with it.

It pulled back for a moment and then it darted in again, looking for the jugular and the king had to stick his wounded hand up a second time. The pain was sharp but bearable—though it was only bearable because he had no other choice but to bear it.

Now the fairies came back. This time they tried using their tough filaments to help. They tied one end to the wolf's tail and the other they wrapped around its exposed snout. This only resulted in a stalemate. The wolf couldn't bite down any harder, but at the same time it wouldn't let go.

"My sword!" the king gasped, pointing with his free hand. It lay just out of reach. The fairies sped to it and began hauling it over by hand inch-by-inch, grunting with tiny voices. Slowly the sword slid across the dirt to him…and then he had it in his hand.

A sad minute later the wolf lay dead after it had endured an awkward thrust through the lower part of its belly. The king stood over it swaying, feeling sorry the poor beast had died the way it did. He had just taken off his shirt to wrap his mangled hand when a great voice spoke above him, "That didn't go as I thought it would."

The mist dragon…or an illusion of the mist dragon sat wrapped around the trunk of an oak. Its words came down and bathed the king in a hot steam, making him go slightly dizzy.

"Go your way, dragon," the king snarled in anger. He couldn't take the chance on this being a fake, so he backed away with the black sword at the ready.

The dragon slithered down and took a fat chunk of the wolf in its great jaws and ate greedily. "Oh that's nice. That's crunchy. The blood is still warm!" It moaned in pleasure as it ate.

Eireden turned slightly away at the sight and said, "Yes, go on and gorge yourself. There are plenty more back that way. Just leave me alone."

The dragon smacked noisily and then stared at the king down its long snout. "Without your lady you're not so haughty. Is she dead already? Did your seed kill her so soon?"

"My seed? What are you going on about, dragon? What seed is this?"

The dragon buried its face in the guts of the wolf and then pulled up a great steaming hunk. After he swallowed at his leisure, he answered, "Just a surprise for you…if you live. Which you won't. Without a fey escort I'll be having you for dessert soon enough."

"Why wait? Come have a taste now!" Eireden roared. Though he wasn't at all at his peak, he worried that the mists would wear him down. This was exactly what the dragon was hoping for.

"No. Not yet. I'll let you marinate in the woods for a few more days and then when you are weak and your head is spinning and you've dropped your sword in some ditch, only then will I..." the dragon snapped its jaws shut to finish its sentence.

"Coward," Eireden snarled. "I knew I was right about you. A dragon can never be trusted."

"Wrong, my tasty treat. A dragon can always be trusted to be a dragon." The dragon took another bite and then said around the remains of the wolf, "See you soon." And then it faded back into the mists.

"Do not fear that silly dragon," Eireden said to his fairies; they shivered against his bare skin. "I'll get you out of here and then I'll make sure we get you some strawberries and cream."

"Crim?" asked a male with green and purple wings.

"Cream," Eireden corrected and started off again, feeling wrong somehow that he was purposely going further from Ella with each step. "You'll like it, trust me."

The idea of something yummy to eat bolstered the fairies and they were less afraid—to a degree. He was able to sing and this further calmed him and his friends, though the song died on his lips at the sight of the Feylands. It was a sight that he would never get used to. Even in the dark his senses were assaulted. It was a land of death.

Yet even this was preferable to the mists.

The king slid and slipped over the sludge covered ground, moving to the center of the valley where he was certain to find Aric. He was wrong. The fey wasn't at the Theater of Ancestral Concordance as expected. It was empty save for thousands of Aric's footprints going in every direction.

"Fairies," Eireden called to the little things that were huddled in the crook of his arm. "Go find Aric. He's a fey with green eyes." They shook their little heads and buried their faces beneath their wings. "Don't be afraid. It'll be ok. Nothing bad can get you here, I promise."

The fairies couldn't believe this to be true and refused to leave him. "Whip-wip would've gone," Eireden grumbled. He trudged on until he had traversed the entire valley. Cursing he started back with his endurance draining away from his many wounds and the poison in the air. He walked half-blind and with his head down. He thought he was following his own tracks back, but when he tripped over Aric he realized he was wrong. The fey was stretched out in the muck moaning in a delirium.

"Come on, get up," Eireden pleaded. His strength was at a low ebb and his left hand was all but useless. "Aric! Please, my friend, get up." Nothing stirred him, not even a slap.

Too weak to pick up the dead weight of the fey, Eireden began to drag him up the long hill to the hated forests. "It'll be ok," he assured the fairies between gasps. "As long as we have Aric, it'll be ok." They clearly didn't believe him and sat on the fey's chest, moping.

Chapter 15

Ella

"Uuuuh!" Ella screamed her hardest. The sound was barely heard even at the edge of the clearing and the gnome smiled showing small brown teeth.

"Do you comprehend? That is that. My instructions are what they are and you are not a part of them. My apologies."

"Uuh!" Ella said in anger. She tried with all of her strength to budge even the slightest muscle, yet she couldn't move what she couldn't feel. The only sensation that she possessed to give fact to her corporeal state was that her heart beat—she could feel it like a small neat watch within her.

That was it. She couldn't even feel herself breathe, though she could force air out to make her pathetic noises. Of her nose and toes and everything in between they might not even be there for all she felt of them.

The gnome nodded at her little noise and then turned away, going about his business as if she no longer existed. He took his strange vacuum-like contraption, folded into an impossibly neat square and then disappeared from Ella's sight. With her eyes frozen in place she could only stare at a section of the river and the trees around it.

The gnome was huffing over something to her right. Afraid, she asked "Uuuh?"

"Do not worry," the gnome said. "You are as you are, and you will be as you aren't as well, if nothing untoward happens."

What did that mean? Was the gnome saying she would be ok unless she wasn't going to be? "Uuuh?" she asked, hoping the gnome would clarify himself.

"If you can wait just a moment you will see!" he grumbled, furthering adding to Ella's confusion. Wearing a beaming brown smile he came back into her vision pulling on the oddest contraption yet. It was a cart of sorts, boxy with odd protuberances jutting at angles that made no sense whatsoever. Underneath were two thin wheels, yet it also had a propeller poking out of the back, while above, rigged to a pole were three blades that looked like they belonged to a stunted helicopter.

"Uuuh?" The sight of the thing made forget her confusion and fears, at least for the moment.

"Yes it is magnificent."

"Uuuh?"

The gnome looked puzzled. "What? You've never seen a chain activated, poly-powered, kinetic slash potential, torque driven, thirty-four spring omni transportator?"

"Uh-uh," Ella replied bewildered by the long string of words.

A hearty, but squeaky, laugh creaked from between the gnome's brown teeth. "Of course you haven't! I just invented it this last week. It now is what it once wasn't, and quite a step up from the thirty-three spring. I could go into the mathematics of it but that tends to baffle the lesser beings."

"Uuh!" Ella said crankily. How did a gnome get off calling anyone a lesser being?

"Don't blame me. You are where you are because you did what you did. I said what I said, yet you didn't have the sense to listen. Instructions are instructions of which you weren't a part of. Now you'll be this way for twenty-four hours, so don't make too much noise. You don't want to attract things that you don't want to attract. Good-bye. Oh wait…"

The gnome approached her and as short as he was she couldn't see what he was doing.

"Had to shut your mouth," he explained with a brown smile as he stepped back. "Bugs will get in there if you aren't careful and then a sparrow might investigate. Let me tell you, sparrows are as bad as they are. Droppings everywhere. Now, good bye."

Just like that the gnome climbed aboard his omni transportator. He sat himself in a triangular seat, stuck his feet onto what appeared to be bicycle pedals and then began pumping his skinny legs.

Despite her predicament, Ella found the machine, with its gears and running chains and bowing rubber bands, interesting. Every part of it seemed engineered to capture the energy exerted by the gnome and transform it into momentum. In this instance to the wheels, yet it was obvious that the device could traverse water, and judging by the blades, the air as well.

Omni indeed, thought Ella as it trundled out of sight.

And then she was alone and more than a bit frightened. What if a wolf or a bear came by? Had the gnome taken that into account? Or what if it rained, or worse, what if a late season snow came up and buried her?

"Uuh!" Ella screamed in just above a whisper. "Uuh!" This last was a scream of frustration. Her screams did nothing for her situation and so dejected, she slumped…in a purely mental capacity.

Twenty-four hours, Ella thought. *That's…let's see…uh fourteen-hundred and forty minutes. Give or take.*

Bored as she had never been before in her life, she tried to figure out how many seconds she had left. *Sixty thousand…plus another, let's see, twenty-four hundred. No wait that's twenty-four thousand, but I also need to add the twenty-four hundred. So…so that's eighty-six thousand, four hundred!*

She had figured it out. *Great.*

If she could've sighed she would have. Instead she watched the shadows of the trees gradually pull in toward themselves as the sun rose higher and her mind lit on every subject save one and that one she so purposely forced herself not to think about that she ended up thinking about it the longest: Eireden's upcoming wedding.

It would be a massive affair, she was certain. Sure, he would want it small, that was his way, and Alseya would want whatever he wanted, but none of that mattered. It would be huge and gaudy. The guest list would be miles long. Every prince would have to be invited, and they would bring along their families. And Eireden wouldn't forget to add his captains and their ladies. And there were the dwarves; Furen would attend and hopefully Gargefrel would come as well. Ella was dying to see what the most beautiful of all the dwarven women looked like…

Ella's mind did a figurative blink as she reminded herself that she wasn't going to the wedding. But what about Whip-wip? The fairy been invited, but had she said yes? Had she checked a "Plus one" on the invitation? Would that be Ella?

Secretly she wished it was so. A part of her longed to see Eireden as king—the way he should be king. Shining armor, raven hair, steel grey eyes…she longed even to see the scars that he wore proudly. Those scars marked him not just as a warrior but also as a man, a real man.

At his image she sighed, mentally, and then shook herself, again mentally. That sort of longing was done with. She was done with all of it: the adventures, the magic, the Hidden Lands and all the unreality that went with them.

Except of course this blasted paralyzation, she thought. *But other than that she was done with it all.* Of course whip-wip picked that moment to come casually floating through the brush to give lie to her thoughts. In her hands she hefted a chestnut bigger around than she was.

"Cook?" she asked, holding it up. The fairy liked her chestnuts roasted.

"Uuuh," Ella said and meant it. She was only trying to demonstrate her current predicament.

"Sis, please. Is good," Whip-wip insisted. "Is yummy."

Ella tried again, "Uuuh."

The fairy's tiny blonde brows screwed up as she stared at Ella in confusion. She then looked at the chestnut, turning it in her hands. "Huh?" the fairy asked, speaking in the language of her new country.

"Uhh," Ella stated.

Whip-wip's eyes suddenly shot wide. "You no talk?"

"Uh-uh."

The tiny blue eyes then looked Ella up and down. "You no move?"

"Uh-uh."

"Oh." The fairy shrugged and then went to work trying to get the chestnut to open. It was a long battle that meandered in and out of Ella's vision, and one in which the fairy eventually triumphed. She came to eat the nut while sitting on Ella's shoulder and getting some sun.

Though her teeth were sharp, they were tiny, yet the sound of Whip-wip gnawing her way through the nut was enough to drive Ella to distraction.

"Uhh!" she exclaimed.

The fairy buzzed her gold and silver wings, coming to hover right in front of Ella's face. "Sis?" she asked, spraying Ella with bits of nut pulp.

Inside, Ella shivered in agitation. "Uuuuh," she sighed unable to communicate even the simplest thing.

Of course this didn't mean that Whip-wip didn't interpret in her own way. "Ella sleepy? Sis. Is nap time." Ella didn't know what time it was, sometime around midday she guessed, and she wasn't at all sleepy. She gave a grunt, which was also misinterpreted.

"Close eyes? Sis."

Ella wanted to protest this, but when her eyelids were pulled down like window shades the feeling of relief was so intense that she practically purred. How long had it been since she last blinked? Three hours, four?

For once Whip-wip interpreted correctly. "You're welcome."

At some point Ella actually slept, but when she woke it went unnoticed; she was still as frozen as before. The sun was on the back of her head by which she judged the time to be late afternoon.

"Uhh!" she called out to Whip-wip. When no answer came, Ella tried a second time. The fairy wasn't near enough to hear the light sound, but something else was.

From behind, something parted the brush. Ella had been about to yell in her pathetic fashion for a third time but she bit it back as a sly step edged closer. Immediately her mind pictured a mountain lion and a squeak slipped out from her lips.

Where was Whip-wip! Ella sent a silent blast out from her mind, searching the forest for the little thing. Like the sound waves of a bat, these mental vibrations ran out in ripples, striking leaf and tree and then bouncing back so Ella had a vague conception of the world around her.

And of the beast creeping up on her!

It was huge. Thick through the shoulders and going on all four with a head larger than the biggest watermelon. It was a cave bear of great proportions and she had no doubt that it wasn't there by accident. That would be just too much of a coincidence, especially as she was trapped in a paralyzed body and blind because she lacked even the ability to do the simplest thing such as…

Ella could have kicked herself. She had her magic. She didn't need to be frozen at all! The first thing she accomplished was to open her eyes one after the other. This was a simple mental exercise—moving her eyes was another thing altogether.

Even as light as her touch was, her right eye swung inward and her vision went doubled. Correcting it the other way had her looking almost out of the side of her head. And there in her befouled vision was the bear, not five feet away! It was bigger than her mind had construed, at least six feet at the shoulder.

Closer it shuffled, snapping heavy branches beneath its dreadful size. If Ella could've screamed she would've, instead she managed to get her right eye basically in sync with its counterpart so now the forest was no longer a blurry mass of greens and browns.

What was easier than moving her eyes was moving her head, and this she did. As her ligaments and cartilage, made stiff from standing still for so long, made an awful snapping and creaking her head turned and there was the….moose?

It wasn't a bear at all. And it certainly wasn't something to fear. Lazily it made its way along the stream bank, eating great mouthfuls of vegetation. Eventually it disappeared in the foliage altogether and Ella had a laugh at herself for her silliness.

Not long after the moose incident, Whip-wip came back hauling a little black ball using a wound strand of her filament. She brought it to Ella's face and said, "Kiwi. Eat." The ball was wet and slime covered; pine needles stuck out from it. The kiwi was clearly well past its expiration date.

Using her magic, Ella tried to speak, "Aw-ba," she said, unable to work her tongue and lips at the same time. The fairy blinked at this, trying to decipher. When she couldn't she popped open her own mouth to encourage Ella and then brought the kiwi closer. Since speaking was beyond her, Ella pushed the fairy and her disgusting offering away.

Whip-wip giggled and then came back for another attempt. "O," Ella said trying to say *no*. When she did Whip-wip almost got the fruit into her open mouth. Barely in time, Ella switched her focus from the confusing interlaced muscles of her mouth and pushed the fairy away again.

This time Ella shook her head back and forth and then said, "O" again.

"No?" Whip-wip asked confused. "Sis. Is fruit." She held it up as emphasis and when she did she saw the pine needles, which she tried to scrape away, hurriedly. Of course when she did her hands came in contact with the slime and she made a face.

The fairy gave the kiwi a shrug and then dropped it. After, she wiped her hands on Ella's shirt. "Move now? Sis?"

To answer would only confuse things, so Ella lifted her hand to show Whip-wip that she could move— a little. The hand and arm attached felt like that of a manikin.

"Good," the fairy said judiciously as if the matter of Ella's paralyzation was an old subject and not one that needed to be discussed. "We is go away. Whip-wip is bored. Sis."

"Aay," Ella said in agreement. Now for the hard part: actually moving. She assumed it would be like walking stiff in a robotic fashion, however she failed to take into consideration the role that her inner ear played in balance. She picked up her right foot and almost immediately the forest tipped over on its side and Ella found herself on the earthen floor of the forest looking through tall grass at the sky.

Whip-wip began a mad cackling and then fluttered down to Ella's face. "Is funny! Sis. Do again?"

"O," Ella replied in lieu of her ability to say *no*. With surprising ease Ella lifted herself using her magic. What was much more difficult was setting herself down again in a way that didn't have her tipping over. What was easier was leaning her stiff body against a tree.

Whip-wip helped by looping a strand of her filament around her and the tree, essentially tying her in place. "Aainn oo," Ella said.

"Welcome," the fairy replied. Then she spotted an insect flying by and without thinking—her specialty— she gave chase. Since it a was wasp of impressive size she was back quickly panting with fear and hiding in Ella's torn and scorched clothes.

From there, Ella's day as a manikin took on a drowsy dullness that had her dozing with her eyes open. When she came to her senses it was dark in the way only a forest can get. Where her friends had always feared the night forest, Ella welcomed it and she settled back—again mentally and listened to the soft sounds of the life that hid during the day and after a time she slept again.

"Zooti!" came Whip-wip's usual morning battle cry.

"Es," Ella said around a recalcitrant and thick tongue that, like velcro, wanted to stick to the inside of her mouth. "Not sho lou...hey! Ip-ip. I can eak. Not sho ud, but shill."

Ella stopped trying since the fairy had long since disappeared. While she waited she attempted to move the rest of her body. It turned out that her recovery could best be described as sporadic. Her left side had the best of it: her big toe, elbow and buttock on that side were fully functional, as well she could also feel her ear, which was cold. Strangest to her was that her left eye could move as it used to and when she tried to look around she felt like a chameleon, looking in two directions at once.

Eventually, about the time Ella could bend her wrists, Whip-wip came back. Her gold and silver wings seemed dull and they drooped as she fluttered up. "Is yuck," she proclaimed, sadly holding up a raisin with tufts of grey mold sprouting from it.

"Sorry...that's better. I can speak! Isn't that great?"

"Sis," Whip-wip replied, dolefully. She gave the raisin a look and then dropped it to the forest floor.

"Do you remember candy?" Ella asked. Her left side was fully alive now and as she spoke she began to work her right arm back and forth hoping that by doing so it would wake quicker. "From back before? When we went to America?"

"Sis. Gum bears es good."

"Well, I promise that once we catch this gnome, I'll get you some...a whole army of gummy bears. What do you say?"

The Fairy's blue eyes grew in eagerness. "I catch gnome!"

Chapter 16

Eireden

The king woke with the sun low on the horizon, burning through the tops of the trees. For a moment he thought that dawn was upon him, but then his heart oriented on Ella—she was south and east—and that meant it was a sunset he was looking at.

"You have slept long," Aric said. The fey sat calmly against a tree with the fairies curled in a tangle of brightly colored wings and tiny limbs on his lap. "It is good that you have. It has taken me many hours to regain my own strength."

Feeling slow in the mind, Eireden sat up and rubbed at his eyes, wiping away the grit. "I haven't slept since the night I saw you last." At this a bearish yawn escaped him.

"You must have quite a tale to tell. Showing up bleeding and half naked, with a gaggle of fairies in tow, how did this come about?"

"There'll be time enough for stories as we travel," the king said as he slowly climbed to his feet.

Aric did not move. "You are not well enough for travel, yet. My goodness. Are those teeth marks? If I had to guess I would say a wolf attacked you and a large one at that."

"A number of large ones, actually. Come on I'll tell you of it as we go. Time has slipped away from me," Eireden said, passing a hand over his weary face. "I was wrong to have slept as long as I did."

"I will not be going with you just yet," Aric replied. "My work is not complete. Until it is I will not leave, though I will heal your wounds. Will you come to me? I don't want to disturb these little beings. It seems they had something of a fright."

"*They* had a fright?" the king asked incredulously.

Aric failed to notice his friend's attempt at humor. "Yes. They even missed their first breakfast. Didn't get up until after nine."

"Those poor things," Eireden said blandly as he came to kneel next to his friend. Aric studied the wounds, making little tsk tsk noises.

"There is much damage and I am still weak. I think it would be beneficial if you slept some more." This he said in such a soothing manner that Eireden blinked, feeling drowsy. "Yes," the fey went on. "Maybe if you close your eyes you would feel better. There you are. Breathe deeply...breathe..."

The next thing Eireden knew was that the fairies were up and whistling in excitement: "Zooti!" they cried as they flew about.

"Huh?" he said groggily, barely noting that his hand had been healed. "Why do they go for fruit at sundown...wait a moment!" The king sat up and looked around at the dim misty forest and noted the sun was still very low, but somehow had spun in the sky. It was in the east.

"You needed your rest," Aric said, still sitting with his back to the tree trunk.

Eireden leapt up in gathering anger. "You! You put a sleep spell on me?" Aric nodded. "Damn! How long have I slept?"

"Your anger is misplaced. You slept only the night and would have regardless of my spell. You were simply too weary to go even if you wanted to."

"The whole night?" Eireden asked, trying to recall where the hours went. "But I slept the night before as well. I can't believe it, I've been gone for two days! What of the battle? Have I missed it?"

"Possibly, but fear not King of the Den. For you there will always be another battle."

"You don't understand," Eireden said through clenched teeth. "Lives are at stake."

"Ella's life, no doubt. As you say, she is a goblin magnet. Do you ever wonder what our lives would be like if we had never found her? I have been thinking on that for some time."

The king didn't have time for Aric sitting around playing: What if? He reached down and plucked the fey to his feet and began dragging him southeast. "It's not just Ella's life that's in danger. It's all of us. While you've been fooling yourself into thinking that you're doing a damned bit of good here, Darhmael is trying to destroy all of the Hidden Lands."

"I'm sure you can handle it," Aric said, making no move to struggle out of Eireden's grip.

"I don't know...there's just so many of them."

Aric laughed easily, uncaring. "Since when do numbers matter to you? I've seen you fight against astounding odds. Remember when you were *Gada* and Lienhart left you in that clearing alone to fight a hundreds of goblins? This will be no different."

"I wish that you were right in this," Eireden said, slowing slightly as a feeling of helplessness came over him. "Unfortunately, Darhmael is leading in person. You have no idea of his power."

"Oh, I have a very good idea. It's why you'll lose eventually. You or one of your descendents. You battle in vain."

"So what would you suggest?" Eireden replied with acid in his voice.

"Surrender. Accept your place."

The simple words of the fey had Eireden seeing red. He stopped and pulled Aric close, so that they were nose to nose. "My place is King of the Den!"

"Yes it is, for now. And for now my place is in the Feylands. I'm responsible for the land."

"Wrong," the king snarled. He then began pulling Aric along at a great pace. "You are responsible for your people, not the land they walk on. Not some damned dirt!"

At first Aric glared at this, then he fought the maddeningly calm look back onto his features. "My people will flourish when they too accept their place. You are right about Darhmael. His power is far greater than any of us know and it's no wonder. He is an elf! The highest form of life on this planet."

In mid-stride Eireden pivoted on his left foot, pulled Aric in and punched him square in the face. It was a savage blow that not only smushed Aric's perfect nose, breaking it with a loud snap, it also knocked the fey unconscious.

"Damn!" Eireden cursed, staring down at the fey in a rage. Had they been anywhere else Eireden would've left him, but they were still in the Forests of Mists and the illusions were only a few steps away.

"Damn," he said, this time in a mutter, before he picked up the light fey and threw him over his shoulder.

Even unconscious the fey kept the illusions at bay, so it was only a simple walk through the forest and Eireden hardly felt his burden. Soon the mists gave way, and the open prairie, that dominated this part of the Hidden Lands, lay before him. Above the blue sky cheered him, and after a glance at the sun to check both the time and his directions he went on with a steady march.

"You may put me down at any time," Aric said, dangling from the king's wide shoulder.

"What is this?" Eireden cried. There was a tinge of embarrassment to his voice and he tried to make light of the fact that he had struck a friend in anger. "Have you been faking this entire time?" Eireden set him on his feet and was glad to see that the fey had already healed himself.

"Faking?" Aric asked, confused. "I don't know exactly what you mean. You were insistent on getting out of the forest. I would have escorted you had you asked."

"I'm sure. I must apologize," Eireden said, bowing his head. "I would that I had not struck you."

"You are forgiven, friend," Aric said touching his face. "Your blow would have felled an ox! I have never been struck in such a way with only a hand."

Eireden bowed his head again. "I find no pride in striking a friend."

"And I find no pride that my words caused you such anger."

"It was the poison in the air, no doubt," Eireden said in reply. "It clearly was affecting your thinking. You seem better now, and the further we get you from its source the better you will feel."

Aric laughed easily and the fairies who had been giving Eireden suspicious looks just minutes before gathered and tittered along. "I feel good now," Aric said. "And you should know that my thinking was not impaired before. I will not follow you on any more of your adventures. They are a misuse of my energies and frankly, a waste of time."

Eireden's hands balled into fists again, but this time he turned to look at the sky trying to find inner calm—it didn't work. "There are lives at stake, as I've stated!"

Aric too gazed at the sky and said, "Yes. Human lives." When Eireden rounded on him in a new fury, Aric put his hands up in peace. "Listen to me, my friend. I understand your feelings. You are king, steward, and shepherd to your flock. You will risk your life for those under your keeping, yet I am not a shepherd. I am fey. I am immortal and thus like the sun above us, should have a much longer view of the world."

Only the muscles twitching along the white scar on Eireden's face gave answer to the fey's words. The rest of him was as rock.

"I have lived fifty-three lives of man," Aric continued. "I knew the last king of the Den who bore the name Eireden. You two are much alike—fiery and noble in equal proportions. He died fighting to preserve his kingdom."

"I can think of no better way to die," Eireden said.

Aric splayed his hands and said, "Yet what has become of his sacrifice?"

Eireden's mouth dropped open in surprise. "What? What has become of his sacrifice? You are mad! The poison has surely ruined your mind for you to ask such a question. The sacrifice of the few is the gift of life to the many."

"Perhaps," Aric said easily. "Or perhaps those *few*, as you put it have all been unnecessary deaths."

"What are you getting at? Are you honestly saying that by *not* fighting we would save lives?"

"Yes."

"Yes?" Eireden thundered. In frustration he stalked into the prairie and kicked at the earth. "Your madness knows no bounds. You refuse to see the true face of evil."

"You misunderstand me," Aric replied. "For their entire existence the Den have fought and clawed and hacked out an existence. And what have they to show for it. That they yet live?"

"That they live free," Eireden countered.

Aric shook his head. "No. You are not free. Your sword has become your master."

Eireden touched the great sword of Aug-Raumon; its blade was blacker than the night. "Bah!" he cried suddenly in disgust. "You know not what you say. My sword is a tool only and I am its master. With it I keep my people alive and free. But what of your sword? Why do you question me when you carry one as well? Is it because you feel that you are so much greater than I? It's true! I see it in your eyes; you actually think that you are greater than I, Eireden, King of the Den."

The fey said nothing to this. He only raised a single eyebrow in answer.

Eireden shook his head at it. "You are not great; not like this. Right now a common, backstabbing filthy goblin is greater than you. And what's more, he is clearly the wiser between you."

"Your insults are low brow and tedious," Aric said with a sigh.

"The truth can be insulting, and the truth is you have lived your entire life as a hot house flower, pampered and indulged at every turn. Every aspect of your life, every tiny particle of it has been perfect. Think on this: have you ever experienced famine? Or drought? Or disease? Your trees bend with the amount of fruit they bear. Your gardens spring forth flowers with the wave of your hand and the earth heaps abundance at your doorstep!"

Aric did not answer this. His eyes were down on his boots, which were tall and grey. They had been muck covered, stained with oil and tar when Eireden had dragged him out of the desolation of the Feylands, but now, like the rest of him, they were perfect.

Eireden went on, "I'd wager you don't even understand the concept of *want*. What do you want, Aric? And don't say peace. You have all the peace you could ever want back in the Feylands now that they've been ruined so utterly. What do you want, personally?"

"I want nothing," Aric said with a tiny lifting of his shoulders.

The king had known what the answer was going to be before he'd asked the question, "And what do you need?" Now, Aric only shook his head. "Exactly," the king sneered. "And that is why every goblin out there is greater than you, the greatest of the fey. You can write endless poems, yet you know nothing of importance. You don't understand the basics of life: want or need. The only thing you understand is *have*! Your life has been one fantastic gift from the moment you were born, yet you look down on the rest of us because we weren't born as lucky as you?"

"Yes, I do," Aric breathed. He couldn't seem to lift his chin and his eyes were heavy.

"And now," Eireden sneered, his mouth tasting of bile at his own words. "And now when you are finally put to the test, when you're faced with the same hard choices the rest of deal with on a daily basis you tell me you want to surrender? You just want to accept your place even though you know in your heart that your place will be as slave to Darhmael? What this tells me is that the great gift of your life has been undeserved and wasted."

The king turned and spat in the dirt: a grave insult among the Den. "At least a goblin will fight for its miserable life." The king began to walk away and then stopped when Aric was just a shadow against the forest backdrop. He asked, "What about the rest of you? Should I waste one more Den life on the fey? Are they all as pathetic as you?"

Aric lifted his face; it was ghostly white. "I can't speak for the other fey. They..."

"Just answer the question!" the king roared in a fury. "Speak for them now, or don't you care about their lives?"

"I do," Aric cried in desperation. "Save them, please. They are not all miserable like me. I don't know what's happened to my mind. Everything has been wrong, whatever I do has been cursed."

"Stop it," the king said, gentle now. "You are not miserable and you aren't cursed. You are Aric Anorian, a great fey. Come with me and prove your worth whether it's in vain or not. Prove that the gift of your life was not wasted."

Aric nodded at first and then changed his mind. "I don't think that it would be wise. Ever since Ella and the Feylands...I have begun to know hate—not for her! Never for her, but for Darhmael, and myself and for others," he admitted sheepishly. "And that is how it started for the elves. Just a little hate, and a little bigotry, and they were never the same."

"You are the same," Eireden said, coming to take Aric's shoulder in an embrace. "Otherwise all of this wouldn't bother you so. I will help you with your little problem and you will help me with a hundred-thousand goblins. That's fair, don't you think?"

Chapter 17

Ella

With a renewed passion Ella went after the gnome. Her previous stint at stalking him, before her bout with paralyzation, had been a walk in the park, comparatively. Now she bore down on him with a will.

No longer was the gnome a matter of curiosity, or a way to cling to her adventures in the smallest way. Now the gnome *was* her adventure. She figured Darhmael wanted something from this gnome—possibly something important.

"It probably is," she said to Whip-wip as they walked along. This wasn't a stroll as before. Ella power-walked and Whip-wip had to cling to keep up.

"What is?" the fairy asked, looking around to what the "it" was. All she saw was forest.

"Important. I think that gnome is after more than just a bauble. But if it is really important why didn't Darhmael send one of his elves to get it? Wouldn't that make more sense? To send one of them to get it?"

"Get what?" Whip-wip asked, trying to get her bottle cap to sit on her head correctly. With all of Ella's jostling it kept slipping lopsided.

"I don't know," Ella said, looking around at the desolate hills and empty forest. "That's the problem. There's nothing here. Certainly not a mall or jewelry store if it was ring or something like it he's after. And would he want a ring? Could he make it magical?"

The fairy shrugged, nearly losing her cap.

"Well I guess it doesn't matter, because there aren't any rings way out here. What could he want in this forest?"

"Zooti?"

"That's what you'd want, silly. Darhmael is after something bigger. I think...but who knows? Maybe it's not so important. Like this is where his favorite mush-rooms grow. Either way, we shouldn't take chances, not with Darhmael, after all he is a master planner. There is a reason he's got a gnome out here and when we catch up to him I'm going to find out what that reason is...whoa."

"Whoa," the fairy agreed. They had just crested a hill and now below them was a body of water of tremendous proportions. It was nearly a mile wide, and north to south it went on further that even Ella's elf eyes could see.

"Well I know where we are, now," Ella said pointing out at the grey water. "That's Lake Roosevelt. Well really it's a damned up river and its going to be pretty cold."

Whip-wip had been fluttering over Ella but now she zoomed down close. "What cold? Whip-wip no swim!" As a rule, fairies loved water just as long as they were familiar with it. They never swam in a strange body of water since there were so many things that could eat them. "Is bridge?"

Ella shook her head and wasting no time, started bounding down the hill. "No, we could be hours from the closest bridge; we cross where the gnome crossed. Don't worry. If you trust me you can ride on my head as I swim. I won't let anything happen to you. First we have to make sure he crossed at all. I don't want to go to all the trouble of swimming across for nothing."

Though they searched for an hour they never found where the gnome entered the water, nor any tracks at all. Eventually Ella decided that she had to cross and so she cinched the elf sword tight to her back, made sure the pistol was secure in her pocket, and just waded into the frigid lake. Even with her magic, the swim was taxing for her and terrifying for Whip-wip.

A breeze with the force of a gale swept continually across the water. Not only did it make white-capped waves that Ella had to fight through, it also threatened to blow Whip-wip from atop Ella's head.

That wasn't the fairy's only fear either. Time and again Whip-wip cried out *fish* or *nymph* and once she even screamed: *Shark*! This last unnerved Ella enough so that she paused in her swim to search the water around her for any evidence of a shark. It turned out to be a piece of driftwood.

With the head winds and the choppy, freezing water, the swim took close to an hour. By the time Ella sloshed up onto the far bank it was late afternoon and the sun was westering over the mountains behind her.

"M—maybe we shouldn't worry about the tr-tracks just y-yet," Ella suggested to whip-wip through chattering teeth. To get out of the numbing wind, Ella hurried to the forest. "I think the current pushed us far south of where we need to be. If we cut to the northeast we can probably find his tracks or if we get to the top of that peak. It'll give a good view."

She pointed up at the craggy slopes to the tallest of the summits. The mountains in this part of Washington weren't like the great snow-topped goliaths found in Colorado. These were older and weatherworn, which made climbing them much easier, but they also seemed closer than they really were.

It was a long, long hike and it exhausted her both magically and physically. The sun had set hours before Ella and a sleeping Whip-wip gained the summit of that high peak. From it the view was less than spectacular: the wilderness around them was a sea of darkness broken only by an occasional porch light from a lonely farmhouse, or the headlamps of a distant car, or nearer, the flicking red and blue strobes of a police cruiser.

Ella watched it's progress with growing concern. It seemed to be heading in the same general direction that she had been traveling before and when she saw a second set of lights racing from the north she knew with a near certainty that the gnome had done...something.

But what? What was out in the nothing forests of Washington State? As far as she knew there wasn't anything of importance out here...surely nothing that would warrant two police cars.

"I'll find out soon enough," she whispered to the night. Despite her exhaustion Ella took off at a run, going down the hills and through the woods like a deer. Since her magical energies were almost tapped out, she had to rely on her elven physicality. And this was up to the test. Faster than any Olympian, Ella ran up and down mountains, leapt narrow gorges and crossed rivers, jumping from rock to rock.
She sped on despite that her lungs burned and her limbs went numb and felt weighted down. Only when she got close to the angry lights did she slow her pace.

"What is it?" Whip-wip asked peaking out timidly from her shirt pocket. "Is dragon?"

"No, I don't think so," Ella said, poking the fairy down deep into her pocket. "Keep hidden...and if there's any trouble, go find Eireden. He'll know what to do."

Whip-wip didn't stay completely hidden. A fairy's curiosity was boundless and her blue eyes sat just above the edge of the pocket as Ella crept closer, going slow, using all the cover she could. And then she ran out of cover completely. The forest had been hacked away making a huge round clearing, all of which was surrounded by tall fences, topped with gleaming, razor sharp barbwire.

Afraid to be seen attempting to scale the fence and being shot out of hand by nervous police officers, Ella decided to sneak close to the gate and when she neared it she saw that lights she had seen from afar hadn't belonged to police cruisers at all. Military Humvees, painted in swathes of green, sat parked in front of an odd building that had been built into the side of a manmade berm.

Another Humvee was parked at the entrance to the facility and as Ella snuck closer she smelled the strange aroma that recently fired guns made; and there was something more, something harsher in the air. Something that could warp metal and turn it black. The gate hung from its hinges; it was twisted from an explosion of some sort.

Next to the gate, eyeing it closely was an officer...or a military policeman to be precise. His face was a mask of anger and fear.

There was no way to sneak around the man so Ella went with the straight on approach and hoped to God that the natural protective charm that Darhmael had instilled in her genetic code would keep her from being shot.

"Excuse me?" Ella said, sweetly, stepping from the trees and into the light. Quicker than a wink the man had a deadly black rifle pointed square at her. She wasn't afraid; though her magic was at a low ebb there was still enough left in her to keep the little safety switch on the side of the gun, away from the word "Fire."

"Who are you?" the MP demanded, nervously. "Give me your name, right now!"

"My name is Ella," she answered plainly, coming closer so he could see that she was only a girl and not some ninja assassin or covert spy. "I'm not your enemy. In fact I'm hunting the person who did this. Can you tell me what happened here?" Her words came slow and easy and were gilded with power—as much as she could afford to use.

It made the man blink slowly as if just waking up. "There's been an explosion," he said and glanced toward the blackened metal of the gate and fencing.

"Is it bad?"

He nodded with bugged out eyes. "It destroyed the gate."

"That's too bad. It was a nice gate, but what about in there? What is this place?"

"It's top secret," he said, sharper now.

Her head had been thumping already as her magical energy drained, and now she had to dig even deeper. With a grunt of pain Ella said calmly, but with power, "That's ok, because I have top secret clearance. What's here that's so important?"

The magic in her words had the man going slack jawed. As if from a dream he said in a slow voice, "Missile silo."

"What?" Ella gasped.

"Missile silo," he said again. "It's a black cat operation. A stray: no agency affiliations. One of the new Archon fours that we keep off the grid."

Ella didn't understand what the man was saying, but she did understand the words: Missile silo. "Are you telling me that there is an atomic bomb in there?"

The man shook his head and Ella breathed a sigh of relief until he said, "There used to be."

Chapter 18

Eireden

The two men strolled across the prairie. Eireden wished to go faster, wished they would run, Aric had healing to do and it wasn't a healing that magic could fix.

"It was the day I first saw Ella's mother," Aric said slowly. "When I saw what sort of state she was in, that horrible trance, I could not get past the fact of her humanity. It was all there. Everything that makes humans so sad: the terrible frailty of age. The ugly misery of pain. The mental weakness."

Eireden cast a sidelong look at his friend. "You are quick to judge. We know not the horrors she faced that turned her so."

"I see that now. I was wrong to judge so quick and so harsh, but I was suddenly confronted with the fact that Ella wasn't everything I thought she was. I had this vision of her as a perfect being that could save the fey."

"I know Ella, she would be the first to decry her perfection," Eireden said with a laugh. "Which of course only makes her more perfect!"

"Maybe you don't know her so well," Aric answered back. "It turns out that she is perfect. She was engineered that way by Darhmael. What power he used, I don't know, but he created her. He made her perfect in every way."

"What is this?" Eireden said, slowing even more. "I know Darhmael is her father, but I would not use the word create. You make it sound as though she was a science experiment."

"She wasn't the experiment," Aric replied. "Those burnt elves, they were the experiment. Those and countless others besides. Ella is the finished product. She was designed with me in mind. She was designed to fool me into loving her."

"Is this truth?" Eireden asked, taken back.

"Yes and I was indeed the perfect fool. I pretended not to see the danger all around her, exactly as Darhmael intended. I took her home to show her off. How proud I was. One thing I am glad for: you were not there to see my stupidity. What a fool I was escorting her around, smiling at my friends, acting as though I had won some great prize, happily unaware of the danger."

Eireden took his arm and squeezed. "You were not at fault in this. If what you're saying is true then I was equally fooled. I loved her as well."

Aric took a deep, harsh breath and said, "No. I saw you fall in love with Ella and...and I saw her fall for you. It was natural and beautiful. Yet I had the audacity to feel sorry for you, because I thought I knew the truth. I thought that since Ella was fey that she would be as shallow as I was and that she would turn her back on you when she found out she was better than you."

"That's not Ella," Eireden said. "She wouldn't do that to someone."

"No, because she's perfect," Aric said with tears in his eyes. "Darhmael did it right. He made her heart pure and...and I looked right past that pure heart and I only saw that her ears weren't pointed and that her eyes could've been a deeper blue. When I found out that she was half-human, that's the only part I could see and it ate at me. And when we were in the dungeons at Rhyoeven and I found out that she been made simply to trick me..."

Aric couldn't continue for a few moments and when he did he couldn't look up at Eireden. "I think I became insane. I couldn't look at her or be near her. And you know the rest. I decided I had to atone for my mistake..."

"Loving Ella wasn't your mistake," Eireden growled.

"Yes, I know that now. My mistake was ever believing for a second that I was better than anyone. Though I did not learn this until you taught me. I was in the Feylands determined to make things like they were: perfect. I thought that my mistake had been that I hadn't been perfect enough and I was determined to be that, only...I discovered the best most perfect fey is still inferior to an elf."

"Hardly!"

"Yes," Aric said, smiling now. "But my mind was saturated with, not only the poison Darhmael had left, but with my own self-hatred. I began to wish I had never met you or Ella. And then I began to wish we had never fought the elves so long ago. I asked myself: what if we hadn't? What if we had accepted our place in their society? I began to fool myself into thinking things wouldn't have been so bad."

"Aye, those are some foolish thoughts," Eireden said, glad Aric had begun to show some wit, but time felt to be running down. He started walking again and gradually picked up the pace.

Aric strolled along with light steps, easily keeping up with Eireden. "What of you, my friend? One day you show up talking marriage and the next you show covered in wounds? Where is that fine armor I saw you in? And what is with these fairies? Why do they stay so close when they haven't eaten?"

At this one perked up his ears. "Zooti?"

"Darhmael has found a counter to the sythie. It's some strange beastie that he's bred strictly for the purpose of killing them."

"So it seems you'll be the Sun King no more."

"I'll be the 'Dead King if he catches us on this empty prairie," Eireden replied.

"I should be able to help both you and this little family." Aric knelt and placed his hands upon the ground; after a moments concentration he looked up gravely. "Things are not right. Eireden, your realm is in grave danger."

Eireden bent to touch the ground as well, but the feelings coming to him were so confused that he didn't try hard to make them out. And it hardly made sense to try when he had Aric with him. "What is it? What do you see?"

Aric's face was white and his eyes blank. "The maug...there are so many. Thousands of them. They're running amok and they're blood-gorged."

"The capital!" Eireden cried, fearing the worst. "Has it fallen?"

The fey closed his emerald eyes for so long that Eireden began to count heartbeats. "No," Aric said breathlessly. "It is safe for now, though I dare not look further. Darhmael is aware. I can feel his mind searching for me."

"Do not look," Eireden said, relieved. "If the capital is yet free we are not lost. In fact we have great hope as long as she lives. Rhyoeven cannot fall. Come, stand and wipe away your fear."

With a shake of his head, Aric's eyes cleared. "What has happened in my absence? Has the world come undone?"

"So it seems," the king replied. He then told the story of the sudden goblin onslaught and how it owed its success to Darhmael's influence. "The only question lies in methodology. The elf's motive is clear: the destruction of the Den, and the fey. I just don't understand how he thinks to accomplish this. His army has burned Tayoeven and Avargard, and I fear that if Hildeoven hasn't already fallen, then it soon will."

"What is not clear? Burning cities won't destroy the Den?" Aric asked in confusion.

"Not if Rhyoeven still thrives and as long as it lives so too do the Den. Still Darhmael must know this. As well he knows that attacking Rhyoeven will destroy his army."

"Perhaps he does what he does to lure you out. Would not Rhyoeven succumb if your army be destroyed? That is what he most likely desires."

Eireden nodded, but his eyes were far away. "I would agree if it were not for Alseya. Her wisdom and vision should not be discounted. She looked upon our enemy and came away with the fear of being trapped behind our very own walls." Eireden paused, again staring, thinking on the opal-eyed fey. Worrying for her. He came to a quick decision. "Come! We must make all haste. It is to Furen and the dwarves I must go at all possible speed. His guidance in all things earthly cannot be ignored."

"You will not attend your capital? What advise do dwarves hold that you deem of such importance that you would not hasten to its defense?" Aric asked.

"Our walls are too great for Darhmael to assault and at the same time his army is too powerful for us to dare meet in open battle. I worry that he intends to attack from another direction."

"Tunnels," Aric said, nodding. "Yes that makes sense. Come, you are going the wrong way."

Eireden had been marching at an incredible pace southwards and now he paused, confused. "But Furen..."

"Is in that direction, yes. However, horses are in this direction, as well as strawberries for our sythie friends." The fairies quivered in excitement.

They came across the strawberries first and the sythie gorged themselves until they were stuporous. The horses were found hiding in a gully and came racing as soon as Aric whistled to them. By the saddles they still wore it was clear they were Den horses.

"This one is injured," Eireden said, pointing to a long gash. The horse, a proud chestnut, pressed himself to the king almost knocking the man over in his eagerness to be near. "What of that mare? Is that her blood?"

Caked blood ran all along the neck of the mare. Aric shook his head, sadly. Wordlessly he went to the chestnut and healed him.

Grimly Eireden mounted the horse, pointed it toward the southern arm of the cascades where the fabled kingdom of the dwarves lay deep beneath and set his heels to its flank.

Though it made sense to travel in as straight a line as possible, roving bands of maug prevented this. Their grey-green bodies swarmed the prairie forcing Aric and Eireden ever eastward until by midday the pair found themselves on a hill overlooking the charred remains of Hildeoven.

"What of her people?" Aric asked. "Where are they all? My kinsmen were here...my mother as well!" Desperately he charged down the hill and would not listen to the king who tried to get him to stop. The fey raced across the battle plain and into what once was the center of town. There he stopped, his face gone white.

Though the bones of the town remained, black timbers jutting from smoldering ash, there wasn't the least sign of death. No bodies, no blood; nothing but the ghost of the town. Aric went from building to derelict building searching.

"We should not remain," the king advised. His chestnut became skittish and danced beneath his hands, eager to leave as well. "There are worse things than goblins about." As if to give credence to his words a howl from the nearby forest went up like a lone siren. "Come Aric! The people of Hildeoven made good their escape before this calamity struck and we should do the same."

"Indeed," Aric said taking to his saddle. They rode out of the town heading south even as a pack of timber wolves entered from the north. There were a great many of them.

"Can you cover our scent?" Eireden asked.

"Yes, but what good will that do us?" The wolves had caught sight of the fleeing horsemen and had set up a dread symphony of howls. The noise made the horse's eyes role white in their heads and the fairies cried and pointed in fear.

"They may be tracking me by smell," the king said. "Me, personally. The other night I had them *all* after me. There was probably close on two-thousand of them all oriented on me in that black night."

The fey nodded and then his eyes went to soft squints as he concentrated on the spell work needed to mask their scents. "It is done. Let's see if it worked."

Riding with their heads turned back they saw the grey pack rush on, closing the distance quickly and then their headlong rush became a confusion. The wolves went here and there with their noses to the ground, trying to catch the scent trail they'd been on. A few eyed the fleeing horsemen suspiciously but did not follow.

"That worked better than I thought it would," Aric said with a satisfied smile. "For them to react the way they did, they must be truly keyed to you and to you alone."

"Wolves have ever been the tool of the enemy," Eireden said and sighed heavily. "I had hoped that they had all followed me into the Forest of Mists and died there."

The pair watched the befuddled wolves for a moment longer and then Aric said, "Come we should not tarry so, for they may come to their senses."

He led them again to the south but angled slightly east, this time for his own purpose, and they took up the South Stream Road. This was clear of enemies and so the two made good time, pausing only once in a slight detour.

"Easa-see?" the king called gently as he came down the hill and into the fairy grotto. "Tissa? Sooni?"

The fairies, who had ridden for so long with them, flew off but not in their usual manner. They flew, keeping low, whistling quietly in their language, calling after their distant cousins. Yet other than the water falling into the blue pool, the land all around was silent and still.

There was no sign of Eireden's sythie family and this struck a note of anxiety in all of them. They decided to water the horses.

"Careful," Eireden said to Aric. The fey had just knelt at the pool's edge for a drink. "There's a nymph living in those waters."

"Oh?" Aric said. He cocked his head at the water and then back to the Den. "And why must I be careful? Have you angered her?"

"Me? No quite the opposite. The watery tart tried to snare me with her song once."

Aric gave a shrug and said, "But is that not what they do? Besides you of all people have little to fear from such a test."

Eireden gave him a little crooked smile. The nymph's song had been a more difficult trial than he liked to admit. He changed the subject, "I fear for our missing sythie friends."

Aric gave the others a look and said, "Perhaps they felt the coming danger and went to the capital to help. After all they do see you as both king and father."

"That is my hope," Eireden said, mounting the chestnut once again. "We shall find out the truth soon enough."

The two, escorted by the fairies left the grotto and took to their journey and for many hours they rode in silence. It was not until the mountains loomed over them and the sun had well set that Eireden asked a question that he had been embarrassed to ask.

"Do you know where the dwarf kingdom is exactly?"

Aric turned, amazed. "Me? I know not. But tell me, are these not the lands of the Den and are you not King?"

"You know these answers," Eireden said, gruffly. "Although I am king it does not mean I am privy to all the secret ways of the dwarves, for they are secretive beyond any. Our emissaries travel this road until it ends and are then led further, and from what is told the way beneath the mountains is an unsolvable puzzle."

"Perhaps there will be door wardens who will announce us," Aric suggested.

"The dwarves do not care for unscheduled visits. They can be suspicious of those who 'walk above, but look down' as they say. I fear they sometimes view even the Den as spies."

"We can only press on and hope that Furen has inspired manners among his people."

With no other options they did indeed press on, following the road ever deeper among the tall crags. Even if it were not night, their path would have been a gloomy one for the mountains squeezed on either side for a long stretch before opening up into a dell. It was a dead end. There were no doors or sentries, only a great flat wall of unworked stone.

Dismounting, the king went and rapped hard upon the wall. This made no more noise and had no more effect than if he had knocked on the side of a mountain.

"Hello," he called out and then looked at Aric, who only shrugged. "Give heed unto me!" he cried louder. "I am Eireden, King of the Den and ruler of this land."

This little speech had a much greater impact than the knock. Suddenly the ground beneath their feet began to shake angrily, and a tremor ran up the walls. The fairies, who had been quietly searching the rocks along the path for berries, now came rushing back to the king as if he could protect them from an earthquake.

Though it was not an earthquake exactly. A large part of the flat wall before them started to fall forward and the two friends were forced to dart back to avoid being crushed beneath. When they were safely away they stared in at a deep hewn cavern, which was filled with rows and rows of dwarves in gleaming metal.

The dwarves appeared in a surly, unforgiving mood and they stared at the two trespassers with beady black eyes that were filled with menace.

Chapter 19

Ella

"What do you mean there was an atomic bomb in there?" Ella asked. Her mind had trouble grasping all the implications in the MP's words. There were so many and they were all so dreadful.

"There was an assault here and a break in," the policeman said, blearily, touching the side of his face. Though Ella hadn't used her power in the last question, the MP wasn't yet recovered from her earlier spell work and his words came out slurred. "A part of the missile was stolen."

Ella felt her heart drop within her. "What part? The bomb part or the rocket part?" If there were any other parts to a Nuclear tipped missile she didn't know, nor did she really care just then.

"The bomb part," the MP replied, blinking slowly. "One of the nuclear warheads. A two stage thermonu-clear war...um, who…who did you say you were with? Are you military or with the Agency?"

"Uh…the Agency, I guess," Ella answered, nearly in as much bewilderment as the spell-struck MP. The gnome had stolen a nuclear bomb? That was the *trinket*? What kind of trinket was that? It wasn't one of course. It was a weapon, an unstoppable weapon.

As if waking from a dream, the MP shook his head, coming to his senses. "I should take a look at your ID just to be safe. It's standard operating procedure."

"My ID?" Ella asked, buying time as she started to pat her clothes. The gnome had a two-hour head start, but as far as she could tell that odd contraption of his wasn't all that fast. And it was only powered by the gnomes skinny little legs, which meant Ella could catch it if she had something faster than her own tired legs—her eyes fell to the Humvee.

"My ID is right here." Ella stepped close and pulled out the little black pistol that she has taken from the dead police officer. She didn't like the idea of threatening a good person like this, however her magical energy was at a dangerously low ebb and she couldn't afford to waste a drop when she had other means at hand.

"Huh?" the man gasped, his eyes going comically large.

"Turn around," Ella commanded. The MP had his rifle, but Ella was so close he wouldn't be able to get it up before she shot. The man wisely turned slowly holding his hands out. Ella took the rifle, a black M16, and after slinging it over her shoulder she pushed the man to his knees.

"You don't want to do this," he said in a controlled voice. "It won't end well for you."

"You're probably right on both counts, only I don't have a choice. I got to get that bomb back. Put your hands together on that bar." She took the man's handcuffs and locked him tight to a sturdy section of the fence. Next she grabbed the keys to the Humvee from his trouser pocket. "Sorry," she breathed in his ear and left him.

The camouflaged vehicle was veritable beast of power. She backed it back away from the gate, calling, "Whip-wip! Let's go." A second later the fairy had zoomed in through the open window and Ella stomped the gas.

The engine roared and she swung the wheel to the west. What little she knew of the gnome had her guessing it would head back to The Hidden Lands in the most direct route. Unfortunately the most direct route wasn't the easiest. Shooting up a long train of dust into the air behind, Ella raced up the dirt road for two-miles and then it suddenly turned to the north.

Immediately Ella stopped the Humvee and hopped out to study the ground. It was clean, which meant either the gnome hadn't gone this way, or it had covered his tracks. "Oh no," she whispered, fearing what she had to do.

With trepidation, she knelt and sent her mind out through the millions of connections along the inter-twined roots of the forest. Always west she searched and then she felt the racing wheels of the strange cart; she felt his legs pumping madly; and then she felt a great numbing static that had her pitching forward into the pine needle covered forest floor.

"Ella!" Whip-wip cried, hovering over her in a soft glow.

"I'm fine," she lied. In truth her head banged and her watering eyes had trouble focusing. In a stagger she made her way back to Humvee and worked it between the trees. The going was tough at first; with the way her head felt, Ella was an erratic driver at best.

But then, just about the time the forest opened up, her mind finally shrugged off the awful fuzz of static and she was able to drive the Humvee as it was meant to be driven.

"My," Ella said in amazement. The Humvee proved to be nearly unstoppable. With it, she charged through the forest, bouncing over fallen logs or smash-ing over young trees with impunity. Once she dropped into an unseen gorge, but just as easily the Humvee, with its huge tires climbed the other slope.

And then there was the gnome, pumping his legs and staring over his shoulder with round eyes. And there strapped across the contraption he was driving lay the bomb, or so she assumed. There wasn't much to it, at least from the outside. The object, about eight feet in length, was cone shaped and painted a bright orange.

Ella gunned the engine, closing the distance quickly, but the gnome was crafty and not so easily undone in his designs. Out of the back of his cart came a grey sack, not unlike a large pillow, and like a pillow it was filled with feathers.

The "pillow" seemed to hang, floating in the air for a moment and then it exploded in a fury of white. The night went from dark to a swirling storm in an instant, blinding Ella. Too late she slammed on her breaks and a second later the Humvee went into a tree that was too large for it to over power. There was screech from Whip-wip as her momentum sent her into the windshield, which, a second later, blasted inwards as an arm-thick branch crashed through it.

"Whip-wip! Are you all right," Ella begged as she pushed aside glass and branches from the interior of the Humvee.

"My wing!" The fairy cried from beneath the mess. A stick had gone straight through one of her delicate little wings and now Whip-wip sat in tears, each twice the size of the eye from which they sprung.

"You're going to be ok, I promise," Ella assured her. "Just not yet. I need to save what power I have left in order to catch that dratted gnome." Whip-wip nodded her little head and then went to hide in the back seat of the Humvee.

Despite the crash, the sturdy army vehicle still rumbled and so Ella backed away from the tree she had ran into. Then she was off again with the night air blowing in at her and feathers spinning oddly around.

Within a minute she caught up to the gnome, which was a surprise and not a good one. She figured rightly that the gnome had more tricks up its sleeve, but she did not understand the full potential of the chess-master mentality of the gnome.

After the fiasco with the feathers Ella decided that to come again from the rear was a mistake so she looked for an avenue between the trees to get at it from the side. And lo, there was just the opening big enough to fit the wide tracked Humvee.

She took it, not seeing the spikes that the gnome had hurriedly hid beneath the leaves. In a second, all four of the tires were in shreds.

"No!" Ella screamed and punched the steering wheel. Her frustration was great, but when she heard the cackling of the gnome as it pedaled away, the frustration boiled into anger. "Stay here Whip-wip," she said, grabbing the M16 that she had taken from the MP.

And then she was off in a dead sprint. Though her magic was weak, her legs had recovered somewhat and she used her natural speed to eat up the distance between her and the gnome. At the sight of her he let out a squeak of fright and pumped his legs for all he was worth, but it soon became apparent that she would catch him.

"I didn't want to have to do this," the gnome said in a huff. He reached down for something and Ella, who was ten yards behind, dodged to her right, thinking he was about try another trick.

He wasn't.

The cart made an odd noise: Whhipp! And then Whhipp! And Whipppp! The propellers above began to spin faster and faster. "That's potential energy, Elf! Thirty-four wounds worth. If you understand, then your understanding should be sufficient to know you can't catch me unless you can fly as well."

"Stop," Ella cried as the cart lifted off the ground. "You can't do this. That's a bomb you have."

"These are the instructions on how to free my family," the gnome replied. "My directives are clear to those who see clearly, which you do not."

"I'll shoot!" Ella said, bringing the M16 to bear. The gnome squinted at it in curiosity, but did not stop, instead he pedaled all the faster, grunting pig-like in his desire to escape. "I said stop!" Ella screamed. "This can kill you. I'm not playing now."

"Only my death will void my instructions," the gnome replied, panting.

"So be it," Ella said and fired the gun. Blam— blam—blam! With the dark and the growing distance she had no idea if she was hitting a thing, but then there came a sound that although wasn't loud it went right to her soul. Ting—ting. She was hitting the bomb!

Chapter 20

Eireden

It was clear that the dwarves were keyed up. They gripped their weapons: great battle-axes, stone headed hammers, and quite a few carried stout halberds that could either spear a rider or cleave a man in two.

Subconsciously Eireden's hand went to the hilts of his sword, but then a jovial voice, like happy thunder, cried out, "Aric! Eireden! What a surprise." It was Furen Traganfel, and his armor was of shining plate and his shield upon his arm was taller than himself, and in his right hand was a hammer that only the stoutest arm could wield. This last he tossed easily to one of his men and then came forward with his hands out in greeting.

He clapped Aric on the back, nearly causing the slight fey to stumble and after a formal bow, did the same to Eireden.

"What is this?" Eireden asked, indicating the rows of dwarves. They were ten across and so deep as to be uncountable.

"This is for you," Furen said with a growing suspicion. "Don't tell you have killed all the goblins that were worrying you and left none for me? I thought we were friends."

"If you knew their number, you would not fret on that account," Aric said.

Eireden stepped forward and inspected the hardy dwarves. "And you say this army is for me? You know of our troubles then?"

"Aye," the dwarf responded. "The Prince of Hildeoven sent a message just ere this time yesterday. He said his city was in danger of being overrun and requested that I assemble all available dwarves. I thought it cryptic, but saw no reason to ignore the call to arms."

Aric, who was eyeing the dwarves alongside Eireden, said, "These are most cryptic times in which we live."

"And you are ready to march so soon?" the King of the Den asked.

"Two-thousand battle-hardened dwarves at your service," Furen said with a wave of his stumpy arm. "I dare not send more. As it is we are cupboard dry in case we are attacked."

"This is impressive, though sadly too late," Eireden said, dropping his gaze. "Hildeoven has been put to the torch as has Tayoeven and Avargard."

The dwarf pulled at his beard in sudden anger and grief. "Hildeoven? And what of Lienhart? What has become of the people, both fey and Den?"

"They fled before the might of Darhmael's army as I had directed," the king said. "Though why they begged for assistance when they knew my mind I do not know. Yet I cannot be unhappy about Lienhart's decision. An army of dwarves will ensure that Rhy- oeven will not fall."

Aric had been listening with narrowed eyes. "If your capital be not surrounded. There is something queer about this."

"What?" Furen asked raising a bushy brow. "There are goblins in need of slaying. What could be wrong? Nothing! My dwarves have been lazing in the mines for too long now. The tunnels can wait. To war!"

"To war! To war! To war!" the ranks of warriors chanted in their deep voices making the walls ring.

Furen nodded proudly. "To war! But first you must meet the queen."

Aric glanced Eireden's way and said, "Are you referring to the Lady Gargefrel?"

As Furen nodded emphatically Eireden began to shake his head. "Do we have time…"

In a quick move Aric elbowed the King of the Den and said, "Time to meet the Queen of the Dwarves? An event that may not occur again in our life time, and may be considered the greatest of honors?"

Eireden bowed to cover his embarrassment at his inadvertent rudeness. "For that we have all the time in the world."

Furen glowed in happiness. "You are in for a treat, my friends. Come!" Leaving all but four of his dwarves in formation, Furen led them through a maze of black caverns, until they came to the beautiful city of the dwarves.

"This is fantastic," Aric exclaimed. The mountain had been carved out and chiseled into great chambers, arched halls, wide corridors, and deep drawing rooms. All of these glowed and glittered and shone with magical fires or gems that sparkled.

"On behalf of all the occupants of the Under-city I thank you. Now, enough gawking there are goblins to slay. Come right through here."

"These are the queen's quarters?" Aric asked in evident surprise. The room they had been led to was an Armory. Short suits of mail in various stages of creation or repair hung all about the low room.

Furen chortled as if Aric had made a joke, while the other dwarves hid their faces to hide their amusement. "No, my friend. I had thought to bring you gifts when I reached Rhyoeven, but I find this would be a better time to present them." He clapped his large hands and the four dwarves came forward and Eireden was a little embarrassed to note they had been carrying boxes all that time. He had been so busy enjoying the city that he hadn't noted their burden.

"Hmmm, mmmh," Furen hummed as he opened the boxes and stepped back. Eireden's eyes went wide and Aric let out a low tone of appreciation and reached out to touch. The boxes held two suits of finely wrought armor.

"These are works of art," the fey exclaimed.

"Aye!" Furen agreed heartily. "And they'll keep goblin swords away from that soft skin of yours. Now let us get you dressed. I can't have you meeting the Queen in nothing but a stained tunic. What sort of manners would that be?"

Though the two had never been measured the armor fit as if it had been hand stitched around them and when they were completely outfitted the two looked radiant for the glint of their shining mail was like white fire.

Eireden bowed low to his host. "This alone was worth the trip. Please accept my sincerest thanks."

"It was nothing, but now you mention your trip as if in passing. Why have you so journeyed with your realm in peril?"

"For answers," Eireden replied and then went on to explain his fear of his opponent using tunnels to attack the city.

"Bah! Rhyoeven sits on a plateau of granite. Remember the dungeons? There was a bare three feet of dirt and then straight rock. Though to be sure a battalion of dwarf sappers could turn it into warren rivaling any rabbit hole given enough time."

This wasn't exactly a comfort to Eireden. If a few hundred dwarves could tunnel in, how hard would it be for ten-thousand goblins to do the same? "How much time are you talking about?"

The dwarf got a faraway look in his eyes and then waved a hand. "Oh, I would think five years, maybe six if we were to do it right. You can't just make a single tunnel and think it'll do. That would be the work of an amateur."

"Darhmael is no amateur," Eireden said, but all the same he was relieved. If it would take the dwarves five years it would take the goblins fifty.

"You are very much correct, yet with dwarves on your side you won't have any worries. We will sniff them out, do not worry." He then rubbed his hands together greedily. "Now we see the queen!"

Only then did it occur to Eireden that he not as yet seen a single dwarf female and truth be told he was highly curious. The females had their own quarters in a separate section of the city and if the male quarters were awe-inspiring the females ones were even more so.

The air was so light and fresh, and the rooms so open and beautifully furnished that Eireden had to remind himself that he was under a mountain and not on top of one. And when he saw the first of the dwarven women, a beguiling lady in waiting with the name of Estrune, he had to hold in his surprise.

The dwarf woman was beautiful and intriguing and very perplexing. She was stone. Her skin was smooth and polished and shone like glass, yet it was green with wavy lines of black running through it. In a sense she was a moving statue and when she spoke, her lips crossed each other with a whisper like water playing on rock.

"The Queen awaits in her audience chamber," Estrune said and Eireden stared.

"Thank you my dear," Furen said. "Come, come, come you two! Why do you stand there like that?"

Aric was the first to gather his wits. "Estrune, indeed. I understand yet I don't."

"What don't you understand?" Eireden asked as they followed the green woman along a corridor; her feet made gentle clacking sounds as she walked and he listened as if entranced. For him there was so much not to understand that to pick one thing was too much for him.

"Estrune is the dwarven word for Malachite. It's a type of green stone."

"Of course," Furen said as if it were nothing.

"But what of the females being named after flowers?" Aric asked. "Oh wait. There it is! Why am I so dull witted?" For all that he had his own wits about him Eireden felt asleep. Aric saw the look and explained, "Many dwarven words have two meanings depending on usage. So the Queen Gargefrel's name can be either interpreted as the silver tined lily or crystal."

"Crystal?" Eireden tried to imagine a being made of pure crystal but could not. And even if he could, his imagination would have been lacking.

"Your Highness," Estrune said in a loud voice, announcing them. "May I present, Aric, a prince of the fey. The Lord Eireden, King of the Den, and the Master of the Mountain, the King Furen Traganfel."

Furen came forward as happy as Eireden had ever seen him and it was good that everyone's attention was on him because Eireden could do little besides stare about. Next to him Aric whispered in amazement, "Look Lapis lazuli. And there's jade. And, my goodness Tiger eye!"

The dwarf woman, Tiger-eye was black and orange and she nodded to Aric for he had been loud. There were so many women and no two were alike, though it was somewhat hard to tell between Red Agate and Red Jasper except when they stood side by side.

Of course the most beautiful of all was indeed the Queen Gargefrel. She was truly crystal and like the mineral was clear through but not completely. The core of her body was flecked in gold and she had gold eyes. These she lowered to the King of the Den, who was slow to come forward to kiss her hand. This was as soft and smooth as anything his skin had ever touched, yet she was also as hard as her name suggested.

"I should be paying you the honors, Milord," she said to Eireden looking up at his tall form. The women of the dwarves were smaller even than the males and not nearly as robust in the girth. "For you are Lord of all these lands."

"It is the highest of honors to meet the Queen of the dwarves," Eireden said, finally coming to his senses enough to show some manners. "Though your beauty shames the silver tined Lily, the prettiest of flowers."

Furen, red in the face, nodded, "It is exactly what I have been saying. When we have defeated that silly old elf I think we should see if Ella can create a flower that can equal my queen."

At the mention of her name, Eireden's heart sought her out; she was far to the east. "She is in the Forbidden Lands and will not return. But that is neither here nor there because I doubt her skill is up to the challenge."

"Enough," Gargefrel said. "If I could blush, I'm sure that I would be now. I need no other flower than the one my dear Furen brought to me." She pointed and the light of the room danced along her skin. There, set in a well-lit alcove, was the flower Furen had risked his life for.

"Though it was always a wonder, it thrives all the greater in your presence, Milady," Eireden said with a small bow.

She nodded back and said, "I feel that your heart beckons its own flower and I wish we had the time to speak on this, but as my husband notes, there is a silly old elf to deal with and I do not wish to keep the warriors waiting."

"Let them learn patience. It's good for them," Furen stated baldly. "You saw how overly anxious they were, Eireden."

He had seen no such thing, but supposed it was a joke when the queen began tittering and it was the sound of pouring pebbles from one hand to another. "Stop jesting, my husband, for time is short," she said and then turned her gold eyes on Eireden. "I am the daughter of the mountain and know much near but less far. And of the Demorlaik even less. Looking into the Haunted City is a sad thing to do, so I do not do it as a rule."

"Why do you talk of the Demorlaik?" Furen asked with sudden seriousness. "Is there something you have seen?"

"I have seen much but shall speak of only this, the maug army," she stated and the room went deathly quiet. "They are beyond count, yet the power of the elf was such that he hid their passage to Tayoeven, even from me. Yet now he does not hide them. Perhaps he wished his actions known? Perhaps he only does so because he wishes to conserve his power? I know not. What is known to me is that the way to Rhyoeven lays open. Save for many stragglers that are scattered, his army marches on Wesgard and may the God above the mountains have mercy on any that yet remain in that doomed city."

"Then I fear we must part in haste," Eireden said going to one knee. Again he kissed her hand. "Farewell," he said and then swept out of the room without a look behind. The idea of another of his cities being burnt had his soul in a rage.

Chapter 21

Ella

Perhaps it was foolish, but Ella dropped the M16 as if it had done something wrong, when she had been the one firing at the nuclear bomb. It clattered harmlessly to the floor of the forest and she backed away from it.

What would have happened if the bomb had gone off? Both she and the gnome would have been vaporized. And the empty forest for miles around decimated but other than that, not much. The real question was what would happen if she *didn't* hit the bomb?

In her mind she pictured Rhyoeven. Without even knowing what was occurring in the Hidden Lands she knew the bomb was destined for the capital. Gritting her teeth she picked up the rifle, sighted down it, aiming for the tiny flick-flick-flick of the propellers atop the gnomes retreating contraption, and then she fired in a long burst.

It was a loud Bam! Bam! Bam! And then, unexpectedly the gun stopped firing. She looked at it stupidly until she realized she was out of bullets—and there wasn't an explosion. "Darn it," she whispered.

Louder she cried, "Whip-wip! Come on, the gnome is getting away!"

Ella waited until she saw the tiny fairy's glow ducking in and out of the tree branches and then she ran directly west until her lungs burned and her legs felt like lead. She went on and on, stopping only at the wide expanse of Lake Roosevelt a great black swath that sat dead in her way.

"Oh jeez," she said. "How could I forget?"

"No go at night," Whip-wip said, nervously from atop Ella's head.

Ella was exhausted but driven. "It'll be ok, Whip-wip. There's nothing in there that'll hurt you. And besides, I have to go." She took a huge breath and waded in. Soon it became apparent that, elf or not, she had done too much that day. The cold water sapped the last of her strength and her clothes dragged her lower and lower until Whip-wip was pulling her by the hair to keep her afloat.

She might have drowned halfway across had it not been for Whip-wip's fear. "Shark!" the fairy cried, pointing. Ella swam to it with arms that barely cleared the water and a stroke that was little better than a doggy paddle. After a few minutes and a great number of cries from Whip-wip, Ella found the "shark" and clung to it as the current slowly pushed her south.

How many miles she progressed in this way she had no idea, but eventually she neared land enough for her to put the final bit of energy into saving herself. She slipped from the log and swam until she felt the welcome softness of the sand beneath.

Her quest to catch the gnome had never seen dimmer. After miles of drifting and hours of freezing she had only made it back to the eastern shore, while the gnome and the bomb were far away on the western side.

Unable to do anything more, Ella crawled into the bush that lay up the bank and passed out.

The sun high overhead woke her and she blinked up at it for some time before her memory of her ordeal came back. And with it came the knowledge of the gnome and the bomb he carried. She sat up and Whip-wip came to her with some tiny green strawberries;

these were so sour that they screwed up her pretty face. Still Ella ate them, greedily.

Then she went down to the edge of the lake and drank, and as she did she eyed the far bank, fearing that another attempt to cross would leave her too weak to travel further. The fairy buzzed the water, skimming a drink.

"Hey, you fixed your wing," she said, happy for her friend. "I wish I could fly. More than anything I wish that, but since I can't I need a car, instead."

"Sis," Whip-wip agreed. "Is there." She pointed back at the forest.

"There's a car?" Ella asked standing. She felt dizzy and nearly dropped back into the sound. "Where?"

Whip-wip squinched her tiny features and tried to look through the foliage. "Is there. By man house."

"There's a house? Oh, I wish I'd seen it last night. You got to show me." Ella began to walk in what was little better than a drunk's stagger, in the direction Whip-wip had pointed. Sure enough, after less than half-mile she came upon a dirt road and there on its edge was a building with a gravel parking lot.

"Holy cow…that's a gas station!" It was a stretch to call the wood slatted building with its single pump and rusted signs a gas station, but she knew of no other descriptors that would do. "They gotta have food." Excited Ella hurried to the building without thinking. "Hello?"

Stepping into the little shop and seeing the usual assortment of junk food had her stomach growling. She almost didn't see the two men standing just away from the counter. Both were attired in old denim and both had woody brown tans and black hair. It was a second before it clicked that they were Native Americans.

"Hi," she said, hoping for a different reaction than the one she got. They stared at her, but not in the usual way. Instead they stared just above her right shoulder and right away Ella thought that Whip-wip had come in with her.

The older of the two, a man of about forty, helped her to understand. "If you're a ninja, I'm sorry we don't have much in the way of cash."

Ella blinked at this. "Ninja? I don't understand." He pointed and she put her hand back and felt the elf sword she had retrieved after the fight in the field. "Oh, this. It's mostly decoration," she said in the lamest lie she had ever told.

"Well it might be good against bears," the younger man said.

"It might," Ella agreed, and then awkwardly began to look around, her stomach hadn't stopped growling since she had walked in. But then a realization came over her, she didn't have any money! Ella stepped to the side of one of the displays and went through her pockets: not one thin dime.

"Well thanks," she said, feeling stupid and heading for the screen door. "Have a good day."

"Are you alright?" the older man asked. She gave him a nod, which he didn't believe. "Here come have a seat. You're white as a sheet." She started to protest but he wouldn't have it. "Sit. Consider that an order. Would you like some water? Or better yet I have tea brewing."

"Tea please, and thanks…I, uh, sort of lost my wallet," she said truthfully.

"And your car?" the younger man asked. "Did you lose that as well?" Ella nodded. She had lost a number of them. "Well, I'm going into town this afternoon. I could give you a lift."

"In the mean time we can get some food into you," the elder said. "Come on around the counter. There's a room here. Sort of a break room. Sorry it's such a mess. Bill over there is a slob."

"Dad!" Bill exclaimed with a significant look.

The father and son were sweet and gave her most of what was going to be their lunch of rice and beans. After she was still so exhausted from the previous days adventures that she could barely stay awake long enough to steal away to get Whip-wip and hide her under her shirt.

Then she fell asleep on a stained couch and didn't wake until close to four. Bill nudged her into wakefulness. "I'm going now if you need that ride."

"Yes please," Ella said, and then paused. "Wait. What town are you going to?"

"Inchelium. It's not much of a town, but it's the closest we have out here on the Res."

Ella had never heard of it. "Is it across the water? I need to cross it, is why I asked."

It was a strange thing to say and she understood that, and thankfully he nodded. Unfortunately he was also very inquisitive. "Why do you need to cross? Does it have to do with the sword?"

Her magic had regained much of its strength and so she opened up a connection with Bill, touching his mind gently. "To see family. It's important to me that I go as far west as you can take me. Will that be ok?"

"Yes," he whispered with a dulled aspect. "Far west. To the ocean?"

"No, not that far. I need to go the eastern edge of the Cascades." She figured that once she got close, she'd be able to either find her way into the Hidden Lands, or track the gnome. As well she figured that by taking a car—there was an old Buick parked behind the store—she would be able to get ahead of the gnome.

"Omak. I'll take you to Omak."

"That would be great." It was in fact a good twenty miles south of where she wanted to be, but it wouldn't matter in the end. If the gnome had rested for six hours that meant it had about a twelve hour head start. That wasn't nearly enough against a car. "How long will it take to get there?"

"The roads are mostly all dirt," he said. "So probably eight hours. We have to swing way south." That was longer than she expected but it would do if her luck held out.

However it didn't.

They were slow getting on the road. Bill's dad had fallen for her natural…or rather her unnatural charm and he tried to load her up with provisions for a trip out to Omak. He kept coming out with armfuls of items: Sweaters in case it was cold. A poncho in case it rained. A fishing pole if she wanted to fish.

Worse than that, the Buick proved dreadfully unreliable. It blew a tire just outside of Inchelium, and then just over an hour later it began venting clouds of white smoke. The radiator had been leaking and now they were out of coolant. They filled it from a pond that wasn't far away, however all they had were three soda cans and the many trips ate up precious minutes.

Every forty minutes or so they stopped to refill the radiator, but thirty miles outside of Omak the car began puffing again, but this time there wasn't water within miles.

It was after midnight by then and so they slept in the car, wrapped in the sweaters and draped in the poncho. Bill wanted to stand guard. He had also fallen for Ella just as his father had, but Ella felt guilty about that and so put him out with a simple spell.

Whip-wip needed to stretch her wings anyways. For most of the ride Ella had snuck raisins beneath her shirt, but when the fairy began to complain, she tried Fig-Newtons, which Whip-wip found enjoyable, and Ella found sticky.

"Go run around and play," Ella said, lifting her shirt and shooing the fairy out into the night.

"Run?"

"Or fly around and play. Just wake me if a bear or something starts sniffing around here."

Whip-wip said something else, but Ella had closed her eyes and sleep sucked her in.

She dreamed of the king and it wasn't what she would call a good dream. In it he wore a shining set of plate mail that Ella had never seen before and assumed that it was what he was wearing to get married in. She assumed this because Alseya entered into the dream and came to stand with him. She wore a flowing gown of white and was more beautiful than ever. The two then went to stand in front of a tremendous crowd who cheered them.

Despite Bill's presence, Ella woke feeling alone. He was a good guy, but he snored loudly, reminding Ella of his humanity.

"Have I become a bigot?" she asked herself, looking down at Bill as he scratched himself in his sleep. She decided the answer was no. It wasn't his humanity that was the real issue, it was the fact that he wasn't Aric or Eireden. Bill was a good guy, but still was just a guy. He lacked that nobility of character, that purpose of life that would have marked him as a true man in her eyes.

"But if I am always comparing men to Eireden and Aric, I'm going to be in for one long and lonely life."

"No! I am Whip-wip. Is friend. No is leave," the fairy said, looking cross at being forgotten. In one hand was a glob of fig from a Fig-Newton and Ella was certain had she been anyone else that glob would have gone in her eye just then.

"Of course, I'll always have you," Ella said and then gave her a little poke in the tummy. "I'm talking about having a man. You know what I mean."

"Sis. Smoochy. Sis." Whip-wip puckered tiny lips and kissed Ella's cheek.

The sun was a bright wheel just over the eastern mountains and the air was crisp and the fairy's kiss left a little wet spot on her cheek that blazed cold. Ella smiled and was, for the moment, happy.

"I shouldn't dwell, for who can guess what the future holds? I could be evaporated today for all we know." Whip-wip screwed up her face at the word evaporated and Ella explained, "It's a bad thing where everything turns to dust. But I don't think it will happen. With this little pistol, I don't think I could hit the bomb let alone accidentally set it off."

"Sis," Whip-wip agreed and showed her lack of understanding or perhaps it was a lack of fear by calmly nibbling at her fig filling. Ella reached into the Buick and quietly picked up the rest of the figs.

"Thank you," Ella whispered. She didn't feel the need to wake him. Bill would have been insistent on coming with her and that would have meant a waste of magic to send him back to his father.

She slipped away, heading north with a hurried pace, while he snored on. As she walked, she nibbled on the figs and wondered what she would do if she actually caught the gnome. What would she do with the bomb? She couldn't leave sitting it in the middle of the scrub-covered hills, and at the same time she couldn't take it with her.

Darhmael would certainly send an elf to get her if she tried and with her beacon there would be no getting away. Unless she got lucky, again.

"That won't happen," Ella said, breathing just a bit heavier as she walked up a steep slope. Already, the Buick was tiny with distance. "I've been lucky; lucky enough for two people. But that can't last. What I need to be is smart."

"Sis," Whip-wip agreed.

Ella gave her a look and then said, "I can't leave the bomb, and I can't take it with me, which leaves what? Detonating it?" She pictured the land decimated and imagined the radiation floating on the wind. "No, that wouldn't be smart at all. Darn it!"

At the top of the slope she looked back and saw Bill moving around the car. With his human eyesight, she knew he couldn't see her. *Now for the gnome*, she thought, and was just kneeling to search the earth for the little creature when the old thought popped back into her head?

Why the gnome? Why did Darhmael send this resourceful, but relatively insignificant, little being to fetch such a powerful weapon? An elf, with all of his magic and super-human abilities would've been much smarter.

"It makes no sense," Ella whispered, leaning there on one knee. "But it has to…maybe the other elves were busy. No. One came after me and I was leaving the Hidden Lands, going in the opposite direction from where the bomb…"

Ella stopped as an idea struck her. Perhaps the elf had been sent in the opposite direction on purpose. Maybe the other two elves had been sent on errands as well. Maybe Darhmael didn't trust his own children.

"I know I don't trust them," Ella whispered. "That's it! Darhmael doesn't trust his children with a bomb big enough that would kill him. I've figured out the mystery, my little Whip-wip! But that still begs the question what do I do with the bomb? I could tear out the wiring but that goofy little gnome would just fix it, or worse, I'd probably blow it up trying."

"No is good. You blow up elf, instead. Is good," Whip-wip stated with finality.

"Ha!" Ella laughed. "I wish, but I'm one of his children, remember? And the one he can least trust. He'd never get close to that bomb with me around."

"Sis."

"Either way we have to find the bomb first, and that means finding the gnome." Ella calmed herself and sent her mind along the root system north and east…and then just north, and when that didn't turn up anything she searched northwest.

She found him and felt his defensive static, but that wasn't what numbed her the most. The gnome was practically in the Hidden Lands!

"Come on, Whip-wip! We're almost too late!" Ella took off in a loping run, but figuring distances and speeds in her mind she realized that she wasn't "almost" too late. She was too late. If the gnome kept going at the same pace, he would make it to the Demorlaik with time to spare and then…

Ella tried to suppress the image of a giant mushroom cloud hanging over the earth, however it wouldn't leave her no matter how hard she ran.

Chapter 22

Eireden

The dwarves pressed on throughout the night, marching in a grim silence and by sunrise they came abreast of Hildeoven. Only then did they mutter curses and scowl. Some shook their mailed fists, while their king swore an oath.

"You will rebuild and I give my word that you can count on the dwarves to help," Furen said. "And this time there won't be a simple wooden palisade as your only defense. No, I'm thinking marble. Young Hortenfel discovered quite a trove of it and I had been wondering how I was to put it to use. Now I have my answer. Tell me Eireden, are you a fan of star or trace works? And I note the lack of redoubts in Den fortification. You should not shy away from…"

The dwarf went on and on about his theories of proper battle-works, but the king was not listening attentively. His own theory was that it was better to defend his walls with men rather than to defend his men with walls. And this was another reason for his uneasiness regarding the mass retreat to Rhyoeven. It didn't suit either his temperament nor his fighting style.

"We are being followed," Aric said with a nod of his head. "Wolves have taken up positions on either side and others went off to the north. We may have a fight before gaining the capital after all."

"…the face of the ramparts should be a…what are you on about?" Furen asked as if it was the fey who was long winded. "Are you sweating a few dogs? Ha-ha! You must be jesting. Look at my soldiers. Not a one fears these dogs and for good reason."

"If there is to be a battle, it will be more than just the wolves," Aric replied.

"Bah! What has become of you, Aric? You've become a mother hen with all your clucking. Ask your friend, the Den if we should fear the road ahead with so many dwarves behind."

The two looked to the king and he surprised Furen by saying. "Aye, we should. Take no offence my friend, your dwarves are a powerful force. It would not be out of the realm of possibility that toe-to-toe they could win out over an equal force of Den, yet we should still look ahead with caution. Our enemy will not fight your fight unless it suits him. He does not squander his goblins like so many captains before him and his reserves are enough to cover this land in their foul bodies."

"Hmmm," the dwarf said in his throat. "You are wise in battle my friend, yet it is clear you do not know the strength of the dwarves when we lock shields and form our phalanx. It would take more than a scrum of maug or even an equal number of Den to defeat us."

For a time, Eireden rode in silence, his mind anxious. "Please, Furen," he said in a whisper so that the marching dwarves would not hear. "You are a great warrior. Hardy and tough as nails, as are your soldiers, I do not doubt. Yet you give too little heed to the enemy. Were I to fight a phalanx of dwarves, I would not slug it out, exchanging blow for blow and neither will Darhmael."

"The dirty goblins know no other way," Furen said dismissively.

"Aye," the king agreed. "Normally, yes. Now they come on in actual formations. They have objectives and well laid plans. What good is a phalanx in wooded terrain? Or at a river crossing. It is in these places that they will attack."

"And you think they will?" Aric asked. "The lady Gargefrel was certain that the main force is far away to the north and that only a scattering remain in these lands."

"I agree with the fey," Furen said. "The Mountain Daughter should not be doubted in this."

Eireden nodded, his eyes searching to the north, seeing in his imagination beyond the curve of the earth. "He is far away. Foolishly so. He goes to burn an empty city while allowing reinforcements to come from the south. We are marching into a trap. I feel it more every day and yet with every passing day my choices are fewer and fewer. And yes we will fight ere we gain the safety of the walls of Rhyoeven."

"Good!" growled the dwarf. "A fight will be just what these lazy soldiers need to shake off the cob-webs. I'll show you, my friend. The dwarven phalanx will not be over come!"

"Hold on, Furen," Aric said, grasping the mailed shoulder of the dwarf. "If what the king says is true, the goblins will not be so easy to overcome."

"We will win the battle, I do not doubt that," Eireden said, his eyes still unfocussed. "If this is a trap as I suspect. Then the battle will be sharp and hard fought. It will be just difficult enough for us fear a larger engagement outside the walls, but not so hard so that we can't gain the walls where we'll be locked up tight."

"Are you certain?" Furen asked, his black eyes filled with troubled thoughts.

Eireden blinked and shook his head as if to clear it. "No. I can't be certain. Nor can I come up with a better plan if I were. We are safest in Rhyoeven."

"We will have to wait upon the future," Furen said. "If a battle occurs and unfolds as Eireden has foreseen then we will have some hard decisions to make."

They lapsed into silence for many miles and all around them the numbers of wolves grew. Aric slipped from his horse and sighed, "The king knows his enemy. The maug which had been scattered for many miles around, have suddenly come together and there are trolls among them."

"Trolls?" the king asked in surprise, looking up to the sky. "Under this sun?"

Furen squinted ahead. "I see nothing. What is their distance?"

"A mile and a quarter. Can you see that forest? They are hidden among the trees where the shade will protect them."

Eireden gazed at the land all about, while Furen stared at the trees. The dwarf turned and barked instructions over his shoulder. In an amazingly short time, the dwarves had swung from a marching formation to a single fighting formation in one great block: the famous dwarven phalanx.

They stood like that in the sun for a span until Furen blew out noisily. "They are right there! Were it not for your prattle about how 'dangerous' the goblins have become I'd march right up and slay them all but now I sit and second guess myself, thank you very much."

"You are king to these dwarves. They will listen if you so command," Eireden said. Furen grumbled at this and blew out some more.

"Then why don't you attack, if that is what you wish?" Aric asked. He seemed at ease, as if the battle would not include him in any way.

"Because I don't want to hear *Mr. High up on his horse* go, tsk tsk when I do! You will, won't you?"

"Do I make that sound?" Eireden asked with a laugh.

"Yes! And it can annoying as a burr in your boot, when it's directed at you," Furen said.

The king laughed again and then explained, "We don't attack for three reasons. One: the sun is high and hot, out here on the plain and the goblins grow weak under its rays. Two: Look at the dwarven phalanx. See how tight they are, shoulder to shoulder, each man's shield protecting the man to his left. In this formation they are like a rock, however if we were to enter those woods, the trees would break it apart and expose them to attack from all sides. And three: we haven't seen their champion."

"Will you fight if it's an elf?" Aric asked.

Eireden didn't hesitate, "No."

"Really?" Furen asked in amazement. "You have slain two of these creatures already, why do you fear a third?"

Immediately his mind pictured Ella and his words echoed hers: "I've been lucky. Those two battles were forced upon me by circumstance. I accepted because I had no other choice. On this field I do."

"What if their champion is a mountain troll in chain mail?" Aric asked. "And what if he's carrying a ten foot tall club?"

"You mean like that troll there?" Eireden asked pointing to a twelve-foot tall mass of muscle and bone with a hide like worked leather and tusks that shot from his lower jaw. The creature stood just inside the forest, waiting.

"Just like that one," Aric answered.

"I wouldn't hesitate," Eireden said. "In fact I'd be happy to, because you see, that troll represents the first mistake Darhmael has made. I'm almost positive that the elf had no idea that I'd be here with the dwarves and he certainly didn't know that I'd be wearing this fabulous dwarven mail and I'd be willing to wager half my kingdom that he didn't know Aric Anorian would be by my side."

"I'm ever at your service," Aric said with a small bow.

"Well if the King Furen will allow me to act as his champion, I'll likely be in need of healing ere too long."

Furen nodded and gave a wave as if shooing the king to his duty. "Aye, go have your fun. Trolls in armor were never my cup of tea."

"My thanks," Eireden said to Furen and to the fairies he cried, "Light me up!" They did and in his new armor he blazed brighter than the noon sun. Like a sweep of wind lightning, he rode his war-horse at a gallop straight at the troll, but turned aside at the last moment.

"Look upon your death," he bellowed riding across the face of the forest, letting the goblins, who were cowering further back in the shade of its leaves, see who it was they had come to fight. For the first time in many months he felt great. He was going into battle, not as a general with the fate of thousands of men dependent on his wisdom, but as a warrior with a revenge fueled blood lust.

At the edge of the forest he turned and raced back, again straight toward the troll and his lust burned hot when the troll took a step back. "I name you coward!" the king challenged. "Turn this instant and crawl back to whatever hole you slunk out of. No? Then prepare to die. Fairies, go to Aric."

Eireden said all of this so fast that the troll was still watching the fairies buzz away when the king kicked his charger at the great beast. His move was altogether fearless since it was well known that trolls were the ultimate killing machines, and with all such creatures their defensive abilities were lacking.

The king's charge took the troll by surprise and it had too little time to strike, it could only raise the club in an awkward parry. Again, the parry wasn't something it practiced regularly, if at all and Eireden had his choice of targets: both hands, the right arm, the side of the head, and the back of the neck.

All of these were armored, which, along with the creature's terribly thick skin did not make them ideal targets. So instead of swinging the great black sword right away, he dropped nimbly from the saddle, went into a roll and came up just behind the beast. Now he swung, quick and hard, aiming for the back of the knee where the skin was thinnest and there wasn't any armor.

In that slash he sheared halfway through the knee, cutting the tendons, and making the leg nearly useless. Trolls do not feel much in the way of pain and this one only grunted as it swung about, leveling his club four feet off the ground. The king moved like a serpent and ducked, bringing his shield to bear, but still the club whipped across the top of it, sending him sprawling.

Luckily the troll went down as well. His useless leg gave way with the twisting motion and he was in the dirt still trying to figure a way up when the king was upon him again. The great sword of Aug-Raumon was like a surgeon's scalpel in the hands of a master. His first strike laid open the flesh across the troll's forehead. Hitting the head itself was like trying to chop down a tree with a sword and so Eireden didn't try, and the eyes were tiny and set too far back, so he opened up a huge flesh wound that poured blood into the eye pits.

Now the troll was nearly blind and he lashed out with the club in one hand while he wiped at his eye with the other. Eireden danced away from the obvious swing and took a vicious chopping blow at the hand in front of the face, taking off three fingers.

The troll bellowed his anger and swatted the king in a clumsy move. Eireden wasn't at all hurt, but he did fall backwards and had to kick himself back away from the descending club, which only missed because the troll could barely move on only a single good leg.

Getting up, the king moved quickly to his left and the troll with its bad right leg couldn't get around in time. It flailed with its club and missed and now Eireden was directly behind it and had it not been armored he would have been able to kill the monster with one swing. Instead it took two.

The first was aimed squarely at the iron collar around the troll's neck, which made a sharp *ting!* And then fell to the ground. The second strike came after another spinning attack from the troll. Eireden sunk much lower this time and the club whistled just over his head—torqueing the troll around so that Eireden was just beneath its chin wear the skin was soft and the arteries were close to the surface. Eireden's sword cut a black line across that throat and for a moment the troll seemed surprised as if it expected more pain, and then blood flowed down into its lungs. It grabbed its throat in vain and then after a few seconds of standing there waiting to die, it toppled over.

Breathing lightly, for the king was unwinded, he gave a simple whistle for his horse to return and after climbing into the saddle he rode back to the dwarven lines to the throaty, deep cheers of two thousand soldiers.

Eireden gave a wave in reply, his mind already on the next task at hand. "Now for the hard part," he said to Aric and Furen. "How many goblins would you say are out there, Aric?"

"Fifteen thousand," came the quick reply. "Not what I would consider a few stragglers."

"My guess as well," Eireden said, removing his helmet and wiping away a trickle of sweat. "The only thing there is to do is to retreat."

Furen's beady eyes went wide. "What? Retreat? But you said that we would win. Why on earth would you want to retreat?"

"I said we would only win after a hard fight, one in which we are made to fear the idea of coming down from our walls. That's how Darhmael thinks this battle will go. Retreating is a much better plan."

Chapter 23

Ella

The half-elf ran across the landscape eating up the miles, but at a great cost. Her physical energies drained from her with every mile and by midmorning she just couldn't go on. Not only physically but mentally as well. It simply wasn't logical. Every time she stopped to catch her breath she felt for the gnome and with every stop it became clearer that she wouldn't be in time to catch him before he made it to the Demorlaik. She was wearing herself out for nothing.

In a strange mixture of hopelessness, grief, and exhaustion she fell to her knees and then laid her head in a flow of soft grasses. Her heart was like a drum, but another sound, a gently thudding came to her ear and she didn't need magic to tell her it was a horse moving in a light canter.

Alarm jangled her nerves and she leapt up, fearing that one of the black elves had found her, but it was only a spotted grey and amazingly she knew the horse. It belonged to one of the scout's from Hildeoven, a young woman by the name of Verissa. But what was it doing all the way out here, she wondered, and where was its rider?

"Cappy?" she called gently. The unbridled horse had prudently stopped when Ella had emerged from the tall grass and now it swiveled an ear at her in clear recognition. "Hi Cappy, come here. That a boy. I have a Fig-Newton for you."

"Hey!" Whip-wip cried at the idea of sharing, and with such a big animal, too. She made to grab the fig but Ella shooed her away.

"I'll get you more," Ella told her. "Don't you worry you greedy little fairy, and besides there's enough to share. Come on, Cappy."

Cautiously the horse came over and took the fig from the flat of Ella's hand. He then allowed himself to be petted and rubbed, only Ella had more than that in mind. She took a fistful of mane and swung herself lightly onto the back of the animal.

"You're a God-send, Cappy. Now let's go! Let's see what you can do."

She kicked the grey into a gallop and rode hard. At steep slopes she dismounted and ran alongside him, and at a very large river, she swam next to him, encouraging him to go faster. At the far bank she allowed the horse to rest and as she did she discovered that she was gaining quickly on the gnome. Faster than she thought possible, and it wasn't until she overtook the poor little creature pushing feebly at the pedals of his omni-cart that she saw why.

His back was a wet mural of blood and there was a neat hole in his little coat just to the side of his spine. It was clear one of Ella's shots had been lucky—at least for her. The gnome appeared to be in a delirium, cursing and muttering while sweat dripped down his rectangle of a face.

Fearing another trap, Ella came at an angle, though it was for naught. The gnome didn't seem to notice her. She slipped off the horse and said, "Stop pedaling, gnome. I've caught you and I won't put up with any more of your tricks."

Using her mind she rifled his pockets and searched up his sleeves, finding all sorts of odd devices, some with wires and some with rubber bands, some with springs, and one, a pokey ball of thumb-tacks. She placed them all well away from the gnome. Only then did she move in to heal him.

"I cannot thank you for that which deserves thanks," the gnome said after the blue light had swept him. He didn't move; he only laid in the grass, at the moment too exhausted to do anything but stare up at the blue sky. "None of this is as it should be. You have turned life into death."

"You are wrong, gnome," Ella said. "You still live, I still live. We can save your family if we try, however you can't have the bomb. Do you understand what it does?"

"It saves my family!"

"Maybe, but at what cost? The lives of tens of thousands of Den? Perhaps more? That's too high a price for their lives or even mine." The gnome shook his head and Ella blew out in exasperation. "Listen, there are other ways. How about I take you to the King of the Den. He is very powerful and he might help you if I ask him."

"He was powerful," the gnome corrected, raising a scholarly finger. "By now he is surrounded and un-free. His choices have all been unchosen for him and he, and they can only await the doom of the master."

Ella glanced at Whip-wip who only shrugged. "Whatever you think is going to happen, this bomb will not be a part of it. I will see to that. Now how do you uh, defuse it?"

The gnome sighed and shook his head. "You wonder if I understand when you should wonder if you understand. There isn't a fuse attached to this device. It does not operate by expanding gases. It operates on the theory of critical mass, which I will not bother ex-plaining as I am sure to be wasting breath that is better spent on breathing."

"I know how it works…sort of," Ella said. "What I meant was how do you keep it from exploding?

There has to be a fail-safe switch or an on off button. Have you…"

From away west, a howl went up, one that chilled Ella to her soul. She swung her head about searching, but saw nothing beyond the tall grass, so she climbed aboard the strange cart. Standing on top of the nuclear bomb she saw a pack of wolves running and bounding toward them.

"How do you get this to fly?" she demanded, as she looked at all the strange levers and buttons on the cart.

The gnome shook his head sadly. "Its wounds are all unwound; its potential energy has been appropriated already. Flee on your horse, Lady and hope the master has only sent the wolves to guard me and not to hunt you."

The wolves were charging now at a full sprint and Whip-wip was screaming and pointing. The horse was dancing, but Ella was calmly looking at the bomb, her mind, seeing beyond the metal, was trying to make sense of the interior of it. Unfortunately it was a mass of wires and strange curled metal rods and things beyond description.

"Ella!" Whip-wip screamed, pulling with one hand and pointing at the inrushing wolves with the other.

She was out of time to neuter the bomb. The best she could do was magically "grab" a handful of wires that ran along its interior and pull with her mind until they all hung loose. Then she vaulted onto the horse and kicked it into a full gallop as sleek grey bodies swarmed past the gnome. By the act of ignoring such an easy meal she knew these were definitely Darhmael's wolves.

In the short run, wolves were the faster than the horse and they came on, nipping at Cappy's tail. Ella pulled her pistol and shot the nearest in a deafening blast. The wolf yelped and then crashed to the ground bowling over a few more that had been too close.

With an inner calm, she then paused as the horse raced for its life beneath her, waiting again until the wolves had formed on her tail before shooting the new leader. The same results occurred and a few more fell, biting and growling at each other.

The wolves were not stupid and so they dropped back, while some ran on either side of the horse and rider. This went on for a minute and then suddenly and with no warning, the ones on the wings wheeled in simultaneously, while the ones in the back sped up. Ella brought the pistol to bear and shot three of them and then the gun was empty, clicking on spent brass.

The wolves saw and somehow understood. Their leering faces seemed to be made of malignant smiles of anticipation, while saliva dripped from fangs too large to have been created by nature.

"They're going to get me," Ella said to herself and was racked by a sudden shiver. She grimaced at the thought of those teeth, but then she set her jaw in determination.

"Whip-wip!" Ella screamed over the racing wind. "Find Eireden. Tell him what's happening." At first the fairy, who was tucked up close to Ella's collar, balked and refused to leave. Ella was forced to pull her off by hand. "Go on, my little friend. You'll be a hero. Go! Go tell Eireden."

The fairy buzzed off crying and Ella could only afford to give her a single wave before she had to go back to concentrating on her escape.

The scout horse was nimble and had endurance to spare, especially with such a light rider on his back. Ella just had to keep the wolves off of him for another mile and she knew they would drop back. With that in mind she headed for the river she had crossed earlier.

It was true that dogs were faster swimmers than horses, but with the horses longer legs it could walk through deeper water and make better time. Ella went into the river until her toes touched and then she pulled the elf sword and turned, only to gasp.

The near bank of the river was covered in grey bodies. Over fifty wolves swarmed in the shallows while more moved to cut them off. Cappy started blowing in fear and wouldn't budge further.

"It'll be ok," she said grimly to the horse and then with her mind she snatched up a river rock the size of a softball. This she sent flying at a wolf swimming after them. On land the wolf might have dodged, but in the water it was a veritable sitting duck and Ella caved its head in.

Almost as one the wolves stopped their ceaseless snarling and they stared at the body of their brother floating away. They then began a fearful howling that had Cappy shivering. Ella cut the noise off. Magically picking up the rocks that lay along the bank she sent them whizzing at any wolf that dared to set foot in the water. And when they retreated up the bank she sent them in a storm until they were yelping and retreating to the woods for safety.

"Go on and run you stinking cowards!" she screamed, brandishing her sword. But they didn't run. They slunk among the trees, using them as cover. Some went up the river and others went down—these crossed to the far bank and sat down on their haunches, breathing heavily and watching Ella and Cappy with red eyes and licking their fangs with hungry tongues.

Ella was trapped.

Chapter 24

Eireden

As the maug began to come out of the forest and formed their lines, the king hopped down from his horse and grabbed a stick that sat close. He waved it at his two friends and asked, "What are the inherent weaknesses in dwarven warfare?"

"What weaknesses?" Furen asked, standing back and looking confused.

Aric raised his hand to answer, "They are too stilted. Historically, almost without exception they fight from a phalanx and do not deviate."

"Why should we?" Furen demanded. "It's a system that's worked for countless generations with very few setbacks."

"Another weakness?" Eireden asked, ignoring his friend.

"They use no stratagem," Aric added. "Everything is basically cut and dry."

Furen began spluttering, but words would not come in his indignation. Eireden held up a hand to quiet him. "And?"

Aric steepled his fingers and thought for a few seconds before saying, "They cling to battle, well past any opportunity of victory. If they have to retreat it is done too slowly and grudgingly. It is a waste of life."

"Stop!" Furen cried holding up both hands. "What is the meaning of this? If you want answers about dwarven battle techniques ask a dwarf not a fey. Why should we use stratagems when we can use steel? And why is it a fault that we do not relish retreating with the same enthusiasm as *other* races? Though the real question is why are you insulting your friends when they come to your aid?"

"I'm not," Eireden said. "All of what Aric has listed is exactly what Darhmael thinks. Remember what I said earlier? He won't allow you to fight your fight. If you form your phalanx he will surround you and come from all sides. Or he'll use trolls to hurl great blocks from a distance, he'll use wolves to come in like lightning. He'll use fire and burn you where you stand."

"And you think a craven retreat is the answer?" Furen demanded smacking a fist into his open palm.

"I think showing him what he wants to see is the answer…with a few minor changes of course," Eireden said. He now drew in the dirt with the stick. "I want *three* phalanxes. The center will hold six hundred men and the wings seven hundred a piece. We have a lot of goblins to contain so our formations have to be long and slim, only four ranks deep."

Furen looked down and then shrugged. "This is your plan? Three skinny phalanxes instead of one good one? With all your talk, I suppose I was expecting more…but why do you have the center thrown out in front of the wings? You know they'll get the brunt of the fighting."

"That's exactly what I'm hoping for," Eireden said.

"And what about the retreat part of your plan?" Furen asked, turning his head this way and that as if the three formations, looking like nothing more than three rectangular blocks in a triangle, was some sort of puzzle that he couldn't figure out.

"The middle formation will retreat slowly and surely to that hill there," the king said, pointing at a little rise a few hundred yards away.

"What of the wings during all this?" Aric asked. "I'm sure you won't be expecting them to just watch. If the center starts to retreat you know the goblins are going to try and crush it entirely and a breakthrough in the center will cut the army in two. From what I understand that's not a good thing."

"Then by all means the center better hold," Eireden said. "That is where I will command. Furen will command the right wing and Hasdrubal, your most trusted lieutenant the left."

Aric raised an eyebrow. "Thank you for not including me in this bloodshed."

Eireden laughed. "I need a response team and I need you to lead it. Magic will need to be countered with magic. Force with force. Any holes in the line will need to be filled. If you see an elf, kill it. Any questions?"

"No," Aric said. "Your plan to kill us all is perfectly clear."

"Ho-ho!" Furen laughed. "I'm in good company if the Good Fey is as confused as I am. What that means is that Darhmael or whoever it is over there is going to be doubly as confused. Or maybe triply so!"

The King of the Den sent Furen to give out his simple instructions barely in time. The maug in a great sweep came rushing forward and the dwarves had to hurry into position. This confusion in the face of fifteen thousand maug should've been a point of consternation, but the king smiled as the goblins boldly struck the six-hundred dwarves of the first phalanx.

As sturdy as the dwarves were they held together by the barest of margins, swinging their hammers and axes with arms grown strong in the mines, yet so precarious was their position that when Eireden called for them to retreat slowly, fighting all the while, they seemed glad to do so. However, when their retreat did not stop as they came in line with the two wings they began to grumble.

"Cease your belly-aching and fight," Eireden bellowed over the din of battle. His steel grey eyes were alight, watching every inch of the bloody front. Back the dwarves went, selling land for lives. For every dwarf that fell, five goblins went down screaming, but still the thousands behind pressed on. They roared like the sea and swarmed like insects seeing their opportunity to rupture the dwarf lines.

If that happened the bloodshed would be marvelous. The dwarf wings would be surrounded and left to fight alone, and they would fall one after the other until none were left alive.

The dwarves were not fools. They saw this as plain as day, and some looked back in anger at the King of the Den as he sat atop his mount. The fairies coming and going with messages from the as yet barely scathed wings did not help the image. He smiled pleasantly to each and thanked them in their language.

How he could be so relaxed when the dwarves in the center fought for their very lives, they did not know. Did the King not hear the ringing of metal and the blood-curdling screeches of the dying maug? Did he not see how desperate the situation had become?

"I admit I am bewildered by this tactic," Aric said as he calmly patted his nervous mount. Though there were a few trolls and some ogres still in the forest none had come out to fight under the sun's bright torch. It didn't seem like they were needed. "You don't want us to fight Darhmael's fight," Aric said. "When are we going to fight our fight?"

"You will see," Eireden said. "I just sent out the fairies with orders. In a minute Furen and Hasdrubal will act on them. Wait here…"

The king rode behind the line of dwarves and shouted, "Now hold! Do not take a single step back! Here is where we have victory." This seemed an amazing thing to say to the hard fought dwarves who were battling against twenty-to-one odds. Some laughed as they hewed about—others went into a frenzy of battle rage, while others looked darkly on the king thinking him a greater foe than the goblins.

And then Furen on the right and his chief lieutenant on the left wheeled inwards. These dwarves were fresh and eager to attack and struck down the goblins who didn't know if they were suppose to keep in formation, facing forward, or turn in response to the attack. Most shied away from the furious assault and pressed inward as if for protection.

"What is this?" Aric asked, watching amazed.

"An ambush," Eireden said as the dwarves swept into the maug on either side throwing them into confusion. "Ambushes occur as a result of hiding a portion of your force and then attacking in the flank or rear. We hid ours in plain sight. The maug were so intent on destroying the force in front and so confident that they could pierce our lines that they gave us their flank."

The goblins in the front ranks, seeing the confusion and panic behind them stopped attacking and now the entire force ceased being an army in a military sense. Their formations disintegrated and they became little more than a mob.

"My," Aric said. His face sank a little. "Their very numbers work against them. They are so packed in they can't even use their weapons properly." It did indeed become a slaughter of frightful proportions. The maug units lost any cohesion, with each side backing away from the stern dwarves hemming them in and although they still held a huge advantage in numbers, the thousands in the center were useless. They were pushed back and forth and if any fell they were quickly trampled.

In minutes the maug were clawing over each other to escape the trap they had set for themselves, but the dwarves extended their lines to encircle their foes completely. Aric turned away at this point. The massacre being a butchery that he did not have stomach for. The dwarves began to sing as they killed.

Eireden clapped him on the shoulder and said, "Leave the killing to us. You just take care of the injured; do the least amount to keep each alive. I'm afraid you are our only healer."

The "battle" ended an hour and half later, and before it was even officially over the king had groups of dwarves preparing pyres for the dead and stretchers for the most badly injured. He took the list of the dead from Furen and stood off to the side running over the fight in his mind trying, to see what he could have done differently to have saved more.

"You are always too hard on yourself," Furen said coming up with a great smile. "We lost only ninety-six heroes! Had I been commanding, it would have been ten times that number. Let me be the first to thank you." Unlike Eireden's, the dwarf's armor was rent in a number of places and was black with goblin blood. He could never keep out of battle.

"Ninety-six is a testament to the hardiness of the dwarves," the king replied. "And we will need more of that hardiness still to come. I know you and your men just fought a battle, yet I have a great desire to get back to my city. I need to know how my own people fare."

Furen made a little noise of dismissal and said, "That wasn't much of a battle, it was more akin to calisthenics. My dwarves aren't the least tired, and any who slack will hear it from me!"

In this Furen did not lie. Despite the battle having just ended, the dwarves had their funeral pyres lit and their injured assembled within the hour.

"These folks are amazing," Aric said. His eyes were a dim emerald. Despite that he was the only one on the plain who hadn't unsheathed his sword he was the most tired. "They bear their pains more stoically than even the Den. And their wounds! There was one young dwarf walking about holding his innards in with a goblin shield. I've never seen its like."

"After seeing the dwarf women it is no wonder that the product of their loins would be so sturdy," Eireden said. "Rock begets rock I suppose."

Hasdrubal had come up just in time to hear the comment, yet took no offence. He seemed to take pride in the comment. "My King," he said. "The men are ready to move out."

Eireden was surprised that Hasdrubal was not speaking to Furen. He glanced to the Lord of the Dwarves, who bowed his head.

"I am but the King of the Dwarves," Furen said. "You are the Sun King and my Liege Lord. All who saw this victory cannot pretend otherwise."

An uncomfortable silence befell Eireden, which he broke by joking, "Maybe I should choose Gargefrel as my bride instead of Alseya."

Aric laughed, but Furen's face grew red and he cried, "Come down off that blasted horse! How can I teach you manners if I can't reach you?"

"I was just joking, Furen. Be not so mad. And besides what happened to me being your Liege Lord?"

Furen reached down and picked up a rock and nailed the king in the side with it, making a hollow clang. The stone bounced harmlessly away. "It was an honorary title and I can change it anytime I wish. Maybe I'll make it Ambassador to kissing my…" Behind them, Hasdrubal cleared his throat. Furen sobered up. "Duty calls. Hasdrubal, move out!"

The dwarves began marching and as they did they sang many songs. Most concerned the recent victory, and many others were about friends who had fallen, and the rest were of their women folk. No matter the subject the songs were doleful and the King found himself picturing Ella's face to combat the cheerlessness around him.

She drew ever closer. He could feel her out there, slowly making her way back to him, or at least back in his general direction and he found himself wondering why. Was it just coincidence that she was coming back in such times? Was she simply regretting her decision about leaving? Was she coming to give Aric a second chance?

The king sighed.

"Ella's heading in this direction," he said out of the blue. "Back to the Hidden Lands. I don't know if you want to know or not. But she is and there it is."

Aric gave him a strained smile and said, "She's picked a bad time."

"Yes."

"Do you know what she wants?"

Eireden shrugged. "I don't. Maybe Whip-wip is home sick…Oh! I do hope Whip-wip's family is ok. It will crush her if they are not."

"What about you?" Aric asked.

"To be honest I'm glad Ella's coming back," Eireden replied, his eyes and his heart pointing east. "She belongs in the Hidden Lands. She's no longer an American."

"I meant, how would you feel if something happened to Whip-wip's family?" Aric explained.

The king felt his cheeks grow hot and he took that moment to adjust his helmet. "I don't, uh, know. I'm sure I'd feel the same as I do now, angry, furious, and very sad." The king nodded to himself; these were his chief emotions…except when he pictured Ella. "So… what are you going to do about Ella? She can be forgiving, you know."

"Like how she forgave you when you refused to run away with her, back when you were a *Gada*?" Aric asked, and then laughed when the king glared. "Ella doesn't forgive easily. She has the fiery temperament of a human coupled with the beauty and elegance of an elf."

"Yes," Eireden breathed. "She's a handful."

"Indeed. Whoever ends up with her will have much on their hands. And that is not including the fact that he will also have to adopt a fairy!"

"There is that…wait. Your words suggest that it won't be you, which I find amazing because I am certain you love her. Are you still hung up on her linage? You said yourself that you weren't thinking straight."

"When it comes to Ella, no one thinks straight," Aric rejoined with a smile. "Yes, I love her, but it is an untrustworthy love. Our relationship began in deceit and ended in conceit."

"Well, you've seem to have gotten over your conceit," Eireden pointed out. "And you were not deceitful in any way, so she should not hold that against you."

"It was her deceit that is the issue."

"What deceit?" Eireden challenged, reining his horse in and glaring. "Ella has ever been honest! How can you say otherwise? You will answer for your accusations! Do not think that our friendship will allow you to…"

Aric put up his hand and Eireden held his tongue though he was red in the face. "I will answer, my friend," Aric said calmly. "Ella told me that she loved me in the Theater of Concordance, when in fact she loved another." The fey indicated the king and Eireden's anger dissipated as if it never were.

"But…but, she loves you now," Eireden tried to reason. "And that should not be discounted. And in truth, you know not the nature of her heart, if you think she didn't love you then. I'm sure she did. It was just, perhaps, not with the same intensity."

"Love is not easily defined, I would agree," Aric said. "It can be fluid, and pulled like the tide this way and that by outside forces or even internal ones such as duty and honor. It is the greatest of mysteries…so why the inquiry over my interest in Ella?"

The question was unexpected and Eireden had to think to come up with the truth. "I want her to be happy." He could picture her smiling and it warmed him. The answer was true but not complete. "And I want her to be taken…loved I mean. Unavailable as it were. She is temptation itself and I am to be married."

Aric's lips went thin at the word married, but Eireden barely noticed. He had just realized he hadn't thought of his bride-to-be more than a handful of times since they parted. Guilt rang like bent metal through his heart.

"I think Ella will be happy with you," Eireden said to the fey and then added quickly, "I *know* she'll be happy with you. And I will be happier as well."

"Am I to be guardian of your happiness?" Aric asked. Eireden gave him a sharp look, to which the fey only raised the soft gold of his eyebrows and asked, "Or is it your honor that needs protecting?"

"You, who knows me so well, need not ask that question," Eireden said stiffly. "I will not dishonor myself whatever Ella decides."

"Then you have a difficult choice ahead of you," Aric replied, and then without a nod to courtesy, he spurred his horse and galloped away along the South Stream Road toward Rhyoeven.

"How dare he, of all people, doubt my honor!" Eireden seethed. In a dark silence that none dared to break he rode to the capital with his singing dwarves and his chattering fairies.

Along with his anger, he felt a need for haste in his soul and he pushed them along at a speed that would have had his Den soldiers flagging, however the dwarves only gritted their teeth and marched on so that they came upon the fair city in the last light of day. Before the gates a great gathering stood cheering and within the city proper, pavilions were set all about.

"Well, some good has become of Aric abandoning us to our walking fate," Furen said. "Is that roast beast I do smell? Ha-ha, it is!"

"Lead your men into the city," Eireden said.

Furen shook his wide head and his beard wagged. "You will lead. After your victory today it is your honor."

The king smiled tightly at the word honor, but said only, "The Den are cheered by our victory, but they are joyful because the King of the Dwarves has answered the call of friendship. Now, lead your army or go home. I will not have it any other way."

Furen bowed and then took his place at the head of his dwarves. The city was jammed shoulder to shoulder with people in numbers Eireden had never seen, and to a man they yelled themselves hoarse.

The king came last, thinking that few would notice, but in this he was wrong. Alseya stood at the gate in a gown of flowing white, so that she appeared an angel and the crowd watched the coming of the king in his silver armor and they drew a collective breath when he went to the fey.

"Your Highness," she said, dipping her head.

Eireden knew his duty and he had his honor intact. Both demanded that he forsake whatever happiness he would have with Ella and cling to this fey woman.

He lifted her chin and kissed her with the entire city watching.

Chapter 25

Ella

The wolves waited and rested, while Ella tried her utmost to make herself disappear. Becoming invisible was the only thing she could think of to get herself out of her predicament. She couldn't fight the beasts, there were far too many. She couldn't fly away. Her furthest flight to date was eighty feet and even then she had been exhausted when she landed.

She tried charming one of the wolves, however its mind was alien and evil with a predatory hunger that wasn't normal.

And that left invisibility.

Which wasn't working at all as she had hoped. This was mainly due to the fact that she didn't know the spell. "There are no spells!" she griped at herself. There was only talent or skill—and she had neither! She tried again, imagining the light bending around her, but all that happened was that her skin seemed to blur and the colors of her coat became muted.

This was something at least, and if Ella had a few more days or weeks of practice there was a chance she could get it right, only she didn't have a few more days, she barely had a few more minutes. New howls went up in the forest and blatting horn answered from the north.

It was a goblin horn.

"Oh jeez," she whispered. The horse blew and snorted and had it been anywhere but shoulder deep in the middle of a great flowing river it likely would have bolted. Instead it danced constantly trying to see all around.

Ella tried to fight this at first, but it was a losing battle and worse, it stole concentration away from what was really important: failing at becoming invisible. She tried again and watched as her pale hand glowed like a rainbow.

"Damn!" she swore and then she whined, "Oh jeez…oh jeez." A company of goblins had just come slinking out of the forest. It was clear they disliked the sun beating down and each thrust a scabby grey arm to shadow their faces from its rays. Still that didn't stop them from coming on, croaking in their foul language and grinning with their yellowed tusks bared at the beautiful girl.

Like the wolves, some made to cross the stream and one slipped and splashed for a moment before catching himself. Another of his fellows picked up a handful of sand and threw it at the wet goblin and laughed nastily as creature nearly slipped again.

Ella's mouth came open as an idea snuck past her panic and ran along her neurons where it formed into a serviceable plan. If she couldn't actually turn invisible she could certainly fake it. "I'm sorry, Cappy. If I could take you with me I would." The horse rolled its brown eyes and she knew it was close to bolting by how much white showed.

She only had seconds.

There were a few things that Ella could do really well with her magic. Things that she had practiced, though always through enjoyment and not as a matter of life and death. How many times had she stirred up a wind to blow Whip-wip around? Plenty.

Ella crouched on the horse's back as a sudden, magical wind rushed along the riverbanks and began churning up the sand, lifting it and spinning it all around like a huge tornado. The wolves whined and backed under the eaves of the forests, while the goblins covered their faces.

And then just as quick as it had come the wind vanished…and so had the girl. The goblins went berserk in their confusion. They charged and Cappy broke and ran with a few wolves snapping at his heels. The goblins ignored the horse and in their rage they beat the water with their swords and stabbed it with their spears, but Ella wasn't even close. Far down stream she broke the surface for a bear second to catch a breath and then she was under again.

Swimming at unheard of speeds was one of the first skills she had learned all those months ago with Aric. She had played in the Pacific, and then it had been a game, now Ella skimmed along the bottom of the stream, holding her breath for close on four minutes, not daring to come a second time until she had to.

Still she could not stay under the water forever, not with the stakes as high as they were. She had to either intercept the gnome or warn Eireden about the bomb. Getting the bomb felt to be a higher priority and so she left the water after a few miles and then immediately began to run. At first she ran straight west to put as much distance between her and the wolves, but after an hour she began to head in a northern direction.

She was close to the border of the Hidden Lands now. Illusions started to pop up and these she saw clearly for what they were: a way to discourage Americans from going any further. Though she was glad to see the familiar illusions, what she liked even better was the abundant vegetation that she had taken for granted and hadn't known was missing from her life until she had walked about the empty forests of Washington. It had been all Whip-wip could do to scrounge for a few nuts.

This was more to her liking and as she ran she snatched plums from trees and grapes from vines, feeding her body's growing needs. She had to have strength left for what she feared would be a desperate fight when she finally reached the gnome and the deadly content of his cart.

Darhmael would send more than just wolves now that his prize had been discovered and he was so close to getting his hands on it. She hoped it would only be goblins standing in her way, but worried there would be ogres and was completely terrified that trolls could be involved. She didn't think she could handle a troll.

"At least there won't be elves to deal with," Ella gasped through lungs that were on fire.

"Are you so sure of that?" a voice said from her left.

On instinct Ella dove in mid-stride, rolling on the soft earth and coming up with sword drawn. There among the pretty trees was the heinous figure of an elf. He was a ghastly shadow beneath the pretty leaves of green and gold.

"Little sister," he said as he reached out for her with its mind and tried to throw her. She went twenty feet in the air and would have gone further but she grabbed a passing branch and clung to it. The elf snapped the blackened stubs that he called fingers and instantly the wood turned supple and wrapped itself around her torso and began to squeeze.

Grimly, she fought back but after the last few days, which were hard indeed, her strength was lower than she would have wished and she was no match for a rested elf. A rib broke on her left side and she gasped. A second one fractured and the sharp end jutted through her skin, sending a run of blood down her side.

The branch continued to crush. "Stop…please," she said in barely a whisper. "Can't…breathe… can't…" The world started to go grey and then amazingly the tree relaxed a touch and she was suddenly able to breathe. Gulping in air she said, "Thanks."

The elf came to stand below her and grinned upwardly showing that although his skin was cracked and shivered in places, his teeth and gums were their natural pink. "Whatever have you been up to dear Sister? I could feel you now for days running here and there all over the state of Washington. Getting in trouble, have you?"

"Yes," Ella admitted though did not elaborate further. If the elf had eyebrows he would have raised one when she didn't continue.

"And?" he asked. She started to shrug and then the tree branch bent and lowered her, with many twigs crackling, so that her toes were just off the ground. "We could do this the hard way."

A line of determination creased her brow and this seemed to make the elf happy. "I'll take that," he said, indicating the sword. It was her only weapon, but the elf took it from her easily. He bent her fingers back until she cried out and dropped it—then he bent them further. "Yes! In trouble," she gasped. "I was in trouble."

"That's what I thought. Now you'll tell me what has become of Darhyel, the onetime possessor of this blade."

Ella was in serious pain from her torture and she saw no reason to lie about the death of their half-brother. "He chased me. I was uh…" It came to her then that it was in her best interest to make her answers as long as possible in order to give her powers a chance to regenerate. "I was in this little town on my way back home. Not to the Hildeoven, but to Seattle. That's where I used to live before all of this. I was a gardener at a little place called…Ow! Stop, please that hurts."

Using his mind only, he bent her fingers back again and now the cartilage around her knuckles made a grisly, soft crackling noise. "It hurts? I guess I'm doing it right then," the Elf said. "Do you think I am a fool? I've tortured so many that I think I can spot a girl who is stalling for time. Now, in ten words or less how did you kill, Darhyel?"

She almost began blurting out words in order to answer his question, however she was sure he would count them so she thought before she said, "A man shot him, while Darhyel tried to kill me."

"Exactly ten. Now, how hard was that?"

"It wasn't hard. I'm sorry about before," she answered, making sure to speak as rapidly and clearly as possible.

"A human killed Darhyel," the elf commented doubtfully. "I have to say I find that so unlikely."

"He had a gun. It's a weapon the humans use. It can augh!" The branch constricted again stopping her breath.

The elf came close as Ella went from red to blue. "I know what a gun is and so did Darhyel," he said, watching the changing shades of the girl. "And the simple fact is that a man with a gun cannot slay an elf. So…?"

The branch loosened and Ella drank in the air, feeling faint. "The…man…had a…hidden gun," she said around great gulps of air. "And Darhyel…thought he was already dead."

"There it is," the elf sneered. "And I'm certain you were doing your best to distract that pompous fool. The master is understandably angered, though it would seem to be his own fault. Wouldn't you agree?"

"Yes," Ella said, quickly, nodding for emphasis, eager to please.

"And would you agree that it seemed a very odd moment to send an elf of such power to chase down a girl?"

Again she nodded and said, "Yes," however her eyes held confusion. Why was it such a bad time?

What had happened…suddenly she remembered the terrible feeling that had come upon her the night before she had been attacked by the elf—the dread and the deep soul tearing fear.

The leering elf read it all in her eyes.

"It was a bad time because we were on the verge of destroying Tayoeven. Oh, I see you didn't really know. You had your guesses, but I'm sure you don't know the extent. Tayoeven is burned to the ground and all its cowardly inhabitants are dead, or worse."

Ella dropped her eyes feeling too stunned to carry on the conversation. The elf lifted her head up by her dark brown hair. "All dead. Save for those tasty morsels that the master hands out for treats," as he said this his hands groped her. She had to fight not to be sick.

"Don't be like that," the elf whispered in Ella's ear. "You might just like it."

"But I'm your sister," she said, grasping at straws. "It's not right."

He smiled and Ella shivered. "Right and wrong are simply points of view. I think we can both agree that it would be a mercy for me to claim you. Trust me, there isn't much left after a pack of ogres have their ruts fulfilled. Yes, you don't want that…but there you go, turning me around. I had questions. What were you running around after? And don't try to lie."

"A gnome…oh…no! Please, stop, please." There was a great and piercing pain deep inside of her, but what was its cause she couldn't tell.

"How many more of these do you have?"

Ella looked up blearily to see the elf holding the rib bone that had at one time been sticking through her skin. He was licking it clean and now it was a grayish white. She started to pass out and he slapped her, turning her face hot and bringing her back.

"The gnome had a bomb," she said quickly. "A nuclear bomb."

"And that is?" he asked as his eyes went to slits.

Embarrassed at them, Ella sniffed back her tears and said, "A bomb makes an explosion that can kill people or destroy an entire building…a nuclear bomb is the biggest bomb. It can destroy an entire city in a great fire. A fire so hot that the sky itself is scorched."

"Are you lying?" the elf demanded peering into Ella's face from inches away.

"No. The Americans figured it out long ago."

"Then why haven't they used this bomb? Why haven't the Den used one of these to destroy the De-morlaik?"

The branch round her torso slowly began to squeeze and Ella spat out, "Because they're afraid of what would happen if the maug got a hold of these sort of weapons."

A bark of insincere laughter shot out of him. "I think you're the worst liar I have ever met," he said casually, and to this she could not comment. The branch was now so tight that talking was a luxury and breathing was nearly impossible. "Your fanciful tales are poorly constructed. You expect me to believe that a device which can destroy a city in fire will somehow leave the maug unaffected? And what of this gnome? How can a single gnome carry a bomb about while you chase it around for hundreds of miles?"

Ella began shaking her head.

"What is it?" the elf asked. "You wish to change a portion of your story perhaps? Maybe you'd like to tell me what you were truly doing out there." When he said 'there' he flicked his hand dismissively.

Desperate for air, Ella nodded and the branch loosened enough for her to drag air into her lungs.

"I could show you," Ella said in a whisper. "The gnome hasn't gotten far." The elf's eyes narrowed at this and Ella cried, "Wait, please listen. It was an acci-dent that I came across him. He had a cart that…" Ella stopped as the elf clearly looked to be losing patience, an attribute that he did not have a large stock of to begin with.

"The master sends one gnome with but a single cart to fetch a 'bomb' that can destroy a city. Do I understand correctly?" When she nodded he added, "Yes, you are very tedious." The branch squeezed again and her remaining ribs began snapping. If she could have screamed she would have.

At some point Ella blacked out. When she came to she found herself on the forest floor and above her the sun had moved across the sky. The elf paced holding his half brother's sword in his hand; he noticed her stir. Immediately the tree came alive and snatched her up.

Before they began to crush again, she called out in a rush, "*You* could be master!" The branches paused and Ella felt shaky at the proximity of more pain—with a twitch the elf could cut her in two. "I'm not lying about the power of the bomb. Darhmael doesn't trust you or any of the other elves, and he didn't want you to find out about it. He…" The branches cut her off.

"As if I wouldn't notice Rhyoeven being destroyed in a great fire," the elf laughed while Ella clawed at the branches. "Oh you are such a child in your lies. And your stratagem to get me to turn on our father is the work of a simpleton. Tell me, dullard, what good would a city-destroying device be against Darhmael?"

He loosened the branches and she spilled to the earth. Beneath her ear she felt the vibration of a horse approaching in a gale.

"Well?" asked the elf. "Would you have me destroy the Demorlaik along with Darhmael? True, I would be master, but master of what? Master of being hunted by the Den? Is that your pathetic, weasely plan?"

He kicked her and she grinned with blood in her teeth. "Why do you smile?" he asked.

"The king approaches!" Ella said, spitting blood. "He is upon you and his wrath is very great."

"Finally," the elf said. "He is slow to come to your rescue…oh I take it by that delicious look of yours that you expected me to be surprised?" He laughed long at this. "Haven't you figured out that you are nothing but a slave to Darhmael? Unwittingly you do his bidding at every turn. The gnome was likely nothing but a ruse to get you here, exactly where Darhmael wants you."

"Why? What's so great about here?"

Smugly the elf sauntered away and pointed west. "We are just far enough from the capital, and Darhmael's army is just close enough that Eireden won't risk his army. He's coming alone, isn't he?"

She had heard but a single horse.

"He is unstoppable!" Ella hissed. "It will be your blood that will spill here today. It is you who should have brought an army."

"Why would I need an army? When I've brought my brother, or should I say our brother. Have you formally met Darhstrai?"

From behind her, another elf came out of the trees. He was slim and smaller than the others, but his eyes were alight with an evil intelligence. "Hello Ella," it said in its high voice. "Just call me Strai."

Chapter 26

Eireden

As though in a dream, Eireden walked the once calm and quiet streets of his city and looked upon thousands of cheering people. Some few he recognized and to these he would give a nod or a smile, but for the most part the people were a blur and seemed strange, for the light around them was not the normal hues of the capital at night.

Above the king a ball of light floated and pulse, casting the people in odd shadows, distorting their features, yet their happiness came through clear.

The ball of light was the fairies, of course, and their numbers seemed incalculable to most. Though not to the king. He knew that the light of his "sun" had dimmed—there were far fewer fairies than he had hoped.

"Easa! Sooni, Tissa..." The king greeted each of his family by name and accepted them as they came in to touch him for luck or love. He smiled, but beneath he worried. Though his family was all accounted for, save Whip-wip, he fretted over the rest? Had they been hunted and slain by the bat-things that had been present at the battle of the plain? Or were the majority in hiding, afraid for their very lives?

"The sun King!" Prince Lienhart roared in greeting as Eireden and Alseya arrived at the palace. The crowd set up the chant of *Sun King! Sun King!* Again

Eireden did his best to show his appreciation, but his mind reeled at the few captains who stood to greet him. Where were they all? Where was Jarlen of Avargard? Or Terwyth, or Gartel, or any of the men from Varisgard?

Beside Lienhart, who looked grey with exhaustion, were the remaining leaders of the Den and sprinkled throughout were fey ladies and gentlemen of note, yet conspicuously absent was Aric Anorian. This added a sour note to his anxiety, still he managed a final wave to the crowds before crossing the threshold of the palace.

"What has happened that they cheer so?" he asked as he handed his shield and helmet to a valet. "The battle today was not but a skirmish compared to what is to come. The truth is we won only the opportunity to add two-thousand dwarves to those already trapped behind our walls."

"Bah!" Furen said, causing many eyebrows to rise at his temerity. "Today was a victory even greater than that which occurred at Hildeoven last year. There you had walls and fairies uncounted."

"From all accounts it was your greatest victory," Lienhart said, solemnly. "And unfortunately it has been our only victory. Prince Jarlen fell on the battle plain of Hildeoven, fighting in a rearguard action. And worse, the 3rd of Varisgard died to a man..."

The king gasped, "The entire 3rd guard? A thousand soldiers? How?"

Lienhart bowed his head in his grief and said, "Darhmael came on much faster than expected. The city wasn't entirely evacuated before the maug came pouring out of the wood. They died to give the people time."

One of the captains of Avargard, a young man with red-rimmed eyes spoke and his voice was harsh, "The elf is the very devil! He drives the maug on and on without pause or rest. Tayoeven, Avargard,

Hildeoven...Varisgard and yesterday, Wesgard. One after another have been overrun. He pushes his army at an incredible rate—forty, fifty miles a day. Even the dwarves would be hard pressed to match that endurance."

This was patently true as evidenced by the fact that Furen did not dispute it.

"But we still have Rhyoeven!" Eireden said. "It is ever the rock."

The prince of Hildeoven sighed tiredly before saying, "And that is why we cheer. The Den are not used to such a string of defeats and when we heard of your victory, as complete as it was, and that you were bringing two-thousand battle-hardened dwarves to our aid, the city burst into a storm of excitement."

Alseya, in her white gown, stepped forward, flowing as if only a gentle wind propelled her. "It was not the victory or the dwarves that so excited our people."

Eireden raised an eyebrow and Lienhart explained, "You were presumed to have been killed or lost forever in the Forest of Mists." The prince paused as though searching for the right words. Finally he blurted, "How did you get past the wolves? And how did you make it through the mists? Did the Lord Aric save you?"

Ever modest, the king began to shrug and so Alseya answered, "You have it backward my Lord Prince. It is the king who saved Aric Anorian. No phantasm can withstand his will, just as no stray dog can bring him low."

"Hear, hear!" cried Furen. "It is as my beautiful Gargefrel says...what?"

To a man the Den had bit back smiles. The name Gargefrel was well known to them and each pictured the dwarf queen in their own way, none of which was flattering.

Eireden held up a scarred hand. "Heed them not, King Furen. They do not understand the loveliness of the queen Gargefrel—and I do not blame them. Such a unique beauty cannot be described beyond simple terms. One must experience her."

Furen's heavy brows came down. "Experience?" he asked in suspicion before brightening suddenly. "Aye, experience. Visually so. Yes she is a dream."

Lienhart bowed and the rest of the gathered Den followed suit. "Please accept our pardon at any slight. We only show our ignorance. Here in Rhyoeven we know of only the beauty of the Den and the fey, such as the Lady Eleanor or the Lady Alseya. It is our loss that we cannot experience your queen for ourselves and understand."

This ended the meeting in a formal sense. The king, allowing for the exhaustion of so many present, ordered the captains of the Den and the dwarves, along with a representative of the fey to meet the following morning at ten.

When they were alone Alseya turned him. "Why do the Den get so uncomfortable when the beauty of Ella is mentioned?" Eireden had noted this as well, especially since he was the most uncomfortable one among them. He was slow to answer and so the fey asked another question. "Where is she? You must know."

He knew exactly where she was. "Ella's out there in the Forbidden Lands. Hopefully she is happy."

"I do not think that likely. She will not be happy until she is home again. Speaking of which, here we are."

She had walked him to his apartments in the palace. Guilt flared within him and he had to fight the feeling since he was doing nothing wrong.

You love another woman, yet you stand so close to this fey. Isn't that wrong?

The king swallowed and said. "Till the morning."

She ignored this and made no move to leave. "I am amazed at myself. I am jealous of the Lady Eleanor." Eireden began to shake his head, but she held up her hand. "My heart tells me that Ella is neither mortal nor immortal, and yet she will be loved for all eternity. While I...I have now. The fates have given me now and that is gift enough."

His guilt was great and his confusion greater, both of which immobilized him enough so that when she leaned in to him with her face to his, he could not help but kiss her.

"Thank you," she said.

In the morning the king dressed alone and ate alone and sat waiting for his staff meeting alone, and lonely. Strangely it was not Ella that he missed just then. Though his heart centered on her as she ran to catch the gnome, and his subconscious fretted over Alseya and her growing feelings, which could never be reciprocated, he thought of Generai and it was she that he missed.

He thought of her faith in him when he was at his lowest, and he thought that, despite her low birth, she would've been a proud queen, a fine wife and a great mother. Had Eireden been human, living with her in the Americas, she would have straightened his tie for him, and folded his socks for him, and scolded him, though none too harshly, had he come home in the middle of the night, knocking into things and smelling of beer. He smiled at the idea, at the simple, yet fulfilling life that would've been.

That wasn't Alseya. If she were human, she would be the paragon of womanhood: stunningly beautiful, accomplished in her own right, with her own skills, her own wants, her own secret needs. She would not only be self-sufficient, but in many ways, self-contained, and because of that, practically unattainable. Yet the man who could manage to ensnare her would find that she was more than he could ever want and perhaps even handle.

And then there was Ella. The king went to his window and stared out, thinking of the girl. Ella's desirability was not because she was the perfect blend of Generai and Alseya, though in truth she was, it was because she was *eternally* what should have been fleeting. What made Ella special was that she encapsulated and lived and breathed and embodied that most perfect of all times spans: the time of falling in love.

The time in which it hurt to be away from that someone special. When all you wanted and needed was to be in their arms. When you couldn't wait to touch their lips again. When you your insides went warm at the thought of her.

That was Ella. She was like falling in love forever.

A knock came and Alseya swept in without an answer from him. She came to him at the window and looked out. "Is she there? Heading home to us?"

There was no use lying to the quick witted fey and so the king shook his head. "No. She's moving north and west now, though I know not why. But that is not so unusual. Were I to draw her course from whence she left us you'd think she was mad."

"I would not think to question her mind," Alseya said. "Just as long as she comes back to you."

Eireden gazed at the fey in wonder before laughing aloud. "Are you the same woman who admitted jealousy only last night? Perhaps it is *your* sanity that should be judged."

She only smiled, and the king came close so they were inches away. "Will I ever understand you, Alseya?"

He had meant it as a joke however she answered somberly, "Yes."

"That is good news," he said trying to get her to smile again. He disliked when she frowned—it was very unnatural on a fey. "Will this understanding come sooner or later?"

Her mood only grew more dim. "Later," she answered, before heading for the door. "Come, you should not keep your captains waiting. That armor seems to be a beastly thing to sit about in."

Eireden allowed himself to be propelled along by the tiny fey woman but he mused as he did, "Whatever you say I doubt I will understand you. I wonder how my great ancestor, Feireden put up with his fey wife?"

Again it was a joke, but he felt the smallest bunching of the muscles in her hand and saw the tiniest movement of her chin as it moved away from him a fraction of an inch.

"What is wrong?" he asked, stopping in the hall outside the grand audience chamber.

"Nothing that time won't cure," Alseya answered evasively. "Now, come and do your duty. Darhmael approaches out of the north. I can feel it in the earth. He will be here by nightfall."

"Then I have time," Eireden said, coolly. Though she pulled at his hand he didn't so much as budge. "There is something that is not being said by you, and I would that it be spoken. You are to be my wife and you should know that I will not abide secrets."

She grew stiff and her chin jutted at him. "Do not presume to tell me my role. I can assure you, that I know what my duties will be as wife, as queen and as mother. And I promise there will be no secrets on our wedding night, but that time is not this time. Until it is my secrets are mine to withhold."

Eireden glared at first and then softened. "You are correct; your mind is your own and I have no right to your thoughts unless freely given. I presume much and do apologize."

Alseya smiled and it was like the sun coming through dark clouds. "I have many to whom I owe duty to, my Lord. Please trust in me that I seek only the good of all in my thoughts and actions."

Eireden made to nod, but a sad voice came lilting down the hall, "For the fey, truth was once a single unbreakable line," Aric Anorian said slowly as he walked up. He wore his dwarven armor and at his side was an elf sword in a silver sheath. "On one side there was fact, on the other...not fact. So simple. Now that is not so."

"Explain yourself," Eireden said, testily. "Are you suggesting that my wife-to-be is a liar?"

"Yes," Aric said, calmly despite Eireden's growing wrath. "She lies to herself."

Eireden was just opening his mouth to let out a roar of anger but now only a squeak came out. "Huh?"

"It is not the time," Alseya said, glaring.

"He has a right to know," Aric countered.

"One of you tell me what's going on," Eireden demanded, but both set their jaws. In a rage, the king slammed open the door to his audience chamber and stomped in. His men came to attention in a great clatter of metal. "Be at ease," he yelled, though with his frustration so obvious none of the thirty or so present took his command to heart.

The two fey followed him, still locked in their silent debate. Their eyes smote like sword blows and neither gave an inch.

"Lienhart, your report," Eireden demanded with an edge to his voice that was well past rude.

"Yes my Lord," the scarred, one-eyed prince said quickly. "With the destruction of Tayoeven, and our losses at the battle of the Hildeoven, and the defeat at Varisgard..."

"Just give me numbers," the king barked.

"We have twelve-thousand, four hundred soldiers fit for service, nineteen hundred dwarves and three-thousand fey...though as you know these are to be used only as auxiliary and not in formations."

At the mention of the fey, Alseya turned her cool, opal eyes to Eireden. It was her way of reminding him that the fey were only his to command if he carried through with his promise. His lips went tight and he asked in as controlled a voice as possible, "And Darhmael? What of him?"

The few fey in the room looked to Alseya and she said, "Near to ninety-thousand maug, five-hundred ogres, and thirty trolls. They march under cover of a great cloud and will be here just after sunset."

"What of his wolves?"

Alseya dropped her eyes. "There are many. They surround the capital but stay well back."

The king turned to Furen. "I'll need to know as soon as possible about any chance their might be tunneling..."

The dwarf held up a flat hand. "I thought that all this lazing around wasn't good on my dwarves; it might turn them soft. *They* might want staff meetings at ten in the morning, so I had them out taking soundings of the bedrock. So far they have yet to discover a single tunnel."

Eireden ignored the jab at the late start he had given his men. He knew his city and its people; everything that could be done had been done. "And what is the state of our granaries?"

Captain Rudyid of the 1st Guards answered, "Only fourteen months with the numbers in the city. We rotate stocks on a monthly basis, so our count is very accurate, however the fey say that they can extend that if they can begin constructing green houses immediately."

Eireden got up to pace. He stopped, facing east, toward *her*. After a deep breath he said, "So we are trapped as snug as you please behind walls that are too great for Darhmael to assault. Quite the stalemate if one believes our adversary to be a fool, which I do not. So what is his plan?"

"He could try starving us out?" Rudyid answered. "Fourteen months is not a long time. Nor would we want to wait even that long if it came to it. Why wait until we are weak with starvation before we come out to fight."

Feylon put up her hand and stepped forward. "If I may. The elf has expended vast stores of energy controlling his forces as he has. This is not something he will be able to continue for a year. Traditionally goblin armies disintegrate long before that. I don't think he'll be able to starve us out."

"What about plague or disease?" Lienhart asked.

This had never entered Eireden's mind as a worry for the same reason Feylon explained, "You have three thousand healers within these walls. Disease will not be an issue."

At the word *healer* the king locked eyes with Alseya and her lips were hard. Again he turned away and again it was to Ella that he looked...she was in trouble...again. He could feel it in his bones. But what could he do, he was in trouble as well. And so was his city and his entire race. In a stew of emotion he spun and caught Aric's eye. Aric was warning him of something.

The king stocked away to the window, threw it open and stood glaring. "I can't have secrets," he said suddenly. "Not now. Out with it!"

The room went deathly quiet.

The king came back to stand before Alseya and with his anger so great he seemed a giant and towered over her. "There is another way in which we can fall. Traitors in our midst."

"You know not of what you speak," Alseya said. "I seek only to serve both of our races."

Eireden turned his glare to Aric. "She is no traitor," the fey said. "And great is her sacrifice. Where she fails..."

"Aric!" Alseya said sharply.

He ignored her. "...is in judging your feeling, my Lord King. She lies to herself that you do not care for her. That you care only for one other. That you won't be hurt if she hurts."

"Explain yourself," Eireden said, his anger deflating. "Who is to be hurt? And why?"

Alseya stood like stone and refused to shift her eyes from Aric, who also would not speak.

"I will speak on this if the fey will not," Ilenwyth E-Den said stepping from the rear of the hall. She had not been invited to the meeting of Eireden's captains, but as former queen and mother to the king she was not to be gainsaid.

"The king has sworn an oath," Alseya said quickly. "He is beholden to it."

"An oath given under false pretense is not binding," Ilenwyth said and there was ice in her words.

"There has been no falsehood given on my part," Alseya said, bristling. "I asked for a union of our two peoples in exchange for fey participation in the attack on Rhyoeven. There is nothing untrue on my part."

"Then you wouldn't mind me explaining to my son what will occur on your wedding night and more importantly what will occur nine months later."

Eireden was speechless. Even his imagination seemed frozen. He couldn't picture what would have Alseya so upset. The lithe fey started shaking her head to Ilenwyth but then turned to her king. "You promised," she whispered.

"What is going to happen?" he asked, but Alseya could not answer. Her mouth came open yet no words came out.

"Life and then death," Ilenwyth said. "I was curious about our ancestor Feireden. All the old tales speak of him taking a fey for a wife, but that was so long ago that it is now folklore. If he had taken a fey where was she? What became of her? They are immortal after all. As did everyone else I thought it more a bedtime story than anything else, yet after I heard of your engagement I decided to research this."

"And?" Eireden's temper was only barely in check.

"Your wife will become pregnant on her wedding night and your baby will kill her nine months later. A fey woman cannot withstand the demands...the unrelenting demands of a human baby within her. It will suck her dry of life."

"I have chosen this course," Alseya said. "And you have sworn an oath."

"Not to kill you," he said, blinking and shaking his head as if to make sense of what was going on. "I never said...I never promised to kill you. How could you ask our child to grow up knowing that he was the cause of his mother's death and that I knowingly allowed it?"

"You have to," Alseya said, quieting the room that had been alive with whispers. "Where do we turn if you do not. We are homeless, leaderless, directionless. The world of man has grown while we have shrunk. Would you have us believe another promise from you that we will be safe when you are considering breaking your last?"

"You ask the impossible," Eireden said, his mind spinning. He was about ask for the courtroom to be cleared so he could think, when a great keening cry shook the entire room. From every door and window fairies burst in a horrendous storm of noise and confusion.

The king was not in the mood for fairy nonsense. "Stop!" he ordered in a voice that shook the windowpanes. Immediately the fairies coalesced into a ball in front of him and their fire was so bright that Alseya had to turn away.

"Look," said Tissa in English, pointing at something in the ball. Eireden advanced into the mass of fairies and felt the thousands of wings caress and sweep over him, and shielding his eyes he saw what they had brought to him.

It was only a simple sythie with gold and silver wings and she bled like a wet sponge from many holes in her tiny body.

"Whip-wip," he gasped. And then louder, he called in a voice that held pain and panic, "Aric, come here!"

Then the fey was there next to him and a second later the blue glow from his hands pushed back at the fairy light. "She lives yet. Look."

"Gada?" Whip-wip asked blinking around at all the fairies.

"What's happened to Ella?" the king asked, knowing already she was in trouble and knowing already he was going to get her. He couldn't stay there in the palace, not with the idea that he would be responsible for the death of his own wife. He couldn't look at Alseya without picturing a baby digging its way out of her ghastly corpse.

"Ella in trouble. Wolves, and bats with stings, and angry elf," Whip-wip said, new tears forming.

"It'll be ok," the king said, feeling a calm, despite the mention of an elf.

Alseya pulled him out of the mass of fairies using her magic—a gross lack of manners in a king's courtroom. "It won't be ok, because you won't go. You can't throw away your life for nothing, just because you don't like the repercussions of your choices."

Eireden began to grow furious at her impetuosity, but then Lienhart said, "I agree. Look, I love Ella, just as we all do. But you can't go, Milord. You're too important. I will go in your stead. I will act as your champion."

"This isn't a challenge!" Eireden steamed. "This isn't a point of honor. And this isn't about my choices, Alseya! I wasn't told that killing you would be part of my choices."

"Then what is it?" Lienhart asked. "Your city needs you."

"Actually it doesn't," Eireden shot back. "You can defend these walls as well as I. So what is my place here? As figurehead? I am not a figurehead and never have been. I don't sit idly by when my people are in danger. We sit here safe as can be, but Ella is not."

"She is just one girl," Ilenwyth put in. "You know how we all feel, but she is still just that."

"In this you are wrong," Aric said in that placid way of his. "She is an elf and has within her more power and potential than any here. The one good elf to be born in two-hundred centuries. I would make the attempt to save her, but I dare not. I am embarrassed to admit that I was saved from corruption by the barest of margins by your king. I cannot again be tempted."

"Then the 1st guard will go," Captain Rudyid said in the silence that followed Aric's admission. "I shall summon my knights if my lord so commands."

The king was looking to the east again, drawn there. "How far off is Darhmael?" Eireden asked.

"Fifteen miles," Feylon answered when Alseya refused. "I'm sorry, but with his army coming down from the north like the wind, you won't make it back to your walls in time."

"That rules out the 1st guard. I will not sacrifice them," Eireden said. "Nor will I allow any Den to follow. Their duty is protecting these walls."

"Have you a horse that will bear me?" Furen asked in desperation. "Any that be small but fast."

The king shook his head. "Sorry my friend." He then turned to the Alseya and the fey. "And what of you? Will you help?"

Alseya raised an eyebrow. "Will you honor our agreement?"

Aric had been wrong with his cryptic message concerning honor and happiness. Sadly, no matter what Eireden choose he would get neither. Where was the honor in allowing his own son to kill his wife? And where was the happiness in breaking an oath?

"I will not be a party to killing my own wife," Eireden said at last. "I will not marry you."

"Then you prove that your words are meaningless. Bind our two races or we will not lift a finger to help."

The Den seethed, but their confusion over the point of honor was such that they could not argue with her, Eireden included. Rather than argue he said to Lienhart, "Get me your fastest horse."

Chapter 27

Ella

"So that fool, that *Gada* comes to us," Darhstrai, the slighter of the two elves said. "It is even as the master predicts."

"Yes," the first elf said, taking his eyes from Ella. "Though what your purpose here is, Strai, I don't know. I can slay this Den with ease, especially coming alone as he does."

"It's because of the bomb," Ella said. "He knows its power and he knows what you two can do if you possessed it. The master is afraid of you."

Strai squatted down next to Ella and poked her with a stick, making her grunt in pain, which he enjoyed. "What is she going on about? What is a bomb?"

"Just tiresome nonsense," the taller elf scoffed, setting the sword he had taken from Ella against a tree and unsheathing his own. "She has a fanciful notion that the humans built a device that can destroy an entire city."

"The humans? How ridiculous," Strai said, standing. He pulled his arm back to toss away the stick but stopped in mid-motion. "However...if it were true, it would explain the master's plans. Wouldn't you agree, Darhrorn? We have corralled the Den into the one place that we can't get at. Something that can destroy a city would be very handy right now."

"Put such thoughts out of your head," Darhrorn said. "The Den approaches." Ella could hear the hoof beats clearly now and her heart sunk. The horse was tired and stumbled in its weariness. This wouldn't be a gallant moment where Eireden came through the trees in gleaming mail upon a white horse to save the day. He was coming to his death, which would leave the world at Darhmael's mercy.

"Yes, put away those thoughts," Ella said, desperately trying to distract the two elves. "That's what the master wants you to do. He gambles that you *two* will do the job of *one* so that he can get that bomb. It has more power than all the fey that ever lived, combined."

Strai looked to consider this, but his brother glared. "You," Darhrorn said to Ella, "be quiet." The tree branches came again to crush her, only this time Ella fought back.

All during her torture she had endured the pain and allowed her body to be abused, and not for a moment had she used her magic in any way. She had held back, reserving it on the off chance she could find a moment to escape.

Now she stopped the branch from curling in.

Darhrorn eyes widened at this display of power, that was only slightly less than his own. He began to force the branch harder and this time there was murder in his eyes, but that was when the king arrived.

It was as Ella had foreseen. Wearing a black cloak, he sat atop a once proud stallion. Now the poor creature shook with exhaustion and made ugly noises in his throat.

The king eyed his two adversaries with a wild look to him—his raven hair went in every direction and his face held a note of chaotic abandonment. It was obvious that he knew his death was near and—it was equally obvious that he didn't care.

"Which one of you is to blame for that," the king growled in a voice that was gritty and sounded as though it had come from the throat of a wolf. He pointed at Ella's broken body.

"That would be my artistry," Darhrorn said, drawing a blazing sword. "You were foolish to have come alone."

"Who said I have," Eireden said and then kicked the tired stallion into a last gallop. As he did he drew the black sword and cast aside his cloak.

Now the two combatants, the elf and the Den, were at least visually complete opposites. The elf was black and burnt. He wore armor of ebony yet in his hand he held a sword of elven make. It glowed a bright silver. On the other hand, Eireden's sword was black as night, a complete contrast to his armor which was afire with gleaming light.

The light seemed to leap out at the eyes as if it wasn't simply the sun glinting off his armor. In a second Darhrorn discovered that it wasn't.

Eireden hadn't come alone. Twenty-three enraged fairies shot away as soon as the king threw back his cloak and they bored in at Darhrorn with a vengeance. Too late he recognized them for what they were and fire shot out from his hands, but they were already peeling away, changing course on a dime.

They had done their job.

Eireden came right behind, the great sword of Ag-Raumon swinging in faster than it seemed possible. The sword made a mockery of physics. It was larger than any normal sword, yet it was also as light as a switch from a willow. It was sharp as razor and yet struck with the force of a sledgehammer.

It had been designed and created with one purpose in mind: to slay elves, and in Eireden's hands it was a fell weapon indeed.

The sword gave Darhrorn no rest, no time for thought, and no way for him to use his magic, save to defend himself from the thunderous blows. Back he retreated from the wild-eyed Den and it would have been a quick death if he had come alone. But Strai attacked from the side and it was all the king could do to parry the blow.

Then the tables were turned for the power of the elves was great. Eireden was forced back and this seemed to suit him. He ducked in and out of the trees using them to cover this flank or that, making the most of his speed and skill. And always the fairies flew by shooting light or hid close, blending with the foliage and stringing their invisible strands to trip up the elves.

Still it was not enough.

Now that he wasn't fearing for his skin, Darhrorn sent branches and vines whipping in from every direction, while Strai set the forest on fire as he shot flames in the air. The fairies scattered, screaming, some in fear, some in pain. And then a root caught Eireden by the foot and held him. Darhrorn lunged in with his elf sword slicing, but the king was a master swordsman, he riposted with a turn of his wrist and the black sword went into the elf a full foot.

The move was textbook perfect yet it left him open for a killing stroke by Strai. In a quick hacking motion the elf sword came at Eireden's exposed neck, but instead of striking and shearing his head clear away the sword struck another.

Ella stood there, fully healed and in a passion of anger and revenge. She had seen the death of two sythie who were family to her and it had sent her into rage. And she was not alone. Tiny Whip-wip spun circles around the tip of the elf sword that Darhrorn had cast aside.

Strai gave her a smug look and then snorted at the fairy. "You should be wiser in choosing your allies. I would..." In mid sentence he slipped his sword at her looking to eviscerate her and she jumped out of reach. This little move set everyone in motion.

Darhrorn used his magic to fly back off the point of Eireden's sword, while the king pressed close, trying to follow up so the elf couldn't heal himself. Their battle was epic, but unseen.

Ella could spare no time for Eireden, not even for a single glance. She knew she had to kill Strai and do it fast before her magic dwindled to nothing. It had cost her much to heal her many injuries and unfortunately she couldn't rely on her superior swordsmanship, since she didn't actually possess superior swordsmanship.

Yet she wasn't without skill and her ability to fight in conjunction with Whip-wip disproved Strai's comment about her choice in allies. They were in tune as if joined in thought. If Ella brought her sword down Whip-wip moved up, and if Ella slid the tip to the right the fairy went left. The effect was mesmerizing and doubly so since Whip-wip's glow matched the light of the elf sword perfectly.

Strai's eyes would frequently slip from the tip of Ella's sword to the little fairy thinking one was the other. When he did Ella would strike fast. Sometimes he would recover and parry, but more often she would draw blood; always just a taste as if she were the torturer now.

In reality she was afraid to commit fully to any single attack. Strai was just too quick and too skillful, and a single mistake on her part would mean her death.

Unfortunately, her very strategy was her biggest mistake. When in battle with a superior fighter the best course is to take immediate and decisive action whenever an opportunity presented. Instead she continued to open up cuts that turned the elf bloody but that did not deliver a mortal wound.

The elf did not make the same mistake. He bled and he cursed every time her blade sliced him up, but he also watched and learned...and saw a pattern. Ella became over reliant on what fencers would call a *Pasatta Sotto*. When Strai would lunge she would drop low and angle her attacks up.

His next lunge was a feint and when she dropped, he ignored the glow of Whip-wip, which was even then fading, and sunk his blade into her neck. Its sharp edge running just along her carotid artery. She could feel her pulse thump against the metal.

He could as well.

"Now what?" he asked in that high voice. "Any more tricks? Any more fairies up your sleeve? Look at them. They seem worried for you."

The fairies sat in a little cloud. Some cried, but the rest seemed to be gearing up for an attack. She waved then away. "Don't," she said in a gurgle of blood, her mind and her magic full on the metal inside of her. "Go...home."

"Oh that doesn't really matter," the elf said. "They will be dead soon. The master is breeding so many of those spider bats. Nasty things." Behind him the sound of constant steel on steel suddenly stopped, and Ella was just able to see Eireden drop to his knees next to a tree.

"And so dies your king," Strai said. "But don't worry for yourself. I won't let such a beauty go so soon. I think I earned a little fun..."

Next to them something warped and strange struck the tree with an awful thump. It was a severed head.

Chapter 28

Eireden

The king pressed the sword of Ag-Raumon against the back of Strai's neck so that the tip began to slide beneath the elf's skin; very bright blood ran free.

"You will desist or your beloved dies," Strai said. He spoke calmly, seemingly not at all worried over the advent of his death.

Eireden stopped the blade, but his hand quivered. "She is not my beloved. She is not mine. I am...I'm spoken for." Eireden and Ella locked eyes for a moment and then the king blew out noisily. "It hardly matters. You will withdraw your blade or die."

Strai gave a little shrug and said, "It matters to me, if it does not to you. If you do not love her then I am at your mercy, while the reverse is true if you do love her. And there really is only one way to find out where the truth is."

A twist of the sword had Ella's eyes bugging and a croaking noise escaped her as the metal in her throat sliced its way through her larynx. She began to gag, but with the sword still in her she dared not do much more than struggle to keep breathing.

"Stop...don't," Eireden pleaded, advancing his own blade into the elf.

The elf obeyed and made a noise like a soft humming while he considered his situation. "Such a dilemma for us both. Whatever feelings you have for this girl is balanced by your devotion to duty. Which puts us at an impasse. I can neither kill the girl nor let her live, for you will kill me either way. Unless..."

"What?" the king demanded.

"Unless we call this little battle a draw. You can even call it a win since you killed Darhrorn, just not a complete victory. I will go my way and you two will go yours. All that is needed is for you to give your word that you will not kill me—a Den's word is gold is it not?"

The king's grip grew tight. "It is. It should be..." His mind begun to spin with visions of Alseya in white and Ella dying in front of him. Right and wrong, honor and dishonor began to become jumbled. Finally he barked, "Ok, just withdraw your blade and set it aside and I will not hurt you."

"That was more of a struggle than I had thought it would be," the elf said withdrawing his blade. When he did Ella gasped and sunk back. "Maybe you don't know where your heart lies," the elf added. "Or perhaps it lies with another."

"One such as you should not question a man's heart," Eireden said and his anger was such that he kept the sword in place.

"You have given me your word, Den," the elf said. "Release me."

Ella healed herself with a sigh, she was pale and her blue eyes were dim. "It's too bad. If there was ever a time to break one's oath, now would be it. Lives are at stake."

After another moment's hesitation, the king withdrew his blade and asked, "Is that the requirement for dishonoring one's self? If it was so, my life would be much simpler." He turned to Strai. "Be gone, elf. Go back to your master and admit your failure, and know I have pity on you, for I am sure that he will not take the news lightly."

Strai backed away from the pair and as always there were calculations in his eyes. "My task was your death, King. And that may still occur. Your walls are far and there are many enemies between you and them. Till we meet again, dear sister." The elf bowed and calmly walked away.

When he did, Eireden hurried to the stallion he had rode in on and began to unbuckle the saddle from its back, while Ella stood holding her throat.

"You're going to have to hurry, for the elf did not lie," Eireden said, throwing the saddle down. "Darhmael's army is almost to the city. Come on, did you not hear me?"

Ella only stood there. "But there is a bomb... a nuclear bomb. Do you know what that is?"

The king was just coming to grab Ella and put her bodily on the horse, but he stopped. He had read about nuclear bombs. "I think so. Do they really do what is written about them?" Ella nodded and Eireden felt his insides curl. "Where is it now, do you know?"

She dropped to one knee and laid her hand in the grass. After a moment she paled to an even greater degree. "It's been too long! The gnome is almost to the Demorlaik."

The word gnome didn't seem to fit with their discussion, but it hardly mattered. Eireden saw Darhmael's plan perfectly, now that it was too late for him to stop it.

"Here's what we're going to do," he said lifting Ella from the earth and setting her on the horse's back. "I will worry over this bomb. You ride straight away to Rhyoeven and warn them. None will truly understand what this bomb can do save my mother and perhaps Alseya."

Ella grabbed him and clung. "You should not make the attempt, the gnome is too far. You will go for nothing and I doubt you'll be able to make it back."

"I don't think I was ever meant to come back."

Just then a howl went up and Ella's face became pinched. "Maybe I wasn't either," she said patting the horse. The poor beast was still in a lather of sweat and it's muscled vibrated from exhaustion. "I should let him go."

At the howl the fairies came down from the trees and huddled close; half went to Ella and half to the king.

"So where does that leave us?" Ella asked swallowing and trying to hide her fear—she could feel the wolves closing just as he could. Despite that she nuzzled Whip-wip and gave her a kiss.

"You go back home to the Americas," Eireden said, looking east. "Take the horse as far as he'll take you. Just don't stop..."

"No," Ella interrupted. "This is my home now. I was a fool to run away. It was childish. But this is my home and I will fight for it."

The wolves were running hard and the stallion really began to blow and skip. Eireden steadied the beast and then said to Ella, "You've chosen a poor time to fight. I fear for us there'll only be one more battle."

Ella slipped off the horse and knelt, laying her hand upon a root. "No, there is time. Straight west. If we hurry we can escape their circle."

"And then what?" Eireden asked. "I could walk to the capital faster than this poor horse. Hell, even if we had fresh horses I doubt we could make it back in time. The only thing that could..."

Struck by a sudden thought, Eireden stopped in mid word and hoisted Ella up onto the horse before jumping on behind, causing the fairies to rise up in a cloud around them.

A startled Ella asked, "What is it?"

"I can still save you," Eireden, said, kicking the poor beast into a sprint westward.

"And what of you?" Ella asked leaning forward over the neck of the horse. Eireden did as well and he became dizzy at the heat of her body.

"Me?" he asked. Feeling guilty, though he had done nothing, he leaned back slightly. "I don't know. One of us has to get through and warn the capital. Besides I may not be welcome."

"What? You are king!"

He was still king and as such none could gain say his honor. Only he could, and on the ride east to save Ella he had done so plenty. "I may be *gada* once again. My word...my honor has been questioned and perhaps rightly so."

"They should worry more for your life."

"Without honor life is not fit to live...now hold your tongue. Look." From the north, through a break in the trees a swarm of wolves swept down. Fortunately they were upwind and the wolves missed them heading away south.

"Now for it!" the king cried, reaching back and smacking the stallion into its last sprint.

"Now for what?" Ella asked. "He can't go on much longer like this." Already the horse labored and the sprint was a pale comparison of what it could have done if fresh.

"We must hope it will be long enough," he said and then Ella looked back at him. Their noses touched and their cheeks lay against each other for the span of one breath. His heart began a thudding that he was sure she had to feel.

"What is it?" she asked. "Why do we ride this poor animal like this."

"To get us some room and some time. I have an idea, but if it's going to succeed I need to know something important." He paused, wondering how he was going to ask. Finally as the horse stumbled and only barely recovered he just blurted, "Are you pure?"

"What did you ask? With the wind I thought you asked if I was pure? Like what? Do you mean sexually?"

Feeling his face go hot, the king said, "Yes."

"Oh jeez!" Ella cried laughing without mirth. "Is it really time to open old wounds?" Beneath them, like a sloppy drunk, the stallion began veering to his left until it grazed a pine.

"That's not what I wish," Eireden said, doing his best to keep the horse straight, but sadly the fine animal was done in.

In a huff, Ella hopped off while it was still staggering on. "Then what is it?" she demanded. Before he could answer she asked, "Are you still jealous of Aric, or do you think a week of running around Washington has turned me into a slut?"

Eireden slipped from the horse as well. "Neither," he said, taken back.

"So do you just want to know if I'll be available— on the side—once you are married? If so you are sadly mistaken!" The king shrank away from her volume and her anger, while she advanced. "Well?" she challenged with eyes that blazed and in a voice that had the fairies staring at him in suspicion.

"I only ask because of the feasibility of calling a unicorn."

"Oh," she said in a little puff of air, while her face went in three directions at once. "Still...I mean it's not something you just ask. It's not really proper."

"My pardon," Eireden said. "I ask out of necessity only."

"I can...I mean I am. I can call a unicorn that is. Only I don't know how. My attempts before did not end well."

With her anger gone so quickly, Eireden was able to relax as well. "That's because you chased. A proper lady does not chase...that's the saying among the Den."

At this she turned red and began to laugh and the fairies forgot their fears and suspicion and began to laugh along.

"Don't laugh," Eireden said, smiling despite the danger and his own attempt at solemnity. "It's what all the mothers tell their daughters."

"I'm sure every mother that had a daughter near you said it doubly so." He could only shrug which had her snorting with laughter and there he was falling in love with all over again. He smiled until his face hurt and the wolves began their howling again.

This sobered them both.

"Here, just like always," he said taking her hand to a nearby spruce. "Picture the unicorn in your mind and just call her."

She began and then flushed. "Maybe you should step further back. You are sort of distracting me."

He had felt it as well. Their heartbeats had immediately synced or rather had entwined and it felt *wrong* when he broke contact and stepped back. The king backed away until he was on the edge of the glade and even that felt too close. He backed until his elbow brushed against a run of white.

The unicorn was right beside him. It was larger than he had expected. In his mind he had pictured a dainty mare, but this was larger than a warhorse and its horn wasn't some pretty accessory. It was golden and long and deadly sharp.

Ella smiled at it and the fairies came to sit on its back like a row of magpies on a fence. They chittered and chattered and couldn't wait to ride.

"You are so beautiful," Ella said as she came forward to gently stroke the muzzle. The unicorn leaned in to her and she hugged its great neck. "Thank you," she said to Eireden.

"She is no gift," Eireden said coming back into the glade. "Ask her to bear you to Rhyoeven. She is the only thing fast enough to get you there before Darhmael's army."

"And I ask again, what about you? How will you get back?"

Eireden gave a glance to the stallion. The poor beast was somewhere between falling in love with the unicorn and dying of a stroke.

"No way," Ella said, laughing in that sparkling way of hers. "Leave him to recover. Come ride with us...that is if you are pure?"

This wasn't a question one asked of men either and when he paused she raised an eyebrow. Oh, there had been many opportunities for Eireden, even in a society as straight as the Den were. Yet as Crown Prince every *opportunity* meant so much more; each being equal to a wedding proposal.

"With your permission," Eireden said to the unicorn. Turning that frightful horn away was permission enough and as lightly as he could he hefted his big frame up. Ella leapt up easily and sat before him.

He took a handful of pure white mane, yet did not dare to set heel to the magnificent beast. Though it wasn't necessary. Just as the howling grew in tempo and the first of the wolves raced into the glade, the unicorn shot forward.

Ella screamed her delight and slid backwards into Eireden's arms, while the wolves growled and nipped close. The king was surprised how near the unicorn allowed the seeming endless pack to get. The grey flood charged all through the forest around them, still the wolves were always too slow.

And then the unicorn snorted in equine laughter and kicked dirt over the leading wolves. Ella laughed along and said, "She toys with them! See how she draws them from the stallion."

It was true. The Den mount was slowly making his way south, alone and unhurt, while the dozens of wolves were all fixated on the fleeing trio. The unicorn allowed them to stay near for a few miles and then she showed what true speed was.

Beneath them the Hidden Lands seemed to flatten and spread as the unicorn's stride lengthened and lengthened until it felt as though they rode a cheetah and not a horse at all.

Ella couldn't stop smiling in joy. "I love this! I care not what is to come because I am in love with right now."

"As am I," he replied.

This only made her laugh again. "You ride a unicorn and that is all you have to say? As am I?"

He had so much more that he would've liked to say, however he was tongue-tied at how close she was, how he could breathe her in and smell her hair as it laid across his chest. Her beauty was intoxicating and he didn't trust himself to speak without stumbling over his words. More than all of that he could feel once more her heartbeat through her hand as she held him for support.

He wasn't unmindful of his situation. He knew his danger and the danger to his city and his people, but like her, he was in love with the now, and when she said, over the wind generated by the flashing unicorn, "I really like your armor. Is it new?" He thought his heart would burst.

Chapter 29

Ella

Nothing in Ella's life could compare to that ride. The unicorn's stride was so smooth it felt as though she were flying instead of running and she had to laugh at herself when she remembered the afternoon she spent chasing after the unicorn.

What a fool she had been—but a happy fool.

There was so much to the Hidden Lands that made her happy. In fact there was only a little that didn't. In its way it was the opposite of life in America. There, the world had an undercurrent of unhappiness and a person had to search for joy.

In the Hidden Lands there was a rhythm to life that allowed contentment and joy in an easy way. Apart from all the monsters and goblins and such, one had to search for problems, or if one was Ella Belmont she only had to be born to have problems.

"It is, what it is and it isn't what it isn't," she murmured to herself, thinking about the gnome. Now that was going to a big problem, she figured, only it was going to be a problem that would have to be dwelt on later for at that moment the unicorn leapt across a river-gorge and the sensation of flying became fact.

It landed on the far side with room to spare and its step was so light it might have just leapt a brook rather than a river. Ella laughed and glanced at Whip-wip expecting to see the fairy smiling if not laughing along, however she wore only a pinched look and stared up into the sky.

Dark clouds hung over the world to the west and the unicorn was drawing ever nearer.

"Now you are too swift," Ella said to her. "I would rather linger in my happiness than race to the sadness that awaits before me."

"I was just thinking the same thing," Eireden said. "If I had my way this ride would never end."

His hand had tightened around her midsection when the unicorn had leapt the river-gorge, now she felt it hot through her clothes. "Yeah, that's what I was just thinking, or saying or, uh…" she said breathing heavy and trying to pretend that hand meant nothing. To change the subject she added, "Maybe, since we are so close, we should send Whip-wip to scout ahead."

The fairy blanched at the idea.

"You know not what you ask of her," Eireden said. "Darhmael has bred some strange beast to destroy the fairies; probably out of revenge for what happened at Hildeoven. Poor Whip-wip only just made it through to the capital."

"Then stay my friend," Ella said touching the fairy's wing. "We have our sturdy unicorn and none can catch her."

"Do not be so sure." Eireden pointed up at the mass of clouds—a portion of which broke off and came screaming down at them. With her sharp eyes, Ella saw that the cloud was made up of thousands of dreadful bat-like creatures with nasty stinging barbed tails.

"Fly unicorn!" Ella screamed, ducking down as low as she could go. They had reached the wide fields of wheat that lay just to the east of the capital and so the unicorn raced as never before, yet it could not the match the speed of the bat creatures.

"Use fire," Eireden ordered just as the first of the bats came up and landed on the unicorn's rear stabbing it with its spiked tail. The king slapped it away and then drew Darhrorn's elf sword that had been strapped to his back. It was smaller and more nimble than the black sword. With it he skewered and slashed at the flapping creatures.

"I don't know how to do a…" Ella began.

Eireden interrupted, "You do! Your thoughts create your magic. Focus on fire. Think about flames and force it out of you."

She tried. She did just as he asked, but she was tired and barely recovered from her earlier torture and battle, while the world swirled with filthy bodied and cries of fear from the fairies.

Ella lifted her hand thinking heat and fire, but the air only shimmied and the bats shied away.

"That was really a great try," Eireden said to uplift her. Above, the bats formed again into a great pinwheeling ball.

"I can't," Ella cried. "I'm too weak."

"You aren't! Ella, you are descended from the golden elves of old. Try! Here they come again." He slashed with the sword and then the bats were all around them and the Unicorn let out a shriek that wasn't in anyway horse-like, and then it began bucking as it was stung over and over again.

Ella didn't try. So angered that the proud unicorn was being hurt on her account she let loose with her mind and the air erupted in flames broiling the sky. The bats let out a high keening of agony as their wings shriveled and burned away. The air went black with burning bodies and poisoned smoke so that Ella reeled and only Eireden's steady hand held her in place.

"Whip-wip, take the others and go," she heard him order. It sounded as though he were far away. "It'll be alright, they are after me. Go! Try to get back." She felt them speed away—even Whip-wip, which left her sad.

Try? Ella had swooned from the poison and her effort, now she squeezed her eyes shut for a moment then opened them blinking. "Oh," she said, understanding what he meant by *try*. She had killed many of the bats, but there were still so many, far too many. They had gone in all directions at her attack, now they were flocking again for another assault.

"Save your energy," Eireden said. "I will keep them off you as long as possible, but you need to swear that you'll save your energy. The capital is near. Look. There are the battlements. Now go and don't look back."

He did not wait. The king slid off the back of the unicorn. Ella tried to grab him. She was still light headed and couldn't follow his line of thinking. What good would it do her to get to safety if he were to die? Where would she be without him?

Even as these thoughts trickled in, he stood beneath the swirling bats and roared out his battle cry. The beasts dove at him and in seconds they had covered him.

"No!" Ella screamed. Up to this point, Ella had ridden at the pleasure of the unicorn, now she was the rider. Without bridle or bit, or stirrup or spur, she yanked the unicorn around and sent him sprinting back.

Where was the king? In the great mass of bodies she couldn't see. But did it matter? Ella pictured the flames and the heat and now the flame she produced was greater than before and the smell and choking smoke even worse.

The unicorn saved her from fainting again. She kicked back against Ella's command and refused to enter the black cloud that Ella had caused. From its swirling mass, bats screamed and spun in odd circles and the king could be seen staggering about. Unceremoniously, the unicorn reared and dumped Ella in the wheat just on the edge of the battle plain.

The girl struggled to find her feet, while the unicorn went to Eireden and lead him out. The king lacked the strength to climb upon the unicorn. He was bleeding from a thousand wounds and he was blind, his eyes punctured and running blood and other fluids.

Ella ran to him and tried to heal him, but she had nothing left.

"Be okay," he mumbled. "Go…go…"

He wanted to fall to the ground and give up, but Ella wouldn't let him. She wouldn't leave him despite her dread and fear, and despite the cloud of bats converging overhead. The brave unicorn wouldn't leave his side either. She walked on with her head hung low so that the king could hold onto her horn and use it to steady himself.

"Are they coming?" he asked. Above the bats were keening louder preparing to attack a third time. There were probably only a thousand or so left but that was more than enough to finish them off.

It was her turn to give false reassurance. "It'll be ok," she said. "I can see the lower gates are opening. Your knights are coming." She wasn't lying. The gates came open and out poured a rush of men in mail—they were two miles away…a six minute ride. The nights would never make it in time.

"Faster," Ella urged and the king tried despite he was leaving a horrible trail of blood. And then the bats came screaming down, stabbing everything that moved. The unicorn reared and kicked and then went down, under a mass of the bats. It tried to roll to crush those upon its back and those indeed died, but the move left the unicorn's soft belly exposed and the bats swarmed it.

Ella could only barely see this. When the unicorn rolled, it knocked her to the ground and Eireden threw himself over the top of her. It was horrible to hear the creatures digging with their spikes to get between his armor. He groaned in pain, but refused to leave her.

And then her world went black as the bats shut out the light. She could feel the horseman racing, and further away goblins running, while closer the unicorn thrashed and kicked and in the air was an angry, fierce buzz that grew and grew and then there was an explosion of light and sound.

The fairies had attacked.

The bat creatures were blind and used sound to track their enemies, but the fairies came screaming in with battle cries of their own, filling the air with such a cacophony that the echoes were useless. Now the bats were truly blind, but they still had the upper hand in size and they had their nasty stingers while the fairies really only had their filaments.

These were used as only fairies could. Coming in pairs, with the filaments strung like tiny steel cables between them. They would find their targets and slash through the air, shearing away the soft wings of the bats or wrapping their opponents so that they would fall to the ground squirming.

The fairies had the upper hand and soon they were hunting their hated enemies from the sky.

And then the knights were there stamping on any of the bats that still moved, while scouts and fey came to the aid of the fallen.

Alseya was there first, but she did not heal either Ella or the king. She only stared with her odd opal eyes. And then there was Aric and he too did not heal Ella, though she bled from scores of wounds. He healed the king and it was left to a young fey with eyes of shining topaz and a smile that dipped at the corner.

"Why are you so sad?" Ella asked her when she could breath normally again.

"Eenaya was a long friend."

"Who?" Ella asked, wondering if a fairy had died in the battle. The fey pointed with her chin to a strange mass of white and red. It took a moment for Ella to realize it was the unicorn. The poor thing lay on her side, unmoving and her fine white coat was rent and bloody. "No!" Ella said, springing to her feet as if she had just woke from a nap.

She grabbed the first fey within reach and demanded, "Heal her!"

It was Aric and he shied back. "Please do not touch me," he said.

In a rage she threw him down. "What's wrong with you! Look beyond your weak will and see that others need you…she needs you."

Alseya came to her. "Your eyes are deceived by your grief. The fair 'corn is dead. She is beyond us now."

The world is always spinning whether we feel it or not and just then Ella felt it in full and she toppled over.

Chapter 30

Eireden

Furen looked at the king with beady black eyes, and in those eyes was judgment and disappointment. "Look at what you've done."

"What?" Eireden asked, staring down at himself. He was bloody and disheveled worse than he could remember.

"If I had known that you were so lackadaisical with your belongings I might not have bothered. Look at that armor! That was months of work. Yes dwarven armor is the best but you just can't stand there getting struck and think it will save you. Really, do you have any inkling what defense consists of? Bah! Take it off and I'll have it fixed, but this is the last time."

"Your pardon, my good dwarf," Eireden said as he began unbuckling the straps. "You could help, you know. We don't have much time."

"Aric must have missed something when he healed you. Did you not see Darhmael's army? Did you not see the hundred thousand goblins that almost caught you napping outside the walls? We have a lot more time than you think."

Eireden shrugged off the breastplate and sighed. Though he had been healed, the armor had been rent in so many places that it still dug into him with every breath.

"And you just toss it on the floor!" Furen cried, picking the armor up and inspecting it. "After this council of war, I'm going to have a talk with your mother."

"Why don't you go talk with her now," Eireden suggested, ushering out the dwarf before sagging against the door. He then went and showered, standing long beneath the hot water. He should have been thinking about a way to find and neutralize the nuclear bomb or a plan to defeat the horde of goblins outside his gates.

Instead he dwelled on Alseya and Ella. Honor and happiness. Right and wrong. He came out of the shower more confused than when he went in.

"For one in so desperate a hurry, you sure do linger long in the shower," Alseya said, making the king jump. He had barely gotten a towel around himself before she spoke.

"Uh…milady…you, uh are here," he stammered out the obvious.

"Yes. I wanted to congratulate you in person on your victory, and also to offer my condolences that you were not able to achieve your goal of an early death."

"You know not what you say," Eireden growled.

Alseya waved a hand, dismissing both his words and anger. "You fool no one. As a *gada* you threw yourself around recklessly, hoping for death. And that has not changed. It is well known that you prefer death before dishonor."

"And what of you? Who are you fooling? I know you've been scheming to keep Ella around and now I know why. Are you offering her as a consolation prize? Do you understand how offensive that is, to her and to me?"

"I want you to be happy," Alseya said. "And I want Ella to be happy. You two could be happy together if only fate would allow, but…that is not meant to be. The fey need you."

"I can't kill you," Eireden said, softening.

A tear came to her eye. "Do you think I want to die? I don't. I really don't. When I stood on that battlement and I saw you two riding Eenaya, I felt that sting of jealousy once more. I've never ridden a unicorn, or seen the ocean, or loved a man." She reached out for him and he took her hands before she could touch him.

"Stop," he asked. "This isn't love. This is murder. Really, even if I wanted to be a party to this I couldn't do it, physically. I close my eyes and I picture you dead…I couldn't if you understand me."

"In that you are wrong," Alseya said and came forward so that she was an inch a way and he could he feel her warm breath on his neck. "I may not be experienced but I know the power of my sex."

Her power was undeniable and he choked out, "Perhaps you are right."

"I am right," she said confidently. "And I am right that the fey need a champion and that you will be that man. Do not be late for your own council." She walked out of his apartments then and he sagged once more.

Yet only for a second. Furen came stumping in again. "I can't understand your mother. First she belittled my ire and then she flew to the opposite extreme. Does being *grounded* mean the same as being stoned? She said she would ground you. I thought it a bit much, but I tell you a good stoning will ensure you learn your lesson and that is…"

He paused looking the king in his towel up and down. "Why aren't you dressed? Wait! Wasn't that Alseya who just left…you dog! I thought you weren't going to marry her?"

"I'm not," Eireden said. Furen's little eyes went as wide as they could. "No, don't give me that look.

Nothing happened. Just like you, she just came strolling in here. Now if you'll excuse, I do have to get dressed for my own damned council of war!"

After escorting Furen out, Eireden went to his wardrobe and stared. Most of his attire represented his station as king: shining steel armor, or dress clothes of dark blue with short cloaks with silver epaulettes at the shoulders. In the furthest corner sat a tired looking suit of leather armor and a stained green cloak—his outfit he had worn as a *gada*.

Hurriedly, he threw on the leathers, but made the ensemble confusing by buckling the black sword to his hip.

People stared as he strode the halls, and his men-at-arms gawked as he passed them entering the throne room, and his captains went stock still, uncertain what was happening. They knew of his promise and of his threat not to carry through with it, but no one had expected this, and no one knew what it meant.

Not even the king.

He was announced by a bug-eyed steward and the assembled captains and lord and ladies of the three races—four if you counted the fairies, the largest contingent—stood respectfully while he came in, though not the fairies of course.

Despite the stares and the worried looks worn by Alseya and Ilenwyth Eden, and the disappointed look that Furen had—it was his opinion that leather armor belonged only on warrior squirrels and not men—it was the sight of the throne that made Eireden reconsider his choice of clothes. It was expected he would sit there, but he never would in that outfit.

"Please sit," he said coming up to dais and stopping on its lowest step. "I asked for this council because our impending doom is worse than we had thought. We've all been worried what Darhmael's next move would be and now we know. Ella?"

"Huh? Me?" Ella sat off by herself, with only Whip-wip for company. "I mean, yes, Milord?"

"Could you explain what exactly a nuclear bomb is," Eireden said. "I'm very sketchy on the details and I want those gathered to have as clear a notion as possible."

Ella stood, entwining her fingers, looking vulnerable and breathtakingly beautiful. "First, I should explain what a bomb is. It's a destructive device that humans use in their wars. A bomb could destroy this palace and every one in it."

Murmurs greeted this. Furen stood, though, coming off his chair as he did, it was hard to tell. "Is it magic? If so, when did the humans grow more powerful than the elves?"

"It's not magic. It's science. A bomb uses chemicals that when set off expand so fast and so violently that it makes an explosion. I've heard that miners hit pockets of natural gas, which can explode. It's like that."

Furen nodded, understanding. "She speaks the truth. We call them Hathyuol spaces, and in order to neutralize their effects we drill, not only perpendicular slag holes, but also diagonal venting lines. This of course depends on the mineral…"

"Furen," Eireden interrupted. "Can I ask that you save the lecture for later? The point is the humans have managed to harness the power of these sorts of explosions."

Ella nodded. "Exactly, but a nuclear bomb is different and much worse than a normal bomb. You don't need to know the science of it, but you have to know that I do not exaggerate when I say only one of these could vaporize this city in an instant."

"And Darhmael has managed to attain one?" Aric asked.

"Yes," Ella stated evenly. "I saw it myself. When I left the Hidden Lands I came across a gnome and curious as to why one was in the Forbidden Lands I went to investigate. He was exceedingly wily and managed to trap me for more a day in some sort of trance where I couldn't move. When I took up the trail again, I followed him to a military facility and learned that he had taken one of these bombs."

Lienhart stood and waited to be recognized before asking, "Do the Americans have many of these bombs?"

Ella nodded. "Yes. Thousands." This had them whispering again.

"The humans have become very powerful," Eireden said, quieting his council. "Clearly too powerful for us to ignore any longer."

"Any longer?" Alseya asked. Her sharp look was enough for Eireden to know that trouble was brewing. "How long have the Den known of this danger and why have they failed to inform the other races?"

"A few years," he answered, evasively. "A blink of an eye for one such as yourself. As for our dwarven friends they weren't in much danger. Nuclear bombs are not very effective beneath the earth."

"I see," Alseya replied. "The Den can decide for the rest of us what is dangerous and what is not."

Eireden shot her a look and said, "The humans do not know we even exist so the danger is negligible. What is incontrovertible is that Darhmael has armed himself with one and has managed to trap all of his enemies in one place."

"How long do we have," Alseya asked. "And is there a counter-force to this bomb? Can it be destroyed?"

Everyone looked to Ella and she gave a shrug. "I'm not sure you can destroy a nuclear bomb…or at least I wouldn't be able to. You can neutralize it by separating its parts. There's a trigger mechanism that is attached by wires and I think if you yanked them all out it won't explode. I did that before the gnome got away, but he's pretty smart. My guess is that he'll have it working soon. Maybe by tomorrow or the next day, but not much longer than that."

"Well we can't stay here," Lienhart said. "We should offer battle with the idea of dispersing so as to minimize the effect of this bomb."

"Dispersing?" Alseya asked. "Where would you have the fey go? The Den can run away to the Americas and the dwarves can go back to their kingdom and shut their doors, but what of us?"

No one had an answer and all eyes went to the king. "The fey have their powers. Why do you always…" he paused and took a deep breath. "I'm sorry, now is not the time. Dispersing would only lead to a massacre. Darhmael's army is too big and too disciplined. He could contain our army with a third of his goblins and still have plenty left to butcher our women and children. He could then destroy the remainder of us at his leisure with this bomb."

Prince Sylra of Wesgard stood to agree, "Or run us down if we try to flee. His maug race like they are being whipped."

"Perhaps we could destroy the bomb before it got to the city," Lienhart said. "We could have fey covered in illusion among the goblins…"

"Excuse me," Alseya said. "The fey are not yours to command. I believe we had this discussion some months ago and I believe we came to an agreement and I believe that agreement has since been revoked."

Prince Sylra glared. "You act as though your duplicity should be ignored. Had the king known you were going to die I am sure he would never have accepted."

Everyone looked to Eireden to answer, but before he could, Alseya said, "That is a baseless argument. We did not agree to this marriage with the idea that both parties would live long and happy lives. How many times has your king put his life on the line without once consulting me or discussing how it would affect our agreement? The answer is zero times. He would give his life for his people as would I."

Ella stood and placed both hands on her hips. "And he risked his life for your people as well. I suppose I don't understand all of this. The Den have always been your protectors, why would you think that would change?"

"It already has," Alseya answered. "Did you not here their plan? Disperse and hide. How does that protect us? The fey would be hunted down and killed one after another. And if we band together? A nuclear bomb explodes us."

Ella dropped her eyes and Alseya went on, "And as for protectors? The truth is that they have been our jailors. And now that the jail has been destroyed, we are their servants not their equals. Did you hear the prince *ask* if we would go down into the camp?"

"We all make sacrifices," Eireden said. "And I don't think any Den looks down upon the fey."

"You do," Alseya retorted. "Look how you dismissed this marriage out of hand. Where was our discussion? Where was the reasoned debate? You used the power of your kingship and threw away a clear promise. How do I know there won't be more promises broken?"

"He wouldn't do that," Ella said.

"He already has!" Alseya stormed. "He is the king of kings. The most revered of you all and he broke his word like that." She snapped her fingers and it was like a branch breaking in the quiet courtroom.

"You could choose from among you to be king," Ella said in a whisper.

Alseya's shoulder's drooped. "We have discussed this. None would presume to put themselves forward."

"Then I will choose for you," Ella said and heads perked up at her temerity. Interestingly the fey did not tell her she couldn't. It wasn't their way. "I choose Aric Anorian."

Struck with a sour feeling of déjà vu, Eireden's brow came down; she had said those exact words in the Forest of Mists.

She went on, "I may have had my differences with him, but he cares for his people more than any. And he is strong and wise."

The fey looked around at each other and none would say no. If Aric wouldn't as well, he would be king. He shook his head so that his gold-blonde hair swayed. "Thank you, Ella, but I cannot accept for the very reason that I hurt you so. I am not as strong as I could have wished and my arrogance blinded me. A king has to able to rule others, which means on some level he must think of himself as above another. I cannot be trusted with this simple concept."

"This is all crazy talk," Furen said, stamping his foot. "Darhmael is out there with a bomb and we sit in here and argue moot points."

"My dear dwarf," Alseya said. "These are not moot points. The fey have come to agree with me that if we are not to be treated as equals then we have no place among the Den. We had planned to leave and find our own way in the world but with this notion of a bomb, we will likely journey to the next life together instead."

"Suicide?" Furen asked, appalled. She nodded pleasantly.

This caused quite a ripple and Eireden felt his stomach drop as all eyes went to him. They bored into him and each asked: *Are you going to let three-thousand fey kill themselves just because you are stubborn*? The answer was easy, no. He would have to find a way to deal with Alseya's death. He was just about to tell Alseya that he would marry her when Furen spoke again.

"If Aric says he is too weak, then you should choose Ella to be the leader of the fey. She's the strongest of you."

Again the fey did not countermand this idea, and everyone looked to Ella. Her cheeks went pink, a rather un-feyish sign. "I don't think so," she said. "I'm not actually a fey. I'm an elf."

"No…no. You are a fey," Ilenwyth said. There were quick calculations going on behind her eyes. "What makes a fey, a fey and an elf, an elf? Only goodness separates them, and you my darling are as pure and innocent a creature as I've ever met."

Suddenly the fey were looking on her with new interest. Aric spoke, "I told you that you were the first good elf in two-hundred centuries."

"And did you not tame the unicorn?" Lienhart put in. "No evil elf could do that, though a fey could."

"And I have always counted you as my sister," Alseya said, looking closely at Ella as if to find the tiniest fault in her. "And my queen if that is what you would choose."

"But I can't be queen," Ella stammered. "I don't know anything about laws, or ruling, or battles or any of that."

Furen laughed. "You don't need to know anything about battles. You leave that to your king." He looked pointedly at the King of the Den.

"What?" Eireden said as his jaw dropped open. He looked at Ella and saw that the pink of her cheeks had risen. His own felt hot. They locked eyes with the very same expression, and he could read on her face the identical question that was running through his mind: *what was happening here?*

"And your child won't kill you," Alseya added. "You are already half human so you'll be perfectly safe when he's born."

"My child?" Ella said in little over a whisper. Now her blue eyes were giant in her face. "I'm going to have a child?"

"Of course you are, my dear," Ilenwyth E-Den, mother of the king said. "And with this bomb coming. You better get cracking."

Chapter 31

Ella

"Excuse us," Eireden said coming right for Ella. She just looked at him as if her brain had come disconnected from the rest of her. It sure felt that way—her fingers felt a mile away from her body. The king pulled her into a small chamber and shut the door and then they went right back to staring at each other.

"What just happened?" Ella asked a minute later.

He started to shrug and shake his head, and one of his hands came out to touch her, but she was a dozen feet away and his feet hadn't moved. "I think you're the new queen of the fey."

"And we're engaged," she added.

Now Eireden nodded quickly, as if understanding had hit. "And you're pregnant…no. You're going to be pregnant before the bomb hits."

"Did we ever figure out the bomb thing?" Ella asked, thinking she had missed a whole lot of the conversation to go from a girl in jeans to queen of the fey in the space of a minute.

"I don't think so," Eireden replied. "So…"

His smile was crooked and his cheeks were ablaze. She suddenly had a thought, which made her step back from him and cross her arms over her chest. "Are we supposed to be…you know…right now. Is that what they expect?"

"No! Uh-uh. No I just wanted to…not be around all of them. I felt like some sort of prize bull out there with everyone staring. I just wanted to talk. To see what you thought about all of this."

Her heart slowed way down at his explanation. "I don't know what to think. I don't even know how I feel, not like a queen that's for sure. I would have to say I feel weird."

"I feel relieved because of the whole oath versus dead wife situation," Eireden said. "That wasn't going to end well. But maybe it all won't end well."

"The bomb?"

"Yes," he said and then sighed. "I can't think of that right now. One thing at a time. So…"

"So."

The silence was thick and strained, right up until she started giggling. Soon she was rolling on the floor. Gasping, "This is crazy! Me? A queen?"

"Just to let you know, you don't look much like a queen at the moment. Not on the floor like that with that fluff in your hair." He knelt down beside her and plucked a downy feather from her dark auburn hair. She grabbed his hand and held it to her cheek, sobering quickly.

Again they were connected—their hearts taking up an easy cadence together. It was her turn to sigh. "You don't love me. I know you think you do, but it's only the rhythms my father put into me. Though I guess it doesn't matter. We have to do this. All those fey; they won't die because of me."

"Right…I get it about the fey. I just don't understand about why I don't love you. You have to explain that to me because it certainly feels like love to me."

"I told you already," she said, getting up and running her fingers through her hair to check for extra fluff. "My father made it so everyone who meets me will fall for me. It sounds great in theory, but here I am with you." She paused to look at his raven hair and rugged scarred chin, and his piercing, stern eyes. "And you only love me because of some sort of magic is making you."

"That does sound bad," the king said with a little smile on the edge of his lip. "Maybe we could get some counter-magic going. What would you think then?"

"About?"

"What would you think if I still loved you?"

Her forehead crinkled. "But you can't…"

"Just answer the question," he said interrupting, stepping closer.

"Then I'd be happy."

"Why?"

"Because…" she was slow to answer. The truth was that every time she was close to him she felt warm right down to her toes and she didn't want to be any-where else. But since there was always someone or something to keep them apart, that feeling was a source of aggravation for her, which made her want to push him away. "Because then we could maybe love each other," she said, finishing her thought.

Now a slow smile spread over his face. "Maybe we could, but unfortunately Furen will get in the way. He's my friend but he loves you, right? He's madly deeply in love with you."

"Why do you mock me? Furen may love me, but not in that sort of way."

Eireden shrugged. "What about Prince Lienhart? He must love you as much as I, but…but he was going to ask Lady Theris to marry him? How can that be if he's in love with you? Maybe he's so in love with you that he can't even think straight."

"What are you getting at?" she asked growing cross.

He laughed and pointed at a spot between her eyes. "I love it when you get all mad. You get three little lines tight there."

She made to wave his hand away but he took her little hand in his huge one. "Didn't you have a point to all your nattering," she said, trying to glare but the cross feeling had already left her.

"Yes I do," he reassured. "If Darhmael has put these rhythms in you they are subtle and relatively weak. Anyone with even a little will power can withstand them or you would have hordes of men battling for your affection."

That was true. Ella blinked a few times thinking: was the impossible so close?

He went on, staring into her eyes, "And you completely discount the idea that someone could love you for who you are. Couldn't it be that even without those rhythms I could love you?"

"I don't know," Ella said in a whisper. "I'm not a lady like Theris or Alseya. Sometimes I don't know what to do when everyone else does. I mean sometimes I feel very American and we don't do royalty. It's sort of ingrained in us to rebel against it."

"Does that matter?" he asked. "I love you for who you are. I remember the first time we met. I felt those rhythms and they made me very curious, but that was all they did. They did not direct my thoughts or my actions. What did was you."

"But Darhmael made me," Ella said breaking away. "All of me. He built me like some sort of robot."

Eireden shrugged. "He did a fine job of it too. You are sweet and kind, and beautiful and lovely. You are talented and powerful yet also compassionate to those in need. You are everything I want and truth be told I should be thanking Darhmael."

"But…" Ella said dropping her eyes, searching her mind for a reason that she shouldn't be happy.

"Yes," Eireden agreed. "There is a *but* in all of this." Her eyes came up quick and she felt a flash of dread in her soul. What did he know? What would ruin all of this for her? "You could marry me for the sake of the fey," he said, touching her face and then sliding his hand behind her neck beneath her hair and pulling her close. "But I'd rather you married me because you love me."

With their bodies pressed together their hearts beat as one and that beat began to pick up in tempo. "I do love you," she said.

He wanted to kiss her, she could tell, however he couldn't stop smiling and so only their noses touched for a span of seconds. Then he kissed her the way a man does when he's in love, hungrily, passionately and she felt the world drifting away beneath her feet and the walls of the room became as nothing to her.

There was only him. They kissed for a long time, uncaring of the world or the coming danger. That could all wait. For now Ella was happy.

Unfortunately the kiss had to end eventually, though neither really wanted it to. He pulled back taking a big shaking breath. "We should tell everyone… wait! I forgot to even ask. Will you marry me? No, wait! I have to do this properly." He went to one knee before her and said, "Eleanor Belmont, Queen of the Fey and ruler of my heart, will you marry me?"

"Yes. Of course I will."

He was up in a flash and they kissed again until he felt a tear on his cheek. "What is it?" he asked looking on her in concern. "What is wrong?"

"Nothing! I'm happy. I'm so happy I could burst. These are tears of joy silly." She could barely breathe she was so happy.

"Of joy? How strange. Is that a symptom of being American?"

"No," she said, punching him in the chest. He was so large that he didn't budge. "It's a symptom of being a girl…but really, am I still a girl? All my life I've felt like a girl, like I was waiting to grow up and find out who I would be and now…now I am a queen. Oh,

Eireden I can't do this! I don't know the first thing about being a queen."

"Then let me help," Eireden said. "The very first thing you need to know is that you are nothing special. You are no better than any one of us."

"I know!" Ella cried, breaking in. "That's why I can't do this."

Eireden shook his head. "You can. Just remember being queen is not about the fancy clothes or the big palaces or the people bowing or kissing your hand. It's about being humble. That's the most important lesson you can learn. Never be fooled into thinking that people bow to you as a person, because they don't. They bow to the position you hold."

"I can be humble," Ella said, grasping at the first idea. "That I can do. In fact, I'm all about being humble…but maybe I'll be too humble. Will that be bad? Oh gosh, I'm sure I'll be so humble that I won't be able to tell anyone to do anything. What kind of queen is that?"

Her breathing started to quicken and he saw the panic building behind her eyes.

"Calm yourself, my love. We all have these doubts. Everyone who has ever worn a crown fears that the title of king or queen is too much for them. That too much is expected; that they will fail to live up to expectations. When that happens keep in mind that if you respect the office you hold, others will respect it as well."

Ella nodded, though the panic was still there, like a butterfly in her chest that could explode with the force of a bomb at any second. "Respect the office and be humble. Got it."

"And remember that I chose you for my queen," Eireden said. "I see in you every quality that I could ever want. So be yourself and the people will love you." He began to lead her to the door and though she dragged her feet his strength was such that he didn't even seem to notice. "You'll need to make it official. I will announce you."

"And what do I do?"

He smiled as confident as ever. "Be yourself," he said before opening the door. "May I present Eleanor Belmont, Queen of the Fey, and soon to be Queen of the Den as well."

He thrust her out and she stared at thirty people—Den, fey and dwarves—all of whom looked suddenly like strangers in her eyes. It seemed to her that they gazed down their noses with sharp judging looks.

She thought she would freeze in that doorway, unable to either go forward because of the strangers or back, because Eireden was right there holding her arm in a gentle grip of iron. However that was when the fairies came to her singing and chirping and whistling in such mish-mash that she had to blink at all the sound and commotion.

Some were congratulating her, while others were complaining about being bored, while the remainder, and this included Whip-wip, were hungry and were asking about zooti.

All of this took her mind off of her fears and so when the first stranger came up, Ella was able to give a real smile. It was Alseya, looking young and beautiful, more so that ever Ella could remember. The slight fey went into a curtsy.

"Your highness," Alseya said. "I am your humble servant."

Just like that Ella froze again not knowing what was right in regard to protocol—surely she didn't put her hand out for a woman to kiss, but what was correct? Her eye caught Ilenwyth's and the old queen of the Den dipped her head and closed her eyes for a split second.

Ella did just as Ilenwyth, and said, "Come, rise. I don't think I can stand too much formality with one who would be as a sister to me." Eireden gave her the tiniest wink letting her know she was doing well.

Each of the people in the audience chamber came forth and greeted her in the doorway where she stood. The last to arrive was the former queen, Ilenwyth.

Her curtsey was slight and came with a grimace of age. "It's about time that my intrigues and machinations bore fruit," she said with a smile. "This is ever what I hoped."

"Maybe now you can retire from the business of scheming," Eireden suggested.

The King escorted his mother back to her seat and then paused in front of the dais to glance at the single throne. Ella stood off to the side, not knowing if it was right to go stand with him; she didn't really want to. The Captains had all filed back to their seats and the same grimness that had held sway over the room began to return and she didn't want to be up there in front of them as though she had some special wisdom greater than theirs.

Eireden thought differently and waved her over, back to business of the bomb. "You understand this bomb better than any. Tell me, how close to us does Darhmael need to get it for it to be effective?"

"I don't know," she answered. "There are many different sizes of bombs, though I think we can trust that Darhmael had the gnome get the biggest he could carry."

"Then we need to intercept it before it gets close," Prince Lienhart said. "Now that the fey are officially on our side we should send out picked teams to watch on the road south from the Demorlaik. Currently the siege is loose and by using illusion we could get twenty or thirty men out without too much of an effort."

"I'm afraid it won't do you any good," Ella said. "My guess is that the bomb will come by air. The gnome had a contraption…a helicopter like device that could fly. It makes the most sense. What do we have beside fairies that can fly to stop it?"

"Nothing," Eireden said.

"So what does that leave us?" Lienhart said in a small voice. "We can't fight them on the open plain and expect a victory and we can't stop the bomb from coming. Do we just sit here waiting for our doom?"

"I say we fight," Prince Sylra growled. "The women and children can either fight with us or they can wait behind the walls. But I can't just sit around not doing a thing."

"I'm with the prince," Furen said. "I'm not going to have my dwarves lazing about before they die. What sort of example is that?"

Ella was looking at Furen with drooping depressed eyes but then they shot open. "Your dwarves! We could tunnel out of here. How long would that take if everyone lent a hand?"

Furen closed his little black eyes as he calculated. "I would say not more than a month. We could set up a relay team of…"

Eireden held up a hand. "That's too long, Furen. Even if Ella had managed to destroy the one bomb, there is nothing stopping Darhmael from getting a second," the king said and then began pacing, walking around the dais in a big circle; the room was quiet as everyone considered options.

Finally the king sighed long and wearily. "Our only choices are fighting to satisfy honor or fighting in an effort to gain the freedom of as many of us as possible. If each fey could take at least two children with them, we could save quite a number."

Alseya stood and gave a glance to Ella before asking Eireden, "If you were Darhmael would you expect just that?"

"Yes."

"And what would you be able to stop it?"

"Yes," Eireden said with his head down. "But shouldn't we still try?"

"And face useless pain and agony?" Alseya asked. "No we shouldn't. If the Den and the dwarves wish to fight for honor let them. But should the fey?" This was directed toward Ella.

"So much for this being a ceremonial position," Ella said with a little smile. "I would say that if a battle is to be fought for the sake of honor and without any other objectives then the Den and the dwarves should not expect assistance beyond the healing of the sur-vivors."

Eireden gave her a sharp glance that had Furen chuckling. "Your first fight. How sweet. I remember my first fight with Gargefrel. She chased me down into this quick silver mine and I fell into a gorge. Two hundred foot drop into an underground river. I had no idea where I was, especially when Gargefrel sealed up the gorge above me!"

"So how did you get out," Ella asked. She didn't like the way Eireden was glaring at her, so she went to Furen and stood behind him. Protected thus she stuck out her tongue, which had the king smiling once again.

"Oh, don't you worry," Furen said looking back at her and frowning when he saw the tongue. "A dwarf never gets turned around when he's underground."

"Never?" Ella said, her mind chewing on some-thing, an idea that was close to forming. "What about in the Demorlaik? Would you get lost there?"

The room suddenly focused on the dwarf and he gave a shrug, "I suppose not. I would know up from down, and east from west, but if you are asking if I could find Darhmael's citadel at the root of the world —I don't think so. At least not in time. Do you not re-call when I gave you that *brief* summary of dwarvish history? The great Dvardfik Tormin himself searched for it and could not discover it."

Eireden agreed, "There is a great dark world beneath the Demorlaik. A maze of tunnels that no one has ever strode."

The idea came fully to Ella now. "You're wrong. There is someone who has."

Chapter 32

Eireden

The king stared at Ella in wonder. "Are you talking about your mother?"

She nodded. "Yes. She has been to the Demorlaik and beneath. It makes sense that she's been to this citadel."

"But she's in some sort of a state," Eireden said, his initial excitement settling within him. "She can't lead us like that."

"Of course not," Ella said. "But if we were to explore her memories, especially her last memories of the Demorlaik, we could see how she came to the surface."

The fey were all silent and none would look up. This was in direct opposition to the Den and the dwarves who were bristling with excitement at Ella's words.

Eireden noted the quietness of the fey. "What is the issue? Is there danger that we should be aware of?"

He had spoken to the little knot of fey, but none would answer. They turned to Ella and she said, "Memories are tricky and dangerous things to play around with. Whoever volunteers to search Elleni's mind will likely confront horrors that turned my mother the way she is now. It will be a nightmare for both. I will do it if none other will step forward."

The king desperately wanted to tell her she couldn't be the one to do it, for many reasons, but did not. In her gown of light blue she was beautiful and the look on her face was a stern combination of elegance and determination—in short she was a queen.

"I will do it," Aric said. Though pale at the idea he stood and gave his new queen a confident look that blinked to something of a confusion when she denied him.

"Not you, Aric. Your job will be a thousand times worse. You're coming with us into the Demorlaik to confront Darhmael and destroy the bomb. And you as well Alseya. I hope I'm not over-stepping my bounds, but the attempt will take the strongest fey. We will find another to search my mother's mind."

"We will," Eireden said, setting his jaw. "But as to the team that will descend into the Demorlaik, you will not be one of their number."

Her eyes flared. "How is that I've just been made queen and yet I can be ordered about?"

The king glanced around and saw every eye on him. With a quick move he took Ella's arm and guided her away. "Because I love you too much to let you go down into those pits," he said in a hissing whisper. "I've been to the Demorlaik. Its evil is more dreadful than you can know."

"You need me," she insisted. "I am no longer the weak little girl that you had to rescue time and again. I've become powerful in my own right."

Eireden was about to voice new arguments but the sound of a footstep near had them both going silent. "You are powerful, my Dear," Ilenwyth said, stepping close. "Just as I had foreseen. Remember what I told you? A queen should be as powerful if not more so than her king."

"I remember," Ella answered. "And as I was just saying I am strong. I should be allowed to use my strength to help."

"And you will help," Ilenwyth said, calmly. "Your power will be needed to protect your child."

Eireden and Ella exchanged looks. "Her what?" the king asked. Had he missed something?

Ilenwyth's smile turned into a chuckle as she watched their faces. "Yes, your child, my Dear. The king cannot go into the Demorlaik without an heir. He has been far too cavalier already, but if he is to have a wife then he will do his duty and produce an heir."

"But we're leaving soon," Eireden said, feeling like his teenage self. He had to wonder who was more red with embarrassment, Ella or himself. Whip-wip seemed to be seeing the same thing. She touched Ella on the cheek a few times.

"Warm," she said.

"You have tonight," Ilenwyth said. "Exploring the mind of poor Elleni will take some time. Take tonight and be happy."

Ella took a step back. "Tonight? But…I…he…we aren't even married yet."

"Then go on and get married," Ilenwyth said and began to push the two toward the main doors to the throne room. "We will hash out the details and the logistics of what must happen in the Demorlaik. Go on and don't come back without bringing me a grandson."

The fact that Ilenwyth was being neither subtle nor quiet had Furen chuckling and Whip-wip explaining to the other fairies what the commotion was about. Soon they were spinning around singing and dancing as if it was a holiday.

"Thank you. Thanks. Ok, that's enough," Eireden said as the fairies began touching the king and queen for luck. There was such a cloud of them that he grabbed Ella's hand and ran. It took a number of locked doors and some fast sprinting to finally rid themselves of the pesky sythie.

"So a grandson?" Ella asked with a smile as they leaned against a door, breathing heavily from the chase. "Does she have something against granddaughters?"

Eireden put a finger to his lips. The palace had been a quiet place for most of his life, but now with the sudden influx there were people around every corner, or so it seemed. "That's my father's influence," Eireden said. "He seemed to be stuck on the idea of a boy. Personally I don't care. I would be just as happy with a girl."

"A girl…wow, this is really going to happen then?"

"Only if you want it to," Eireden answered hastily.

Ella looked down at the floor and she nodded. "I do…but so fast? It's just…I know there is the bomb to deal with, and the Demorlaik, and Darhmael, and…" she started smiling…"And the goblins, and the ogres." Now she began to laugh and it was half-sad and half-merry.

"We could wait until…"

Ella interrupted turning serious, "No! If there's no tomorrow then we had better make the most of today. Come on. Where do we go to get married?"

Eireden shrugged and spread his arms. "We could get married anywhere. We just need witnesses."

"Then how about on the battle tower? With the sun setting I bet the view would be fantastic."

His smile faltered as he pictured the battle tower. He hadn't been back up there since Generai's death. "I'd rather not. What about at the main gates? It would give the men something to talk about besides the goblins."

She agreed and they hurried through the palace. The rumor of their wedding had spread like wild fire and as they walked they collected hordes of fairies and hundreds of Den and fey and even some curious dwarves who were filthy from digging or training or whatever it was that dwarves did to keep themselves busy. They were always busy. Eireden had never seen one so much as lean.

By the time they reached the gates there was a crush of people around them, which only made the fairies, go crazier still. Above the couple they burned so bright that the sun setting was a forgotten thing.

"Open the gates!" The king called over the din. "We shall let the goblins see what they are missing!"

This brought out a cheer that shook the walls. Beneath it Ella asked, "This is how you get married? Isn't there a ceremony?"

He pulled her in close, meaning to speak into her ear but he kissed her instead and the crowd seemed to like this even more than opening the gates. Eireden laughed. "Each couple decides their own ceremony. All that is needed is a public declaration of love and an announcement of marriage. Everything else is just pageantry."

Ella pointed to the crowd. "This is more like a parade that pageantry, but I love it. And I love you."

The people nearest started pointing and shouted, "She said it!"

"That wasn't it," she yelled back, laughing. "That wasn't official! If you want to hear me tell your king that I love him then you need to quiet down!"

Half the crown quieted but it wasn't until Ella unexpectedly jumped up on a water barrel and waved Eireden over that the rest held onto their tongues.

"See this man you call king?" she cried pointing down at Eireden. This brought on another round of cheers and when they had quieted again she went on, "He is no longer your king! I'm sorry, but he is not. He is not your king because he is mine! He is my king and I love him with all my heart and I defy any of you or any of those goblins to say otherwise. I could search all this world and never find a finer man and I love him. Fate has given him to me and I do love him."

It wasn't at all like a normal ceremony which usually was filled with flowery prose, but there had been no time for either of them to prepare in the least, yet the crowd roared their approval nonetheless and the fairies flew among them enjoying the chaos. Eireden couldn't help but smile at her and she beamed down on him.

When the crowd hushed, the king didn't climb onto the barrel with Ella nor did he jump to a railing where he could have towered over her. Instead he only stood so that she was on a pedestal.

"See this man whom you call king?" he called, pointing to himself. In his leathers he wasn't the dashing figure that he would have cut had he been in his shining armor. "Once I was nothing. Once I was a gada. But somehow, by some miracle this beautiful woman fell in love with this nothing. While at the same time, I fell in love with a woman worthy of being more than a queen. If she will have me as her king I will be that. If she wants me as a stable boy, I'll be that as well. I will be her anything and everything as long as she will have me."

Now he leapt up to stand on the barrel. "Eleanor Belmont, Queen of the Fey, will you have me in marriage eternal?"

Ella smiled and her blue eyes were like glittering diamonds that would have the people talking about for hours to come. "Yes, King of the Den. I will."

The crowd cheered and the sound was a force that smote the two of them as they kissed. They kissed long and the sun set and the fairies grew tired and sank onto the shoulders and hats of the people of Rhyoeven.

"That was nice," she said when they finally broke for air.

One of the soldiers near whispered to a friend on the other side of the now closed gate, "She said it was nice."

"Time to go," Eireden laughed and began to pull her through the crowd, waving to the people he knew and smiling to those he only barely knew.

"Are you going to show me to your stable, stable boy," Ella asked, making sure none could hear.

"I don't know if I'm up for it," he said, stretching and opening the door to the palace for her. "I've had a pretty big day after all. This morning I woke up engaged to one woman, I fought two elves and a horde of bats, rode horses and unicorns back and forth across the kingdom, and ended up getting married to a different woman at the end of the day. And tomorrow I'm scheduled to save the world. I have to say, I'm pretty tired."

"You're not up for it?" she asked raising an eyebrow. "We will see about that."

"What about her?" Eireden asked, flicking his eyes to Whip-wip. The fairy sat upon his broad shoulder and had thoroughly enjoyed all the kissing. She was a sucker for romance.

"Sorry Whip-wip. Tonight you sleep with Furen and this time don't put bumble bees up his nose if he snores."

Chapter 33

Ella

The queen of the fey dreamt of a little boy with thick dark hair and marbled green and blue eyes that looked like the earth from space. He was a happy toddler and he laughed and giggled when the fairies dropped flowers on his face. Ella awoke crying with joy in the pre-dawn light and for a second couldn't place where she was.

Then she realized she lay in the king's bed…in her bed rather, and she was alone. A part of her wanted to find Eireden, but a lazier part wanted to lie there longer. She was deliciously warm both inside and out.

But her tears and the dream were still fresh and so, slipping on her dress from the day before, she padded barefoot, down to the throne room where she knew he would be.

He and his captains were off to the side staring down at a crude map. "Your highness?" she called from a good twenty feet away. She was somewhat embarrassed at her appearance and the fact each of the men had to know what had occurred the night before.

"Ella! Why are you awake? You should be sleeping," Eireden said coming over to her. He was weary from stress and too few hours rest, yet his eyes were bright and warm for her.

"I just wanted to be the first to congratulate you," Ella said. She had to quickly blink back tears that strained at her eyes. "You're going to have a little boy."

He laughed aloud and then kissed her fiercely, but it was brief due to his exuberance. "I can't believe you know so soon. A normal Den woman wouldn't know for weeks."

"Well I am not a normal Den woman am I?" she said, and then glanced toward the map spread on a table. "What's going on?"

"We have to coordinate our break out. If we ride straight out of the front gate I think Darhmael may try to stop us. Come take a look." The map was that of the city and the surrounding battle plain and forests. "We're going to send out riders from all four of the gates. Three groups per gate and all with fey illusions covering them."

"And at the same time," Lienhart said, eyeing Ella's mussed hair with a barely suppressed grin. "We want the fairies to go haywire all over the place. They need to cause as much confusion as they can. If you could coordinate that we would appreciate it."

She nodded. "That won't be a problem. They should listen to me now that I am Mrs. Sun King."

War councils were not usually the place for such talk, but Ella was Ella and she was a breath of fresh air wherever she went.

"Congratulations to you both on your marriage," Lienhart said and went into a bow. All the captains bowed and that was when Ella saw the stern looking countenance of Furen. She had missed him among the tall soldiers of the Den.

He blew out noisily, as well as pointedly.

"What did Whip-wip do?" Ella asked, nervously.

That the captains knew was evident from there snorts and smirks. "That dratted fairy tied my beard to my eyebrows! I woke in such a state you have no idea.

For a moment I thought I was being attacked by a badger."

"I'm so sorry," Ella said, putting her hands out to him. The dwarf would have none of it, especially with the other captains carrying on.

"You two find yourself a new babysitter the next time you two, uh…the next *time* that is," Furen said. He then pretended to be overly interested in the maps.

Eireden thought that this particular council should be a boys only council and he hinted that she should go find Whip-wip and practice some maternal discipline. Instead she found Whip-wip and went to watch the sunrise with her. As she did she rubbed her stomach absently. A tired Ilenwyth found her just as she decided that it was time to have breakfast with her husband—a word she found suddenly strange.

"Good morning Ilenwyth…or should I call you mother?" Ella asked the old woman, who blanched at the word.

"Maybe not today. It is your own mother whom I'd like to speak to you about. My news is not good, I'm afraid."

Ella's eyes went wide. "Is she dead? Was the strain too much?"

"I wish that were the case," Ilenwyth replied, sadly shaking her head. "Your mother is a remarkably strong woman. She is tough like a piece of gristle, and that is what makes this so difficult. She fights us with everything she has. I'm sorry to tell you this but they're going to have to take her with them."

"That's too cruel," Ella said. "Don't you see that she won't understand, she'll think she's being punished."

"We understand better than you. I have glimpsed her memories—I have been to the Demorlaik in her mind and it was a horror beyond description. It is why I have come to ask your permission."

Ella nodded. "On one condition. She is to be killed the moment they find the bomb. I cannot subject her to a second more of pain. If any question this let them know that her death is on my head."

"So be it. You are queen now and none would question you, though in this case none would. All feel for your mother and pity moves them," Ilenwyth answered. She made to turn away and then stopped.

"Yes, you will be a grandmother," Ella said without being asked. "I carry the King's son."

"That's what so many of us find so lovely about you, Ella. The world could be falling down around us, yet you can always bring a smile. Come let's tell Furen. He's been in a black mood for some reason and I'm sure this will cheer him up."

As they went down the many steps, Ella explained Whip-wip's mischief, which had the old lady wheezing in laughter. The news did indeed cheer the dwarf up. They found him eating an immense breakfast with one hand as he used the other to shoo fairies away from his strawberries. "You here that Whip-wip? I'm going to be an uncle and you're going to be an aunt."

"No, me is sythie," the fairy explained to Furen. "No is ant. Ant is small. Whip-wip is big." She puffed herself up with a big breath.

Ella left her to have breakfast with her husband and as she did she dwelled on the word husband. "So what is my last name? Am I Ella Eden? Are you Eireden Eden?"

He smiled over his eggs. "Officially you are Queen Eleanor Eden, however you can asked to be addressed as Queen Ella or even just Ella, but I would reserve that for close friends. I am King Eireden of the Eden line. And our son…what shall his name be?"

"Feyden, like your long ago ancestor," Ella suggested. "Wasn't he the son of Eireden?"

"No. Feireden was the father of Feyden. It is not a bad idea except you are not exactly a fey. Though that doesn't mean you should try to name him Elfden. You might have a riot on your hands."

Ella looked at him close before saying, "On *our* hands is what you meant. You are coming back, do you hear me? In fact you should probably think of a name while you're gone and tell me when you return."

The king shook his head. "A name is too important and a father should have some input."

Despite that their dining room was long and spacious it was filled to capacity and everyone saw the tears spring to her eyes and everyone heard her say, "No. Don't be like that! You have to come back to me. We'll discuss the name then. When you get back."

Eireden reached across the table and grabbed her hands. "You draw me on, Darling. Even from the Demorlaik I'll be able to feel you and I'll…do my best to come back." She began to shake her head and tears came. The king let one run to his finger. "Our son is not even this big and I know his name already."

"Tell me when you get back!" she cried.

He shook his head. "Elleden."

"A fine name, Milord," Lienhart said to the general agreement of the dozen warriors sitting in uncomfortable silence near their tearful queen. "It sounds like the perfect mix of mother and father."

Prince Sylra stood with a mug in his hand. "To Elleden…long live the king."

Long live the king was echoed by everyone save the queen. She sat there with shaking shoulders crying, letting her dark hair hide her face. Her husband, the man who had her heart exploding love; her child's father was leaving and he wasn't coming back.

With a wave of his hand, Eireden cleared the room and when the last chair scraped back and the room was empty he went to his beloved and held her.

"I can't live half a life," she whispered. "I need it all. I need you and the baby."

"What promise can I possibly give that will satisfy both you and my honor?"

There wasn't one of course, which made it all the more frustrating for Ella. "Always it's about your honor! What about your duty as a father and a husband?" Eireden only stared at her, growing tired around the eyes. She grabbed him and clung. "I'm sorry. I know you only do your duty to protect your people and me as well, but this is your fault for marrying an American girl. I can't help that we wear our hearts on our sleeves."

"I'm not asking you to change," he said looking her dead in the eye. "I fell in love with an American girl and when I get back I had better find that same girl."

"You will," she promised.

Just then Ease-see came into the room humming a tune. After plucking a forgotten grape from a plate he went to the king and said, "It time."

"Thank you, Ease-see," the king replied. "Tell them I'll be down as soon as I suit up."

When the fairy left, nibbling on the grape, the king and queen stared at each other for over a minute and neither could put into words everything they wanted and needed to say.

Finally the king stood and after kissing her once again said, "As much as I love my American girl, I think I would like to say farewell to the Queen of the Den at the main gate. It would be better for the men not to see too many tears."

"I understand, my love. I have my own duties to perform and my own honor to uphold. Just know that your American girl will be there beneath it all and she'll be loving you with every beat of her heart."

Chapter 34

Eireden

The king kissed his new bride at the main gate once more and this time only a few fairies made a fuss over it. The rest of the city was in too grave a mood to give a single kiss much thought.

News had spread about the bomb and while some discounted the idea, most looked to their king's actions as guide and the thousand horsemen preparing to rush at the endless horde of maug spoke of desperation and not of confidence.

Though this was not from a lack of trying on Eireden's part. His dwarven armor had been repaired and once again it shone in brilliance and any who looked upon him could not help feel buoyed in spirit.

"I'll be back soon," he told Ella, touching her cheek.

"Pick me up something nice while you're gone?" she replied jokingly with an odd laugh. "Maybe some flowers? Oh, and do something about that silly bomb while you're out."

Despite her bravado, he saw the dread behind her eyes and felt the fear in her touch. "I will, my Queen."

He turned to Whip-wip. "And you my darling fairy. It's time to go cause some chaos. Go!"

This should have been a great excuse for the fairies to go wild, but they understood, in their own primitive manner, the seriousness of the situation. They shot up into the sky with a buzzing of wings, but not a single laugh. They flew as the color of dark sky and the goblins did not know.

"Signal the illusions," Lienhart called.

The fey began their work and all thousand horsemen disappeared, becoming invisible and Eireden felt Ella reach for him with shaking hands. He could see her just fine and he took her hands and kissed them.

"Open the gates," a voice called.

"Goodbye, my love," Eireden said and nudged his horse down the causeway and onto the battle plain. There he waited for the next part of the plan, which was not slow in coming. Down from the four gates, an endless stretch of horses and men came boiling down in a fury. These many thousands swept by Eireden and his little group and charged with a great yelling at the goblins circling the city.

The maug cried out in their own warty, croaking language and prepared to meet the rush, but the attack was illusion only. The images rolled over the maug leaving them bewildered and standing about slack jawed—and that was when the real horsemen attacked. The thousand knights, each with his own fairy in attendance, appeared out of nowhere and plowed into the milling goblins and sent them screaming away in fright.

"Let's go," Eireden said to his small group and they cantered after the horsemen. The attack had made a gaping hole in the lines that would not last. Even as the men hewed about them and killed with great flourish, many more thousands of maug were running to fill the gap. The king's men raced through it, invisible and silent.

"That was not so bad," Lienhart said when they were well past the goblins. Already the horsemen were turning from the mayhem they had caused and were racing back to the safety of the walls to a cheering that was only a small sound with the distance.

"Speak for yourself," a sweating and red faced Furen said. His hands were white-knuckled on his reins while the rest of him was literally tied to his saddle. "This uncouth beast makes me long for the Demorlaik."

"Mark his words," Aric said, flashing a smile. Before him sat Ella's mother. She too was tied in place and as an added precaution she had been gagged. Aric undid the gag and said to his friend, "I'll wager that you'll be missing that mare by this time tomorrow."

"Let's not worry over tomorrow when there is still today to deal with," the king admonished. "Let's button it up and put some miles between us and the goblins."

By twos they rode due north, keeping well away from the one dirt road that ran to the haunted city. Next to Eireden, on her sprightly grey, sat Alseya. She began a soft song that was taken up by the other fey. There were six fey all told, one to compliment each warrior in the group and Eireden hoped the combination of swords and sorcery would allow them to prevail against Darhmael.

Furen rode next to his long friend, Aric. Behind her son went Feylon Darania with Prince Lienhart looking tall, high up on a charger beside her. Prince Sylra came next paired with Aziel a fey known for his strength of mind and a cousin of Alseya's. Captain Rudyid, with his muscles and his dreadful scars, looked like an ogre next to the tiny fey at his side. Yurel was small even by their standards and had a voice like songbird, but was valued for her ability to weave illusions.

Last came the only pair that was mismatched in the opposite manner. Harfel was the only dour fey Eireden had ever met and his night probing Elleni's mind hadn't helped. He was grey and pinched, and his song was harmony only and this came at odd intervals when he bothered to look up.

Next to Harfel was young Tharaden, a distant relative of the king's. Unlike the other warriors, Tharaden did not wear armor and his sword wasn't a great hacking blade, instead it was a thin rapier. From all accounts he was as fast as any fey and as deadly as a viper, though one would not know this from his appearance for he was sweet in disposition and smiled so much that he was nicknamed *Sunny*.

This was all Eireden had to work with. The fey had grown weak. None could match Aric or Alseya in strength or spirit, while most grew weary after a few minutes of complex illusions, and even fewer would carry a sword. Though a hundred or so had volunteered to go into the Demorlaik, only the six that trotted up the road with him were made of stern enough stuff.

"It'll have to do," he said to himself.

Though the king rode quickly, he did not ride boldly. Every few minutes one of the fey would drop from their horse and feel the world around them, searching for the least hint of danger. There was very little to note, not only of danger, but of anything at all.

The goblins had swept through all the Hidden Lands and killed or drove off any living creature. Even of the birds above there were scant few. The land was empty and sad. It was quiet and their horses seemed loud in their ears.

Here and there, the group would find corpses or various body parts. And they rode through long stretches of blackened earth or burnt forest where the remains of the trees stuck up, bare and forlorn like unnumbered grave markers.

Yet nothing challenged them nor barred their way and so it was mid afternoon when they gazed down at the foul city of the dead: the Demorlaik, and even it seemed as empty as the rest of the world.

"There are rumors that Darhmael has emptied his city in a last ditch effort to destroy us," Prince Sylra said, gazing in wonder at the twisted and shadowed streets. "Perhaps we are lucky and this time the rumors are true."

"They aren't," Eireden said with authority. "The dead will not leave their city. You saw the army, which surrounds Rhyoeven. It is made up of goblins and ogres and all the rest. What's down there is much different and much worse. Ghouls, ghasts, the living dead, things that should not be and cannot die...at least for good."

"Then how do we fight them?" Rudyid asked. His face was hard as stone, but Eireden knew him well enough to know that the stonework hid a worry that bordered on fear.

"We don't," Eireden replied. "Fighting them is useless. Our one chance is to get through the city as fast as possible and get down into the maze beneath."

"Won't they just follow us?" Alseya asked.

"I don't think so. The two times I was fool enough to go into that city I noted that the goblins feared the ghouls almost as much as they feared the Den. They were nervous about being in the city itself. My guess is that the two do not ever mingle."

There was a silence among them as they each looked down at the path they had chosen for themselves. Despite that it was afternoon the city hung shrouded in such dark clouds that it could have been night beneath.

Eventually the king gave a sigh and pointed at Elleni. "It's time. Who will look into her mind first?"

Feylon came and knelt in front of the old lady. "Forgive me," she whispered, closing her eyes and placing her hands on Elleni's. Almost immediately the fey grunted and her hands tried to pull away.

"Not yet," Alseya said, holding Feylon's hands in place. "Look for the way down."

Feylon twitched and moaned in tune with Elleni for long dreadful minutes and then she yanked her hands away. "Enough! I saw it! No more…no more."

"It's done Feylon. Look at me," Alseya said. Everyone looked, not just Feylon. There had been power in her words and there was power in her in her strange white eyes. Feylon stared, growing calmer as she did.

"I saw it," she whispered. "The way down is not hidden. In the center of town is a great black pit, like the mouth of some tremendous beast from the depths. That is the beginning of the tunnels."

"Are there guards or a gate of some sort?" Lienhart asked.

Feylon cackled in an eerie manner. "Why would there be? Only a fool would ever go in there."

"It'll be alright Feylon," Alseya said again in her calm voice. To this Feylon nodded and accepted her son in an embrace when Aric went to her.

Uncomfortable with this show of weakness and affection the Den stood and looked to their mounts. "We should be going," Eireden said softly. Feylon nodded and then gathered her strength to leap onto the back of her mount.

She pointed to the city. "If we go straight along that ridge we will come to a bridge. A road runs from it to the center…to the hole."

"Then let's get to it," the king said and pointed for Elleni to be put before Aric once more. "We go straight through. Rudyid, take up the rear. If any shall fall or become overwhelmed you will need to leave them. The true danger is down at the root of the world and we will have need of you. That goes for everyone. Do not turn back for anything."

He did not wait for questions. The king gave his warhorse a kick and rode for the bridge, a bridge that was not unknown to him. He had crossed it before to great pain and great shame. It was here that his dear friend and cousin, Lord Harowyth had fallen trying to save him, and it was here that he had led his men into a death trap.

He had been over confident—and he hadn't changed. To go down into the under belly of the Haunted City took someone with confidence that bordered on the reckless. To be timid would be to invite a quick end to their desperate gambit.

Eireden looked neither left nor right, he aimed for the bridge at the fastest possible speed, which wasn't near as fast as he could have hoped. Already Furen lagged. Next to him, Rudyid, sweating and red, yelled instructions: "Sit further up! Grip with your knees! Come on, or I swear I'll leave you behind."

"Do what you need to do," snarled the dwarf.

Rudyid didn't leave him and nor would Eireden allow his team to get strung out. Instead they rode slowly, at first, and then quicker and quicker as Furen began to get the hang of riding, though to be sure it was more likely his mount got used to balancing an ungainly, cursing dwarf upon his back.

The bridge was their first real test. It should have had a guard upon it, but the tower was empty and the gate open. They rode across it to a great thundering, but the noise was nothing compared to the sudden shriek that Elleni let out. It was blood curdling and Furen's horse shied away threatening to spill it's rider in the black water beneath.

"Quietly Elleni," Aric crooned. "Close your eyes and sleep, you are safe with us."

She closed her eyes and slept, however many more eyes came awake. The riders could see them peering through windows. They were large eyes and blank were their stares, yet there was also an unholy black fire in them that burned with hunger and greed.

"The dead," Furen said, pointing.

"Do not look upon them!" the king cried. "Ride and leave the dead behind."

This was easier said than done. The streets filled with walking corpses with ice for breath, while overhead ghasts began to form themselves into beings of phantasm. Eireden plowed through them and despite his warning not to fight he laid all about him with the black sword, hoping to make less the danger of those behind.

It was a hope in vain. Minutes into the city the first of their horses was pulled down by the grasping hands and biting teeth of the dead. It let out an almost human shriek and despite his talk Eireden spun his warhorse like a top. It was little Yur-el's dun mare being eaten alive even as he watched.

"Go on!" the king yelled to Alseya, however she hadn't slowed even a wit, which he thought uncharacteristic of her. Didn't she care that Yur-el was even then buried beneath the avalanche of bodies? Eireden did for certain. He had lost too many good men to this city not to care and he went into a charge, racing past the other members of the party until only Rudyid was left riding in an odd fashion, as if he was also being pulled down from behind.

In a wrath at the loss of the sweet little fey, the king went right at him with sword raised.

Rudyid bellowed something that the king could not hear. There were bodies everywhere and the dead had begun a howling like the wolves of Darhmael. Yet the commotion did not affect the captain's judgment, he swung away from Eireden so that the king could rid him of the beast clinging to his cloak.

Eireden went for a savage killing strike only to practically drop his sword in surprise. What clung by one hand to the speeding captain's cloak wasn't one of the undead fiends. It was Yur-el!

Somehow she had leapt away from her steed just as it had gone down and now she pulled herself hand over fist to come sit behind the giant of a man. There wasn't really enough room and so he reached around and picked her up as if she were nothing but a child and set her in front of him.

Eireden saw all this as though from a passenger in his own body. Without thinking he had checked his momentum and turned the warhorse back the way he had come.

Yur-el raised an eyebrow as he passed. "I thought we weren't supposed to go back if any of us fell?" Although she teased she was at once frightened beyond anything she had ever experienced and happy that men such as Rudyid and Eireden wouldn't give up on her. The king read this clearly in her eyes in the split second it took to pass the pair.

"I am king," he called back over his shoulder. "Even though I make the rules it doesn't mean I have to follow them."

Even with the danger, the men laughed and the fey smirked. They had passed their first test and all were still alive. And what was more, they had reached a point that their speed was keeping them ahead of the hordes converging on them.

Eireden took the point once again and rode, standing in his stirrups looking all around. He saw the center of town now, however of the opening to world beneath nothing could be seen for the ground rose sharply from the avenue they traveled upon.

It was a steep hill but the slope wasn't the reason he had to set spur to his horses flank to get her up. It was the cold. Nothing in his life, not even his previous trips to the hell of the Demorlaik had prepared him for it.

This wasn't the cold of a nasty winter. This was the ultimate cold of death and he felt more and more lethargic the closer he got, while his horse began to scream and rear. Behind him the other riders were in the same boat, with the worst of the lot being Furen.

His problem wasn't the cold—while the others ranged from pale to paper white, the dwarf was his usual ruddy self—his problem was his lack of skill in managing a horse over anything but the flattest earth in the most simple of conditions.

This was anything but.

However the horse did come on pushed by its fear of the advancing horde. The undead saw the dwarf as its next meal and they converged.

"Forget the horse!" Eireden yelled. "Get off and run."

"He can't," Lienhart cried over the moaning wind. "He's tied in his saddle, remember?"

The king nodded, locking eyes with his Prince. Nothing needed to be said and they rode back down the hill. "You get the dwarf," Eireden ordered and ignored the look Lienhart gave him. Getting the dwarf was the easy part. Dealing with ten thousand living corpses was the tough part.

Eireden rode right up to them and then turned on a dime and danced away keeping just out of reach. He tried to draw them away—only there was just too many, and hundreds kept on after Furen.

Slightly up the hill Lienhart had a hold of Furen's reins and was using the strength of his steed to pull them along. It was going to be very close, Furen had fallen out of his saddle and dangled precariously off the side of his horse.

Still, Eireden saw they had just enough of a lead and so fought his horse on up the hill and topped it just as Alseya's grey had enough. The poor animal, like all of them, was dancing and rolling her eyes in fear, and then without warning it bucked nastily and bolted, leaving the fey to leap to safety.

This seemed to signal a stampede mindset among all the horses and they went wild, bucking and lashing out with kicks and teeth. In pity Eireden yelled, "Let them go! They can't come down into the tunnels anyway."

Everyone dismounted and away the horses went. It was too sad a thing to watch. There was nowhere for them to go but straight into the onrushing horde of undead and their cries were dreadful. But a new cry arose that overshadowed all else.

"Furen!" Lienhart screamed.

The prince had almost made it to the top when the horses bolted past. His own fine charger broke and fled with the rest and as the superb horseman he was, Lienhart landed easily and safely. Furen, however was still tied in his saddle and when his horse fled, it fell, rolling down the hill with the dwarf attached.

The two did not roll far. Their momentum was checked by the other horses who had run from one horror to the next. Furen's mount barreled into another and both went down and were instantly covered by the bodies of the undead, who began to fill their bellies.

Eireden took one step down the hill, but Rudyid grabbed him. "No. I'm sorry but this is one you can't save."

In a daze the king was pulled away from the awful sight and was drug down into the pits beneath the world where he began to wonder if Furen had been the luckiest of the group.

Chapter 35

Eireden

"Damn it!" Eireden cursed, staring up from the opening at the ring of earth. "He shouldn't have come. I knew it. I knew he couldn't ride worth a lick, but he was so insistent. He said he had to come...and now..."

Alseya touched the king's face and despite the size difference between them, she led him away. "And now he is with others of his kind, and if I know Furen he is stamping his feet and yelling for you to go on."

"That's the Furen I know," Aric said with a sad smile. "Except he would likely add some colorful language with that foot stamping."

"And he'd say Bah!" said Rudyid. "And he'd blow out so that his mustache would flitter."

"I thought him a strange dwarf," said Yur-el. "Though to be honest I only just met him. And really I don't know any other dwarves." Everyone looked at her with odd expressions and she explained, "His mannerisms are what I am referring to. He was so very angry with that fairy and then a second later he kissed her good bye."

Tears had been threatening to overwhelm him, but now Eireden barked out a laugh. "He kissed Whip-wip?"

"And patted her head," Yur-el added.

Now the king cried and laughed at once. "That fairy will be very sad," he said and then glanced around in confusion. They were going down into a dark passage where the smell made him ill, however there was something beyond that, which had him asking, "What happened to the cold?"

Aric glanced back and of the opening there was nothing to see. They had gone too deep already. In front the passage opened into a dimly lit cavern that held so many stalagmites springing up from the rocky floor it seemed like an underground forest. "I suspect the cold is what keeps the undead from coming down after the living."

"Yes," Alseya agreed. "And now we have come to our first choice of paths. I will speak to Elleni's memories."

"Not yet," Feylon said, holding out an arm. "I saw more than I wanted to earlier. Over there," she pointed to the right where the shadows seemed deeper than the rest. "Our road is there. We go down."

Going through the rock formations was tricky as the ground sloped upward at each, however it was easy compared to the twisting corkscrew of a road that delved down into the world. The path was sloped at a sharp angle and was wet with goblin excrement and more than one of them slipped. Especially at risk was Prince Lienhart who carried Elleni over his shoulder. Her catatonia was complete and she moved not a muscle on her own.

"This is where I really need Furen," Eireden said. "He loves the dark...I mean loved. Either way. I have no idea where I'm going. Can anyone see anything?"

"We can," Alseya answered. "The fey can see in low lighting, though not in full dark."

"This should help," Aric said and pulled out the elf sword that he had carried from the first moment Eireden had met him." It glittered like a thin slice of sun and was so bright after the heavy dark that it made the Den as equally blind as before.

Eireden tried to squint around it and he saw a flicker in the shadows off to their right. "There is someone with us," the fey Harfel intoned, calmly. "There was a face leering at us from near that wall."

To a man the Den drew their swords and Eireden advanced in front, but there was nothing to be seen but a hole in the wall that wound off to who knew where. "There is a passage here. Did you see this in Elleni's memories?"

"No," Feylon answered.

The king cursed under his breath. "Hasfel search Elleni's mind. We have to know for certain where out next route lies, we don't have time to back track. Aric, feel the wall. Try to tell me what the hell is out there."

The fey prince reached out for the wall, but snatched his hand away with a strangled noise in his throat. "These walls are not natural. This passageway...everything about this place was built with blood and cruelty. I cannot use it as a conduit of my thought."

"Then we are blind in more ways than one," Eireden said. "Let's hope Elleni does not fail us."

Hasfel had listened to their conversation as Lienhart lowered the woman; now he touched her and his face contorted in pain seconds later. "He hates her," the fey said in a choked voice. "He whipped her right here...why? He whipped her up this passage and he whipped the baby..."

"My baby!" Elleni shrieked in a voice that echoed in the dark. It gave Eireden goosebumps. She was talking about Ella.

"You have to look past that, Hasfel," Alseya advised. "She will dwell on the pain to the exclusion of aught else."

"There is only pain," he whispered. "He hurt her every step of the way out of here."

"I know it's difficult," Alseya replied, calmly using her power to soothe. "You have to track it back. Where did she come from? How did she get here?"

"A door...he broke all my fingers in the door. I was going crazy with the pain and I could barely..." he left off and Elleni finished.

"...hold Ella. She slipped and slipped because my fingers were all broken."

Alseya touched her and Elleni went limp. "Find the door Hasfel. Where is it?"

The fey pulled his hands away. They shook and he massaged them as if they were in pain. "Further down. The fourth door will lead to a passage, he...he did things..."

"No," Alseya told him. "Put it out of your mind. It's only a memory and a borrowed one at that. It will fade."

Eireden helped the fey up and gave him a quick once over with the light from Aric's blade. "You'll be fine," he said, not knowing at all if that was truth. The king then barked out orders. "Rudyid get the rear. Aric with me up front. Tharaden take Ella's mother. Carry her if she won't walk and gag her if she gets loud...but don't be too rough. The rest of you fill in and keep your eyes sharp."

The fourth door was hundreds of feet down the spiral passage where the air became stifling and the smell of excrement and waste and decomposing flesh was over-powering. Clearly they were nearing some sort communal dumping sight for the maug and they were all happy to get through the door—all save Hasfel. He cringed when he went through.

The dark passage beyond the door started as a purposeful thing, hewn from rock and it went that way for over a mile before the walls became slanted and the way tortured and cramped. "This isn't right," Hasfel said. "I don't remember any of this. We missed something. Go back."

"Are you sure?" the king demanded, anxiously. He felt time slipping away and every pause made his stomach churn.

"He has to be correct," Aric said "This bomb of yours wouldn't be able to fit through here, would it?" He could stand straight in the passage but the Den were all hunched over.

The king shook his head impatiently. "No, but that hardly matters. There's probably more than one way to get down to the lower portion. Turn around everyone. We need more light...wait, what am I think-ing!" Eireden reached down and touched the pearl he always wore and it sprung to life in a white glare.

Aric smirked and touched his own gift from Whip-wip—it lit up his handsome face. He took it off and gave it to Hasfel who held it aloft by its thin fila-ment letting its light direct him.

"Here it is," the fey said in confusion. "I did not see this before, did any of you?" Most murmured 'no' however Yur-el in the back with Rudyid nodded that she had. Eireden hadn't, although it was hard to tell, everything was black and shadowed, and there were so many doors and corridors and crevices along their path that he was very much turned around and missing Furen more and more with every step.

"Is that the right way, or not?" the king asked, pushing his way through to look at a wet hole of a tun-nel that sloped away into a black depth.

"It is, only I should have seen it," Hasfel said, looking sick beneath the light of the pearl. "I guess it doesn't matter. We take this down and ignore all of the different side passages; it will end at a cross section. After that I don't know."

"Ok, you did very well," Eireden said, taking the pearl back. "Since it is a straight shot, I will lead." With the light they proceeded quickly along, yet de-spite this he grew more anxious with every step.

"Something is missing, something is wrong," he said. "In Elleni's memories was this place so empty?"

"That's right," Prince Sylra said. "The pits of the Demorlaik are supposedly stiff with monsters of all sorts."

"It was not empty," Feylon replied. "There were creatures, and not just maug and ogre. Strange and horrific they were, but they cringed back at our passing." Hasfel agreed, but said nothing.

"Then where are they?" the prince wondered. "So far we've seen only a face and that was a shadowed one at that. Maybe it was nothing but your imagination?"

"I do not use imagination in such a way," Hasfel replied, stiffly. "Imagination is used behind the eyes not instead of them."

"Of course not. He meant no slight," Lienhart said, diplomatic as ever. "Maybe it was a spy. It could be that our enemy has these monsters lying in wait for us. Never was a place more suited for ambush than this warren."

"In that case let's button it up," Eireden ordered. "I see the cross section ahead. Tharaden put the lady down over here, it's a little less wet. And let's have Aziel next. I want to keep you as fresh as possible Aric, but..."

Yur-el suddenly spoke in a panicked whisper, "Aziel's gone!"

Everyone turned and Eireden rushed back a little ways with his pearl held up as if the little light would show them Aziel sitting there quietly, but of the thirteen who had left Rhyoeven that morning only eleven remained.

"Aziel," Eireden called down the passage in not more than a loud whisper. He paused listening, when nothing came to him but the heavy breathing of the Den he ran back the way they came and and shouted in a voice that could carry above a hurricane, "Aziel!"

The others hurried to him. "Do we go back for him," Lienhart asked.

"No," Alseya said, flatly.

"Yes we do!" Prince Sylra countered. "He was in my care and I'm not going to leave him behind."

The king went between them. "Stop," he ordered. "No one's going anywhere unless I say so. We don't even know how long he's been missing. When's the last time anyone saw him?"

They looked back and forth among themselves until Yur-el said, "He was on the winding passage. I saw him there, but I don't think he was with us when we had to backtrack up above. Everyone filed past me and...I don't remember him. I'm sorry."

"That long?" Eireden asked in a hollow voice. "Is there any way he would just wander off on his own?"

"No," Alseya answered. "He knew the danger of the Demorlaik and what lay beneath just we all did. He was either drawn away by something, or he was taken."

Taken...Eireden got the chills at the idea. He stared down the corridor the way they had come for a moment and then bellowed at the top of his lungs, "Aziel!" No one spoke. They held their breath straining to hear anything.

When the silence went on and on, mocking them, the king said in a voice that held acid, "We go forward, and this time we button it up tight! By twos. Sylra you're with Aric, and don't you lose him." Grimly—on the part of the Den, and sadly—with regard to the fey, they drew together in pairs.

"Face outward," the king barked as though speaking to new recruits. "It doesn't do any damned good looking at each other. Yur-el, it's your turn with Elleni."

With small tentative steps the littlest fey came forward, clearly fearing what was to come. Eireden didn't blame her and in fact felt sorry for her. She swallowed audibly and knelt before the stiff and dreadful looking human. As the others had, she reached out to touch her, but unlike the others there wasn't the immediate reaction of fear or pain.

"There's a bridge ahead," Yur-el said in her piping voice. "We go to the right and another right and there's the bridge and a tunnel."

She was so calm that Eireden felt comfortable asking, "What's after that?"

"More black," Yur-el answered in a far away voice. "There's more black beneath the bridge...deep, deep black. And after it there's pain...always pain. And death. Always death. Death for the weak and pain for the strong."

"Come back, Yur-el," Alseya said. "You don't belong in those memories. Come back."

The little fey leaned away from the crone and blinked uncertainly. "You did great," Eireden said reassuringly.

"No, I didn't do great. She did," the fey said of Elleni. "She is very brave."

Eireden couldn't understand this so he gave her a smile, but it was a shabby thing from worry over Aziel, and sorrow over Furen, and sadness over the fact that he knew he would never see Ella again.

In a softer voice of command, he ordered, "Ok, let's move out. And keep it tight, please."

They took the right at the intersection and then the next right as Yur-el had told him, and this curved to the right and curved and curved, cork-screwing ever deeper. Frequently he glanced back to make sure his charges were all accounted for and he wasn't the only one. The other Den were extra vigilant, with giant Rudyid going so far as to hold onto Yur-el's cloak to keep her close.

Though all of this wasn't needed. The fey kept much closer than they had been. Where before they might glance into a room or sniff at a fissure or glance down one the thousands of lanes that went this way and that at every angle, now they huddled inwards.

Eventually the corkscrew path flattened and joined others to become a regular road, which tunneled right to a steep edged shelf of rock. They were at the bridge.

"It has changed," Yur-el said coming forward to look. "The bridge used to be of stone and there were rails."

The bridge now was made up of only two parallel ropes with a run of very rickety boards attached to each. It looked questionable if not downright perilous. The king, feeling ill at the idea of stepping a single foot onto it, inched closer to the drop over which it stretched and held out his pearl.

An inky black swept downward to an unknowable depth. He stepped back with a big shaky breath and Alseya walked up calmly. "Not too bad. I'll go first."

"What? Wait..." the king said but before he could do more than reach out for her, the fey walked out onto the rickety construct, stopping midway. There she gave it a little bounce, causing the men to hold their breaths. "It is none too sturdy," she added calmly. "I'd go one at a time."

"Tell her to stop bouncing," Rudyid said in a choked voice.

Eireden glanced back and found the rest crowding him—the Den eyeing the bridge in trepidation the fey, curious as to the drop. "I'll go next," Lienhart said. When no one stopped him or asked to change places with him, he went to the bridge, set his jaw, and strode across.

Immediately the ropes went tight and began making fearful sounds, while the boards beneath creaked alarmingly. But worse was the fact that the bridge began to sway and tip. Eireden jumped to the edge of the bridge and grabbing the first board, and fought it back to center.

With it somewhat stable, Lienhart hurried across and when he got to the other side everyone went limp in relief. "Aric can you take Elleni with you? I'll go after you."

Ever since Yur-el had looked into her memories, Elleni had been walking on her own—though to be fair it was the shamble of a robot and not what one would consider a normal stride. Still she preceded Aric across with less fuss than Lienhart.

Then it was the king's turn. It wasn't as bad as he had feared. With Lienhart holding one end steady and Rudyid the other, he made it across with a minimal of swaying.

And so it went, fey and then Den until only Rudyid and Yur-el were left on the far side. Rudyid stood next to the bridge, frozen in place like a child twenty feet above a pool on the high board for the first time.

"I think you should go first," Yur-el said. "I'll be right here, ok?"

"But what about you?" he replied in a higher octave than usual. "I'm probably going to break the bridge. I'm too big." This wasn't just nerves talking. The bridge had sagged with each crossing and more than one of the boards had snapped.

"Oh, don't worry about me. I can practically leap across this little gorge. You just need to catch me when I do. Can I count on you to catch me?" Despite her size she was perfect in every way, as all the fey were, and Rudyid looked on her as something to protect and cherish.

He nodded that he would catch her and then crossed the bridge. Even with Eireden straining to keep it steady, the bridge yawed and the ropes made evil twerking sounds—but still Rudyid crossed safely. Sweating but jubilant he turned with a huge smile to Yur-el, only Yur-el was nowhere to be seen.

Chapter 36

Ella

The queen watched the attack of the thousand riders with a face set in regal elegance and those around her saw the calm and their fears were allayed and their spirits buoyed.

She watched the swirling battle yet saw none of it. Her heart and her mind and her magic was on the king as he rode away under cover of illusion and it was only when a somber cheering went up that she seemed to even notice the warriors returning.

Her attitude wasn't one of uncaring. They knew their jobs and they were fell and deadly, and they had their own leaders who directed them in battle. She didn't know the first thing of war. Her value to the effort was strictly in her presence and just being there on the wall was trial enough for her.

How badly she wished either to ride with her king to whatever fate was to befall him, or run and hide back in her bed. On the wall she felt useless and did not want to see the bloodshed. It hurt her to see the empty saddles and the crippled and the dying men, but it was the fairies coming back mournfully with their own dead that nearly cracked the porcelain veneer she had constructed to cover her true face.

"Who are they?" Ella asked Whip-wip. But the fairy could not speak and she buried herself in Ella's bosom crying.

None of her family could speak and it was a young male with black and gold wings who told her the names. There were many. Forty-two names to go along with the ninety-six from the battle the day before. It was too much for many of the fairies to hear and instead of flying around they huddled on the walls in ragged clumps.

As queen, Ella listened to each of the names and they were cold stones piling in her heart until she thought she was just about full, and she feared that one more would kill her, but then the fairy spoke the final name: Ease-see and Ella did not die. She wished she could. The pain at losing the brave little fairy was that great.

Just then she wished it was over. She wished she could have her king back and that they could lie together and pass on to whatever awaited them in death.

But she could not do these things, because she was queen. She knew there were fey even then seeking life beyond death, and she knew that there had been among the Den those who had been hurt in mind and spirit to too great a degree and these had rode with the thousand with no intent to return.

But that was them. They were not queen; they had choices where she did not. The queen had her duties to attend to and these included not just mourning the dead but uplifting those that still had hope even when hers was nearly gone. The king had been her hope and it was clear from the drawn looks of the men and the pinched anxious looks of the fey they felt the same.

"I feel done in, Whip-wip," she said to the fairy as all around them the people watched the maug begin to close their ring. The goblins in great formations advanced to just out of arrow range and then began to dig. Though the thousand riders had their losses, the maug had been butchered horribly and so now they dug trenches to keep the horsemen from again charging.

"I'm like a balloon that's been deflated," Ella said to her friend. "What do I do?"

Whip-wip did not understand. She puffed up her cheeks and floated up slowly. "Is balloon? Fly is high, sis?"

"I'm not a real balloon, silly. And I can't fly." The best she could do was float for a while or jump great distances with the aid of her magic. Real flying still escaped her.

A captain of the Den approached, a man unfamiliar to her. As he was in armor and they were at war he did not bow and she did not offer her hand. He nodded only and held out a piece of paper. "The men who did not make it back, Highness. A hundred and three. The advantage was with us, and our sythie allies were very brave and thusly we slew twenty times that number."

"You should be congratulated in a proper fashion," Ella said. "When the king returns I will share with him your exploits and the courage of your men."

He bowed his head again and made to turn away, instead he paused. "If he returns," the captain said, without looking her in the eye. "The men will not admit it, not out loud, but I hear their rumors. They fear the Sun King will not come back from the Demorlaik. It casts a shadow upon their hearts."

Ella had the very same fear, but she hid it from the man and grew angry that he would dare to bring it up. "Perhaps the problem isn't in your men, maybe it is their leadership that is lacking," she said with cold steel in her voice.

"I did not mean to be insulting in my words..."

"Then what was the point to them?" Ella demanded icily, her face haughty. She held his gaze like a basilisk and all the while felt like an imposter—she was no queen. She didn't know the first thing about what it took to be a real queen.

"Ahem..." Behind them Ilenwyth Eden came strolling up. "I don't mean to interrupt, but I have an urgent message for the queen." The captain was only too willing to get away and after a brief nod and a strained smile he left.

"Well?" Ella asked when Ilenwyth only stood there. "You had a message?" Desperately she wished it was from Eireden.

"Yes, it's from the former queen. She wanted me to mention that you are not her and that you should not try to be like her."

For a span of seconds Ella's face grew imperious and color rose in her cheeks, but then the words sunk in and her mask broke. The high queen melted back into the American girl and she stepped close to the old woman and confessed in a whisper, "But I don't know how to be a real queen. It's all happening too fast. I'm suddenly a wife and now a mother, and a queen. It was one thing to smile prettily next to my husband, but he's gone and everyone looks to me and I'm just a nobody. I'm just a girl."

"Stop that talk," Ilenwyth snapped. "No matter how it happened or whether or not you are ready, you are queen and you must act as one, even if it is only an act."

"I was trying," Ella said.

"You were trying to be me," Ilenwyth replied. "It is not something you are suited for and besides, being me isn't always a pleasant experience. As a queen, I was respected but rarely loved. The trick to being queen is that you need to be yourself and not yourself at the same time."

"I don't know how to be either," Ella replied with a smirk.

"See," Ilenwyth beamed. "Being sweet and charming is your gift. Use it. And enough with this 'Girl' business. You are a woman, with all the power of a woman. Use that as well."

"And the part about not being me? If you don't want me to act like you, who should I act like?"

Ilenwyth shook her head. "It's not what I meant. You need to step away from whatever is limiting you. The men need you, the people need you, and the entire city needs you...even the sythie need you. Or rather they need you to become something more than a sweet girl in a nice dress. Remember, what I said about the power of a queen?"

"I must be as powerful as the king if not more so," Ella replied. Ilenwyth nodded, curtseyed as deeply as her aging knees would allow and left Ella to figure out who she should be and who she could be.

"This is all very confusing," she said to Whip-wip. "I'm supposed to me and not me when I barely know who I am on a daily basis. What do you think? Who am I?"

The fairy squinched her nose as she stared up at Ella—it was her 'thinking' face. "Ella is queen, sis."

"I know I'm queen, but what sort of queen should I be? I'm not good at being the Ice queen like Ilenwyth used to be. And I shouldn't be the cutesy queen as I feel when Eireden is around. He's lucky. He's the 'Sun King' thanks to all you fairies, but what am I?"

The tiny nose stayed squinched until Whip-wip nodded. "Sis. Ella is Sun Queen."

"As long as I have you, I will be," Ella answered, though inwardly she was still confused and sad and stressed nearly beyond her ability to cope. She made to whistle up her family of fairies but they had all disap-peared and she supposed they had left to eat or sleep or mourn but they had not.

They had left to fashion a coffin for their fallen brother and now they brought it to her. It was tiny and blue, fashioned from woven petals of *Forget-me-not* flowers. She blinked rapidly but still the tears came like hot rain on her cheeks and her breath struggled to come.

They set the coffin in her hand and then one after another the fairies came and gave their light to it and then it was Ella's turn. She started to say, "I don't know how..." but bit the words off. She had never made light before but that didn't mean she didn't know how. She just had to imagine it.

Ella closed her eyes and pictured first a candle but that didn't seem good enough for such a brave fairy as Easa-see. She then thought of the sun, but that was too much. Finally she thought of her husband and how everyone called him the Sun King. From a hundred people she had heard the story of the battle of Hildeoven and now she could picture him beneath the light of ten-thousand fairies. She could see the brilliance in her mind clearly, how the gathered fairies looked like a fallen star hanging just above the earth.

Suddenly someone cried out, "The Sun King! He returns!"

Ella's eyes snapped open in excitement, but she had to shut them again from the glare—a golden light rippled all around her and pushed back the gloom of the dark day. She had made that light and it flared off of her in a radiance too bright to look at. Quickly a buzz sounded in the air and a snapping and crackling and Ella squinted, looking up to see the fairies of the city rushing to join in a great thrum above her.

"No, it is not he," the same voice said in a yell as people from all over were hurrying to see the light, and the commotion was great. "It is she! The Sun Queen!" And many voices took up the cry.

"So that is who I am?" she asked herself. "I thought I was to be just a girl with a dream of flying but I suppose I am now the Sun Queen."

"Sis," Whip-wip agreed. Even she had her blue eyes mostly closed from the glare of both the fairies and Ella. "But why you not fly too?"

"Because I can't..." Ella stopped. It was true she couldn't fly, not yet and perhaps not ever, but she could float. With her mind she lifted herself high in the sky above the gate and floated there. And below the people gathered and cheered, and out on the battle plain the goblins in their fresh trenches covered their faces and quailed in fright.

Higher Ella drew so that all could see and the streets were filled with people straining their heads back. She hung there as a beacon of hope until the strain proved too great and then she gradually came back to earth to be Ella once again.

But she was not the same Ella at least not to the people of Rhyoeven. She was no longer the American girl, she was their Sun Queen.

As she walked back to the palace she was a sight, for the dress she wore was of a beautiful white, em-broidered with spun gold and now it glowed gently as though it had absorbed too much light. Along the way she smiled at the people she met and nodded to the soldiers who lined the streets as they stepped back to allow her to pass and in their eyes was not the gloom of earlier.

There was hope.

She made her way into the palace and went first to the throne room and saw the great throne on its dais. With the king absent she was within her rights to as-cend the steps and seat herself there, in fact it wasn't just a right, but a duty.

Despite that the room was peopled with staff offi-cers, dwarves, and fey staring at her, Ella felt utterly alone as she walked with silent steps to it and sat, feel-ing very small and sad despite its grandeur.

"Captain...I'm sorry but I don't recall your name," Ella said to the captain she been brusque towards.

He hurried forward and bowed low before an-swering, "Captain Gairad, your Highness."

"I'd like to apologize for earlier. I was out of line in how I spoke to you," she said, but the captain only shook his head to say that an apology wasn't needed. "And I have a request," she added. "Our allies, the sythie need weapons."

"Weapons?"

"Yes, weapons. There are still many of those bat creatures about and the fairies are practically defenseless if they have to fight one on one. I think spears would be best."

A dwarf hurried forward and after a stiff bow said in an excited voice, "You wish the spear? It a thought in my head. Now is command and is good. For the fairies good too is well."

Most of the dwarves could barely speak word one in English, but this was Hasdrubal chief lieutenant of the dwarves and friend to Furen, so Ella understood him even as Gairad looked upon him clueless.

"Yes, spears; a thousand of them. Probably sixteen inches long and very light. And make sure they are sharp, thank you."

The dwarf bowed again and hurried out of the room calling to others of his kind in excitement. Ella turned to a sleepy Whip-wip and said, "We'll keep you safe."

She thought the process of making so many spears would be a job of some days, but by late afternoon, a parade of dwarves came into the throne room in a strange solemn procession. With them came a fey that Ella had met once before.

"Hello Archera," the queen said with a quizzical smile. "I'm glad to see you again. May I ask what is all this?"

"Our friends the dwarves do not speak English well and have asked that I interpret for them."

"Good...but what is all this? And why do they seem so grave?"

The fey laughed easily and for no good reason—a normal thing among fey—and explained, "They are to present a gift of great importance upon you and upon our friends the sythie." The fey said this and then nodded to Hasdrubal who came forward with a long box of inlaid wood that Ella guessed would be a spear for herself.

"For the Sun Queen. Eleanor the Pure," Archera translated from Hasdrubal's thick language.

Ella smiled to accept the gift, but the smile froze when the dwarf opened the lid. It was indeed a spear. Its shaft was of worked silver and it shone but the head of the spear was of gold and it was a shock to see that it had not been crafted by man nor dwarf.

"I can't," Ella said, pulling her hand away. "That is Eenaya's horn. You...you desecrated her body?"

The dwarves began muttering and Archera spoke quickly to them in a calming tone. He then turned to Ella. "I think you misunderstand. This is a gift from Eenaya herself. She gave her life for you, which is the rarest of things. She wanted you to be safe from your enemies."

"But her body..."

"Has been burned to release her soul," Archera explained. "We could not allow the maug to despoil it so we brought it here and when she was burned only the horn remained. And no one knew what to do with it since it cannot be destroyed or melted in any fire."

Ella eyed the beautiful horn and tried not to cry when she thought of brave Eenaya. "But do you really think she would want us to make it into a weapon?"

"It was a weapon already," Archera said. "And now it is the weapon of the Sun Queen—if you will accept it."

"I will," Ella said. "Please convey my apology for my hesitation." When the fey did, Hasdrubal smiled and then came forward to present the spear, but Ella didn't immediately take it. Instead she stooped and kissed the dwarf on the cheek. He turned tomato red in an instant. Only then did Ella take the spear from the box, surprised at how amazingly light it was.

She thanked the dwarf and then the others came forward to present the smaller spears to the fairies, and whether they wanted them or not each of the dwarves were kissed as well, but not by Ella. The fairies took their cue from the queen and each kissed the dwarf presenting them with their gift.

When all thousand spears had been presented and the fairies had finished their impromptu battle with each other and had been healed of their wounds, Ella and whip-wip left the palace and went to the battle tower.

People stared at their passing but she did not notice. The long day was drawing and she had only fear in her heart—the king should have made it to the Demorlaik hours before and it was only a matter of time before they knew if his mission had been successful.

She decided she would await her death or her joy at the top of the tower so she would know first which way the world would turn. She watched to the north and her spear became a beacon as the sun began to set. The golden horn shone with a warm light that should have filled her with joy.

Instead she felt empty, as though her heart was already dead. There in the sky was an odd contraption with whipping blades. It was heading straight for the city.

Chapter 37

Eireden

"Yur-el!" Rudyid cried and the word echoed in the gorge beneath them. The sound made the gorge seem endlessly deep and Rudyid took a step back. But it was only a moment's hesitation and then the man stepped onto the bridge.

Eireden, who had been at the edge holding the bridge, leapt up. "Rudyid, don't..." But it was too late. The captain was making his way across with his sword drawn and eyes staring into the dark.

"Come save her," a velvet voice said ahead of him. It was Darhmael, tall and handsome, full of a radiance that stopped the captain in his tracks. "Are you man enough to save her?" The elf had Yur-el by the throat and dangled her over the edge of the gorge.

"I am. Put her down and face me if you dare," rasped out Rudyid. He took a step forward and the bridge began to pitch. Eireden dropped to his knees and grabbed the boards to keep the captain from going straight in, while behind him the others gathered close.

Darhmael smirked at this and moved away from the bridge, but not away from the gorge. Rudyid took another step. "Rudyid don't," Eireden said again. "We can't win this fight, not here. The way's too narrow."

"I won't leave her behind," the captain said. "He'll fight me. His honor depends on it."

The elf only smiled the more and beckoned him on and all the while Yur-el's face had gone from blue to purple in his grip.

"He will fight you and he will kill you!" Eireden said. "Please stop, damn it! We said we wouldn't go back for anyone. Yur-el forgive me please, but Rudyid I order you to come back."

The man shook his head and was practically to the other side when he said, "I know my fate is death, as may be hers as well, and I will share it with her if that is to be."

"Oh it is," Darhmael agreed. Casually he tossed away the fey as if she were a piece of trash. The girl disappeared down into the black of the gorge with a cry and it was a blessing that they did not hear her when she hit the bottom. "Now come share her fate."

In a rage the huge captain made it to the other side of the bridge and attacked the elf with hammering blows. Lienhart made to cross as well, but the king grabbed him.

"No. It's what he wants. Remember the Battle Tower? He can flick you into the gorge with a thought. Or set fire the bridge while we're trying to cross."

"Then we do nothing?" Lienhart demanded, watching as the elf toyed with Rudyid, slashing and slicing him so that he was slick with blood, letting the fight last to entice the others to cross.

"No, we do what we came here to do," Eireden said, taking the prince by the arm and dragging him away from the shelf of rock. "We get to that bomb and stop it. Hurry now. Hasfel and Sylra watch our backs. Everyone else don't look back."

The king grabbed Elleni by the waist and in a smooth move swung her onto his shoulder. He then rushed down the tunnel trying his best not listen as Rudyid died slowly, grunting with each wound the elf inflicted. With every step Eireden felt more and more to be both a traitor and a coward yet he knew in his heart that running was the right thing to do.

The tunnel went straight and it was dark and close and no one listened to the king's orders about looking back. They all did, with fear in their eyes, wondering when the elf would come for them and begin the battle in earnest.

But Darhmael stayed hidden so that they soon began to suspect a new trap would be waiting for them, ahead.

When the tunnel came to fork Eireden set Elleni down and moved forward slowly with his pearl raised, both tunnels seemed unremarkable. "Alseya, find out which way we need to go from here," he said over his shoulder.

"The one to the left."

She answered so quickly that he turned in confusion, wondering how on earth she found out so fast. The answer was that Elleni told her. The old woman stood with her face slack and her eyes unseeing, yet with her arm out pointing to the left tunnel.

"Could this be a trick?" he asked. "Could Darhmael be controlling her with magic?"

"No," Alseya reassured. "There are no enchantments upon her."

"Then I guess we take the left fork," Eireden said, marveling over the strange woman. Gently he lowered her arm and picked her up again, this time with a little more reverence. After a quick count of the remaining nine of them he went down the tunnel with Alseya at his side.

This tunnel went up and down with turns here and there, and everywhere there were new openings that the group crossed cautiously, fearing another sneak attack. At each the old lady remained motionless, until they had gone for ten minutes and then she moved in his grip.

They had come upon another intersection identical to the last. Again she pointed to the left. The king peered down both before taking Elleni's suggestion. Again came a maze that had them all bewildered, but then the tunnel opened up.

"Oh my, look at this," Alseya breathed, staring up at what could only be the Citadel at the Root of the World. A great castle, lit with flickering ghostly lights sat in the middle of a cavern of epic proportions. Still it was not tall enough to fit the citadel's highest towers; these seemed to meld with the stone above.

The ground in front was flat and smooth, but there was a moat just prior to the castle and a single bridge sat across it. In his arms, Elleni pointed at the bridge.

"I think I got it from here," Eireden said, as he set her down. He turned to the others who all gazed up at the citadel. "Let's be careful. Real tight. Remember, if one falls, we all go on."

Each nodded and they set off across the plain with Eireden leading and Elleni next to him, pointing as she shuffled along. At the bridge he paused in indecision and a growing fear. The bridge was of stone and at the far end an iron-barred portcullis was raised. The way forward seemed clear, however the moat beneath was terrifying. It held a thick tar like substance that gave off an awful smell and Elleni shivered at the sight of it as they waited to cross.

"Will he attack when we cross?" Lienhart said, leaning forward slightly and staring into the black substance. "I'd hate to end up in there. I bet it sucks you under."

Eireden was just having the same unhappy thoughts. "I think we should link arms so he doesn't try lifting us up with his mind and tossing us in. We'll go three across and we'll hurry. If he comes, we fight him on the other side." Across the bridge seemed an open area like a courtyard.

"There could be an ambush on the other side," Alseya said.

"I'd take that over fighting on this bridge," Lienhart said, anxiously trying to link arms with Eireden, but the king pulled back.

"Alseya and I will take Elleni with us," he said. "We might still need her."

Lienhart turned to link arms with Aric, but the fey was already linked with his mother and Tharaden. Unhappily Lienhart linked arms with a grinning Sylra and the dour Hasfel.

"Do not fret, my fellow Prince," Sylra said. "The three of us are the heaviest group. It's the king who should be worried. My armor weighs more than Alseya and the human lady combined." Indeed the three at the rear had little fear of being thrown into the moat by the elf since combined they weighed upward of seven hundred pounds.

Yet it was the very weight that became an issue. The king set across at a brusque pace his eyes darting quick and his feet light. Alseya was just as speedy and the two dragged Elleni along with Aric, Feylon and Tharaden trailing close. The third group was only steps behind, however it proved fatal.

Twenty feet from safety, the portcullis dropped, screaming down on rusting chains. Without pause for thought both Eireden and Alseya dashed forward hauling Elleni along like baggage. Aric and Feylon were equally quick and Tharaden was no slouch. With a cry of warning they lunged ahead, racing as fast as they could, but still Tharaden was nearly impaled by the sharp ends of the iron bars as they came down.

The other three were trapped on the wrong side.

"Alseya watch our backs," Eireden ordered. He stared around and saw a door in the castle wall that wasn't far. "Feylon, you and Aric see where that door leads. We need to find the winch that'll raise this..."

"No!" Sylra said with hard eyes. "Leave us. You're spreading your group out and that's what Darhmael wants."

"We have to at least try," Lienhart said, grabbing one of the bars and straining against it with all of his strength. "Come...on!" Sylra did the same as did Hasfel and Tharaden.

"It's coming up," panted Lienhart. Eireden joined the effort and the heavy bars lifted with a squeal of metal and an odd grinding noise.

"What the hell is that?" Lienhart asked. His one remaining eye was big and round in his face. Just then the noise, like two boulders running against each other, increased and a vibration went through the bars. "The bridge!" yelled Lienhart.

Beneath them the bridge dropped suddenly, sinking into the black moat. Hasfel let out a cry and sprinted back the way they had come, while Sylra took two half-hearted steps and then stopped as he saw the uselessness of running. Already their feet were covered in the black tar.

"Lienhart! Grab my hand," Eireden yelled, reaching through the bars and taking his prince's arm. Sylra tried to reach out as well but his feet were glued in place, while further down the bridge Hasfel had fallen and was on his hands and knees with his face inches from the black.

"I won't leave you," Eireden grunted as the bridge continued to drop.

"Please don't," Lienhart gasped. "I don't want to die like this! It's not right."

"You won't," Eireden said straining to hold Lienhart up. Next to him Tharaden grabbed the prince's other arm. "Aric! Aric, take my cloak and...and we can cut it into strips. We'll tie Lienhart in place, until we can figure something out. Maybe there's some rope..."

"No," Lienhart said, suddenly. His face was white and his mouth shook but he grew resolute and suddenly pushed away from the king. "It's too late, go on. Leave us."

"No," Eireden growled, pulling harder. "I can still save you."

Lienhart looked back to see Hasfel straining to keep his face out of the black, the rest of him was covered, while Sylra had his sword out and was trying to use it as a wedge against the tar to free one of his legs.

"You can't save me, my King," Lienhart said. "But you can save others...the ones we fight for. Go! Don't watch me die this way."

Sylra sheathed his sword—the black was up to his waist and poor Hasfel had disappeared. "Remember us as we fought, not how we died."

"I will," the king said in a whisper.

When he didn't move, a hand grabbed his collar and he was yanked away. As he stumbled on, his mind filled with a rushing noise and all he heard beyond it was his own guilty heartbeat in his ears. He was pulled along because he couldn't seem to focus. "My men aren't supposed to die like this, drowning in black sludge," he said as though speaking to himself. "They were supposed to fight toe to toe with Darhmael—not be eaten by the undead, or thrown in endless ravines, or taken in the black unknown...

Alseya touched him and said a word—suddenly his fatigue and his anxiety grew less, while his spiraling sadness was pushed to the back of his mind and the great pain in his heart withdrew into a bitter kernel.

"We will mourn their passing in time," she said. "Now we must have our wits to deal with Darhmael."

Eireden blinked, coming back to himself—his grief was still within him, like an animal eating him from the inside out, but Alseya had made it bearable. "Thank you. I was…confused. And mayhap I still am. Why do we not head to the main doors. The elf is likely up there," he said pointing at the tallest tower.

"She points this way," Tharaden answered. "And she has yet to steer us wrong." Elleni pointed at a low building that had thick walls and a gated door. Eireden's first thought was: *It's the dungeon*.

He wasn't wrong. They passed through an empty guard chamber and down a lit twisting stair and with each step the smell of decomposing flesh grew. They wrapped their faces in their cloaks and followed after Elleni as she pointed with vacant eyes.

Three levels down she made to open a door, but the king hesitated, holding her back. From deeper below a chain rattled. They waited listening, but when nothing came the king challenged, "Darhmael! Fight me if you have any honor!"

The words echoed back to them.

"Another trap is my guess," Aric said. "One we should avoid, and besides Elleni is getting anxious." Like an automaton, the old lady marched in place, being held back by Tharaden with ease.

"You're right," Eireden said, with little emotion. "Come Elleni, show us the way."

It wasn't far. A minute later she stopped in front of a cell with her hand out, pointing. Most of the other cells held stick-thin corpses of various beings—goblin mostly, but this one was empty.

Curious, Aric stepped in and poked at the brittle straw with his toe. "Does anyone suppose there may be a hidden passage?"

"I can look into her mind," Alseya said. "Though I do not believe we will find any passages."

"Home," Elleni said in a voice like dry crackling leaves. Everyone stared in surprise.

"What does she mean?" Eireden asked. "Does she think this is her home?"

Tharaden stuck his head into the cell, glanced around for a second and then stepped out again. "If so we should not waste our time indulging this. The elf is near."

After a pause for thought, Eireden nodded to Alseya, "Go ahead, please. Search her mind." As the fey pulled the human down to her knees and took up her hands, the king gave a glance at Tharaden. "She did not ask to come with us. If this will make her happy in some way then so be it."

"She doesn't look happy," Tharaden said. He was right, both the human and the fey were crying in silence.

Eireden made to break the connection but Aric put a hand on his arm and said, "Not yet. Alseya is in control. Her mind is stronger than any and if she wishes to break the connection she will."

"She thought this was her home," Alseya said in a whisper. Her opal eyes were still closed and she still clutched the woman. "She wants to find out where she came from, but it is far, far in the past where she cannot see." The fey went quiet and minutes ticked by and then Aric pointed.

The old woman was as catatonic as ever, but now her face was split by a grin. Soon Alseya sighed and stood, drawing Elleni with her. "We have delved deep and have discovered who Elleni Feyden was before."

"Who?" Eireden asked, intrigued.

"Mary Welsley, an innocent. Darhmael took her when she was four years old."

Eireden had been expecting more, which, upon reflection didn't make much sense. Elleni, or rather Mary was only a human after all. "She seems happy, so I'm glad for her and do not count this as wasted minutes. Now we should go, we have little time left I fear. Do you know the way?"

This he had asked of the woman but she only stood and smiled. Alseya took her by the hand. "I don't think we will have trouble finding the elf from here. He is in his citadel and he waits for us."

Eireden nodded. He felt the same sort of sensation in the air. Darhmael had whittled down the group to a point where a straight fight didn't look winnable for the survivors. Still they could not turn around and go back to await the bomb, so they left the dungeon and with hands gripping weapons they went to the main doors of the castle and flung it open ready to fight and die.

Instead they gaped.

The difference between the outside and the inside of the citadel could not have been more startling. Where outside everything was dark and loathsome, and the air foul and full of fear, the inside was bright and inviting.

The walls were white with finely carved crown molding, the floors polished and gleaming marble, the sconces were of shining brass and the artwork, masterful. The air smelled of cinnamon and baked apples, and it swirled gently with music.

"Is this an illusion?" Eireden asked, not trusting his senses.

"No," Aric said in a small choking voice. Eireden turned at the sound and saw that his friend was pale.

"What is it?"

"Darhmael," Aric said, pointing an unsteady finger.

Just inside the double doors was a wide-open area, where, if anyone ever visited, guests would be greeted. Beyond that was a grand staircase of lacquered wood. The elf stood upon them, smiling down on them.

"Eireden!" he said with a chortling laugh. "Come. Bring your friends. I have refreshments, for I suspect you are weary. Though, please put the human outside, I don't want her to make a mess on the floors."

Eireden ignored the elf's words and started to advance, creeping slowly his nerves taut and his reflexes keen, at no point did he take his eyes from his bemused opponent. He pointed to his left and said, "Aric take the left flank, Tharaden the right."

"I don't think I can," Aric said in that same choked voice. "Something's not right."

"He isn't wrong. It's the walls," Darhmael grinned. "They're made of iron; pig iron really. This was supposed to be Aug-Raumon's final refuge. He thought his end would come at the hands of an elf, so he built this citadel out of iron—grating isn't it?"

"Yes," gasped Aric. Behind him Alseya looked green and Feylon wobbled on the verge of passing out. Aric blinked hard and said, "I can't fight here."

"Exactly," Darhmael agreed. "That's why I invited you up for something to eat. You can relax up here and watch the festivities. Come." Without waiting for them the elf went up the stairs with light steps.

Tharaden hurried to the king's side. "Can we fight him? Just the two of us?"

"What choice is there?" Eireden replied. He turned and looked at the three fey. "You will not waste your life. Take Elleni and make it to the surface."

"And die in the Demorlaik instead?" Alseya asked. She set her jaw and drew her sword. "We will stay with you Sun king. We have sworn upon this fate."

He saw that there would be no dissuading her, "So be it. Do what you can. We shall sell our lives bitterly."

The five, followed by a drooling Elleni, went up the stairs ready for battle and found Darhmael in what had once been a tremendous throne room. Now it was partitioned into something cozier—something that resembled a sitting room. There were luxurious couches, soft ottomans and low tables arranged with food. Yet what drew their eye the most was that one of the walls was stark white and upon it was projected a picture of Ella. In it she stood on the wall of Rhyoeven overlooking the main gate wearing the same dress she had worn when they had left that morning.

"Please, eat," Darhmael suggested. "I can assure that no goblin touched any of this."

"You are mad if you think we will dine with you," Alseya hissed. "Come and meet your fate at the hands of the king."

"My fate?" Darhmael mused, making no move to attack. "How can any know what their fate is? Eireden probably thought that his fate was to save the world, but perhaps that is to be my fate instead. I am already fated to rid this world of the goblin menace once and for all."

"What do you mean?" Aric asked. "They are a part of your army...will they attack? Do you expect them to lose?"

"No, he doesn't," Eireden said, seeing the elf's plan clearly now. He had been distracted by the picture of Ella, but now the plan clicked in place. "It's why this place is empty. Darhmael plans on killing them, along with everyone in Rhyoeven, by using the bomb. Though that doesn't sound like saving anything to me."

"No, it's ridding the universe of a plague," Darhmael said. "I should be thanked if not praised. Really I should be worshipped. Yes, don't give me that look, Aric Anorian. I have often wondered how the world will look when I have my day—when my enemies cower and kneel before me, when I stand victorious—and I have decided that I will be a god."

"You are not a god," Eireden scoffed. "You are little more than a bully."

"Then let the real god stand forth...where is he?" Darhmael spread his hands wide. "I'm the closest thing to a god this planet has ever seen. Look at her," he said pointing at the picture of Ella. "I made her. I created a perfect person in this pit. Think what I can do above in the sun!"

"And what of the humans?" Aric asked. "Will you be their god as well?"

"No. They are ill mannered and ill made. They are viscous and vengeful and would probably kill themselves off even if I did nothing. But I am tired of waiting. I will ensure they are eradicated soon."

"Then you will be the god of nothing," Eireden said, mockingly. "Who will worship you if you kill everyone? And who will cower before you on your great day? It will be none of us, I can assure you."

The elf shook his head sadly. "You seem to mis-understand fate. It is not a matter of wishful thinking. You can't change it by thinking you have some sort of monopoly on goodness. The fact is that you have been beaten at every turn and you live simply because I wish it."

"Why would you want that?"

"Because you have not suffered enough," Darhmael said with a black look behind his beautiful eyes. "If you thought it was painful to see your friends die one after another, wait until you see your city an-nihilated."

"That's not going to happen," Eireden answered. "We won't allow it. You aren't as strong as you want us to think. If the fey have lost their magic then it stands to reason that you have as well. Is that why you've stood around running your mouth? Are you trying to stall so that you can get your bomb away?"

"Since you are insistent," the elf said, drawing his sword. "Come let us see what your fate will be today."

Eireden gave a nod to Tharaden who moved off to the left of the elf while Aric worked his way to the right. When they were in position, Eireden began the attack with a hard hacking blow with his black sword, but his blade swung through nothing but air—the elf had completely disappeared only to reappear behind Alseya and Feylon.

The white-haired fey spun to her right narrowly missing being sheared in half. Feylon was not as quick and the elf ran her through. He then turned and dueled

Tharaden one handed, while at the same time he sent a storm of knives at Eireden and Aric.

They both dodged, but with the pig iron affecting him, Aric was slow to react and went down with two of them sticking out of him.

"You were a fool to rely on fate," the elf commented, easily matching Tharaden in swordsmanship. "As you may have noticed, I retain my full power. After fifteen…" here he paused to turn aside Tharaden's blade before sending his own through the Den's neck. "…thousand years I have built up a tolerance for iron. I don't like it mind you…"

Eireden attacked from one side and Alseya the other in a beautiful tandem of speed and power. Blades flashed and slashed so quick that even a great swordsman would be hard pressed and Darhmael was indeed great. Back he went, fighting in silence until he ran out of room and had he been human he probably would have died there.

Instead he switched from fighting physically to fighting magically. With a twitch of his great mind he sent the king flying back and with a snap of his fingers Alseya froze in place, paralyzed.

"Fate can be so very cruel," the elf said coming toward his lone opponent. "Especially when you make the mistake of relying on her, for she can be fickle. Come, Eireden, King of the Den, kneel before me and as a boon I will end your life quickly."

That would never happen. The king got up from the blood-splashed marble and attacked alone. It was a short, sharp fight and in the end the king added his blood to the floor.

Chapter 38

Ella

High above the city, the strange gnome device came nearer and Ella sent out the force of her mind in the wild hope she could pull more wires and disable the bomb before it detonated.

In a flash of mind-numbing pain her hopes were dashed—the gnome technology that had kept him hidden from her had been applied to the Omni-cart. And now there was nothing for her to do but wait for the inevitable flash of light that would mark the instant of her death. From what she had read about nuclear bombs, if one detonated this close she wouldn't feel the least pain—she would be dead too quick.

And so she waited and waited as the Omni-cart came closer and as she waited she found herself grimacing and shying back, but the Omni-cart didn't explode. It actually landed on the roof of the battle tower, and upon it was not a bomb but three small beings that she recognized as gnomes.

They hopped off in their stiff legged fashion and approached Ella. The leading gnome was a female, or so Ella guessed. She had softer features and though she wore clothing similar to the other gnome Ella had met, beneath her shirt she had breasts that were somewhat square.

"It cannot be doubted that there isn't two whom meet the description of Eleanor, Queen of the Fey," the gnome said. Like her male counterpart she squeaked when she spoke, only more so. "Are you she who is undoubtedly her?"

"I am," Ella said. Behind the female were two smaller gnomes and between them they hefted something that had Ella going dizzy. "Is that…" she could not finish.

"It is what not else is, that is to say, in plain that it is singular," the gnome answered. "It is the sword of Aug-Raumon. We are sworn to deliver it to the Queen of the Fey, for the master wishes it destroyed and can't abide it."

The gnome lady signaled to the smaller gnomes and they brought it to Ella and she took it with numb hands. The sword in its scabbard, though large was light. Still it dropped from her hands to clatter upon the roof. "Is he alive?" she begged of the female gnome.

"Of *he's* there are many, but of *him* there is not. If your reference is to the king, then yes he lives. Your death will be his pain, however soon all shall share your fate."

"Are you saying…is the bomb coming?" Ella asked, knowing in her heart that it was.

"Soon, a few hours," the gnome replied with her head down. It was hard to tell on her stiff features, but Ella guessed that the gnome was sad. "You had mismanaged what Fela-thire had managed and his repairs are slow. Though he is slow because he is not fast."

Talking to gnomes wasn't easy. It was as though they spoke a language that was a cousin to English and had to be translated before she could understand. "So Fela-thire is going slow on purpose," Ella said. "Why? Slow or not, our doom will not change now that Eireden has failed."

"Because Fela-thire did not say what could not be said." When the gnome said this and Ella's brows came down, the little creature went on to add to her confusion, "Familial contractual obligations are considered implied within the bounds of all contractual obligations…"

"Maybe I can help," Ilenwyth-Eden said from the door to the stairs. She was out of breath and leaning on the rail for support. "Gnomes are single-minded when contracted for labor, except that said contract must not run counter to any other contract, including the social contract between husband and wife."

"Clearly," the gnome said.

"But," Ilenwyth went on, "When they do, the family contract takes precedence. The gnome is going slow on fixing the bomb to give his family a chance to escape."

"Exactly," the gnome added.

"So what do we do?" Ella asked. She glanced down at the black sword but did not pick it up, instead she went to the railing that ran around the rooftop and gazed out at the goblins as they dug their deep trenches.

"There is nothing that can be done," Ilenwyth replied. "We can't even attack. Hasdrubal says any chance to break out was gone hours ago."

The dwarf captain had explained this to Ella as well. "So why do the goblins keep digging?"

The gnome answered. "They do not know what is known. Their fate will be all of our fates." The two women turned on the gnome and she explained in her manner. "The master is to be master of all and all is to be one."

"He plans on killing the goblins as well," Ilenwyth said. "I suppose in its way that is a good thing."

Ella shrugged. "I can't see good in any of this." She then turned to the lady gnome and nodded her head. "I wish I could find it within myself to thank you for bringing me the news of my husband's failure but I cannot. I am weak in this, sorry."

Ilenwyth's lips went tight. "I would that you do not use the word failure in regard to Eireden. His death alone will announce failure. Until then we should get you to safety. If I'm not mistaken, this contraption can fly? Is that how you planned on leaving?" she asked the gnome.

The gnome bent her head slightly. "My plans have been unplanned. I will stay because I cannot go."

"I understand," Ilenwyth said and then turned to Ella and explained, "She cannot live without her husband and chooses death, which means you can use this thing to escape."

"And where am I supposed to go?" Ella asked. "These are my people now. I shouldn't leave them so easily."

"It won't be easy," Ilenwyth shot back. "*Our* deaths will be easy compared to what you must do. You are carrying the heir to the throne within you, and possibly the only one who can stop Darhmael. You must protect that child so that one day this world can be free. You must teach him magic and swords and how to be brave, like his father."

"Can I take anyone with me?" Ella asked, now suddenly hopeful of living and at the same time afraid of being alone. "Will you come, Ilenwyth."

The gnome creaked her head back and forth. "That would be in excess of weight parameters."

"A gnome just called me fat. How do you like that?" Ilenwyth said trying to put a smile on her face. "No, you must go alone and you must go now before it's too late. Take Whip-wip and don't look back. I will see that the other sythie are sent as far away as they will go."

"But…" Ella said as Ilenwyth began to push her toward the Omni-cart.

"No buts," Ilenwyth stated. "For a day you were a symbol of hope, however the sun has set on that day. Now, you must hide, and quickly. That is my grandchild you carry—the future King of the Den—and he must live."

Ella nodded and after setting herself awkwardly in the tiny seat, she listened as the gnome began a series of bewildering instructions. Ilenwyth brought over the black sword and laid it across the cart, atop Ella's spear. "You cannot defeat Darhmael without it. Good-bye sweet, Ella. Be strong and brave."

She felt suddenly lost and more afraid than she could ever remember. All of her friends were either dead or held prisoner beneath the Demorlaik, all save this one lady who cared for her more than she feared death.

"I will try," Ella said, biting the inside of her mouth so her lips wouldn't quiver.

And then the gnome touched a button and the Omni-cart's blades began to spin about and the contraption began to rise. Suddenly Ella had a new fear to drown out her old—within two seconds the omni-cart was fifty feet higher and now she was out over the city.

Ella turned back to wave a final good-bye to Ilenwyth and then the city was behind her.

"Oh my, we are high up," Ella said staring around the edge of the rickety wooded cart.

"Sis," Whip-wip agreed from inside a fold of Ella's dress. She had peeked out once at the spinning blades and had not come out again.

Almost as an afterthought Ella began to pedal the cart, though she had no idea if it was helping in any way, and then she began to contemplate steering. "I don't know where to go," she said. Though she spoke to Whip-wip her mind was on Eireden. "I'm lost without him. Can you believe that? I'm married for one day and suddenly I can't stand the idea of being without him. Or even living without him. How am I supposed to do this? How am I supposed to raise a child to fight Darhmael?"

"I know no," Whip-wip answered. "You is strong, sis. You is magic, sis."

"And I'm supposed to send my baby to fight and die just like I sent his father?"

"I know no," the fairy said again.

"You know no because you know I won't be able to do it," Ella said. "Jeez! I'm starting to sound like a gnome. I know myself better than that. I'll go hide and I'll never let that boy out of my sight. And Darhmael will grow stronger and stronger and then…" she paused remembering her dream of the sweet child growing inside her. He was too precious to let die at the hands of a fiend like Darhmael.

"I won't be able to do it," she said. "I won't send my child to fight and die, which means what? That Darhmael wins? I don't know. I don't know what to do! I can't go back and I can't go on…so where do I go?"

"Home?"

"There's no home for me if it isn't here," Ella said, feeling a resolve starting to grow within her, one that gave her chills to even contemplate. "What did I say when I first got in the Hidden Lands?"

"You say you like Whip-wip's wings," Whip-wip answered.

"No that's what I said when I first met you. What I said on my first day was that I wasn't going to be the damsel in the distress...I know what I'm going to do. I'm going to the Demorlaik and then beneath."

"Sis," Whip-wip said and then the tiny fairy got the shivers.

"I agree," Ella said, gritting her teeth as she turned the cart north.

Too quickly for either of their likings the haunted city could be seen. Despite that it was only a shadow in the daylight it let off an eerie glow at night that was a warning to anything living to stay away.

Ella came on regardless and as she did the omni-cart began to descend lower and lower, strangely it felt to be gaining weight around her. Pedaling helped, though it was difficult in her fancy dress, but still she knew she would not make it to the center of the city. From high up she had seen there was a great opening which she assumed was her destination and the cart came down with a heavy thump in a bizarre world blocks away.

The Demorlaik was a twisted and dank nightmare and Ella was hurrying down the street on foot as soon as she landed. On her back, hanging by its sheath strap, was the black sword and in her hand was the golden tipped spear—this she kept from glowing too brightly. She could hear things moving in the buildings and didn't want to attract attention to herself.

Eventually attention came anyways. Whip-wip whistled a warning and pointed to a building just in front of them. A man or man shaped thing stepped from a doorway and began to amble toward them. Even with the shadows Ella grew afraid and ducked around a corner.

"Can you distract him?" she asked Whip-wip. The fairy started shaking her head but then Ella reasoned, "You can fly, but he can't."

"Oh sis," Whip-wip said in relief. She then flew off glowing like a lamp and this definitely distracted *them*.

Suddenly there were dozens of the things—zombies they were in Ella's mind. They shambled after the fairy, but unfortunately for Ella, hundreds more came stumbling from all the buildings around. They had initially been drawn to the light of the fairy, but when they caught sight of Ella they forgot all about her and turned to the queen with dreadful moans.

Ella ran. She hiked her dress with one hand and carried the spear in the other and was thankful that the Den women weren't into fancy heels. She sprinted through the city, thinking she was well ahead of the creatures but then Whip-wip came down at her like a shooting star.

"*Monstas* ahead," she said pointing. Ella tried one side street and then another, yet both were filled with the creatures while behind they moved like a beastly undead wave toward her.

"Here! Here!" Whip-wip screamed, pointing at a tall building across the street. It seemed to be empty and Ella dashed across to it with the undead army close on her heels. She proved the quicker and gained the entrance. In a flash she sent out the power of her mind and mapped out its interior—a staircase was two doors down and she booked to it with an idea forming.

She went up four floors with the creatures right behind and then she burst into an empty corridor. Had the structure been in America she would have de-scribed it as an apartment building and like one, there were many doors entering onto the hall. She chose one with a north face and was through it before the first of the zombies could enter the hall.

"Ella!" Whip-wip cried as Ella went to the win-dow and jumped. "You no fly!"

She didn't need to fly; she just needed to land softly enough not to get hurt. And this she did, break-ing her fall with the power of her mind and landing in the same street she had just vacated, but this time the zombies were behind her and not blocking her way to the great hole in the city.

Again she didn't dare even to pause for a breath, she ran, as around her the creatures began to drop from the sky, uncaring of hurting themselves. Down the street was a strange hill that marked the center of the city and this was her last hurdle. She took it in fast strides and when she saw she would beat the hordes a smile broke her face.

"We can make it Whip…"

Her words choked in her throat. Halfway up she came across the decimated remains of a number of horses—all that was left were splayed rib bones and shredded saddles.

She knew the king's saddle…and Lienhart's…and the light blanket that Aric used instead of one…and there on the ground was Furen's iron cap that he always wore.

Ella detoured to pick it up and saw that blood was pooled in it. "Whip-wip, look," she said, holding it up. The blood poured out of it and Ella began to cry.

"Is no time, sis!" Whip-wip said pointing. Zombies were moving to cut her off left and right, and there were more up the hill. A line of them blocked her way to the hole—they had been waiting for her.

She realized that she never had a chance to begin with and that all of her running was for nothing. Despair swept over her, but right behind that came anger and she took up her spear to slay as many as possible. The ones on the hill charged down and Ella charged up blasting the lead ones with light—when that didn't do much she tried fire.

Unfortunately the zombies did not feel pain and they came on like dreadful human torches. She swept them back with her mind but there were too many and when one was thrown down another took its place and as her strength began to fail they pressed close and Ella was surrounded in the heart of the Haunted City.

Chapter 39

Ella

Ella pulled the black sword and for a second the undead hesitated—it had been the sword of their creator—however the hesitation did not last and when they attacked, Ella let out the battle cry of the Den and hacked away the hands that reached for her.

And then a new battle cry thundered in the city and there was a dwarf-zombie attacking with a huge war hammer. It was the body of Furen come alive. He was a horror to look upon—covered in blood and hanging shreds of flesh from every edge of his armor. He laid about him in a confused manner knocking down zombies left and right and then he grabbed Ella by the arm and dragged her in close with his mouth wide.

He was so close that her spear and her blade were all but useless and so instinctively she kicked him in the crotch.

Air shot out of him and he groaned, "Why would you do such a thing?"

"Furen! You're alive," Ella gasped in disbelief.

"It doesn't feel like it," he gasped while his eyes began to water.

"I'm sorry," she said. "Come on." She dragged the dwarf away as the undead began to pick themselves up. The top of the hill was close but with the dwarf huffing and puffing and cursing under his breath they made it just ahead of the zombies. Going down was easier and soon the horde backed away and refused to come closer as Ella and Furen entered the cold.

"This will end soon," Furen said, recovered somewhat. "Just a little further."

The bitter cold went right through her dress and even Whip-wip found little warmth snug in her bosom. "I wish I had stopped to put on something other than this." The dress was white with flowers of spun gold and so far it was little worried by her run through the city.

"I think it is fetching," Furen said. "Much better than me. Look at my armor!"

"You are a mess," Ella said but then looked ahead —searched ahead, really. "Is Eireden with you?"

"No, I am afraid they left me, but through no fault of their own. For some reason I was saddled with a horse that wasn't very well trained. I wonder if it was even a Den horse. When those ghasts came after us it would not keep its head and ended up falling down that hill with me still in the saddle. I was pinned beneath it and before I could get up another horse came down atop of mine!"

"Were you not crushed?" Ella asked.

"Crushed? By a horse? No, but two horses made it difficult to draw breath I suppose. Eventually the ghasts ate away enough of the horses that I was just fine, but what a mess they made! I wonder if I will ever get this cleaned up."

"I'm sure you will," Ella said in disbelief at what parts of the story he found most difficult to deal with. "But how did you fight all those things? Those ghasts?"

"Oh that. When there was just shreds of the horse left atop of me I just jumped up and ran. They seemed surprised that anyone would be alive under a couple of horses."

"How silly of them," Ella said dryly. She then smiled and resisted the temptation of hugging the dwarf—he really was foul. "So how do we get through this maze?" she asked eyeing the dark tunnel.

"I was hoping you knew," he answered. "Do you not have a plan?"

"No…I was just going to wing it." She then went on to explain about what the gnome had told her.

Furen frowned as she went on. "It doesn't look like we have much choice but to wing. However I'm afraid we will die of starvation long before we find Darhmael. I've explored some of the lands down here and it is a wonder anyone could find their way. Here, let me show you."

He led her until the tunnel opened into a wide cave that went back further than she could see. "There are fourteen different tunnels that open off this little cavern, and each of those immediately branch again and then those branch as well. Do you begin to see the issue?"

"Yes, but look at this," Ella allowed the unicorn horn to emit more light and she pointed to the ground.

"Oh aye, that is fine work. I can tell Hasdrubal's handiwork. Though I would have…"

"Don't look at the source of the light—not the spear. Look at what it lights up." In the scant dirt of the rocky cavern a boot print that was larger than a dwarves could be seen.

The dwarf went down to his hands and knees and squinted. "I see a print! Do you think you might be able to track them in this way?"

"Or by smell," Ella answered, taking a deep breath and catching that unique odor of Eireden's, which had always been a comfort to her.

The dwarf stepped back. "You can smell us? Maybe I should go behind you."

"And take his sword. It will make it easier on me."

Ella had never tried to track someone in such a way, however once she started she was able to pick out the individual scents with ease. She had some difficulty on the spiraling stairs because of the fetid, overpowering odor emanating from the depths, but she found the door they had taken and from there it was smooth sailing. Even when they backtracked at a certain point she picked up on it quick.

"Uh-oh," she whispered as she came up on the bridge. The smell of blood was strong. "Someone died here," she said.

"Is that right?" Furen answered vacantly. His eyes were on the rickety bridge. It seemed exceptionally narrow for someone of his bulk.

"Rudyid, I believe. Though it may be Yur-el. Her scent is strong, though I am afraid it's coming from there." She pointed to the black gorge.

"Oh what a shame that is," Furen said, sadly. "She was one of the few fey that I could see eye to eye with."

For whatever reason the two were morbidly drawn to the edge. They peered down into the darkness and Ella breathed out a sigh of relief that she could not see any of the bodies of her friends.

Furen sighed as well and just as he did a voice spoke from the gorge, "Ella?"

"Wha!" she screamed and jumped back.

"Ella? Is that you?" came the voice again.

"Yur-el? What…where are you? Hold on, we can't see anything. Whip-wip can you find her?" The fairly looked skeptically at the black gorge, but with a nudge she lit herself and floated down. There, about thirty feet below the edge of the shelf was Yur-el clinging to a little outcropping of rock.

"Hi Whip-wip," the fey said. "I'm awful glad to see you." The fairy rubbed herself against Yur-el's cheek.

"Just hold on," Ella said looking around. She could lift the fey with her mind, but she was only just getting her strength back and she wanted to save herself for her fight with Darhmael. The bridge! She pushed Furen to it and said, "You have to cross. When you do we'll cut one of the ropes and use that to haul her up."

"Ho, wait! Shouldn't we discuss…Ella!" The dwarf scrambled to hold himself back. He turned and for the first time ever Ella saw fear in his eyes. "I don't know about this. I'm not good with heights and look at that thing! It'll crumble beneath my weight."

"We don't have time for this," Ella said as calmly as she could. "You're not too heavy. If Eireden crossed you can as well. And Furen listen to me, I won't let you fall."

The dwarf shook and trembled and when he put one of his stumpy boots upon the bridge he pulled it right off again. "Ok," he said and then turned to Ella. He whispered, "I can do it but you have to swear you'll never say a word about any of this."

"I swear," Ella said.

"Ok." Furen took a deep breath and then shocked Ella by getting down on his hands and knees. He then commenced to crawl across the bridge. Whip-wip went into a fit of laughter and flew up to ride Furen's back. "Get that dratted fairy away from me!" he roared, his face red.

Ella used her magic and pulled the fairy back. Whip-wip just laid in the gentle hand of her magic, weak from laughing.

Furen made it across and wanted to just lay there for a moment, but Ella was anxious. "Cut the other end of this rope," Ella said as she used her spear to shear away one of the ropes.

"How will you cross?" Furen asked. Ella would never have done this back in America but she was not the same girl. Without answering she scampered across the single rope as Furen stared.

"Quick," she ordered, when she had reached the other side..

The dwarf cut the rope free and dangled it for Yur-el who came up as easily as a spider monkey might. She gave Ella a hug but when she saw the state of Furen's armor she only gave him a smile and a sincere thanks.

"What of Rudyid?" Ella asked.

The smile left her face. "He fought and died like a hero. Darhmael proved the stronger in arms, though not in love."

"And what of the others?" Ella asked, fearing that her love had died here as well.

"Aziel was taken somewhere in the upper chambers; we know not where. And I was thought dead by everyone. I was just able to catch a hold of that rock, but with the walls so shear I could go neither up nor down. And with the elf holding such an advantage the others had to leave us and I blame them not. Though I look upon you in wonder, good dwarf. Are you so tough and hard that even ghouls find you inedible?"

Now that he had crossed his bridge Furen was all smiles and as they walked he told his story. Ella barely listened. Her anxiety grew with every step and when they came upon the wide plain before the citadel she wanted to rush forward. Instead she only picked up the pace so that little Yur-el practically jogged along.

However when she saw the bodies on the bridge, Ella couldn't stop herself and she ran until she came to the edge of the moat. The portcullis was back in its original position and the bridge had been raised again. And there, to her horror were three corpses. They were so covered in a black tar that she couldn't make out their features.

"Who are they?" she cried anxiously. "I can't tell by smell and they are too covered to know."

"This is Hasfel, my dear friend," Yur-el said pointing to the smaller of the three. "That is Prince Sylra. You can see the eagle design on his shoulder plate—he liked eagles. He told me so once. But that person furthest away...it's either the Prince Lienhart, or the king. They were of similar size."

Ella couldn't tell either. "Then it's the prince," she said through clenched teeth. "I'm sorry but that is the way it is. And…and…his sword! It *is* the prince. See he's still wearing his sword…"

Suddenly overcome, Ella felt her hands go numb and her knees buckled and she wept there on the edge of the bridge and they were tears of sorrow for she loved the prince very much. As well they were tears of relief. There was still a chance.

"I wonder what happened here," Furen said, standing next to her. "Did the bridge sink?"

"It appears that the portcullis must have dropped in front of them, and then the bridge dropped," Yur-el said. "See how there isn't a speck of tar on the bars?"

"Then how do we cross safely?"

Wiping away her tears, Ella got up and looked at the situation. "Hand me the king's sword and stand away." Taking the black sword she backed up a dozen paces before dashing forward so that her dress trailed and then she leapt as pretty as a gazelle clearing the thirty-foot bridge with room to spare and with only the slightest use of her powers.

She stuck the sword point down in the track where the bars would normally slide. "Come on," she hissed. Furen ran at full speed, which wasn't the least quick, while Yur-el loped along beside him, and the bridge was quiet and the bars remained in position.

Ella handed back the sword to Furen. "This it," she said.

They were in the courtyard and above them the towers soared. She began heading for the main doors but an oddity in the scent trail made her pause. "They went this way first. And see there is a change in their prints."

Furen shrugged, looking down at the ground while Yur-el only raised an eyebrow and asked, "Should we follow in their path and veer off on this tangent, or head straight in? Whatever occurred in there did not avail them."

"Then perhaps they missed something," Ella said. "I say we walk just as they did." When neither of the other two second guessed her, Ella went to the dungeon door and paused there with it opened. Beneath the smell of decay, and the light odors of Eireden and the others, there was a scent that she nearly recognized but not quite—it was like a forgotten word that sat just on the tip of her tongue. It was such an annoyingly curiosity that she bypassed the third floor where Eireden and his group had gone and went deeper.

Four floors down the scent grew and as it did the faster she went, passing cell after cell with their dead occupants, and then she stood in front of the last and she gasped taken back.

"Do I know you?" she asked of the man who stood at the far end of his tiny cell. He was tall and thin and his eyes were purple glass and his hair was copper.

"Yes," he answered with a lilting voice. "I am Strai. Now please leave me. I do not wish to be stared at so." Ella blinked not realizing until then that she had been gaping at the half-elf.

"Who is this?" Furen asked. He stared, unabashedly so.

"My brother," Ella answered.

This only made Furen stare harder and then he blinked. "This is one of the elves! What does he do in this prison?"

"I have been left here to starve like the rest. Father says it is because I failed him, but he makes excuses only. The truth is, he has decided that when the humans are extinct he will create a new breed of elves and he will be their god. In such a world, Ella and I are no longer welcome."

"We go to fight him, now," Ella said. "You may join us and change your fate."

"Hey, now wait just a moment!" Furen said, gently pushing Ella away from the cell door. "There is no way we can trust him."

"And there's no way we can win without him," Ella shot back. "If Eireden couldn't finish Darhmael, how can we? We lack the fire power."

"You can't win even if I threw in with you," Strai said. "Father is at the height of his power in his citadel, while we will be at our weakest. The entire fortress is made from iron, just as these chains are."

Ella hadn't even considered that a possibility. "Then we really do need you."

"Ella!" Furen said, stamping his foot. "What is the one thing we know about elves? They hate dwarves, they hate Den and they hate fey. They probably even hate the sythie."

"Of course we do," Strai answered reasonably. "But ask Ella what is the one thing we hate worse than all that?"

They all looked to her and she answered, "They hate themselves. It's why they torture themselves with fire."

"Still…"

The elf cut in, "And there is something we hate even more: Darhmael. He did this to us. He made us like this, so close to perfect and so far from it. That's why I would fight with you. If we lose, what have I lost? Nothing, I am to die either way. Though what I gain if we win I'm not exactly sure."

"I guarantee you won't be harmed," Ella said. "I can even guarantee a fresh start."

"We will see," Strai said. "We will settle on a truce for the time being. Now, release me."

"Hold on!" Furen said, blowing out fiercely. "I am against this but I respect the lady. Let it be said here and now that I will slay you, fiend if I feel for a moment that we are being double-crossed."

Strai nodded and said, "I would do the same." He motioned to Ella, who opened the locks with her mind. He then stepped into the corridor and held out his hand. "I'm going to need a weapon."

"The king's sword!" Furen asked in a fury. "Oh my goodness, Ella please. I have a dagger he could use." Even Whip-wip looked askance at the elf's request. She held up her little spear for him, but Strai was adamant about the sword.

Ella took the sword from Furen and handed it over. She then said, "So how do we do this?" No one had a clue beyond attacking hard and fast with everything they had. This didn't sit well with Ella.

"We may be fast, but we aren't particularly hard. In fact, Yur-el I want you to consider not fighting at all."

"What?" she asked in surprise. "Am I to wait here to see who wins?"

"No," Ella said, her mind suddenly burning up neurons. "I have a different plan for you. We will fight, but we won't fight Darhmael's fight."

Chapter 40

Ella

Furen stood outside the citadel doors and with great relish he struck them three crashing blows with his war hammer. He then stood back flexing his muscles. In his right hand he held the hammer and from his back he unslung the shield that always gave him the appearance of a beetle and strapped it across his left arm.

He waited with the patience of his kind.

It was not a long wait. The doors swung wide and Darhmael stood just within them. "What is this?" he asked. "You found your way through the maze. I am impressed."

Furen was on his toes, ready to move at the slightest provocation. "I have come for the king."

Now Darhmael laughed in earnest and stepped forward so that he was just inside the doorway. From where he stood he could see neither Strai nor Ella who stood on either side. He had absolutely no reason to believe they were there.

"Come on in," Darhmael said, still chuckling. "I can set you up with the same accommodations I have given them—front row seats to the destruction of Rhyoeven."

"I think we should settle this here," Furen said. "There's no reason to make a mess of things."

"If that's the way you want it," Darhmael answered and before the last syllable had been spoken
the elf sprang forward with a speed that astounded
Furen and he only just got his shield up in time. The
next attack was faster still and the third drew blood,
despite the dwarf's finely crafted armor.

"Yes, let's not have you bleed all over…"
Darhmael started to say but a flicker of movement to
his right had him turning instinctually. "You!" he cried
at the sight of his son. They crossed blades in a shower
of sparks.

Strai was fast and strong yet was no match for his
father even with the black sword, but he had Furen
swinging his mighty hammer next to him, and the two
had Darhmael retreating slowly to the safety of his
citadel where Strai would weaken in an instant.

Yet this was not unexpected and in fact it was
hoped for. Ella had slipped inside as soon as Strai had
attacked and now she waited with sweat on her palms.
Back Darhmael came and Ella was in the perfect position and with all her strength she drove the spear
straight through the elf.

He screamed in shock and pain, while throwing
himself forward. Had she been better trained in the use
of the spear she might have ended the battle right
there. However she was slow to follow up and he
blasted her away so that she flew up the stairs. Pain
spiked down her back and her breath shot from her
lungs.

Now the momentum shifted. Strai wavered as he
stepped into the citadel and Furen, with his short legs,
was slow to get around him. This was all it took for
the elf to heal himself. He stood tall again and behind
the dwarf and the half-elf the citadel's doors closed
with a great crash.

"So many surprises for one day," Darhmael said.
"Let us see if there are any more."

Ella suddenly felt herself lifted off the ground and she flew toward the elf who raised his sword to split her in two. Though her strength of mind was a tenth of what it had been just minutes before outside the citadel, the power of the unicorn horn was still intact and she used it to send a blast of light at the elf.

She dropped like a rock, practically at his feet as he threw a hand to his face. Seeing her chance she jabbed awkwardly with the spear, but even blinded the elf could feel all of her movements with his mind and parried the attack. And then the spear was magically yanked from her hands and sent flying; now she was defenseless.

Ella began kicking herself backwards but the elf did not bother to follow. Furen and Strai were charging at him and they battled to a great ringing of metal. Ella couldn't waste a second watching the melee unfold; she had to get her spear, however her back shot through with pain with every movement.

She could only crawl up the stairs, grimacing as she went, and when she reached the top, the sight that unfolded before her nearly stopped her breath. The room was a blood-covered horror.

There was Feylon with her throat slit. And Tharaden hewn to pieces. Aric was a pincushion of knives; she could count seven of them sticking out of him yet still he rolled a bleary eye at her. And Alseya—the lady in white, was white no longer—she was a deep red and did not stir.

And there was Eireden, King of the Den. Gone was his shining armor. In its place he wore a sheen of fresh blood and gore, yet still he stood with Yur-el's sword in his hand. The little fey had stolen up the stairs to give up her weapon and was now hiding with only a Furen's dagger to attack with.

And strangely there was Elleni standing like a statue off to the side. She was alive and unhurt, and amazingly she wore a smile on her face that made her look years younger.

But of her spear naught could be seen. Behind Ella the clash of metal ended and Ella turned to see Darhmael slide his glittering elf sword from Furen's barrel chest. The dwarf wore a look of surprise before he toppled backward to land next to Strai who knelt clutching his innards.

"Look how lovely you are in that dress," Darhmael said as he slowly came up the stairs. Ella began backing away coming to a stop with her back to one of the couches. "We don't get such beauty…"

Just then Whip-wip couldn't stand the danger to Ella for a second longer and she came shooting out of her hiding spot. Casually Darhmael sent a wave of fire over her and she spun past Ella screaming. The queen turned quick and composed—she had expected this very thing—and before the fairy even hit the ground behind the couch Ella had healed her, though the magic use left her weak and shaky.

"So sad," Darhmael commented. "Though to bring a pet to a battle is just foolish. And speaking of fools." The elf looked to Eireden and took the sword away from him with just a thought—it went clanging down the stairs. "That's better. Now sit."

Against his will, Eireden was forced backwards until the back of his legs struck the far couch and he plopped, ungracefully down. Darhmael then considered Ella.

"So many surprises for one day," he said for a second time, eyeing Ella with a gaze that went right through to her soul. She felt her mind open like a box. "What other surprises do you have hidden? What is this? You are pregnant?"

"Stop it!" Ella yelled, grabbing her head as if that would do anything to stop the elf's intrusion.

Darhmael chuckled. "What a fool you were to come here with the only heir of the Den within you."

At the moment it did seem very foolish and it didn't help that Eireden flicked his eyes to her just then. Ella rallied at the notion that she was being judged by either man. "And hiding would've been wise? Could I have hidden from the plagues you'll unleash on the humans? Or the wars you start to eradicate them? Or would it have been better that I sit and wait to die without a fight?"

"Spoken like a true Queen of the Den," Darhmael answered. "Too bad you'll hold that title for only another twenty-five and a half minutes. The gnome is even now up there putting the finishing touches on his omni-device. Most ingenious it is—it will fly, pilotless to Rhyoeven and no power, not even my own will be able to stop it. The good news is that we can watch the destruction of your city right here and after you have cried and cursed me, I'll kill you."

Ella's face contorted in a spasm of anger, but it did not last. Despair hit her—she was out of ideas and had the strength to perform only the simplest magic. Her allies were either powerless and cowering, or dead or very close to it.

Eireden struggled to stand and when he did he swayed from blood loss. "The Den do not wait to die. Fight me, fiend."

Darhmael considered this. "Yes. I will. Killing you in front of your beloved will add to her suffering and we do have a little time on our hands. An excellent idea."

"My sword," Eireden asked, clutching the arm of the couch for support.

"By all means," Darhmael laughed. "You want to go down swinging. How very heroic." The black sword came flying up from the bottom of the stairs and smacked Eireden in the side of the face, knocking him down.

"Why are you so cruel?" Ella hissed.

"Before you speak to me of cruelties, look at where I've been imprisoned for the last fifteen-thousand years! And look who I've been imprisoned with. And are you so quick that you forget my entire race, and all of my family have been killed? I think I have a right to my cruelties. I deserve the joy they bring me."

"You deserve what's coming to you," Eireden snarled and then swallowed hard, making ready to fight. But then he held up a hand. "Wait...Ella, I've changed my mind. If we have a girl, I want her name to be Generai."

Ella blinked at this strange request. Generai? But they were having a boy—he knew this. And why Generai? Was this his way of telling Ella that he secretly loved...suddenly the "request" clicked in her mind as she remembered how the scout had died.

With dread at what he was contemplating she began to shake her head, but he set his jaw and said, "To my last breath, I love you."

"Love you too," she answered, knowing in her heart that he would not be stayed from his course.

The action was short and savage. Eireden had strength for only a few passes of his blade and then, just as Generai had done on the Battle Tower of Rhyoeven, Eireden let himself be impaled on the elf's sword and at same time he tossed the weapon of Aug-Raumon to Ella.

She snatched it in mid-air and with a fury driven by her overpowering sorrow sought to cleave the elf from head to toe. However Darhmael stepped aside easily, leaving his weapon stuck through the Den king. His unexpected move overbalanced her and she sent up a shower of sparks as her sword smote nothing but the marble floor.

And then Darhmael kicked Ella's legs out from beneath her and landed atop her with a dagger to her throat. "Do you think that I would so soon forget the name Generai?" he said, grinning from ear to ear. "It was a nifty trick then, but I won't be fooled twice."

"You know Generai, but do you know who Whip-wip is?" Ella didn't have to look to know her friend was coming.

Darhmael's mouth came open just as the fairy—colored snow white to match the backdrop of wall behind her—came zipping at him. In her hands she wielded the foot long spear that Hasdrubal had made specially for her. It was like the world's sharpest knitting needle and this she sunk four inches deep in Darhmael's glittering right eye.

The elf sat up, roaring in rage and pain, and with his right eye blind and his mind on Ella and the fairy, he didn't know that Yur-el had come sprinting from her hiding spot behind the couch. He didn't know until she sunk Furen's dagger up to the hilt beneath his collarbone.

He screamed again and now Ella reached over to grab the black sword, but Darhmael yelled, "Enough!" With the word came a wave of power that sent the fey flying, while Whip-wip smacked up against a wall. He then pushed down Ella's hand.

"You are persistent," he hissed dripping blood down upon her face. "But in the end it won't be enough. Your kind is too weak."

"What…of the…human?" Eireden asked in a wet and bubbling whisper. He did not stir more than to speak. "What of Mary?"

"Mary?" Darhmael asked, his one good eye grew in puzzlement at the sound of the name. And then it went wider still as the horn of the unicorn shot out from his chest in a burst of light and blood.

Elleni Feyden, also known as Mary Welsley stood behind him and finally there was life in her eyes and a spear in her hands. "Don't hurt my baby," she said in a voice that cracked.

A look of intense pain swept Darhmael, but just as before he had the magical power to hold onto life long enough to push himself off the horn, only this time Ella was right there and she gripped the silver haft of the spear and would not let go and he was stuck upon it as his life ran out of him.

"No," he said and then died, slumping over Ella.

With a grunt, Ella heaved him off and for just a moment she rejoiced at her victory, but then the butchery of the room had her reeling. Everywhere there was pain and death—all save her mother; Mary was already back to her statue form, though now the smile was greater than before.

"El," came a whisper.

"My king!" Ella cried dropping to her knees and tearing up at the sight of him. His wounds were many and grievous.

"The bomb," he whispered.

"But…"

"Leave me," he said. If she did he would die and if she didn't, thousands would. Such was her love for this man that she hesitated selfishly, though for only a second, and then she bent and kissed him.

"Hold on, my love!" she cried running, leaving him to his fate.

There had been stairs going up at the entrance and so she ran past Aric and the limp form of Alseya. She leapt the sad parts that used to be young Tharaden, and there was Furen, the dwarf who could not be crushed by two horses. He lay on his back with his eyes closed and his normally grey face a pasty white.

"All the way to the top," Strai told her. He sat slumped against a wall, with his cloak thrown over himself to hide the gaping wound. "If our father was correct, you have two minutes."

"Oh jeez!" Ella whispered. It was all the breath she allowed herself to waste. Two minutes and a twenty-story tower didn't match. If both were correct she would never make it.

"Ella, my wing," Whip-wip said with little tears on her face. One of her four gold and silver wings was bent near in half, and she flew at an odd angle because of it. "Fix sis."

"Gnome," Ella said in a breathy whisper as she sprinted up the stairs. She was only halfway up and already her lungs burned. "Stall…him."

Broken wing or not, Whip-wip was a good flyer and she sped up and out of sight. She was back quickly. "Is glass," she stated matter-of-factly.

Ella had no clue what she meant and couldn't spare even a sip of oxygen to ask. Her legs began to feel like weights fighting against her and still she pressed on, but now she went slower and slower until she staggered up the final flight.

She had expected the tower to open up and that she would be able to see all of the vast cavern that the citadel sat in, but instead the stairs ended at a heavy glass door and there was the gnome beyond it. He sat on what looked like half a bike—it had a seat and pedals and a chain, but no wheels and was without handlebars.

The gnome was pedaling like mad and checking a device he held in his hand. The device was connected by wires to his large version of the omni-cart.

"Gnome!" Ella cried, pounding on the door. He jumped in surprise and a squeak shot out of him. If Ella thought he was pedaling quickly before now he went at it so that sweat flew. "Stop!" she yelled. "The master is dead. You don't have to finish the bomb."

"I cannot undo what cannot be undone," he said huffing.

"But…but, he's dead. No one needs to be killed. I mean no one else." The gnome did not pause at this line of reasoning. "I met your wife," Ella said, trying a different route. Desperately she tried to remember the lady gnome's name, but she hadn't offered it and Ella hadn't asked, which she really regretted just then. She did know his name, however.

"Fela-thire, you have to stop. If you don't she will die. Please, can't you hear me?"

"I may only stop when it has begun and that will be in thirteen seconds."

Thirteen seconds! The seconds ticked away and finally the gnome stepped off the bike. He went to the omni-cart pressed one button and the blades began to whip. Ella pounded on the glass for all she was worth, but the gnome ignored her until the blades were spinning too fast to see. He pressed a second button and then calmly strode for the door as the omni-cart rose gradually into the air.

"Hurry, damn it!" Ella cried, however nothing hurried the gnome. He opened the door and stood aside as Ella ran into the room and looked up. Far above her the Omni-cart was steadily rising through a smooth shaft that had been cut through the rock. It was a straight shot to the surface.

"How do I stop the bomb?" she demanded of the gnome.

"You cannot stop the bomb, I'm sorry. It cannot be affected by the magical means of affectation."

Ella didn't try though she desperately wanted to. She was outside the citadel now and there felt to be a volcano of energy within her—just then however it was a useless volcano.

"You could stop the chain activated, poly-powered, kinetic slash potential, torque driven, thirty-four spring omni transportator," the gnome mused. "That is if you could do what you most certainly can't."

"What can't I do?"

"Fly," the gnome said in the simplest terms he had ever uttered.

"And if I could?" Ella asked, feeling the power within her. It wouldn't be enough. She didn't have the strength. No one did.

"Press the red button, of course."

No one had the strength, no person alive…but maybe an elf would. If she had bad enough need.

You need to step away from whatever is limiting you. Ilenwyth had told her. *You are a woman, with all the power of a woman.*

"I can be the Sun Queen if I let myself," Ella said in a whisper. She then bent her knees and jumped into the air and before gravity had a chance to pull her down she shot upwards using the volcano inside her to project her up through the shaft.

"You is fly!" Whip-wip cried happily from beside her.

"Really I just jumped," Ella said. She was going so fast that flight was not the best term. A bullet fired from a gun couldn't really be said to be flying, yet it did the trick and she came up on the cart in a scream and she had to put on the mental breaks just to keep a hold of it.

"Find a red button!" Ella yelled—there were many buttons and more levers than could be good for her.

"Red, sis," Whip-wip said as she was about to press a blue button.

"No!" Ella cried. "I said red. That was…never mind. Here it is." She punched it and the blades above came to a stop and the cart began to fall like a rock. "What the…"

Not knowing what to do, Ella hit the button a second time, which restarted the blades. They kicked in just twenty feet above the ground and they landed with a heavy jolt and too late Ella realized she had been holding onto the nuclear bomb for support. She jumped away from it.

The gnome seemed very pleased and he clapped his wooden little hands. Ella went down to one knee and begged, "How do we stop the bomb? You built... or you fixed it, so you must know how to unfix it."

"I made it non-unmadeable. It will remain in this state until it no longer does."

Ella studied it, looking for seams or rivets or even screws, but it was a solid chunk of metal. "How much time do we have?" she asked

The gnome glanced up at a clock that sat above a tool bench. "Eighteen minutes and forty-one seconds."

"Oh jeez," Ella said going back to the bomb and staring at it as she thought. Eighteen minutes wasn't long enough to run away. And after her brief stint at flying she was weak and shaky. Another flight would be impossible and even if she could fly, she couldn't leave the king. Not to be killed...if he wasn't already dead.

"I have instructions for you," she said to the gnome. "Do not touch this cart or anything on it until I come back. Whip-wip, guard him." Ella took off for the stairs and immediately felt the pig iron surrounding her; it made her want to be sick.

Still going down was twice as fast as going up and soon she came upon Furen staring at her from the floor. "The bomb?" he asked.

"It's at the top of the tower," Ella said hurrying past and running up the wood stairs that led to the throne room and found Yur-el kneeling over Alseya and crying. "Is she?"

"I live for the moment," the opal-eyed fey said in a whisper.

"Then you live forever," Ella replied with a strained smile. She went past her mother and went to the king. Yur-el had removed the sword from his stomach and had shoved a torn piece of her cloak into the wound.

She thought him dead, but he cracked an eye. "I saved the city," she said. He smiled through pale lips. "Only, I have doomed us. I stopped the omni-cart thing, but I can't diffuse the bomb. It's going to explode in seventeen minutes. What should I do?"

"Take…cart," he whispered.

"Take the cart? Where?"

"Home."

Ella looked at him as if he had just lost his mind and then she realized what it was he asked. "You want me to leave the bomb and take the cart?"

"Destroy Demorlaik."

"Yes! Oh my God, Yes!" Ella made to get up and then she thought of the stairs and everyone around her. None but Yur-el would make it besides Ella. "We can heal you!" she said, coming up with an idea. "Yur-el, do you have the strength to heal the king if we took him outside?"

"No, I used everything I had to keep him alive as long as he has. Using power in this place is draining."

Ella dashed to Alseya's side. "What about you? If I took you outside…" the fey shook her head. Gritting her teeth in panic and frustration, Ella crawled to the king and said, "I don't know what to do. I barely have any strength left and your wounds are so grievous that I could not heal them all even if I were at my full power."

"Leave me," Eireden said. "But kiss me first."

"I can't leave you!" she cried gripping her hair and pulling hard. "Not after everything. I need you."

"They need you. Kiss me so I can sleep."

Ella bent and kissed his lips and they were already cold. "Love you," she whispered, but he did not speak again.

The queen stood and swayed, her mind threatening to go blank with her grief. She had the littlest bit of power left and so she went to Aric, and with tears dripping down his face, she began to slide him along the floor to the entrance. Yur-el followed with Alseya.

When the dark air hit her Ella began to bawl and she knelt over Aric and healed the holes in his arties and veins, it was all she had strength for, but since his wounds were less it would do. "Go to the top," she said and then stood feeling her head go light with the effort. Next to her Yur-el went to a knee having pushed herself to the limit in healing Alseya who was still dying but only slower.

"You must go," Alseya warned. "And quickly."

"I don't want to go at all. I thought I knew what love was….I had this vision of it. Flowers and walks holding hands, and making love, and smiling, and being happy. But now I know what it really is. Love is a poison—and the only antidote is him. Without him I will die."

"You must live," Alseya replied in a whisper. "You are queen! And mother to the king. You have to live. Live for that baby within you, and live for your peoples."

Ella nodded, but she nodded with a dead heart. In the doorway, Furen watched her through eyes that leaked around the edges. Because of the pain of his heart, he could not speak. Despite his injury he heaved himself up and headed for the stairs leaving a trail of red.

Now Ella tried to pick up Alseya, but the poor fey was slippery with blood and had it not been for Yur-el the fey would've been left with the king to die. Instead they took her together and brought her to the stairs and there was the elf, Strai.

"I'm sorry but I have nothing left," Ella said in a monotone. "Can you heal yourself?"

"I don't want to," Strai answered. "I'm not meant for your world. I would always be the monster. I would always be the one despised and blamed and ridiculed. I don't want to live like that."

"We also have beaches," Ella said, though she knew not why. She then went to the stairs, but not before taking one last look at her king, hoping against hope that he would stir and beckon for one more kiss. If he had she would have run to him bomb or no bomb. However he just laid there as still as death and she went up the stairs.

When Ella, Alseya, and Yur-el finally got to the top, they saw the bomb was upon the rock floor and everyone, including Elleni sat huddled on the cart waiting. Ella didn't hurry. She helped the fey aboard and then, taking the last empty spot, told Whip-wip to hit the red button. "No, I said red. This one."

And then the cart did what it was designed to do. It went up through the tunnel and floated out into the night. For long minutes everyone stared back and just when Ella began to wonder if the bomb would go off there came a strange gout of light and fire shooting straight up in the air.

She then turned to the far off lights of Rhyoeven and these blurred as she cried.

Chapter 41

Beyond

"What do you think she meant by beaches?"

Eireden blinked slowly as his mind came into consciousness even slower. "Excuse me?" he asked and realized only then that he could breathe again. For so long, as he had laid there after his losing battle with Darhmael, his lungs had filled with blood and each breath had come with an awful bubbling from somewhere deep inside him. Now he took a very great breath and gave a little cough.

"I said beaches, or rather she said beaches. I just don't know what to think of that."

"And who are you exactly?" Eireden asked. The man was tall and thin with sharp purple eyes—they were like twin amethysts.

"I am Darhstrai…your brother-in-law, I suppose. We fought briefly yesterday?"

Eireden stared harder, but could not see the resemblance between this beautiful creature and the burnt elf that he had been. "And are we supposed to fight now?"

They were outside in the courtyard of the citadel and after a brief glance up at the tower, Strai answered, "No. Not just yet. But I did bring your sword, just in case. To be honest, I don't know what I want. I healed you to spite my father, since it would be the last thing that he would want, only now I don't know what to do with you."

"You do seem confused," Eireden agreed.

"Yes. A few minutes ago I was set to die but then Ella mentioned beaches and now I'm not certain I'm ready to die just yet. There's a bomb up there. We should get clear."

The elf helped Eireden up and they began walking for the bridge. At the sight of his two dead princes and the fey Hasfel, Eireden paused. "We can't get clear in time. How long do we have?"

"Nine minutes or so. So we better get moving." The elf began to run across the plain.

Though he ran very fast, Eireden didn't think they would get near far enough away. "We only delay our death," he said running easily without his armor and only the black sword to carry. "Even if the blast doesn't get us, the caves could very well collapse. And then there is the radiation—do you know what that is?"

"Yes, Father bragged about it before imprisoning me," Strai answered. "Have you ever been to the ocean?"

"I have. It was beautiful."

"That's what I've heard. Here's my dilemma: I don't know what to do with myself. For so long I've plotted and planned, even schemed. With always the goal of taking my father's place as ruler of the Underworld. That's what we call this place…stop, don't go that way."

Eireden had veered off, heading in the direction they had come. Strai took them to the right and the king could do nothing but follow and hope for the best.

Strai went on talking easily despite the sprint they were in. "I plotted against my brothers and against my father, but not against you. I've rooted for you every step of the way. It's probably why I didn't kill you just now, though even that makes little sense."

The king gave him a look of surprise. "You rooted *for* me? Was it because I was trying to slay your competition? If so, I'm not too assured by this. Won't you just start plotting against me next? And what of Ella?"

"Down here," Strai said. They went through a sharp-sided gulch and ahead the king could hear rushing water. "I hope you can hold your breath for a long while, Den. Do not try to breathe until you see light."

In front of them was an underground river and its waters raced. Strai gave a little wave and then jumped in; he disappeared in wink. With no other choice Eireden followed suit. It was a terrifying ride in a darkness that seemed to go on without end. His skin was bashed, bruised and shredded by the time he saw light and he came up gasping and spluttering.

He wanted to scramble to the edge, where the lichen glowed eerily, to rest but the elf drew him on where the going was slower than before but still quicker than running. "That's just it," Strai said, taking up exactly where he left off. "My father did too good of a job with her. When we fought I could've killed her, easily. Yet at the same time, I couldn't. Or I didn't want to. I allowed myself to be fooled into thinking that her innocence equated to weakness—that I could always kill her at another time."

Just then a rumbling crept through the rocks and shivered the river. "We should leave the water," Strai said. "Here, take that path."

A path came off the water's edge and wound off into the black. Eireden was virtually blind so Strai went forth with his elf sword giving a pale light.

"So you love Ella?" Eireden asked.

"I don't know what I feel," Strai confessed. "I've been so long stuck beneath this damned rock being fed on hate and rage that now I don't know what is what. My dream is gone. The bomb has surely destroyed the citadel and it will eventually turn all of this deadly with radiation…do you think we got far enough away?"

"I would think so. We have to be three or four miles away by now and there is enough rock between here and there that radiation won't be a factor at least for awhile."

"Good, but that still leaves me with a future to worry about," Strai said. "I had very much wanted to just sit there and let the bomb end me, but then Ella mentioned a beach. I would like to see one. And there are other things I would like to see. The truth is that I enjoyed the surface when I was there. I asked myself: why can't I go back? Why can't I do what I want now, time is getting on don't you know."

"I don't," Eireden said. "Immortality is a concept that only immortals truly understand. The Den are long lived compared to humans, but we are still mortal."

"As am I," Strai replied. "I am closing in on two-hundred and I begin to feel it. Why do you give me that look? Do you really think that Darhmael would allow any immortal besides himself? I sometimes think that was part of his enmity with the fey."

Eireden shrugged a little. "It's not that. It's just I always assumed that Ella would live on well past me."

"And she will, but she won't live forever," Strai said.

They trekked for a long while in silence and always the path went up and up, and on many occasions Strai would remark about new formations caused from the blast or he would search for the right trail among strewn rocks until finally he paused.

"Now for the hard part," he said. They were at the cavern just down from the opening to the Demorlaik.

"If we run the entire way we stand a very good chance," Eireden said.

Strai shook his head. "Not that. Oh, why do I confess this, it makes no sense? We will be once again mortal enemies. We struck a bargain, Ella and I to confront a mutual enemy, and that time is over. And so now what? With every second that passes I grow more confused. Did Darhmael have me under a spell? Was it just that his hatred was infectious? I don't know, save that I feel tired of hatred yet at the same time it is there within me like a shard in my soul. I can't say for certain what the future holds."

"Who can?" the king replied. "But if you are need of direction or just in the need to kill, I have a hundred thousand maug to deal with."

"You don't have much to worry about there," Strai replied. "They are under orders not to attack until the 'signal', and of course there is no signal. They have food for about three days. After that they will begin to fight among themselves. I'd say in a week they'll be mostly back in the Underworld getting radiation poison."

"Then if you just need to talk," Eireden said, putting out his hand.

The elf gave it a look. "The American way? Why not?"

They shook hands and then after an awkward silence the two went up into the Demorlaik. Eireden had expected the hordes of undead to be close at hand, but they were far off, climbing over themselves to be near the heat and the radiation of the nuclear blast—he didn't want to know what it would do to them, nothing good no doubt.

They left the Demorlaik and parted ways with a quick nod. The king traveled south, but bypassed his city. Even from afar he could see the trenches ringing the battle plain and he knew that it would be suicide to try to get past them. Instead he continued south until he grew tired; he spent part of the night and the first few hours of the morning sleeping in the crook of a tree.

When he woke he continued on, passing the burned out remains of Hildeoven and he didn't know his destination until he crossed over the steep hill and went down into the grotto of the fairies. This place had always held one of the happiest moments of his life and he needed that sort of serenity to heal his mind and soul. He had seen too much and been through too much in the past week, and he needed to regain his strength in order to begin the job of rebuilding his kingdom.

For three days he lounged near the pond, letting the sun warm him, and eating of the fruit when he grew hungry. He was lonely, for the fairies were gone and he disliked that the nymph was always trying to entice him. So on the fourth day he decided to go home, however he had barely made it to the top of the hill before a flash of light caught his attention.

Quickly he ducked among the underbrush and watched as a women, dressed in shining silver armor, descended from the skies. In her hand she carried a glowing spear and about her were a constellation of lesser lights.

She landed beside the pond and smiled in a sad way as the lights around her ceased their glowing and flew about whistling joyously about being home. "You see?" Eleanor, the Sun Queen, said. "Rumors are just that. Who would believe that a half-naked giant roams these hills? I think you just wanted me to escort you home."

The fairies had much to say about this, however seeing as they spoke over each other to such a degree that they were all incomprehensible, she turned to get a drink.

One fairy was too insistent to be ignored. She pushed the queen's face from the water and pointed with much hooting at something in the sand. It was a human footprint—a very large one.

In a literal flash, Ella turned, bringing her bright spear up at the ready. "Who is there?"

"Only a sythie," Eireden said.

"Show yourself," she demanded. "I want to see the sythie that possesses such large feet."

He stood forth and her eyes went wide, but then they quickly narrowed. "Who are you?" she raged, advancing with her spear.

"I am your husband and you are my queen."

She began shaking her head and then she grew stern again and sent out a wave of power that swept over every inch of him. And now she stepped back in confusion. "What are you? You are not him, so tell me now before I grow angry. What are you?"

"I am the Sun King."

The spearhead—a golden unicorn horn—had lowered, but now it shot up. "He is dead! You are an imposter."

"I am not," the king replied. "What do you think Whip-wip?" The bravest of the fairies had slipped out of her hiding place and now she floated near.

She eyed him close and then kissed him on the nose and said, "Sis, is Sun King." This was good enough for the other fairies who swarmed him and touched him.

"But aren't you dead?" Ella asked. "You have to be...I left you for dead. I gave up on you. So how?"

"Do not take this on yourself, Ella," he said coming closer. The spear tip waivered and he gently pushed it aside. "I told you to leave because I wanted you safe. You and the baby. This baby," he added touching her stomach.

Even through the metal of her armor, the connection was there, the instant love. But now there was another connection and they both marveled.

"I can feel him," Eireden said of his unborn son.

Ella had tears in her sapphire eyes. She placed her hand over his and said, "I can feel you. It is you. But how? How can you be here when you died…wait, never mind for now. There is only one thing I want to hear now."

"I love you," he whispered. They were so close, practically touching noses that he didn't need to speak louder.

"Love you too," she said and then kissed him long and deep to the great delight of the fairies, who danced around them.

The End

*

Author's Note:

If you've enjoyed The Hidden Land series may I suggest The Trilogy of the Void? The first book in the series, *The Horror of the Shade* was inspired by one of the paranormal events that I've been connected with. Quite simply it was a two second ghost sighting, witnessed by me and two of my brothers.

So how is that extrapolated into a proper trilogy? Step one: Remove me and my two brothers; we would just get in the way after all. Step two: Change the ghost to a demon, add a hot, but diabolical witch. Throw in a hunky seventeen-year old and his hell-powered schizophrenic sister and you're in business. Oh, I forgot to mention there will also be: Gypsies, exorcisms, blood, bullets, a nice sprinkling of sex, sin, murder, and a couple of trips into the wonderful vacation spot known as Hell...and did I mention sex? Right, check that off the list.

Step three: Churn these all up into non-stop action, until you realize what you have is nothing more than a family in dire peril. What is this story about? What every story is about: people. People in love, people in danger, people fighting for their very souls.

Peter Meredith

P.S. Finally, on a self-serving note, the review is the most practical and inexpensive form of advertisement an independent author has available in order to get his work known. If you could put a kind review on Amazon and your Facebook page, I would greatly appreciate it.

Fictional works by Peter Meredith:

A Perfect America

The Sacrificial Daughter

The Apocalypse Crusade War of the Undead: Day One

The Apocalypse Crusade War of the Undead: Day Two

The Horror of the Shade: Trilogy of the Void 1

An Illusion of Hell: Trilogy of the Void 2

Hell Blade: Trilogy of the Void 3

The Punished

Sprite

The Blood Lure: The Hidden Land Novel 1

The Sun King: The Hidden Land Novel 2

The Sun Queen: The Hidden Land Novel 3

The Apocalypse: The Undead World Novel 1

The Apocalypse Survivors: The Undead World Novel 2

The Apocalypse Outcasts: The Undead World Novel 3

The Apocalypse Fugitives: The Undead World Novel 4

The Apocalypse Renegades: The Undead World Novel 5

The Apocalypse Exile: The Undead World Novel 6

The Apocalypse War: The Undead World Novel 7

Printed in Great Britain
by Amazon